THE YOWLING OF THE DAMNED

AUGUSTUS H. FURLOUGH

skullhoundpublishing.com

Copyright © 2024 Augustus H. Furlough

ISBN: 979-8-9919224-0-1

Library of Congress Control Number: 2024923135

Cover Design: Evgeniia Gurcheva

Interior Design: Michael Vito Tosto

Editor: Sean Leonard

First Edition: December 2024

Printed in the United States of America

Published by Skullhound Publishing

Visit us at skullhoundpublishing.com

Contact: skullhoundpublishing@yahoo.com

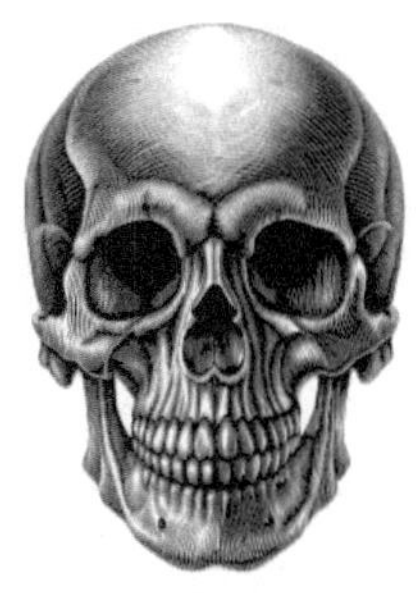

I.

Dark and treacherous landscapes fill the void as far as his mind will allow him to see. A disconsolate blackness bereft of light permeates the atmosphere, stripping away even the smallest fragment of hope or sense of comfort. Jagged mountains tower in decrepit execration, casting spells of hatred and damnation, piercing his mind and injecting his thoughts with a poisonous, feverous lust for demonic salvation. Looming in magnificent elevation are the cordillera-shaped formations—structural evil, a backdrop of black and red-tinted peaks—massifs of horror that no known mountain range possesses. For thousands of miles they stretch into the nightscape—if only night could define these illustrations.

The world he bears witness to is deprived of the sun's life-giving rays. A sun-like star does not even exist, only the frigid, lifeless darkness; a land of soul-starving bleakness saturated with forbidding vistas, barren and pleading for deliverance. Here the creatures of the past dwell, waiting in abhorrent, seething hatred, silently loathing in unbridled hostility. They are resentful of the dimensional abduction of their domain, perpetrated eons ago by the gods of ancient times. They know the hour is at hand; retribution will follow—pure, cataclysmic retaliation.

A sudden pain abruptly severs his cogitation as his ability to reason fades into a maelstrom of agony. As his misery proliferates, his awareness inverts. The realms of ancient enlightenment molest his subconscious, sending him spiraling into a virtually comatose state of madness and despair. The pain transforms into a searing burn and the defeat of uncompromising despondency reaches the meridian.

He suddenly, without sound reasoning, finds himself standing on a cliff somewhere deep in the timeless bleak context. Perched high upon the precipice he stands, feet grounded atop black molten rock, as he gazes silently into the dark and mountainous landscape. No signs of movement can be seen, nor can any sense of life be felt—there is only the tormenting embrace of fear to contemplate. Panoramic mental despair is his only companion in this abominably desolate domain, truly a torturous revelation for his inflamed spirit to behold.

Instantaneously, a beast of untold proportion swiftly rises from below the crag, shattering the palpable suffering into shards of fragmented mourning. It seethes with a loathsome foulness incalculable in its vastly iniquitous ways. The deliberation of this creature conjugates the rift between madness and sanity. A hell of fangs and demon's breath vomits maledictions into the spirits of all entities who greet its ghastly essence, assuming the beings who have experienced the displeasure have, in fact, endured. As the horrid entity contorts in sordid undulation, the spectator is hypnotized by the vulgarity of its hatred for humankind. The smell of rotten flesh exudes malodorously from its scaly, reptilian plates, poisoning the air with a sickening profanity. A teardrop forms on his cheek as the monstrous being stares into his terrified soul with dozens of pupil-less black eyes. Surrounding its eyes are orbits consisting of protruding sections of jagged, curving frontal bone portions, a contour which conjures sentiments within the mind of hellish intent. They are of immense size and depth, enclosing each optic with an envelopment of archaic, serpent-like quintessence. Surrounding the creature's dreadful countenance is a skull of horrific proportion, its centuries-old visage colossal in magnitude. The face of this being is far removed from either human or beast, echoing instead a demonic and unearthly essence—skinless, scale-covered, and horned.

The measure of the remaining portions of its body is unknown. Even though the man can only see the upper region of this beast's form rising above the edge of the cliffside, he is sure the rest of its body stretches far beyond the gully below. The creature descends its elongated neck, bulging with girth, promising undiluted agony with each passing movement. The creature positions itself to the front of the man in one timeless movement as if space itself made way for the iniquitous stirring.

Now poised with statuesque dominance, the beast towers above the man's pathetic human form. Stories tall and drooling with venomous bile, it opens its skeletal jaws to reveal rows upon rows of glorious fangs, soiled and stained with the gore of a millennium's worth of kills. Slowly and fluidly the massive jaws open, aching with an ancient decrepitude. A monumental growl erupts in blasphemous volumes from its hellish maw, stripping the tears from the man's face with a foul and stinging gale, reverberating waves of heat that somehow darken the atmosphere further.

Accompanying the thunderous roar is a tremendous flash of lightning striking beyond the black mountains in the distance. The violent luminosity exploding forward through the bleak context rivals that of a nuclear warhead, blinding the man with its deathlike intensity. As the landscape beyond is illuminated, it reveals a topography of corpses as far as the eye can see, rotting in majestic profusion. For a brief moment, the man's attention is stolen away from the great beast before him, temporarily diverted toward the ghastly sight filling the backdrop. Millions of mutilated human bodies litter the landscape beyond, filling the man's heart with a dread unsurpassable.

The light from the flash begins to wane as the man's eyes strain to catch an impression of the fading view. Still fixated on the evaporating vista, his sight is redirected once again as the great beast now lunges toward his cowering being, the velocity violating his imagination. He throws up his hands in a pathetic attempt to protect his body, more so out of instinct than for protection. He can feel the radiating heat from the enormous jaws encapsulating him, searing his skin with a blasphemous fulmination. His terror is boundless as his senses culminate in a pinnacle of magnificent exoneration.

Charles violently bursts forth from his slumber, drenched with sweat and hyperventilating from fear and fascination. His lungs, still burning from the sulphureous vapors of his dream state, gasp for air as he slowly gains composure. He glances around his opulently decorated bedroom, still trying to convince himself he is back to reality. Morning rays of sunlight creep their way through black velvet curtains in his chamber-like room, glistening on the polished marble floor while creating hues of melancholic ambiance around the room.

Charles carefully removes the black and red Siberian white goose down comforter from his body and stretches his arms, slowly shaking off the edginess from his sleep. He rises from his tufted platform bed with mechanical prowess, flexing his broad muscular frame flooded with adrenaline from his nightmarish dream. Shuffling down from his bed, he marches past the black candelabra statues that stand guard in front of his elegant if not imposing resting space. He swiftly makes his way through the hallway connecting his bedroom chamber to the master bathroom. As he moves through the hallway, he yields a passing glance toward the bleak medieval landscape portrayed in the painting on the west-facing hallway wall, a disquieting reminder of times now past. The black walls of his bedroom accentuate the starkness of the illustration, creating an ambiance of unease. One of many paintings throughout the home, this one conjures an especially delectable feeling of dread within Charles's mind.

As he passes through the black wooden doors of his palatial master bathroom, he pauses for a moment's reprieve. Charles's truest ambitions toy with his subconscious, mocking his every waking breath. He gathers his composure and flips the light switch inside the bathroom. The switch is housed within a heraldic armorial crest, an ode to the dark, arcane times of human history. He steps inside his expansive bathroom and takes a left turn, walking briskly past the black marble bathtub in the middle of the floor. Charles takes a deep breath and stares intently ahead, focusing on the image reflected before him. A baronial Venetian mirror adorns the eastern wall of the washroom, garlanded with black diabolical creatures lurking and swirling in barbarous savagery. The reflecting image within the mirror is no less vexing than the mirror itself.

At six feet tall, and framed in a stout, muscular eminence, Charles's appearance commands a level of respect from his peers. His high cheekbones and chiseled, square chin garner no lack of attention from the women he passes on the streets. The blondish-brown hair always kept neatly combed in a timeless side part atop his head conjures a sense of reverence and composure within the imagination of the outside interpreter. Intense blue eyes stare deep into the souls of his fellow man when he speaks, accentuating his smooth facial features and demanding the attention of those who stand before him.

Charles is well-known at the firm he oversees as being a cold and calculating hedge fund manager. He has no qualms concerning the execution of unscrupulous deals, with little to no regard for the financial suffering he may inflict upon his clientele. But what would his coworkers think of the scars that cover his chest, carved in reverence to the beings he pines to embrace? Tormented flesh envelops his body, evidence of ritualistic debauchery—a sadistic testimony to his devotion to the dark side. As his candescent blue eyes scan the image before him in the mirror, he contemplates his longing to catch a true glimpse of the world he knows only in nighttime reverie. Those dismal creatures of the black abyss, the rightful proprietors of our world, have been banned from this plane of existence for far too many eons. His sympathy for their plight is the impetus for all his deeds in this lifetime, and the scars upon his chest bear witness to this claim.

"It is the strange fate of man, that even in the greatest of evils the fear of the worst continues to haunt him." A quote from Johann Wolfgang von Goethe churns through Charles's mind as he pulls his favorite cashmere Bergdorf Goodman suit from the wall beside him and prepares for the day ahead. It is not the fate of man that haunts his mindset, however, but rather the fear that his ambitions for the downfall of humanity will never be achieved.

Making his way down the extensive and winding staircase that leads to the main hallway connecting the parlor to the foyer of his classical-styled mansion, Charles quickens his pace. Tucked away in an isolated hillside of the Berkeley Hills in the Pacific Coast ranges of California, the homestead provides a discreet location for the heretical diabolism of Charles's vulgar pursuits. The location, while befitting of his obscure occult fascinations, does not make for a short commute to and from the Financial District in San Francisco, where his firm Prometheus Capital Management is located. On this morning in particular, Charles is anxious to get to the office where a new, exceptionally vulnerable client awaits his arrival.

Charles exits the entrance of his home through ornately carved oak doors. They sit beneath an illustrious arched window section filled with stunning architectural stained glass. He turns left and heads for the gray and black-tinted limestone two-car garage to the east, one of three garages that house his collection of luxury vehicles. Pulling a set of keys from his pocket, he advances toward the open garage and steps alongside his black Jaguar F-Type Project 7.

While his deepest infatuations involving those blackest dwellers of the nether realms hold claim to his innermost desire, his proclivity for extravagant material possessions is a close second. At just thirty-nine years old, Charles has afforded himself a life that most men his age can only fantasize about. After earning his MBA from Dartmouth College, no time was wasted on unaffiliated avocations, as Charles took to pursuing "the buyside" with an unparalleled fervor. His unwavering pursuit for success, coupled with his unconscionable lack of moral or ethical concern, has served him well in the cutthroat world of finance. This shrewd ability to accumulate wealth has afforded Charles the means to reach beyond the limits of most men's desires, to touch and embrace things which the wholesome detest.

Abandoned at an infantile age to the foster care system due to the untimely passing of his birth parents, young Charles Alexander Kepler was forced early on to carve a path of his own unyielding obduracy. His mother, Margaret Kepler, a woman of devout Catholic observance, was a shy and nurturing homemaker born of Irish descent to parents fleeing the faltering economy of Northern Ireland in the 1950s to England. Her abrupt demise, which accompanied Charles's birth, was a tragedy for her burgeoning family which only consisted of herself, her husband William, and the newly born Charles. No less tragic than her passing was the death of William only six months after Charles's birth, meeting his quietus in a mysterious murder still unsolved to this day. William, also of Northern Irish ancestry, was an electrical engineer by profession. Hard-working and obstinate in his willfulness, he, too, was a dedicated Catholic who made his late wife's acquaintance at St. John's Cathedral in Portsmouth, England.

Shortly after his father's death, Charles spent several years in Westminster Children's Home in Fareham near the northwest end of Portsmouth Harbour, a market town between Portsmouth and Southampton in southeast England. After a confusing and tumultuous triennial, he was approved for adoption by Richard and Judith Hassner at the age of three. The two moved young Charles into their affluent manor house in Tonbridge, England, a luxurious homestead bequeathed to Judith after her parents passed away. Soon after adopting Charles, several bad business dealings forced the family to sell their estate. Richard moved the family to Palo Alto, California, during the tech boom of the mid-nineties, where they remained for the rest of Charles's adolescence.

Judith was heir to an oil fortune; her silver spoon upbringing afforded her a lifestyle of opulence and fostered an attitude of intolerable arrogance. Her stern demeanor and admiration for discipline commanded an unsettling respect from her peers and Charles alike. Richard, a devious and uncompromising stock investor whose keen sense for financial affairs helped champion Charles's shrewd tendencies toward fiscal success, was not without an unwavering tendency to disciplinary action himself. Together they guided Charles's will throughout childhood with ferocious determination, ensuring that excellence would prevail in their adopted son's existence through castigation and austere conformity.

Richard and Judith's relationship was not one born of love and companionship however, built instead upon a mutual affinity for wealth. Greed was paramount in all their endeavors, rising far above any semblance of compassion between them. Thoughts of divorce never strayed far from the minds of either Richard or Judith, and neither were strangers to the vice of infidelity.

Many of Charles's earliest memories were laced with scenes of abuse and debauchery. On one occasion when Charles was only six years old, he bore witness to his adoptive father engaging in sodomy with Judith's own sister in the wine cellar of their home while Judith was out of town. This instance of depraved revelry made a vivid and lasting impression upon young Charles's mind, but it would not be the last time he would experience such lascivious misdeeds.

Another licentious instance, this time involving Judith, occurred when Charles was eight. While Charles was restricted to his bedroom most afternoons, on this day he managed to sneak from his upstairs confines and make his way downstairs for a midday snack. As he fumbled around the pantry, precariously reaching for the cookies on the shelf above him, he heard a noise coming from the pool area on the outer side of the kitchen. He slowly peeked his head out the kitchen window which provided a convenient view of the poolside patio. Upon scanning the area, he caught a glimpse of Judith crouched down near the edge of the pool. She was accompanied by two of Richard's business partners that Charles had seen many times at the home before. All three were fully undressed, Judith kneeling vulnerably between the two standing men, engaged in depraved fornications that no child should ever behold. Charles learned on this day what was meant years later when his teenage friends would jokingly refer to a "golden shower."

His surrogate parents' tumultuous relationship took a final sinister turn just after Charles's fourteenth birthday, a turn that would alter the course of his life forever. On the sixteenth of June, the Palo Alto Police Department received a missing person's report filed on behalf of Judith Hassner. Richard had reported the disappearance of his wife the night before. For several days following, detectives combed the streets and sifted through leads, trying in a series of failed attempts to locate the vanished Mrs. Hassner. Weeks later the search died down, the police never locating Judith or providing any clues on her where-abouts. The truth of Judith's disappearance, however, was far more unsettling than anyone could have imagined.

Weeks before the missing person's report had been filed, Richard and Judith's sordid marriage had come to a direful culmination. Their union, already bordering on the brink of collapse, came to a ghastly impasse the night Judith threatened divorce. Richard, terrified of the prospect of losing half his wealth, took matters into his own hands. He devised an insidious plan to disencumber himself of his marital dilemma by means of murder. As if this plot was not diabolical enough in its own right, the barbarity was multiplied by the inclusion of young Charles in the perpetration of the crime.

The night before Richard reported Judith missing, he slipped sleeping pills into her cocktail. After she fell unconscious, he suffocated her with her beloved lynx fur coat, a *coup de grace* highlighting his spiteful detestation for her threatened betrayal. Together, he and Charles loaded her in the back of Richard's sedan and disposed of her in a shallow grave in the woodlands of the Monte Bello Ridge.

Following Judith's murder, Charles's upbring was a direct reflection of Richard's rapacious callousness. Richard subjected Charles's teenage mind to the voracious greed and apathetic mindset of the business world and all the material and carnal pleasures associated with it. He molded Charles into a man of unyielding determination and willfulness to the absolute best of his avaricious ability. Despite his sadistic upbringing, Charles felt a strong admiration for his surrogate father, viewing him as a man of strength and tenacity.

Charles adhered to his adoptive father's strict censure and guidance out of fear of retribution, but his cold, loveless castigation over the years built inside him a firm resolve—a resolve that would serve him well throughout his life. The upbringing he experienced in those darkened years of adolescence was paramount in his aptitude for business. His childhood experiences gave him the ability to make large-scale deals with clients without having consideration for their financial or emotional well-being.

Richard's indifferent outlook toward humankind, and his unwavering drive for success, created a lasting bond between the two until he fell ill just before Charles's twenty-eighth birthday. As Richard lay dying in his final hours, he imparted one last vestige of contemplation for Charles to consider. While on his death bed, he whispered this one final utterance: "In order to have true wealth and power, one must never help the weak, and one must never feel guilt." As Richard lay there suffering, Charles took the pillow from underneath Richard's head and suffocated him with it.

Turning the key forward in the ignition of his Project 7, Charles takes a moment to admire the roar of the engine's reverberation throughout the garage. He smashes the pedal to the floor and lights up the turquoise marble flooring underneath the tires, leaving a thick, black layer of rubber spanning the distance between the bay door and the street.

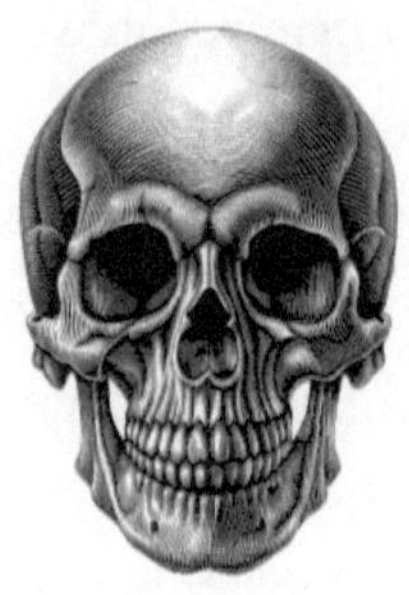

II.

"What now, *bitch?*!" Jessie shouts as he repeatedly pounds his fist into Jake's face. "Fucking pussy. Not so tough now, are you?" He transitions now to a whisper into Jake's ear in a semi-casual tone between continuous blows to the side of his jaw.

"Man, I'm sorry, stop," Jake wearily replies, exhausted from his failed attempts to shield himself from Jessie's barrage of blows.

"Come to my house talkin' that shit, *motherfucker*! *I didn't rip you off*...punk ass bitch!" Jessie, furious at the perceived slight of Jake's accusation moments before the fight started, knows that the punishment must be severe, as anything less could provoke feelings of weakness toward him from his peers.

The stinging of Jessie's knuckles against Jake's mouth rattles his concentration as he attempts to speak in between punches. "Bro, sor— Sorry. I didn't... *Fuck*! Mean it," Jake barely manages to stammer, blood dripping from the corner of his mouth. The fact that he did indeed cheat Jake out of his money was trivial to Jessie; the audacity of Jake to do something about it was of great consequence, however. Jessie pushes himself away from Jake, shaking off the soreness of his swollen and blood-covered fist as he stands, convinced that the beating was sufficient. One minute before the fight erupted,

Jake and two of his friends had pulled up to the front of Jessie's home, honking and shouting obscenities from the windows of Jake's car. A week before the fight, Jessie had ripped Jake off for two hundred dollars, providing him with a bag of baking powder instead of the cocaine he expected to receive.

As Jessie surveys his surroundings, he individually meets the gaze of Jake's two accomplices, currently staring in disbelief at the results of the relentless beating that just occurred. "Pick your little *faggot* friend up from my yard and get your bitch asses out of here, *now*, before I fuck you up too," Jessie growls, turning to head back inside. As he walks through the front entrance to his home, he slams the door behind him, his body still surging with adrenaline. As he steps into the living room, he hears the screech of tires echoing from the street as Jake and his friends angrily and shamefully speed away from the house.

Jessie is no stranger to confrontation. He is known in the neighborhood for being tough and exceptionally well-built for an eighteen-year-old who never touches weights. His muscular frame and wide shoulders are enough to intimidate his peers alone, but the giant grim reaper tattoo spanning the entirety of his back accentuates his already dominant appearance. Not one to typically start fights, Jessie is most certainly the one to finish them. Scamming Jake out of his money was not representative of Jessie's usual dealings, however. In this case, Jessie was attempting to impress some girls at a party by bullying a weaker associate. To this effect, he was successful; later that night he brought both girls home for a drunken *ménage à trois*.

No stranger to the affection of women, Jessie is gifted with charisma and appealing looks. His short blond hair, bright green eyes, and charming smile are a magnetic force for the high school girls to cling to. Strong, handsome cheek bones punctuate his smile, an irresistibly pleasing quality for his many suitors to adore. Standing six feet and one inch tall and abounding with lean muscle mass, Jessie clearly has a body built for athleticism. Rarely, however, does he participate in sports as he had in the earlier days of his youth; by the time he reached high school, the partying lifestyle had taken hold, becoming infinitely more important to him than physical pursuits or an education.

Born in Manhattan to Jessie Bower Senior and Amanda Olson, Jessie's unwed parents moved him frequently throughout childhood. Lynchburg, Virginia; Lancaster, Ohio; Fort Worth, Texas; Gunnison, Utah; Fairhaven, Oregon; and finally, Eagle Rock, California, where Jessie Senior took a job as a mechanic while Amanda stayed home with young Jessie and his older brother, Derek.

Jessie was never problematic for his parents. His father, although strict—never one to abstain from corporal discipline—was a dedicated patriarch. Jessie's older brother is another matter. In and out of correctional facilities from the age of sixteen, Derek is no stranger to the legal system; the local police knew him by name before he turned fourteen. Jessie always looked up to his older brother regardless of the grief he bestowed upon Amanda and Jessie Senior. When Jessie was eight and his mother left to pursue a secret romantic interest, Derek was always there for Jessie while his father worked long hours to provide for the family.

Jessie, making his way down the steps to his makeshift bedroom located in the basement of his father's home, pauses to feel for the pull string hanging from the light at the bottom of the stairs. He throws his shirt to the side of the bed. The Nike logo on his white tank top lands emblem side up, now spattered with blood from the fight just moments ago.

He flops down on the old brown couch along the back wall. A hand-me-down from his older brother Derek, it is now a semen-stained relic, covered in years of spilled bong water and cheap beer.

Jessie grabs a Bic lighter from the table in front of the couch and touches the flame to the glass bowl clenched between his lips. Inhaling a potent cloud of Gelato, he holds it in as long as his lungs will allow until the irritation causes him to burst forth an exhalation of cough-inducing smoke. As he takes another hit, he hears footsteps shuffling down the stairwell. Looking up from his blue and red-striped glass smoking utility, he sees Blake and Shawn through the haze of marijuana smoke. "What up, bitches?" Jessie slyly whispers, a semi-stoned smile spanning his face.

"Sheeeiiit, sup wit you?" the first newcoming guest replies as he lumbers toward Jessie, hand outreached in anticipation of a cordial fist bump. Jessie stretches his arm toward Blake, his acquaintance of several years now, his fist starting to swell, with dried blood caked across two of his knuckles where the skin scraped off against Jake's skull.

"Not much, bro. *Chillin'...* Hittin' this weed, resting my hands... *Ouch! Easy*, brooo..." Jessie bemoans before transitioning to a whisper, his speech mellowed by the effects of the marijuana as his swollen knuckles meet Blake's fist.

"What happened to your hand?" Shawn cuts in, the second arrival into Jessie's basement abode. Pushing his glasses back up to the bridge of his nose, he awkwardly awaits Jessie's answer with a clumsy smile about his face and the look of self-doubt coloring the remaining portions. Always the concerned one of the bunch, Shawn is consistently panged with anxious sentiment. A good friend to have in one's corner, even though Jessie and Blake mostly keep him around for his car and drug money.

Taking another hit from the pipe, Jessie smirks and meets Shawn's insecure eyes. "Nothing a little green can't fix... Had to put the hands to that punk Jake today," he manages to struggle out while holding in the smoke.

"Word?" Blake incredulously responds, snatching the pipe from Jessie's hands. "Lemme hit that..." Blake breaks from speaking to inhale the smoke, straining to hold the marijuana within as he struggles between choked utterances to finish his thought, "Fuck...that guy. So...you ready for this eclipse or what, my dude?"

"Eclipse?" Jessie responds, puzzled by Blake's question. "What eclipse?"

"Bro...you haven't heard? Big event..." Blake pauses again to hit the pipe. "Only...happens like once...every three hundred years or some shit," he manages to mumble, trying to hold the smoke in his lungs as he speaks. "How do you *not* know, brah?" Blake stutters, simultaneously exhaling a fog of Gelato.

Shawn hesitantly chimes in, "Yeah, man. Should be *pretty* cool... Gonna be happening in like a week or something. A total solar eclipse. I heard about it on the news." A nervous look crosses his face as he silently hopes the pipe gets passed his direction.

Jessie thinks for a moment with a bewildered contemplation, pondering briefly whether or not he cares in the least about a solar eclipse. Settling on indifference, he changes the subject. "Sounds sick. Y'all ready for that *party* Friday? Gonna be *dope*... Tons of bitches there, bro!" He has been excited for the upcoming party this weekend. A decidedly beautiful young woman he has been trying to hook up with for the last couple weeks assured him that, should he be there, chances are good he will get lucky.

With an abrupt excitement in his voice, Blake fires back, "You *know* it, *man*! Don't know if *Junior* here will be there though."

"*Hey*... If my dad lets me... I mean...I'll *be* there," Shawn hesitantly replies. Jessie and Blake are both well aware that Shawn's mother and father don't approve of their son befriending the two, a fact that does little to suppress their association with him.

"You *better* be there, homie. Don't want to be a virgin forever, *do you*?" quips Jessie, followed by chuckling from both he and Blake.

"Yeah...whatever," Shawn replies with a scowl, quickly following it up with a cheerful smirk. "You gonna pass that pipe or what?"

Blake glances in Shawn's direction with a slightly empathetic gleam. "Chill, bro. Just fuckin' wit ya." Then he passes the glass pipe diplomatically in his direction. Blake redirects his line of sight toward Jessie and slowly exhales a cloud of smoke. "Yeah, bro. We'll be there for sure."

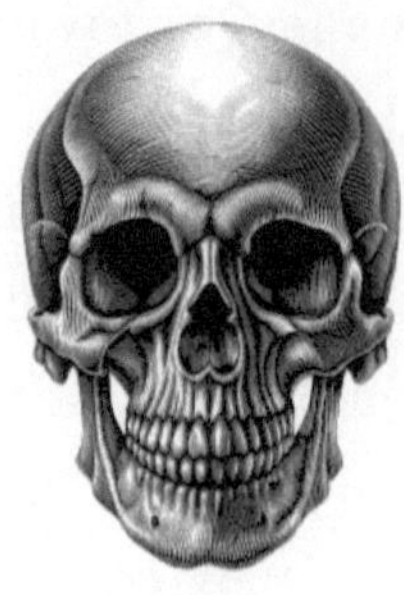

III.

As Professor Martin Patterson hastily scrawls the Klein-Gordon equation onto the chalkboard in front of him, he takes a brief repose to gather his thoughts. Turning back toward the class, he draws an extensive breath. He has grown to despise explaining the behavior of scalar fields to his students. It is not out of spite for the mathematics contained therein; the elegance found within the equations captures the very quintessence of his devotion. For the lack of comprehension that seems to greet his explanation of the principles, however, Dr. Patterson, over time, has grown increasingly weary.

Gathering his courage, Professor Patterson points to the equation hastily scribed upon the board behind him. "Now, who can tell me how mass plays a role in the four-dimensional generalization of the Laplacian operator in three-dimensional space-time?"

"Ahem-hm," a student clears his throat in the back of the class, momentarily raising the hopes of Professor Patterson. Aside from the sounds of a throat clearing and students shuffling about in anxious apprehension, his question is answered with the cold, empty embrace of silence.

"*Okay*, guys... Let's call it a day. We'll do it again on Friday, yes?" he cheerfully pipes, tossing the chalk onto the desk beside him.

As the students begin filing out of the classroom, confused mumblings echo from their lips. As Martin shuffles back to his desk to gather his things, he overhears two students commenting on their confusion with his lessons for the day while they exit the door. Collecting his papers and filing them into his brown leather briefcase bag, he reminisces about times past when students seemed hungry for the mysterious world of quantum physics. *Imagining the luminaries he held in such high regard: Bohr, Heisenberg, Feynman, Planck, Einstein—all seemed so unquenchable in their thirst for knowledge. Today's practitioners in the fields of science have lost their fervor for the wonders of physics,* Martin thinks to himself as he exits the classroom. *Or perhaps it is just me.*

Born in Carlyle, Illinois, fifty miles east of St. Louis, Martin Patterson spent his youth reading books and performing makeshift scientific experiments in the basement of his parents' home. The eldest of three children, he was known as the quiet one in the family. While his younger siblings, Kimberly and Daniel—both born in two-year increments after Martin—were playing sports and forming friendships with the other children in the neighborhood, Martin was busy learning basic chemistry and studying Newton's laws of physics into the small hours of the night.

On one prognosticating evening, young Martin, only eleven years old at the time, nearly burned down the family home while experimenting with methanol in a chemistry study gone awry. The scientifically inspired gaffe resulted in scarring on his right hand still visible to this very day. Soon afterward, his parents confiscated his makeshift laboratory. But the fever for science never waned, and as a result, Martin dove deeper still into alternative disciplines. He soon discovered the wonders of quantum mechanics, and the captivation he experienced has since never diminished.

Born into the loving embrace of Howard and Barbara Patterson, Martin's parents believed in the wholesome family structure of which they were both nurtured. They, too, were born in Midwest, USA. God-fearing, good-hearted, and generous, they were convinced that the Bible and good morals were the way to salvation. As a result, Martin and his siblings were never at a loss for encouragement and warm family values, an authentic household of true Christian virtue.

His childhood, however, was by no means perfect; times of trial and struggle certainly abounded throughout his life as an adolescent. When Martin was in his late teenage years, his parents nearly separated due to infidelities on Barbara's behalf. A short-lived fling with a coworker nearly caused Howard to file for divorce. He was eventually able to forgive his wife for her extramarital endeavors and they remained married until he passed away, his wife joining him the following year.

While his parents' more egregious marital hurtles were mostly isolated to that one salacious instance, his family was beset still by other challenging dilemmas. The summer before Martin was preparing to enter his first year of college, his sister Kimberly—sixteen at the time—failed to come home after spending the evening with her boyfriend. Days went by, followed by weeks, which in turn became months, and still no sign of Kimberly or her boyfriend Tom. Missing person's reports were filed, posters were hung, countless search efforts were made, all without success.

Six months following Kimberly's disappearance, she finally showed up to the family home. Six months missing and six months pregnant, Howard and Barbara were awestricken with disbelief by what their beloved daughter had enacted in her time of absence. But forgiveness ran deep in the Patterson household, and with time, they extended the principles taught to them through the lessons of Christ and all was eventually forgotten.

Martin was exceedingly fortunate to grow up in a household full of love, compassion, and unwavering forgiveness, a luxury not afforded to all. Named after his ancestor Martin Davis, who fought and died in the famous skirmish of Lexington on April 19, 1775, during the Revolutionary War, Martin embodied from an early age the determination and spirit of those men who long ago fought and died for their independence. A young mind wielding a disciplined and unyielding tenacity, Martin earned a full scholarship to the University of California, Berkeley, at just seventeen years old, graduating first in his high school class one year early.

After earning his Bachelor of Science in Applied Physics, Martin proceeded onward to graduate school, directing his efforts toward a master's degree with a focus on theoretical physics. Once again graduating at the top of his class, Martin was able to procure a research grant before entering his doctoral studies. Four years after obtaining his masters, Martin earned the title Dr. Patterson, receiving his PhD in theoretical physics. His stunning dissertation, "The Dynamics of Gravitational Fundamentals Arising from Perturbative Fields," not only earned him a doctoral degree, but the respect of the university and, more importantly, the physics community *en masse*.

Martin's implacable determination to understand the essence of matter, down to the very basic particles of nature, has always been the driving force behind his indomitable quest for knowledge. His love for helping others understand these principles, coupled with his inherently altruistic nature, is what prompted him to accept an offer for a professorship at Berkeley University, his beloved alma mater. A renowned educator and leading team member for various research projects within the institution, Martin has distinguished himself over the years as a man of extensive knowledge and a champion of revolutionary physical concepts.

A jovial and highly approachable gentleman of science, Martin's agreeable nature and affable appearance make it easy for students and colleagues alike to gravitate toward his friendly persona. A small, somewhat portly fellow, Martin's five-foot seven-inch husky frame lends to the notion that he spends a little more time behind a desk than at the gym. A slightly rotund belly and a full beard of white and gray, accented by round wire-framed glasses, conjures images of a jolly St. Nick, minus the red suit and reindeer, naturally. Sixty-two years and counting, Martin is as sharp as ever; quick with a quip and a consistently pleasant smile adorning his bearded countenance, he can often be found enjoying a pipe while thumbing through the pages of a paperback novel.

While Martin has managed to achieve much in his lifetime, failure has intermittently beset him along his long and arduous journey. Now divorced, his ex-wife of twenty-three years simply could no longer tolerate the strain that Martin's dedication to science was putting on their flailing marriage. Martin met Christine while perusing the aisles of a local antique shop near his home in Pinole, California. Thirty years old at the time, and two years into his professorship at Berkeley—a relatively young age for a professor in his field of study—Martin finally had a chance to breathe and enjoy some pastimes other than research.

Martin never had much luck with romantic engagements. One of his passions, apart from physics, happened to be antique collecting, a hobby that rarely affords one the opportunity to meet single women. On a sunny, unassuming Saturday afternoon, he happened down an aisle of his favorite local resale shop hoping to find some old blues records or possibly a vintage porcelain vase in decent condition. Spotting an old flip-top pipe lighter behind a glass encasement, Martin hastily reached inside to remove it only to accidentally knock two glass ornaments sitting next to it onto the ground, shattering them into numerous pieces. Feeling a fool, he nervously looked around to see who might have witnessed the awkward event. Just then, a beautiful young cashier with flowing brown hair and glowing blue eyes came round the corner to investigate the sounds caused by the breaking glass. After a nervous apology, some uneasy small talk, and an embarrassingly inept invitation, Christine agreed to meet Martin for coffee at the local cafe. Two years later, they were wed, and young Elizabeth Patterson was born.

Science is an unequivocally cruel mistress. Slowly, increasingly, and unfortunately, the communication decayed between Martin and his better half over the ensuing years. His research and unwavering dedication to work caused an unmendable rift between his beloved wife and himself. Still, they managed to squeeze twenty-three years out of their disconnected marriage. Christine gave every ounce of energy she could to sustain what little they had between them. For Elizabeth's sake, she endured, putting in the work of two parents while Martin immersed himself in his research. Ultimately, Christine filed for divorce just four months shy of their twenty-fourth anniversary, the same year Elizabeth entered her first year of college. The departure of Christine never really haunted Martin's conscience, however; he was well aware that he was too engrossed in his work to provide the emotional presence necessary to sustain a healthy marriage. Nevertheless, lamentation abounds within his spirit, despite his apathy for Christine's parting—from the day his wife decided to leave, he never heard from Elizabeth again.

Deeper still, Martin dove into his work, plummeting to the very depths of his mind's erudite capabilities. With nothing left to blockade his voracious craving for knowledge, he took his exploration of the fundamental nature of the universe to greater heights. Awarded several academic honors for his research in gravitational physics and his various books and papers on the dynamics of string theory and quantum mechanics, Martin became one of the leading contributors to the field of theoretical physics. The compact, slightly corpulent fellow, bearded of white and perpetually smiling, became the face of modern physics in the Berkeley science community and even to some parts of the world beyond.

Stepping off the sidewalk and onto the blacktop of the faculty parking lot, Martin stops to reach for his Savinelli billiard pipe. He tucks his briefcase bag under his left arm and pauses before fishing out his lighter, allowing the summer sun to warm his face. With the briefcase still tucked in his armpit, he pulls his lighter from his pocket and lights his pipe, taking several short puffs to get the embers inside the blue friar wood bowl glowing red. Savoring the sweet mixture of vanilla and latakia-flavoring, Martin proceeds toward his car, reflecting on the day's lecture.

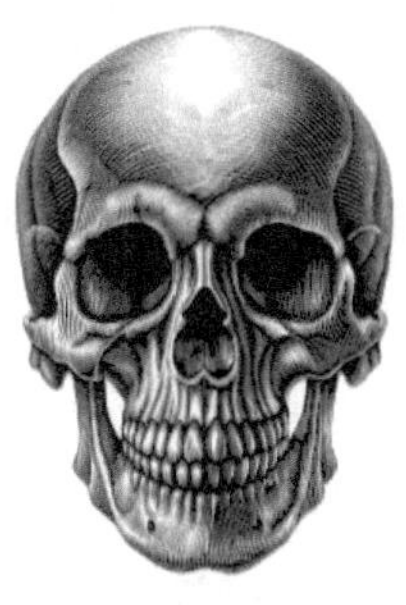

IV.

A mosh pit erupts in a frenzy of thrashing bodies as violent guitar riffs ring out from the stage, inciting the crowd to attack one another in a murderous, slamming conjunction of musical reverence. Lightning-fast double bass beats pummel eardrums and assail the chests of those in attendance as the snare unleashes a blasphemous bomb blast, damning the audience with an anathema of audio hellfire. Abruptly, silence ensues from the stage—a respite echoing sentiments of a momentary ceasefire. Smoke fills the room as fog machines dim the atmosphere with a chilling and foreboding sense of mysticism. The silence is violated as a viciously evil riff ignites from the right end of the stage, foreshadowing the mayhem that lies ahead. A figure in black appears from beyond the mist—bullet chain belts crossing his chest, spiked gauntlets on his arms, and a sordid, ominous smile spanning his countenance. One hand raises in the sign of the horns, the other grasps a microphone so tight the veins in his hands swell, surging with blood and adrenaline. With a demonic swiftness, the hand previously raised in the sign of the horns sweeps down toward the earth and meets the other, dually gripping the microphone as it pivots upward toward his jaw—now open—and unleashing an inhumane, ear-piercing scream. An unholy blitzkrieg of auditory obliteration explodes as the vocalist violently bangs his head, sending hair flying in dizzying circles as once again the pit ignites, incited by the band's brutal musical assault.

The haunting, chaotic soundscapes produced by Nokturnal Skies bewitches the showgoers for the duration of the festival, holding them spellbound for the entirety of their set. The headlining act for the Embrace of Darkness tour, this spot in the lineup was an offer Matt and his bandmates were more than happy to accept. Fresh out of the studio after recording their latest record, *Hymns to the Primeval Ones*, a national tour in support of their latest effort was precisely what the band was hoping for. Their latest offering is Matt's most esteemed work thus far—a concept album framed around his greatest passion. That passion—one of an inherently dark and imperiling nature—being the observance of knowledge practiced in archaic times of demonic wisdom and ancient celebrations concerning spells, incantations, and forbidden teachings mostly lost through the centuries and, perhaps rightfully, forgotten. Matt has been captivated by esoteric subjects since childhood, a fascination that not even he can fully explain.

Twenty-five years ago, Matt Beasle was born out of wedlock, cocaine-addicted, and six weeks premature. His mother, Christine Beasle —a lifelong crack cocaine and heroin user—fell victim to an unidentified assailant, a rape for which no one was ever charged. More the parent than the son, Matt spent more of his childhood playing caregiver than he did playing with other children his age, forced to care for and protect—to the best of his adolescent ability—his mother, who could barely provide for herself, let alone Matt and his two siblings. Doing his best with what little they had, Matt oftentimes found himself in situations that required him to fend off drug-crazed boyfriends, dealers, and other random lowlife associates often found hanging around their neglected home in Richmond, California. His younger sister Samantha died at twenty-three, just two years ago, another victim of the ever-present and increasingly deadly fentanyl crisis. Jacob, his youngest sibling, is a current resident of the California Department of Corrections; the judge, tired of seeing him in court for the same drug charges, decided that a lengthy prison sentence was the cure for his addictive dilemma.

Through the utter chaos of Matt's childhood and teenage years, he still managed to graduate from high school, even going on to community college and earning a few credits in general course studies before dropping out to focus on music. Throughout his strange and hectic lifetime, he increasingly found himself drawn to ancient studies focusing on the esoteric, Egyptian mythology, occult rituals, past civilizations, and anything involving old religions, demonology, or the like. Fascinated by the possibilities of strange worlds beyond the average human's comprehension, his ruminations on the unknown are not born purely out of curiosity. Matt has always had a strange sense of cognition about the world around him. From childhood, he would experience sudden bursts of visual enlightenment, accompanied by the feeling that he was seeing the true nature of the world and what lies beneath the fabric of what everyone else sees on a day-to-day basis. On one occasion he attempted to convey his experiences to a school counselor after a particularly disturbing vision. The results of his confession consisted of a three-week stay in the psychiatric wing of the local hospital, accompanied by several prescriptions for medications and a year of mental health appointments mandated by the state. No longer comfortable sharing his experiences with others, Matt instead dove into the mysterious world of ancient writings and occult literature in a feverous attempt to gain a better understanding of his otherworldly episodes.

Extreme metal music was an easy art form for Matt to gravitate toward, with many of his favorite bands incorporating the same dark elements that he was interested in and—to a disturbing degree—was intimately familiar with. Meeting some fellow like-minded individuals in high school, Matt and a few friends formed a band, giving him an outlet for his thoughts and strange meditations. Seven years later, Nokturnal Skies has found moderate success in their musical endeavors, affording them the opportunity to record and tour, even seeing a small return on their sonic investment. Over the years they have built a strong following—a flock of metalheads whose enthusiasm for the music is wholly blind to the actualities of Matt's lyrical allusions and underlying conceptual realities. Three albums later, the band has made their name commonplace amongst local heavy metal discourse. Jacob's effortless skin-bashing skills, Steven's pulsating bass notes, Erik's driving guitar riffs, and Matt's captivatingly evil stage presence and vocal abilities have given credibility to their dark sounds and relentless brutality. A name in the metal scene drawing reverence and respect from its oblivious fanbase, Nokturnal Skies is, quite simply, a musical expression of Matt's arcane knowledge and unexplainable experiences.

Matt's slender form stands in respectable repose upon the stage after a long and chaotic show. His skinny, lengthy frame appears much taller on stage as he scans the audience one more time before bidding farewell, scowling with finality to ensure the crowd takes with them a piece of the concluding frenzy. Long black hair swings well past his shoulders as he thanks the crowd and turns toward the back of the stage, quickly making his way to the stairs. Two young women dressed in tight black leather skirts are standing to the right side of the stairway as he exits, the leftmost female staring lustfully into his eyes. His lengthy dark hair provides a dull contrast to his true gray eyes, a rarity amongst the human population. Stepping down from the back of the stage, Matt briskly makes his way over to the bar located in the far corner of the club.

Grabbing the leg of a nearby stool with his leather combat boot, he drags it closer and takes a seat at the farthest end of the bar. Signaling the server with a subtle hand gesture, Matt orders a bottle of Heineken and pulls a pack of Marlboros from his right pocket. While fumbling around in his pockets for a lighter, he is interrupted by a smooth feminine hand with painted black nails inching toward his face. The flick of a lighter clicks and a flame greets the cigarette hanging loosely from his lips. He looks to the right to see the woman who previously caught his gaze, once again leering carnally into his soulless gray irises. "Great show tonight," she whispers into his ear, the warmth of her breath caressing his skin with a rapturous radiation.

"My pleasure... Are you a fan of our music?" Matt slyly replies, a lascivious grin adorning his lips.

"I am now," she responds in a soft, prurient voice, her hand reaching up toward Matt's lips. She removes the cigarette from his mouth and takes a long drag, exhaling the smoke into the thick barroom atmosphere.

A sensual voice casually and suddenly appears from the other side of his face, carrying with it an unanticipated but warmly welcomed pleasantness. "We were wondering if you would like to come back to my place," she whispers into his ear, ending with a subtle inflection of tone. "We were thinking we could maybe have some drinks...light some candles..." She wantonly trails off with a salacious smile.

"I think I may be able to accompany you two lovely ladies," Matt answers with a smile, tilting the bottle of Heineken toward his lips. As he sets the bottle on the bar, the server simultaneously places three shots of whiskey in front of him, ordered by the two women prior to their appearance. The woman to his right picks up one of the shots, her painted black nails carefully embracing the glass. Matt glances downward toward the shots to find that only one remains, the other resting against the lips of the woman to his left. He watches her tip the glass upward, finishing her drink without even a hint of irritation. Slowly turning his head to the right, his eyes fixate on painted black nails curving upward toward the ceiling as the first woman swallows her stinging libation, setting the glass atop the bar while licking her crimson-hued lips. Taking Matt's hand, she gently prompts him from his stool, her tight leather dress swaying seductively while she guides him toward the exit.

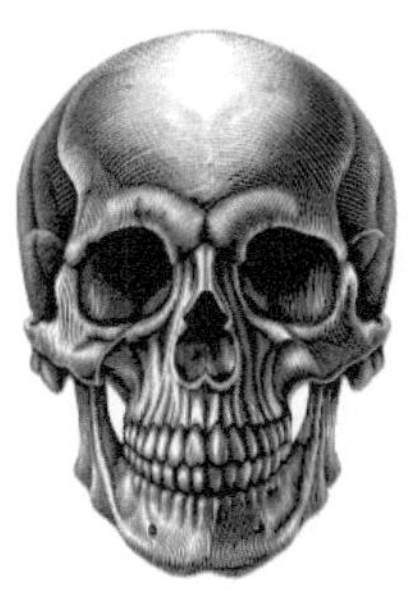

V.

A restless anticipation grips the attendees of the physics conference at the University of California, Berkeley, announced just two days ago at the behest of Dr. Phillip Jennings, the head of the particle physics department. The waves of excitement are palpable amongst the scientists here gathered, the possibilities innumerable as postulations and theories surge in the minds of the men and women in attendance. Whispers of doubt and consternation among some; nods of agreement and smiles of exhilaration amongst others. All await in unshakable suspense for the arrival of Dr. Jennings to give his presentation on the recent discovery.

As Martin enters the conference room, he scans the seating arrangements for an empty chair. The chatter among his colleagues is boisterous, resounding with sentiments of excitement and enthusiasm. Picking a chair near the far end of the long table centered in the room, he takes a seat, eager for the discourse to begin. No sooner than he is seated, Dr. Jennings enters the room. A nervous silence graces his presence as he walks to the front of the conference hall and gently sets his papers on the table before him. Those gathered for the conference are aware of the reason they were summoned: talks of a newly discovered fundamental particle have had the rumor conveyor rolling, and Martin has had his fill of the speculation over the last couple days.

Dr. Jennings looks around the room, a slight smile forming in the corners of his mouth. "Good afternoon, everyone. I know many of you have heard some rumblings on the recent discovery at Athena Laboratories." The silence in response is stifling; every member of the conference holds their breath in restless prospection. "It appears that a new fundamental particle has indeed been detected using the Max Planck Accelerator. Researchers and scientists at Athena Laboratories are proposing that the particle is, in fact, a graviton." The silence is now replaced with an overabundance of response so thick and voluminous that a single coherent thought can barely be discerned.

"So what does this mean for the unification of Einstein's theories and..."

"Is the gravitational force at the quantum level..."

"How does this affect string theory in relation to..."

Several members of the room shout in unison before Dr. Jennings has an opportunity to finish his opening statement. "Please, everyone... I know the excitement is quite—" Once again, he is shut down by the incessant clamor of two dozen overenthusiastic scientists, and Dr. Jennings pauses his presentation to allow for the impassioned ripostes to gradually die down.

Martin, in his reserved and reverent mannerisms, sits quietly in peaceful observance, awaiting his opportunity to add to the unceasing questioning. As the probing begins to relent, Martin casually raises his hand, eyeing Dr. Jennings from across the room with an innocuous smile extended across his lips.

"Yes, Professor Patterson?" Dr. Jennings inquires.

"What energy levels were achieved to create the conditions necessary to observe these particles?"

"Well... I am not entirely sure, Professor Patterson. We don't have a full data summary at this time... But...the discovery report seems quite convincing."

"It seems to me that the consequences—" Before Martin can finish his sentence, he is interrupted by another round of disruptive probing from his overzealous fellow colleagues. Mired in the overwhelming notions of his own inquiry and the infinite possible causalities inherent to his speculations, Martin sits in silence for the remainder of the conference, unable to free himself from his obsession with that single fixed idea.

Two exceedingly energetic and tumultuous hours later, Dr. Jennings ends his assembly and the group disperses. Thoughts abound in Martin's mind of the implications surrounding this new discovery. The idea that the unification of the four fundamental forces of physics may finally be within reach grips his mind with an overwhelming embrace. *Einstein's final quest for a unified theory of everything could quite possibly be upon us*, he contemplates, pulling his pipe from his front pocket as he exits the physics hall.

Walking down the stairway leading to the faculty parking lot, Martin flips the top open on his lighter. Thoughts of the Max Planck Particle Accelerator interrupt his motions before he can place a flame upon his pipe. He is well aware of the facility located within the Sonoran Desert. Athena Laboratories currently houses the world's largest particle accelerator, three times the size of the Large Hadron Collider in Switzerland. Martin was involved in the development of the facility, as were most of the well-known physicists at the time of its inception. Designed from new alloys created from materials found deep within the earth, the ultra-sensitive detectors and super-conductive magnets contained within the accelerator are an astonishing feat of mechanical and electrical engineering. The fifty-one miles of closed-loop beam pipes forming the circumference of the collider ring, located six hundred feet below the desert surface, are awe-inspiring to say the least. No less astonishing are the expansive computer infrastructures, exhaustively wide-ranging control systems, and the high energy injection mechanisms comprising the rest of the massive framework that forms the world's most advanced particle collider. Years of painstaking construction, thousands of scientific minds in laborious integration, and enough raw materials to construct an entire municipality, has provided the means for the Max Planck Particle Accelerator to become one of the greatest collaborations of science and engineering mankind has ever witnessed.

From Isaac Newton's laws of motion and gravitation to the insights provided by quantum mechanics and the hypothesis of string theory, and now, with the discovery of a particle that describes the framework of the very smallest units of mass attraction, mankind's most fundamental understanding of gravity's true nature could, quite possibly, be within mankind's grasp. Thoughts swirl with unyielding rapidity inside Martin's head as he ponders the impact that this remarkable achievement in scientific history will have on humanity. He opens the door of his Nissan Altima and sinks into the cracked leather seat. Remembering the lighter still clutched within his sweat-covered hand, he strikes the wheel with his thumb and ignites the pipe resting laboriously between his teeth. Puffing away at his favorite briar bowl, he turns the key to his ignition and tunes the radio to his favorite classic rock station, listening intently for something to relieve his overstimulated mind.

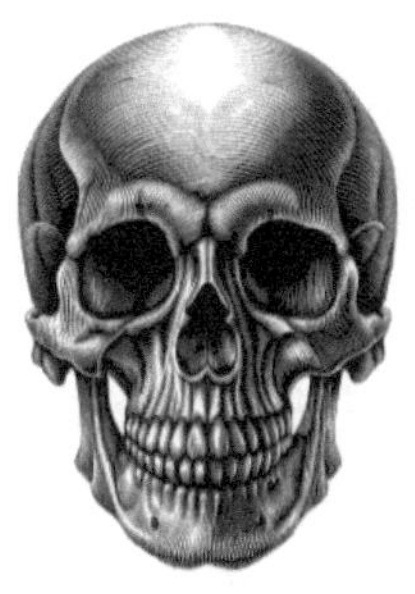

VI.

The bass from the subwoofers in the trunk reverberates through the entire car, violently shaking the rearview mirror and pounding within the chests and bodies of the two moderately intoxicated occupants. Jessie reaches toward the stereo and turns it up another notch, as trap beats echo throughout Sunset Strip, emanating loudly from the windows of Blake's Camaro SS. An older model vehicle, Blake's car is not without a few cosmetic inconsistencies—a primer-colored left front fender, some dents along the rear bumper—however, it is fast and loud, enough to attract the attention of the high school crowd that Blake's peers primarily consist of.

Between Jessie's legs rests a bottle of Patron, purchased earlier that evening by Blake's older brother after almost ten full minutes of pleading by Jessie and Blake. Headed first to pick up Shawn from his house, then to a party hidden in the woods on the outskirts of town, Jessie and Blake are already buzzed, a mixture of marijuana, tequila, and teenage hormones, amplified by the hopeful prospects of a party atmosphere and sexual fulfillment, coursing through their veins.

Pulling up to a red light at the intersection of Sunset Boulevard and Holloway Drive, they look to their right to see two attractive women in a black BMW M8 stopped in the lane beside them. Reaching over once again, Jessie turns the bass up four more units, the pounding low frequency shaking both Blake's Camero and the BMW next to it. Jessie looks over toward the two women, who appear to be in their early thirties, with a cocky smile across his mildly intoxicated face. Blake's head comes creeping into view as he slowly leans forward, a farcical, half-witted smirk smeared along his countenance. Annoyed by the thumping reverberation of the trap beats overwhelming their conversation, the two women look over to see two stoned and semi-absurd faces staring intently back at them from the car to their left. The two women look back ahead as the light turns green, speeding ahead of the two men in an attempt to escape the loud music and creepy vibes given off by the gazing teenagers.

"You scared the bitches off again, bro!" Blake jokingly asserts, grabbing the bottle from Jessie. "Lemme fuck wit dat... *Whew...* Damn, bro... That shit *hits!*" Blake stammers, slamming down a large gulp of tequila, allowing a stream of liquor to dribble from the corner of his mouth and down his chin as he struggles to conceal the afterburn.

"Quit wasting that shit, *lightweight.* You got more of it on your chin than in your mouth," Jessie fires back as he snatches the bottle from Blake's hand, carefully scanning the area for police before taking another swig. It's just past sunset and the breeze through the windows of Blake's car feels cool on Jessie's face. The last couple days have been hot, even for Los Angeles in July, and the two of them have been cutting grass for Blake's older brother's lawn care business all week long.

Blake glances over at Jessie with a facetious smirk, wiping the alcohol from his mouth. "So...who's this chick you're supposed to bang tonight... *I mean*, meet up with?" It's followed by a snarky chuckle. Jessie had mentioned her to Blake a few times previously throughout the week, seemingly excited at the prospect.

Jessie looks over with a furtive smile across his face. "Some girl my boy Blue told me about. Remember that dude's house we were at a few weeks back… He had those mushrooms…then a couple girls and some dude rolled through and got a bag off him?" Blake looks over from the driver's seat with a puzzled grin on his face, trying through liquor-distorted reasoning to recall the event.

"Oh…yeah, *yeah*. One of the chicks had green hair on one side of her head or some shit."

"Yessir… The other one…Olivia, the brunette. That's the one. Blue told me she thought I was cute or some shit. Told my dude to hook me up with her name. Then I found her on Instagram."

"Word, my dude. So, she'll be at the party tonight for sure?"

"That's what she said. I got this molly… Figured we'd take some and see what happens. Know what I mean, bro?" Jessie quips, pulling the bag of pills from his pocket and glancing down at it with a mischievous smile.

Pulling onto Clearview Drive from Benedict Canyon in Beverly Hills, Blake turns down the radio as they head up the hill toward Shawn's driveway. They've been warned before by the local police about the loud bass pulsating from the trunk of his car—complaints from the neighbors regarding past visits over the previous months. An open bottle of Patron, a pocket full of ecstasy, and myriad other paraphernalia scattered about the car heightens their awareness of possible police presence on this particular summer evening as they cruise insidiously through the neighborhood. Veering into the driveway of the Modern Movement-style home, Blake screeches the tires to a halt, stopping the vehicle mere inches from the rustic wooden garage door.

The car doors slam as Jessie and Blake exit the vehicle, the driver door creaking as it shuts due to the denting on the front end where the panel was replaced. Sauntering in through the back gate near the rear patio, Jessie flings the gate open, causing it to crash into a trash can on the other side. "Whoops," Jessie mouths flippantly, stumbling slightly as he steps through. Blake follows clumsily behind, tripping over the steps leading up to the side entrance, buzzed from the huge slugs of Patron he was taking on the way over.

Jessie hesitates before ringing the doorbell, checking his breath and straightening his shirt as he smiles farcically into the camera on the bell, trying ineffectually not to look inebriated. Working through a slight pang of anxious apprehension, Jessie unenthusiastically presses the button on the doorbell, silently hoping that Shawn answers and not one of his parents. A dark figure appears behind the door, a brooding, sluggish pace accompanying its presence. Listless, squinting eyes slowly come into view through the windowpane, followed by a bright sobering light over their heads as the floodlight clicks on above the doorway. The inside door opens and a tall man—donning a suit, tie, and scotch on the rocks in his left hand—presents himself through the storm door. "Hello, Jessie. Hello, Blake," he drones in an indifferently dispassionate tone.

"Hey, Mr. Townsend... Is...Shawn here?" Jessie nervously stutters. He and Blake cannot stand Shawn's parents, mostly due to the fact that they've made it clear over the years that they do not like, nor do they respect, Jessie, Blake, or either of their families. A household consisting of Mr., a successful stockbroker, and Mrs., a savvy real estate investor, Shawn's parents have done exceptionally well for themselves, and it vexes them profoundly that their son cannot seem to find better accompaniment than the likes of Jessie and Blake.

The idea that Jessie and Blake even have a friend living in Beverly Hills is perplexing in and of itself; the result of a friendship that Jessie and Shawn formed several years ago at a Christian fellowship for teens. Starting innocuously enough when Shawn was fourteen and Jessie thirteen, over the ensuing time their interests grew apart and the friendship became less amiable and more manipulative. As they entered their later teen years, Jessie got more involved in drugs and the party lifestyle, with Shawn aimlessly following behind in a lost and semi-desperate struggle to maintain the relationship. The last two years have been more of a test of endurance than a friendship—Jessie and his friends using Shawn for his financial means and Shawn holding onto the nostalgia of times past, nourished by a total lack of self-esteem.

"Shawn is downstairs in the theatre room… Just what exactly are the plans for tonight, gentlemen?" Mr. Townsend questions in an austere and imposing tone, standing in authoritative obstinance, raising his scotch toward his lips.

"We thought we…uh…we'd meet up with some friends. Maybe… see…a movie?" Jessie hastily conjures, fabricating the first thing that comes to mind. Jessie looks over toward Blake's direction to find him nervously grinding his shoe into the natural granite flooring of the kitchen, looking downward in awkward silence.

Mr. Townsend takes another drink and eyes Jessie with an incredulous scan. "A movie? I see. What's playing?" he inquires, knowing full well that a movie is not on the agenda for the evening. Mr. Townsend had already been informed of their intentions, questioning his son earlier that afternoon with a lengthy and thorough interrogation. Shawn is usually straightforward with his father—an expert at spotting his son's deceit.

Knowing he is caught, Jessie quickly rearranges the dialogue. "Not…really sure… Did you say he was down there?" Jessie adds with a rapid succinctness, sliding swiftly past Mr. Townsend and toward the downstairs entryway. He briskly makes his way through the hallway leading to the basement with Blake following closely behind, ending the escape with an abrupt slamming of the door in a hurried thud.

The sound of their trampling feet rushing down the steps causes Shawn to look back from the TV.

"What's up, guys?"

"Your dad is a dick, bro," Blake angrily retorts, strutting his way over to Shawn and plopping down on the leather couch next to him.

"I know," Shawn mutters in a low and shameful voice as he looks back toward the TV.

"Hey, does your dad use mouthwash?" Jessie asks with mischievous seriousness.

"Yeah... Why?"

"Is it the yellow kind?" questions Jessie, a sordid, wide-eyed look emanating from within his visage.

"I think so," Shawn replies, a confused look forming on his face.

"You should fucking piss in it!" Jessie slyly suggests, followed by a nefarious chuckle.

Blake bursts forth with a brief and uncontrolled cackle. "*Haaa*! So, anyways... Let's raise up out this piece, *dawg*! I don't want your *bitch-ass* dad coming down here...being all inquisitive and such!"

"Hold up, let me save my game real quick," Shawn implores, manipulating the PlayStation controller in his hands as he hastily maneuvers through the menu screen. He presses the button to open the save section, and suddenly the screen goes dark. "*What the...*" Shawn looks up to see Jessie standing next to the TV, his finger slowly moving away from the power button on the side of the screen.

"*C'mon, fucker*, let's roll," Jessie loudly asserts with commanding dominance and a devilish grin as he advances assertively toward the stairs.

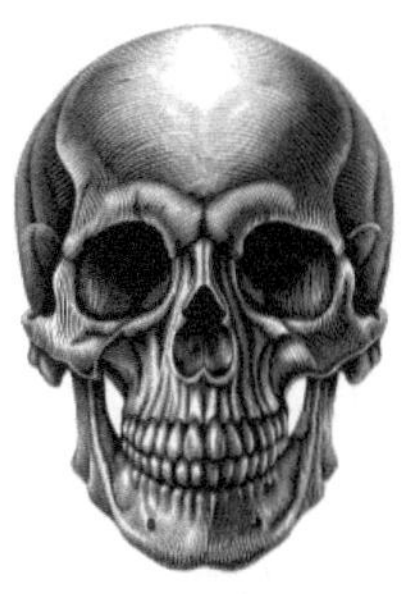

VII.

"How many times is it gonna take for you to get that *fucking* intro right? *Jesus fucking Christ!*" Matt snaps loudly and belligerently at Erik, frustrated with his multiple failed attempts to properly play the introduction riff to their new song.

"*Fuck you, Matt!* You play it, *asshole!*" Erik fires back, setting down his guitar and picking his beer up from the top of his amplifier.

"Chill, guys. Let's take a break, drink some beers...then back at it in a few," proposes Jacob as he places his drumsticks down on his snare.

Matt, now feeling like a jerk, exhales deeply and turns to Erik. "*Fuck...alright.* Hey, bro, sorry. Not trying to be a dick. Just frustrated," he explains, picking his bottle of Heineken up from the floor. An unnaturally despondent ambiance fills the rehearsal room this evening. A disquieting mood tempers the emotions of the band members—they are all feeling it, yet no one mentions the strange, unnerving aura of perturbation filling the air.

The other members of the band know Matt to be an unrelenting perfectionist when it comes to his lyrics and vocal arrangements. Countless times before they have witnessed this very dilemma in Matt's deportment. They can tell all too well that his unease is due to his frustration with the lyrics to their latest musical effort. His irritation during this night's rehearsal stems from the feeling that something is missing from the new song—something abysmal and disquieting—a translation to a newly discovered ancient text that he cannot seem to weave appropriately into the next line of the chorus.

Oftentimes in the past, his fellow bandmates have been the unfortunate observers to drastic and morbidly abrupt changes in Matt's mood when conceptualizing his lyrics. On one ominously prophetic occasion, Steven happened upon Matt in his bedroom—unresponsive—his eyes rolled back in his head, only the whites exposed, and a haunted, belabored breathing emanating from his lungs. Matt had been working feverishly for days on end, pouring over translations of ancient Sumerian texts in an obsessive and frantic attempt to complete the lyrical structures for their first official release. Unsure of what to do and gripped with a panic-stricken consternation at the sight of his incapacitated and beleaguered friend, Steven violently shook Matt in a feeble attempt to awaken him from his unresponsive state. Matt's reaction to the impulsive shaking was eerily cryptic, his head turning ever so slightly with the whites of his rolled-back eyes meeting Steven's disturbed and disbelieving gaze. What happened next still troubles Steven's cloudy recollection, and to this day, he is not quite sure that what he witnessed was not a fabrication of his distorted reflection. Of what he recalls from the macabre and distressing experience, Steven is not completely certain, yet what he thought he heard sounded like an unearthly growl erupting from Matt's gaping jaw between the rasped, spectral breathing of his besieged, phantasmal respiration. The inhuman growl Steven wishes was the sole dreadful happening of this horrifying occurrence, for what followed truly defies explanation and haunts his memory with a nightmarish retrospection. It appeared—at least to his feeble, distressed observation—that a whirling mass of hideous, demonic entities of the apparitional sort accompanied the monstrous growl, spewing forth from his mouth with a foul, barely visible stream of ghostly emittance.

Moments later, Matt awakened from his passive state, unable to recall what had happened, nor did he remember at what point he fell away from reality. Steven never mentioned to Matt what he witnessed; he was not even sure that what he saw transpired as he recalled it. Locked away in his subconscious, the memory remains, any hint of remembrance stuffed deep down in a dank mental cellar of denial and skeptical rationalization.

Outside of the rehearsal space, in an unused, crumbling parking lot across from an abandoned brewery, Erik finds Matt shuffling about, knocking around small broken pieces of pavement with his boot, tilting back his beer in between kicks. "The fuck's going on, man?" Erik asks with a forced layer of sympathetic concern. "I can tell you're pissed off about something. Writing these lyrics getting to you or something, man?"

Matt gently kicks another broken-off chunk of cement with the tip of his boot and stops cold, glaring up from the ground with an empty and solemn appearance. "The latest texts they've discovered are intense," he replies, taking another drink from the green bottle clutched between his thumb and forefinger. "Nothing like the stuff we've done before... This stuff...it's dark...vast...*singular...*" He trails off, taking another sip from his Heineken while gazing into the night sky. The band's lyrical concepts have always been conceived of ancient mythology—arcane and esoteric translations of old religions and forgotten beliefs. Recently, two new ancient writings had been discovered in Egypt: a strange mixture of Sumerian script, Egyptian hieroglyphs, and a form of writing that is highly advanced for its time and speaks of strange ancient worlds and demonic spirits undocumented until recent months.

The texts were discovered in a strange tomb isolated from civilization, buried in the desert three hundred and fifty miles southwest of the great pyramids, just outside the town Qasr Farâfra in the Al Farâfra district of Egypt. The tomb was discovered by mistake when a team of archaeologists stumbled upon it while searching for artifacts relating to the army of Cambyses, fifty thousand soldiers that disappeared in sixth century BC after being sent to destroy the Oracle of Amun. It is an ongoing process, with new texts being discovered by the month. Some have been released to the public and others have yet to be discovered. With the help of a large language model, namely the TIA (Translations Interpretations and Analysis) AI platform, archeologists have been able to translate the texts and release them to the public at a rate that was never possible in pre-artificial intelligence times.

Erik looks solemnly toward Matt; he loathes to see him in this mindset. "Look, bro. I fucking hate it when you get like this. Our music...these lyrics...they're not that important. You can write our lyrics about *anything*. Doesn't have to be this *weird*, old shit. You always get yourself so fucking worked up trying to get them perfect—"

Angered by the implication, Matt cuts Erik off, raising his voice in defiance. "*Fuck that*! These concepts, these ideas... They're a fucking part of me! I can't write some *fairy*-ass bullshit about some fantasyland, make-believe nonsense... We're not fucking *Slayer*...fucking *Pantera*. I want something FUCKING REAL! The ancient civilizations that wrote this shit... They lived it, worshipped it, *sacrificed* for it!"

Unsettled by the verbal lashing, Erik, too, now raises his tone. "*Yeah*...and look what it does to you writing it! Immersed in this *shit* like it's all that matters!"

"Fuck you, Erik! Go join some other *pussy*-ass band if you can't handle this shit. Nokturnal Skies is about more than just music. It's a window into the ancient worlds. I want our fans to experience what I experience… The *fucking* blackness…the cold…the abyss…" Once again, Matt trails off, tipping his beer toward his lips—empty, the last drop sliding from the edge of the bottle across his tongue. Angered by the thought of his beer being depleted, and frustrated by Erik's impassioned intervention, Matt hurls the bottle toward Erik, shattering it into hundreds of pieces just inches from his feet.

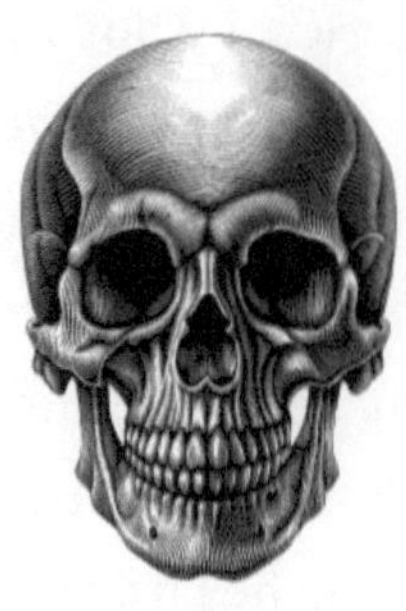

VIII.

Tormented screams resonate within the mortared stone walls of the cellar, filling the already foreboding atmosphere with a superfluous dimension of ghastly devilry. The woman's cries of agony are not pleadings for help, however; any semblance of hope has long since faded away from her consciousness—all that remains is the agonizing reality of her stark, irremediable dilemma. The screams amplify with each embrace of the blade, her skin giving way to the steel in an almost reverent display of subservience as Charles gracefully carves the ancient signs into her flesh, languidly and with great deliberation—the details must be exact for the ritual to be of satisfactory effect.

Stripped of clothing and dignity, she hangs helplessly, crudely, from the wooden archway of Charles's antiquated and dismally lit wine cellar. Black candles line the floor of the crypt-like vault, scantily illuminating the cavernous room with flickering hues of hellish orange incandescence, as if twisting souls were dancing amidst the flames. The rocky masonry of the damp cellar walls is spattered with blood droplets near where her body hangs. The crimson essence of her life appears quite black in the faintly glowing candlelight, creating a ghoulish backdrop for the barbaric events underway. The wine bottles that line the walls of the cellar are covered in dust and grayish-silver webbing, adding a clarifying contrast to the blood-red-splattered walls. The vinification of these bottles occurred centuries ago, a testament to olden times and antiquated ways—an extraordinarily appropriate landscape for the ancient ceremony taking place.

Her suffering is palpable; Charles can sense the essence of her lamenting spirit—an overwhelming sensation of wonder as the horrors of mystical enlightenment unveil their darkened secrets before him. Charles utters ancient ceremonial chants, last spoken by a forgotten and undocumented civilization—syllables and phrases not hissed since primeval times. These words have long since been forgotten, erased from the memory of modern man and unearthed by the unspeakable creatures of dimensions hidden away from human consciousness. With each symbol he inscribes upon her twisted body, her screams grow louder, as if every successive insignia summons the torment of yet another tortured spirit released from unknown confines by way of her mouth. His vision blurs and the signs of the ancient ones gradually come into focus. A kaleidoscopic panorama of carnivorous tribulation unfolds before him—a tapestry of demonic commands, compelling him to carve further still into her innocent flesh.

The ritual has been underway since dusk, and dawn draws near. Numerous times now the woman has lost consciousness, only to be revived through smelling salts—sal ammoniac, an elder concoction named after the patron god Ammon. Charles must not allow her awareness to fade during the ritual, for it is her suffering that allows the spirit world to grant him vision beyond human sight. Her body is covered from head to toe in lacerations and she is becoming weak from loss of blood. Charles takes great care not to carve too deeply; if she dies, he will not be able to finish the ritual. The sacrifice must be carried out within the confines of the ancient doctrine in order to obtain a vision of the translational progress.

The translations are paramount in Charles's blasphemous endeavors. The ancient documents recently discovered in Egypt are more than simple relics of the past. They were never meant for the living, buried long ago within the tombs of kings, rulers of the dark underworlds of archaic times. The archeologists currently working at the site in Al Farâfra are ignorant of the grave implications surrounding their discovery. The texts they have stumbled upon in that strange tomb of granite and sandstone construction hold the secrets of a black era, wiped from human history with deliberate intention.

Charles has witnessed this dark past in his dreams; time and time again his nightmares have bestowed upon him ancient knowledge of horrific times—times that mankind dares not dream of—horrors that were not meant for our fragile minds to comprehend. In his nocturnal reverie, he has beheld the slavery—the torturous revelations of mankind's past. What we were before—what he longs for man to become once more. Mutilation beyond comprehension pervades his subconscious. The enslavement and brutalization of men, women, and even children—the truth of our existence is more damning than even the most depraved mind can conceive of.

The last years of Charles's life have become more revealing, his dreams becoming nightmarishly vivid and more intense with each successive slumber. Archaic beings are beckoning his subconscious and influencing his motives, a carefully executed transgression since conception, his birth and childhood no mere coincidence of fate. His twisted youth and past experiences have been but a fabrication of sinister design, wrought by forces of magnificent power and unyielding strength. They provisioned the means—a test of human durability—

providing a blueprint for the most vile and debaucherous will to manipulate in a trial of human life. Countless times over the last several thousand years these dark influences have attempted to summon into existence a man of Charles's diabolical deportment. The most corrupt minds of history's sordid past were simply failed attempts at a conjuring, to be considered unsuccessful rites of profoundly blasphemous iniquity. While the greatest minds of dissolute and abject evil have perpetrated some of these beings' most cherished and favorable inhumanities—mass exterminations, genocide, global warfare—they were still undeserving of this ancient blessing.

Now, it seems, a singular being of human ancestry holds the qualities deserving of their demonic benediction. After countless eons of profane dabbling, their trans-dimensional reach into our world has finally gripped the spiritual inadequacies of our primordial roots. That ancient human will—so malleable and easily influenced—documented since biblical times, proves once again the template for a serpentine persuasion.

Blood drips steadily from fresh wounds about her left breast, the only remaining unmarked region of her body. Her terrified screams grow louder, as does Charles's chanting, creating a sickening symphony of tormented wailing and indecipherable ancient dialect as the blade etches the final symbol into her skin. The candles in the room begin to glow brighter now, as if some unseen force is stoking their morbidly incandescent flames. Inexplicably, the room grows darker as the candlelight burns brighter, causing the cellar to seem even unholier than it previously appeared. The darkness is not an absence of light; a black presence can be felt by both Charles and his terror-stricken victim. Sounds of damnation fill the void, echoing with reverberations of monstrous hostility. Growls of epic ferocity fade in and out of perception, like an entity comprised of a malicious resonance is attempting to break through to our spiritual plane of existence. A pulsating vibration can be felt by both occupants, rumbling with vehement undertones and eerie oscillations. A wave of misanthropic radiance engulfs the darkened cellar, saturating the air with a stifling constriction, and for a brief moment, all is forsakenly vacuous.

A droplet of blood trickles down her left breast, exiting the laceration from which the final sigil was hewn. It slowly makes its way underneath the curvature of her chest, running in an unsettling line down her abdomen with a languid, otherworldly pace. It stops for a brief repose, resting peacefully above her navel. The momentary respite is broken as it continues once more, only to stop a final time at the base of her labia. An almost serene confluence of fluidity and desolation abounds throughout this momentary suspension of horror as if some preamble to an undetermined final judgment was underway. All is still—all is silent—barren emptiness—nothingness.

The blade comes rushing from below with an infernal velocity, penetrating her vulva in a forward trajectory with such incredible intensity that it completely slices through to the rear of her sacrum. Charles thrusts the blade upward with an exceedingly tremendous force, such that it causes the two halves of her being to split into separate sections, creating a lateral duality of wrenching human portions and thrashing limbs. The blood flow is phantasmagorical, the quantity seemingly endless in volume. The sounds of her torso crudely halving is sickening, surpassed only by the demonic growling building in exponential layers with each successive inch the knife travels. Her skull separates and the divisions of her partitioned corpse disperse, leaving two human halves dangling in nauseating morbidity from the wooden archway.

With a transformational continuity, the low moans and maleficent growls metamorphose into a spectral vision, as if a dynamically shifting scenery was revealing itself to Charles's awareness. His resplendent blue eyes are wide now with wonder, the impressions before him presenting a scenery of segmented omniscience. The ritual is now complete, and his reward, the infernal blessing of sight. Charles bears witness to the progress of the archeologist's work. The Al Farâfra project nears completion—he has now seen it within his own mind. Tossing the knife to the ground, Charles turns away from the sanguinary dishevelment he has left in the cellar, the grisly remains of his victim wholly meaningless to him.

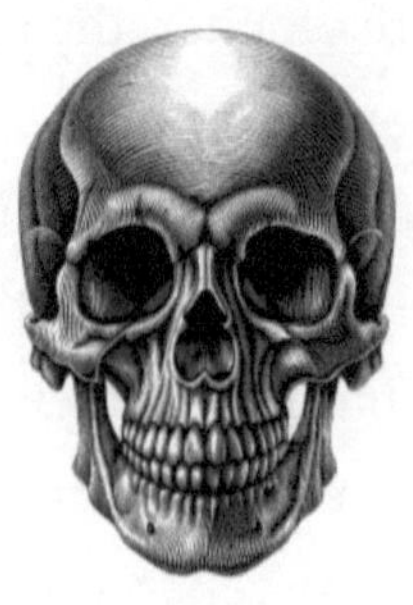

IX.

As Martin pulls into his driveway, he turns down the radio and switches off the air conditioning, an ingrained habit he has always adhered to but never fully comprehended. His modest ranch-style house in the middle-class suburb of Pinole in Contra Costa County, California, is a place he has called home since the divorce many years ago. A man of significant means by way of his professorship and multiple published writings and scientific journals, Martin has never found it necessary to inhabit a larger home, instead feeling quite content to reside in a smaller, more manageable residence.

Aside from the peace of mind accompanying his three-bedroom, one and a half bathroom, low-maintenance dwelling, the view from the back deck provides Martin with a significant sense of ease. On a clear day he can just see the edges of the San Pablo Bay, a particularly alluring amenity that he has always cherished, even though only the faintest outline of the waters can be seen.

Walking through the doorway to his home, Martin pauses to switch on the lights to the living room. He tosses his brown leather briefcase bag onto the couch beside the wall and makes his way forward toward the kitchen, famished after a long day of lecturing. He sets his black, wire-framed glasses on the faux marble kitchen countertop and rubs his nose with his thumb and forefinger, a pang of anxiousness building as he suddenly notices a headache fast approaching. Perhaps it is his hunger spurring his cranial discomfort...or maybe it is the incessant overthinking prompted by the recent discovery at Athena Laboratories he has been overwhelmingly preoccupied with. Opening the drawer to his right, Martin pulls a butter knife from the utensil organizer, the thought of a sandwich relieving some of his angst.

Closing the drawer, he is suddenly redirected by the vibration of his phone buzzing intermittently from his pants pocket. Hesitantly, Martin looks downward toward his screen, followed by a brief consideration to press ignore, the thought of making a sandwich sounding far more appealing. As Martin reads the contact's name across the screen, he is surprised to see Dr. Jennings calling him this late in the evening. Once again, the option of ignoring the call appeals to him, his stomach gurgling in a vociferous, rumbling cacophony of hunger-induced growling. His conscience besting his appetite, he reluctantly hits the answer button on the screen.

"Greetings Dr. Jennings!" Martin exclaims in his most amicable, yet fraudulently genuine voice.

Martin's artificial conviviality quickly turns to sedate concern upon hearing the tone of Dr. Jennings' voice at the other end of the conversation. Martin stands in his kitchen in abject silence, the butter knife still in his other hand, listening to the ominous perturbations preoccupying Dr. Jennings' reasoning. Martin listens intently, albeit dubiously, to the strange details concerning the implications of the call. A particular brand of fear begins to well inside his gut as he digests the words and phrases pouring clumsily and perplexingly through the phone, the kind that he would get as a child when his parents would argue and he could not help but feel that for some unknown reason he was to blame for all their troubles. Jennings explains that he was contacted by officials at the Central Intelligence Agency regarding matters that require further investigation of a scientific and analytical nature. Martin feels a peculiar incertitude rising within his mind, accompanied by a wearisome nervousness building atop the fear in his stomach, as Dr. Jennings continues to describe the situation, feeling all the while as if there is something that Jennings is perhaps afraid to state directly.

Dr. Jennings' vague utterances and seemingly evasive detailing prompts Martin to interrupt. "Am I or one of my colleagues in some sort of trouble?" The phone call goes silent. It is unclear to Martin whether the call was dropped or if his question posed implications warranting grave consideration. Finally, the silence is broken by a calming reassurance from Jennings that he would simply like to gather a small team of academics familiar with the types of problems the CIA are facing to "collect their thoughts" in an attempt to adjust for mathematical anomalies in the data that has been gathered. He assures Martin that some irregular incidents are being reported and some officials within the government would like to assemble a small team of professors to look over the data. Feeling a small yet comforting level of relief quelling his disquietude, Martin takes a breath, finally placing the butter knife on the kitchen counter, realizing he has been gripping it so tightly that his hand was beginning to cramp. Dr. Jennings pleasantly ends the conversation, following the assurance from Martin that he will be at the scheduled conference in two days.

Turning his attention back to his sandwich, the thought of a glass of wine suddenly overtakes his desire for food. As he pours the cabernet into his favorite glass, Martin returns once again to his scientific musings, a contemplation of past triumphs that often possesses his thoughts. Ruminations abound as he takes a sip from his glass, the fragrance of blackberry intermingled with the revolutionary ideas set forth by Galileo's heliocentric planetary model infusing his mind with limitless optimism and fathomless exhilaration. He imagines what it must have been like for Galileo in his time of scientific discovery—the persecution and imprisonment he faced for his findings, concepts too radical for the Church to accept. The thought of the upcoming solar eclipse, just one week away, suddenly occurs to him. *What fools they were to deny Galileo's concepts in light of such obvious and incontrovertible evidence.*

As Martin lies on the couch, his eyelids become heavy. A long day, coupled with a generous pour of cabernet sauvignon, is beginning to take effect, forming a potent elixir for sleep. Martin begins to doze off—glass still in hand—while barely holding onto his thoughts. Still pondering the concepts of planetary models and eclipses, contemplations of the ancient Egyptians creeps into his mind's view. As he fights to keep his eyes open, subtle and ominous considerations invade his free-falling cognizance. The ideas of old and the fears of impending doom that accompanied the eclipses of ancient times nudge his approaching reverie as he nears sleep. Martin closes his eyes a final time for the evening and drifts slowly into slumber, the images of an ancient civilization cowering before an apocalyptically eclipsed sun burning into his consciousness as it fades into darkness.

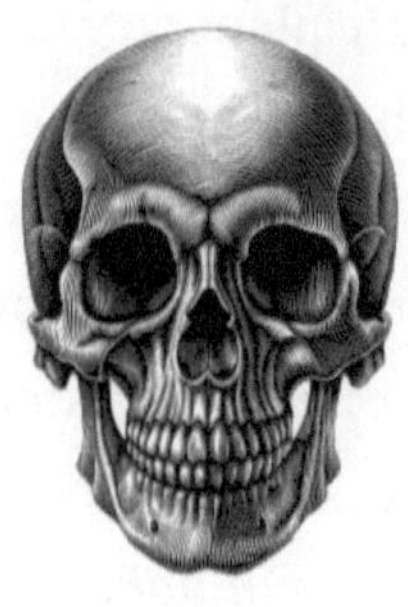

X.

On the outskirts of the Angeles National Forest in Arcadia, California, a small bonfire blazes, dimly lighting the clearing in the woods where a small party of teenagers have gathered, assembled for the purposes of fun and dance, augmented by alcohol, techno, and a choice selection of illicit substances. Around twenty teens have thus far accumulated, but the night is still young, and more are steadily arriving as twilight settles in. The moon is almost full tonight and the beats from the speakers thump steadily, creating a potent atmosphere for dance and flirtation, but perhaps more importantly, drug use and alcohol consumption.

A small pickup truck is parked in front of the fire and in the bed is a set of large monitors, a laptop, a turntable, and a burgeoning DJ dancing behind the platters to a mix he created specifically for tonight's occasion. A few strings of Christmas lights have been hung precariously around the makeshift DJ booth; a somewhat lackadaisical approach to stringing the lights was undertaken, it seems, yet the effect produced is enlivening nonetheless.

The forest floor in the clearing provides a suitable, if not uncertain, dance floor for the half-dozen or so attendees currently flittering to the repetitive beats. A few moments were spent clearing sticks and debris from the area when the hosts of the gathering first arrived, providing the means for the assembled partygoers to step fervently to the beats. It has not rained in a couple weeks, providing for a dry layer of dirt-covered dancefloor, an improvement over the last event held in this location which was rendered almost unusable by rainfall in the days leading up to the occasion.

This particular section of wooded area is newly discovered by the ever-watchful teens. They are always on the lookout for a new spot to party, the cops becoming aware of their haunts after the trash begins to accumulate and complaints from the public start to mount. Being that it is only the second time for a rave in this location, the organizers are vaguely confident that, at least for now, they are free from the perturbation of police presence.

A short distance from the epicenter of the soiree, a pair of headlights can be seen fast approaching through a clearing in the trees. Tires spinning across the leaves and sticks of the forest floor along the old service trail crackle and snap as the car makes its way through the scattered brush, careening through the woods in a manner typical of a fearless, perhaps inebriated, youth behind the wheel. A couple of the partygoers take notice and turns their heads toward the vehicle speeding along the underbrush, curious as to who has come to join their ranks. One of them, familiar with the owner of the vehicle, spots the primer-colored left front fender and immediately asserts that Blake and Jessie have arrived. As the Camaro draws nearer, those on the dance floor—or dirt-laden forest ground—are temporarily thrown off tempo, the bass from Blake's subwoofers overcoming the DJ's smaller, less powerful speakers. Passing the crowd of partygoers in an arrogant display of recklessness and over-abundance of speed, Blake finds a suitable place to park, roughly fifty yards or so from the center of the gathering.

Blake skids to a halt, throws the car into neutral, and yanks upward on the emergency brake as all three occupants prepare to exit the vehicle. Slamming the doors behind them, Jessie and Blake strut toward the crowd with a swaggering bravado, howling at their friends along the way while stopping to bump fists and bro-hug with their friends, leaving Shawn anxiously lumbering behind. The skunky aroma of marijuana and burning logs from the firepit hits Jessie's nostrils and he instinctually pulls a joint from his pocket, lighting it as he walks toward a small crowd gathered near the DJ's truck. "What's up, people?!" he shouts, sauntering over toward the group of teens gathered near the pickup.

"Hey, Jessie... Blake," a young woman sporting pigtails and a fedora hat shouts back from the group.

With a cunning smile, Blake gives a subtle nod. "*Whassup, Madison?* Where's your girl Chloe at tonight?" he asks, curious as to the whereabouts of a girl he's been interested in since the previous summer.

"I don't know. You guys just get here?" she questions with an innocent grin, looking downward at the joint in Jessie's hand. Feeling shunned by Madison's lack of interest in his inquiry, Blake heads off into the crowd to see if anyone has a beer he can freely procure. Eying Madison with a not-so-modest taunt, Jessie slowly raises the joint to his mouth.

"I bet you want to hit this, don't you?" He smirks, taking a long, slow hit, trying his best to arouse jealousy within the mind of his acquaintance.

"I *sure* do," Madison replies, a sly smile forming across her lips. "Pass that this way."

"Under one condition... Where's your friend Olivia?" Jessie coyly inquires, waving the joint around Madison's face, exhaling his smoke in her direction in a teasing, semi-flirtatious manner. Jessie had been looking forward all week to meeting up with Olivia. Since their introduction several weeks ago at his friend Blue's house, he has only chatted with her via social media, but tonight he's hopeful that she will come back home with him after the party.

Madison points her finger to her chin in a teasing manner, pretending to think about her friend's whereabouts. "Maybe she's here, maybe she's not," she responds, tilting her head and grinning as she snatches the joint from Jessie's hand. As Madison takes a puff from the pilfered jay, she casually tips her head to her right side, nonchalantly signaling that Olivia is across from the fire.

"Ha *ha*! Thanks, babe," Jessie hurriedly quips, seizing back his spliff as he gambols away, laughing teasingly while shooting her a mischievous glance. Making his way over toward the fire, Jessie eyes several small groups standing several yards removed from the flames. The night is young, and the day's humidity is still lingering; standing too close to the open blaze is not ideal on an evening such as this. Using the heat as an excuse to showcase his tattoo, Jessie removes his shirt, exposing the large skeleton and scythe tapestried across the whole of his back. He takes another glance around the small clearing in the woods, searching the obscurely lit woodland for the girl he came to meet. Spotting Olivia on the far side of the clearing, just outside the fire's blaze, Jessie puts his joint back in his mouth, making certain that upon approaching her he looks cool and collected, a tactic that he feels is sure to impress.

Before he can start in her direction, an annoying voice sounds abruptly from the edge of the woods. "*There you are...* I've been... You guys left me behind!" Shawn nervously stammers, interrupting Jessie mid-stride while stumbling clumsily from the bushes on the side of the pathway.

"*The fuck, Shawn?*! Where the hell did your goofy ass come from?"

Jessie sputters, not expecting to be abruptly approached from the low-lying brush.

Shawn looks to the tree line. "Over through there," he replies, pointing with one hand toward Blake's car while straightening his glasses with the other. "Where's Blake?"

"*Fuck...* I don't know. Chill, bro. Trying to head over to this bitch, bro. Just...fuck off for a bit, let me do my thing," Jessie blurts in response, perturbed by Shawn's sudden appearance.

"Can I at least get one of those pills?" Shawn goggles with an ungainly smirk, an almost puppy dog look filling his eyes.

Jessie sighs and reaches into his pocket, willing to do anything at the moment to rid himself of Shawn's presence. "Yeah. Here, man. Just do me a favor and chill for a while. Tryna put the mack on this chick. Feel me, bro?" Jessie removes the baggie containing several pills of ecstasy, proceeding cautiously so as not to drop them on the faintly lit forest floor. Shawn greedily snatches the pill from Jessie's hand and walks away, barely muttering an acknowledgement as he saunters toward the wood line. Tired of Jessie's indifference to his presence, Shawn decides he'll disappear for a while, thinking perhaps a walk in the woods will help relieve him of his present affliction. He tilts back his head and swallows the pill, straining to squeeze it down the back of his throat. Jessie watches from a distance as the light from Shawn's phone suddenly flashes on, then slowly fades away as he disappears into the forest.

Turning his attention back to his original objective, Jessie focuses his eyes back toward the group near the clearing. As he makes his way over, he checks his posture, making sure his shoulders are square and his chest is flexed. Just as he nears Olivia, her head turns toward him, laying eyes first on his muscular chest, then on the joint hanging loosely between his lips.

"*What's up, girl?*" Jessie confidently declares, pulling the spliff from his mouth and passing it in her direction while his green eyes meet hers in the dim firelight.

"*Heyyy...* For me? Thank you," she replies, taking the jay from his hand and putting it to her lips. "You just get here? Who'd you come with?"

"Yep, rode with Blake, the guy I was with the first time we met at Blue's," he explains, reaching up and running his hand gently through her hair before reluctantly adding, "Shawn's bitch-ass is around here somewhere too."

"That's cool," she says, her barely visible brown eyes meeting Jessie's with a suggestively carnal glance. Before Jessie can respond, the DJ drops a new beat, abruptly causing him to change his train of thought.

"*Shit, girl...* That's my jam. Wanna dance?" Jessie quickly requests, pointing his head in the direction of the DJ.

She hands back the joint and slowly exhales, simultaneously raising her eyebrow and flashing him a tempting smile. "Sure." Taking her by the hand, Jessie leads her over to the impromptu forest dance floor, her skin-tight low-rise shorts swaying seductively behind him as she follows. Stopping at the center of the dance area, Jessie pulls the baggie containing the molly pills from his jeans. She looks down at the baggie with a timid smile, the blue streak in her hair hanging teasingly down the side of her face.

"Say 'ah.'" Jessie smiles, placing a pill on the tip of her tongue, staring intently into her eyes as he drops the tablet inside her mouth. Taking two additional pills from the baggie, Jessie swallows them down, followed by a long, slow inhale from the joint still clasped between his fingers. Both begin to dance to the repetitious electronic beat, rhythmically pulsating to the techno cadence while several other teens gather amongst them, summoned subconsciously by the contagious, hypnotic sounds. For the next hour they dance and chat, with Jessie seizing every opportunity he can to cop a guileful feel, trying his best to get Olivia into a libidinous mood.

As the night stretches on, the effects of the MDMA take hold, prompting Jessie to feel light-headed and causing his heart to race inside his chest, its erratic beat pounding with rapid pulsations. Not wishing to seem weak in the presence of his suitor, Jessie slyly excuses himself to find a spot away from the crowd to rest, silently hoping that his feelings of indisposition will soon subside. Finding a tree near Blake's car, far removed from the sight of his fellow revelers, he seats himself on the ground, resting his back against the trunk of an old, far-reaching oak tree.

From the ground looking upward, the expansive limbs of the tree cast strange shadows amidst the moon's unsettling light, arousing disquieting apprehensions and morbid fears within Jessie's altered sense of reality. He closes his eyes to block out the dreadful vantage, which, for the present moment, seems to alleviate his substance-induced misgivings. In the distance, he can faintly hear the incessant techno drumbeats throbbing with a sickening permeation—infecting his mind with an odd assortment of lucid delusions. *Is a feeling of sickness overcoming me, or is a drug-laden episode of panic setting in?* he wonders, trying his best to hold together his rapidly diminishing sanity. With that rumination, his fears are solidified, almost as if the very idea of deliberating his rationality seals his impending neurotic fate.

A feeling of unprecedented alarm sweeps over him in a wave of physiological and mental manifestations, triggering his mind to twist in eerie contortions and his heart rate to increase further still. The overwhelming sense of foreboding anticipation seizes his acumen, holding him hostage within his own prison cell of flesh. Heightened sensitivity culminates in a frightening pinnacle of trepidation, leaving nothing to experience save the mind's own instinct for self-preservation. All goes black in a merciful gesture of exoneration as Jessie faints, falling into a state of fear-induced unconsciousness, his mind no longer able to cope with the crushing weight of its own consternation.

Jessie awakens from his blackened state to find himself lying on the ground surrounded by darkness and an ominous quiescence, otherworldly in its desolate blankness. Confusion encapsulates his mind, followed by a slow restoration of memories leading up to his unconsciousness. Bracing himself on the dirt and leaf-covered ground, Jessie pushes himself upward, leaning once more against the old oak tree, his efforts in doing so causing him to heave with an exhausting sigh. Unable to discern the time of night or how long he has been out, he reaches into his pocket for his phone only to be stopped cold by a disturbingly curious realization. An unearthly silence permeates his surroundings—no sounds of revelry echoing from the party, no music emanating from the DJ's sound system, not even the twittering of crickets chirping in the foliage encompassing the area—nothing but the chilling embrace of a frigid and hollow stillness extending though the disconsolate woodlands surrounding him.

Jessie cautiously rises to his feet, feeling unsteady from a mixture of dizziness and the disconcerting feelings miring his mindset. In the distance he can see the faint glow of the dying firelight, flickering mournfully through the tree line. Making his way through the brush to avoid the long walk through the pathway, he observes an additional disturbing realization: Although no people can be seen or heard, the parking area is full—the vehicles of his fellow partygoers remain, lining the woodland edge just as he last remembers.

Once again, that sweeping alarm grips firmly upon his being and his chest suddenly tightens under the surmounting forces of panic-induced anxiety. *No, this isn't right,* he thinks to himself as he instinctively starts running toward the fire, ignoring the thorn bushes digging deep into his arms. Trying as best he can to convince himself that all is well, Jessie sprints through the underbrush, frantically surveying the area for the presence of anyone as he draws nearer to the fire.

Finally reaching the source of the waning flames, he stops to survey the area, straining his eyes in an attempt to espy the scarcely lighted proximity. The lights on the DJ booth are no longer illuminated, leaving only the embers from the firepit to cast any radiance upon the area. Jessie squints his eyes as he focuses, barely able to make out the darkened shapes jumbled amongst the wooded scenery, the fire now hardly an adequate source of lighting. He pulls out his phone and swipes down with his thumb, unlocking his screen so that he can switch on the camera flash. As the light emanates from his phone, it shines a scarce illumination upon the area, and a dismally horrific backdrop appears within his view. Jessie's mind shatters beneath the weight of the appalling images before him—blood and flesh strewn across the landscape—so shockingly vast in magnitude that he nearly faints once more.

As he closes his eyes to block out the view, he questions his sanity, thinking—praying—that perhaps it is the drugs he consumed earlier that are causing his inconceivable observations. Gathering his courage, he opens his eyes, first one, then the other, surveying once again the ghastly environs enveloping his surroundings. Upon closer inspection, he notices slices of flesh and bone littering the area, crudely torn from the bodies of the partygoers. The carnage before him is impossibly fierce—parts of limbs separated as if they were ripped off without the use of tools; eyes still connected to their adjacent pieces of skull; fingers split off from their accompanying regions in odd sections, suggesting inhuman force was applied. The bloodshed is beyond comprehension and so obscenely voluminous in proportion that his nostrils are overwhelmed with the scent of death.

Only one thought remains in Jessie's frantically overstimulated mind: *RUN*! Utilizing his phone light as a guide, he sprints along the pathway by the fireside, his adrenaline pumping with a dizzying ferocity. Bolting through the bushes next to the DJ's truck—now spattered with blood and tissue—he makes a sharp left toward the clearing entrance, nearly crashing to the ground as he trips over the crudely torn chest cavity of the DJ's vulgarly separated body. Regaining his footing, he picks up his pace, once more achieving full sprint.

In the nocturnal obscurity of the forest brush, his phone light barely provides a clear view of his pathway causing him to repeatedly stumble amongst the scattered limbs and weeds entangling the forest floor. Determined to escape his hellish environs, Jessie soldiers onward through the bloodied wooded maze, slowing once more to navigate through the chunks of torsos and partially separated body parts blocking his escape. The carnage now behind him, Jessie struggles to see his way toward the dirt road from where they entered, the only route in or out of the thick timber fortress. As he twists and turns though the labyrinth of brushwood, he finally spots the tree-lined path. Again, his adrenaline surges, the prospect of escaping the thicket fueling his desire. Only a few yards away now, the road to freedom just within reach, Jessie takes a running leap through the last stretch of shrubbery separating himself from the horror in his wake. Just as he is landing, a figure appears on the periphery of his phone light's luminescence, moving incrementally into his trajectory. Jessie collides with the mysterious interceptor, causing them both to crash violently to the ground.

Thoughts scatter sporadically within Jessie's shattered mindset and again panic reaches the apex as he frantically searches for the phone knocked free from his grip. Spotting the light a few feet to his right, he reaches toward it just in time to witness it slowly rising into the air. The camera lamp points upward, casting a dim illumination upon the face of the stranger holding it, initiating a slight relief within Jessie's hysterical emotional state. Shawn's face appears within the radiance, a feeling of annoyance from the collision clearly painted across his visage. "*What the hell, Jessie*?!" he shouts, scanning the ground for his missing glasses which were knocked off during the impact.

"Shawn... *Thank God*! You... Back there... *I... I...* So much blood...it was *everywhere...* They're...they're all..."

Shawn looks up at Jessie with a mixture of doubt and irritation. "Bro, calm down," he starts, still scanning the area for his missing glasses. "What the hell are you talking about?"

"*EVERYONE IS FUCKING DEAD, SHAWN!*" Jessie screams, grabbing him by his shoulders while looking him straight in the eyes. Shawn, steeped in confusion, pauses his search for a period of contemplation. For the moment, he cannot tell if Jessie is joking or high. For the past several hours, Shawn has been wandering about the woodlands by the light of his phone, enjoying the effects of the ecstasy he consumed earlier in the evening and completely oblivious to the happenings back at the party site.

"What do you mean they're *dead*? C'mon, man... Let's head back to the par—"

"*NO!*" Jessie interrupts. "We're not going back... *FUCK YOU, BRO!*" Jessie releases his grip on Shawn's shoulders and takes off once again, sprinting with a look of desperation down the maintenance trail toward the main road.

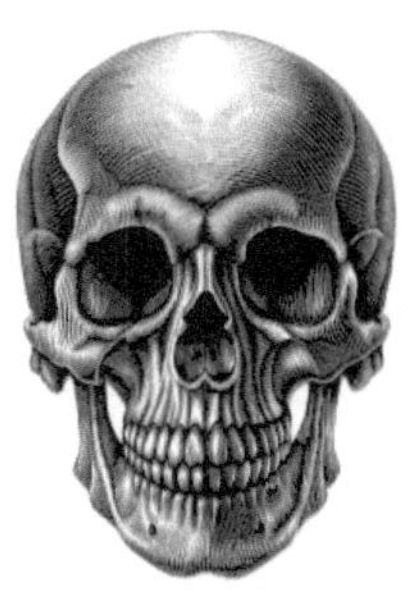

XI.

Prometheus Capital Management towers above most of the other buildings on California Street in the Financial District of San Francisco, looming menacingly over the surrounding structures and casting upon them shadows of dominant omnipresence. Once belonging to a large property management entity, the building was acquired eight years ago by Charles and his associates, who, upon making the purchase, successfully turned it into one of the most lucrative investment firms in the country. Little is known about Charles's partnership, however. An obscure consortium of mysterious partners and cryptically secretive entities comprise this lot of individuals and groups, about whom not many questions are asked, and if inquiries were to be made, they would not be answered.

When one first enters the building from the ground floor, they might be taken aback by the spaciousness of the reception area and the lavishness of the glass walls that partition the rooms with a shining elegance allowing natural light to penetrate the entire area in a deceivingly natural and wholesome luminescence. Just past the front desk, a stunning glass sculpture of intricate design and architectural appeal steals one's attention away from the walls. It stands twenty-five feet tall and spans the height of nearly two full floors, stretching upward through the center of the building's interior. The sculpture is of immaculate design, engineered and created with elegant complexity, illustrating the skillset of a master artist.

By taking the elevator past the trading floor and up one level above the meeting rooms, one will arrive at the research department. A curious area awaits any visitors to this particular floor, as the elegance of the ground floor is exchanged for plainness—the analysis department. The research conducted in this area is utilized in investment decision-making and provides the data needed to make sound, strategic business dealings. The analytical surveyance of stock trends and market sectors is not what makes this department so curious, however.

Walking through the vast matrix of cubicles and around the corner past the resource center, the entrance to the analytics room can be seen. There are dozens of computers and servers capable of providing advanced market models and trend analysis data sets, all running on the most up-to-date software systems available. Still, the interesting thing about this department cannot yet be evidenced, for the strangeness of this otherwise placid and uneventful portion of the large firm is not with the department itself.

In the very farthest end, around the corner of a long hallway, is a small IT room loaded with servers and routers, wires and cables, and a heat so thick that a large industrial cooling system was installed to keep the room chilled. Only a handful of employees have access to this area—mostly IT professionals and a couple members of the administration—as the need to enter is not a common occurrence. On occasion, however, the need arises, and the small anxieties that accompany that necessity, while seemingly foolish, do exist in the minds of the appointees, nevertheless. Whispers of spectral inhabitances and ghostly coincidences pepper the conversations amongst the IT team regarding this room. Most brush off the rumors and laugh at the suggestion of haunting, attributing the insinuations to overactive imaginations and a dull grasp upon reality. Stranger still than the trifling rumors and imaginative rumblings is the oddly shaped star insignia painted upon the wall in hues of dark red, barely seen behind the massive entanglement of wires and cords, instigating further the irrational amounts of whispering hearsay.

Taking the elevator up several more floors, past the data center and legal department, one will eventually arrive at the executive level. Here another echelon of primacy greets the visitor; an aura of superior preeminence pervades the atmosphere with a grim avariciousness that is both visually and spiritually palpable. A spacious and open area awaits when stepping out of the elevator and onto the polished black marble floor of the administrative level. The floor itself is a testament to the opulence of the firm, its construction comprised of material sourced from distant mines in areas renowned for their exquisite raw materials. Various manners of artwork and grandiose sculptures adorn the walls and walkways of this floor, exuding a sense of wonder and intimidation to those of lesser concern.

Walking in between the giant white and grey Carrara marble sculptures, formed in the images of the Greek gods Plutus and Hermes, one will pass the risk officer and operating officer's suites. Farther still down the marble aisleway, just beyond the Van Gogh on the right side of the wall, are the CFO and CIO suites, both nestled across from one another beyond illustriously carved oak doors adorned with handles fashioned from crystal and shaped into the form of imperial dragons.

Straight ahead one will find a concluding ornate entryway comprised of two antique grand scale carved French doors, intricately crafted, with the images of great beasts and medieval mounted horn blowers etched timelessly into the woodwork. Here resides the CEO of Prometheus Capital Management, *Charles Alexander Kepler*, as read on the inscription of the nameplate outside the office threshold. The doorway cracks and in walks a secretary, timidly and cautiously, as if she is fearful of entering the room. She walks past the 15th century stone gargoyles guarding the entrance on the other side of the door and gradually approaches the large mahogany executive desk at the far end of the suite. The office space is filled with a myriad assortment of the finest artwork and sleek décor, obviously meant to instill awe and domineering authority within the observer. Not that she would notice the arrangements within the office, however, as she can barely lift her head to meet the eyes of Charles, who is seated behind a row of monitors staring ominously in her direction as she approaches.

Without lifting her head to meet his gaze, she sets a file of papers on his desk, straining to raise her voice loud enough to be heard. "He— here's the account you asked for, Mr. Kepler." She immediately turns to leave without so much as a moment's pause to ensure that the folder rested securely on the desk after placing it down. Charles eyes her as she walks back toward the door, annoyed at the bothersome disruption of his work. Charles's cold, emotionless demeanor is unsettling to most of the employees of the firm. His incandescent blue eyes stare pitilessly into the souls of his subordinates, resulting in very few interactions between him and the others, save for the members of the administration, whose freezing glances and dispassionate temperaments match his own.

The doors to his office creak unsettlingly as they close, and Charles turns his attention back to his work. His cell phone rings, and a scowl adorns his face. "*What now*?" Looking down at his phone, he sees *private number* scrolling across the screen. Charles answers and hears a familiar voice at the other end speaking in a low and abjectly professional tone. It is a scientist from Athena Laboratories, one of whom his acquaintanceship has provided invaluable amounts of assistance and support throughout the last several months. He tells Charles that the preliminary experiments have begun on the Singularity Project and the first round of trial accelerator runs have been successfully completed. They speak for only a few short moments, as the man on the other end knows that Charles despises being bothered and is a person of few words and limited composure. The scientist keeps the conversation short and to the point, making sure to thank Charles for the substantial donation on behalf of Prometheus Capital Management. He ends the call with an expression of gratitude for Charles's beneficence toward science on behalf of the scientific community. Charles provides an amiable yet apathetic acknowledgement and asks when he can come in to observe the second rounds of testing and runs. The man says the next line of trials will be ready for observation in just a few days, and the final experiment should be ready on the morning of the eclipse. Charles thanks him and promptly hangs up the phone.

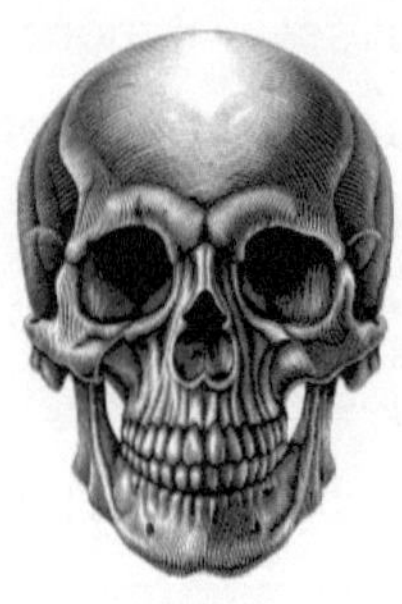

XII.

The walls of Matt's bedroom in his apartment in Oakland, California, are draped in nostalgia, covered with heavy metal icons and bands to which he gives great reverence and admiration toward. Interspersed amidst the collage of posters and memorabilia are cracks and holes, spattered with dried blood in some spots, remnants of lost tempers and bouts of fury stemming from stress and alcohol-induced rage. Matt has lived in this apartment with his guitar player Erik for two years now; a tumultuous living arrangement for both at times, it still provides a respite from his previous accommodations. No longer able to cope with the non-stop insanity of staying with his mother in his childhood home in Richmond, Matt and Erik utilized some of the earnings from their debut album to put a down payment on the apartment located near the Fruitvale District of Oakland. Known for its large Hispanic population, Matt chose the Fruitvale location due to its close proximity to their band rehearsal space, nestled within a small industrial complex not far from the Port of Oakland. The apartment is certainly not one of luxury or rich in amenities, but the neighborhood is decent and a far cry from the chaos surrounding his childhood residence.

As of late, Matt has been spending considerable amounts of time alone in his room, locked away in taciturn solitude, working tirelessly on the lyrics to the new Nokturnal Skies album. Often, he can be found in this singular perspective, trapped within his own mind in a self-indulgent state of obsession, his sole aim being to penetrate realms beyond thought. Pouring laboriously through the transcriptions of the texts unearthed in the Al Farâfra district of Egypt, Matt struggles to properly formulate a verse for the lyrics he is currently working on. Hours have passed since he began writing late last night and it is now well into the daylight span. Lately, sleep has been far from a priority, with food and proper hygiene also low on the list.

Over the last few months, Matt's obsession with ancient writings and occult-inspired philosophy has gradually nudged out all other interests. These musings on archaic beliefs and demonic entities have slowly possessed his consciousness to an even greater degree than previously throughout his life. Concerning himself only with the blackest of revelations, his mind has become immersed in dark contemplations and doctrines of a sinister fascination. Matt has become increasingly aloof from his fellow band members, and their concern for his well-being has been voiced repeatedly in recent memory. In times similar to these, Erik and the rest of the guys have successfully been able to reach through to Matt's sense of reason, but this time things are forebodingly disparate, their concern for him becoming progressively immense.

In a feverishly compulsive pattern of thought, Matt sifts endlessly through printouts scattered along the floor, surrounding himself in a cluster of translations and strange drawings detailing the recent findings. Like a frantic being in the throes of mania, Matt searches amidst the piles of papers, checking and rechecking, flinging papers and picking them up, searching for something to fill the lyrical void. Several notebooks lie about the room covered in barely legible scribbles and eerie pictures sketched impulsively in places where words could not describe his thoughts. Matt vacillates between hasty writing and re-petitive scanning, desperately combing for hidden meanings within the ancient texts.

While shuffling around piles of paperwork, he notices a strange star symbol peeking out insidiously at him from beneath a stack of pa-pers. He picks up the printout from underneath the pile, scattering the pages atop it along the floor. His eyes, blurry from lack of sleep, strain to focus on the image before him. One of several articles he printed off the internet, this one shows the image of an archeologist standing be-fore the unearthed tomb recently discovered southwest of the great pyramids. Outside the tomb, carved into the granite and sandstone construction, is the likeness of a star, eerily disproportionate in sym-metry. Matt stares absorbedly at the photograph, fixated on the rep-resentation before him. He attempts to steady his blurred vision, but the strain of sifting endlessly through mountains of papers and old texts for the last several hours has taken its toll. Yet, still he stares on-ward, blinking his eyes and trying to focus, the thought of something beyond a mere photo wrestling with his fast-failing sanity. Matt wants to set the page down but his mind refuses; something inside him whis-pers to continue onward.

With a surreal fluency, the blurriness within his vision transitions into bizarre distortions, transposing his semi-self-aware mania with a sense of concern. Finally lifting his eyes from the page, he takes a deep breath and glances around his bedroom, horrified by the spectacle that greets his sight. Objects within his room begin to take on an amor-phous yet organic structure almost as if they are alive, vibrating with a strange and metaphysical oscillation. Shadows appear to breathe, and the room seems to whisper, divulging secrets of a blasphemous nature. Panic grips Matt's senses for the briefest of moments, then suddenly subsides in an odd yet calming wave of trance-like serenity.

Reality fades away and a new worldly structure seamlessly metamorphoses before his eyes, occurring in an ethereal context as if time was absent from the transformation.

A scene of ghastly carnage plays out before him unlike anything he has experienced in past reverie. Matt envisions an otherworldly struggle for the benefit of a dark influence bearing witness to a spiritual warfare so profoundly cataclysmic that he can detect with ghoulish intuition the suffering at hand, a sight with which causes his body to withdraw in revulsion. Human flesh is being tormented in fashions that are unfamiliar to his worldly knowledge and with a torturous barbarity so pronounced that his mind refuses to comprehend the notion. He can feel the hatred as if it were a wave of heat from a blast furnace pulsating toward his being. Creatures of vast enormity and disturbingly vile essence inhabit this world, and somehow Matt can sense that they are the rightful rulers of this dominion. The suffering of the victims is of monstrous proportion, a cruelty so legendary that words cannot define the atrocities tormenting his blasphemous vision.

Running concurrent with his otherworldly and out of body excursion, the door to Matt's bedroom suddenly flings open and Erik walks in, hoping to question Matt about the rehearsal plans for the evening. Erik looks downward and sees Matt sitting on the floor with his legs crossed and his long black hair sweat-drenched and hanging partially in front of his face. Matt's eyes are wide open but rolled back in his head, triggering an unsettlingly vivid sense of déjà vu within Erik's memory. His mouth is open as if locked in a silent scream, and his arms are outstretched with his palms facing upward like he is immersed in a state of horrified meditation. Blood is running steadily down Matt's hands and dripping onto the carpet, flowing copiously from slash marks that have been carved into his wrists and lower arms. Erik, shocked by the sight of his friend profusely bleeding, rushes across the bedroom to retrieve a towel from the bathroom located in the corner of the room. He quickly grabs two cloths and bolts back toward Matt, kneeling beside him so that he can wrap his wounds.

As Erik ties the linen tight around Matt's left arm, he scans the bedroom floor for a knife, thinking all the while that Matt must have attempted to take his own life. To his consternation, no knife or sharp objects can be seen, initiating further a sense of astonishment within him. Turning his attention back, he begins to wrap Matt's other arm in the second towel, ensuring that the dressing seals tightly around the wounds. Suddenly a chilling realization occurs to him. Glancing down again at the cuts on Matt's lower arms and wrists, Erik takes a closer look at the markings. They do not seem to be slashes, but instead resemble a series of symbols etched precariously within his friend's flesh. Erik pauses for a moment then hesitantly begins to unravel the towel on Matt's left arm, curious to see what lies beneath. The other arm, too, bears the marks of strange design, fashioned with crude precision as if carved into his skin with deliberate proficiency. Frozen in a voiceless scream, Matt sits motionless all the while with eyes rolled back into his head and wrists bleeding from hideous sigils engraved in his skin.

Once again, Erik's concern returns as he quickly wraps the removed towel back around Matt's arm then turns his attention toward the other, wrapping it as tight as he can in an attempt to stop the bleeding. As Matt sits rigid on the floor in a seemingly comatose state of fixed animation, Erik struggles in contemplation as to what he should do next. Unable to form a sensible decision, and frantic in his rationale, he reaches backward as far as his hand will extend and swiftly brings it forward, slapping Matt across the face, endeavoring to wake him from his apparent loss of consciousness. Matt's lengthy black hair flies to the right side as Erik's hand greets the side of his head, immediately snapping Matt back to reality.

Looking about the room in a dazed state of confusion, Matt strives to comprehend his current situation. He looks at Erik standing before him and tries to understand the words coming from his mouth. Incoherent whispers, jumbled and stuttered, slowly fade into phrases that his mind can understand. As Matt tries to conceive of what Erik is muttering to him, he looks down at his arms to investigate the cause of the pain afflicting his skin and the weight that pulls them downward. He sees the towels enveloping his arms, and upon noticing the blood spattered about the floor of his bedroom, he lets out a cry of terrified consternation. Erik repeatedly asks him if he is okay with words that finally penetrate clearly into Matt's sense of reasoning. The incessant questioning from Erik finally prompts Matt to answer; however, his responses are framed in questions alike. Erik has no more answers than Matt does, and Matt repetitively emphasizes that he cannot remember a thing about what has transpired, only the vague recollection that something horrific has just occurred.

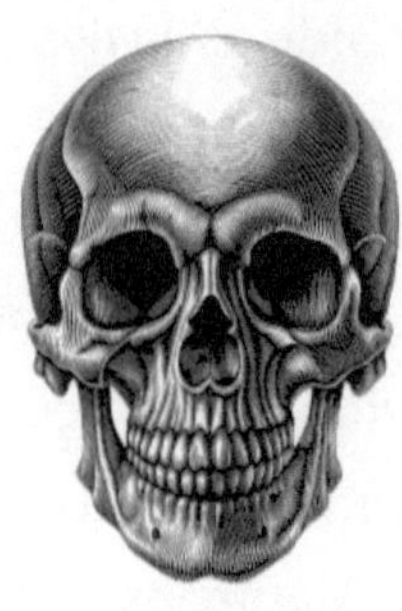

XIII.

Interrogation Room Three at the Arcadia Police Department is chilly, and Jessie shivers without the covering of his shirt, which was lost in the woods as he ran to safety. For the time being, he and Shawn are considered suspects for what the police are referring to as the Angeles Forest Incident. Thirty-one dead and four considered missing; the police, however, are not entirely certain that the missing teens are not simply scattered about the carnage, the dismemberments being so intense that crime scene investigators and the forensics team are having a great deal of trouble piecing together the bafflingly horrendous mutilations.

Interrogation Room Two where Shawn is currently seated is no less frigid, as he sits in restless anticipation, chewing on his fingers as the detectives watch him through the video surveilling monitor. Drinking their coffee and musing upon his actions, the detectives can't help but wonder if his tears are ones of remorse or sheer panic stemming from the situation he has become inextricably involved in. His parents are on their way to the station—with a lawyer, no doubt—and the anxiety is completely consuming his present mental condition. He has no idea how he is going to explain the situation to his dad or how he will react, creating an overwhelming sensation of hysteria within his already overstressed mind.

The door to Jessie's room opens and a detective walks in, holding in his hand a thin blanket for Jessie to cover his upper body with. Still in shock and shaking with fear, he reaches his unsteady hand toward the blanket and snatches it from the officer's hand. "Can we get you something to drink, Jessie? Soda, water?" Detective Moore warmly asks in a manner befitting a semblance of empathy toward Jessie's fragile emotional state. Jessie has been at the police station for several hours now with little contact from the investigating officers, who have mostly been busy talking to crime scene officials and focusing their interrogation efforts on Shawn.

Gazing up at the detective with a confused look upon his face, Jessie suddenly breaks free from his stolid and trance-like state. "*What*? I mean… Sure. S—soda would be nice," Jessie stutters, focusing his attention as best he can. A petite woman of forty years wearing a blue tailored blazer and straight trousers, the detective quietly strides out of the room to fetch Jessie a drink. Following her exit, Jessie returns to sitting in dismal stillness, tormented by an acute mixture of despondency and restless unease. The images of his friends and acquaintances torn to unrecognizable shreds torture his thoughts, solidifying and underpinning an unprecedented level of fear the likes of which he has never experienced before. The notion that the police currently suspect he and Shawn are complicit in the mass killing compounds his alarm and adds an incomprehensible mass to the gravity of the situation. Terror-stricken and beset by an ever-increasing sorrow for his losses, Jessie sits in the interrogation room in confounding silence, wrapped in his cheaply made jailhouse blanket, shivering at the prospects of his uncertain fate.

"I… I *swear*, I had *nothing* to do with this! I was in…in the woods the whole time!" Shawns cries in between outbursts of hyperventilated breathing and squalls of tears. "I never even saw the bodies. *Jessie...* He was...he came running out of the woods... Ran into me, he was running so fast!" The atmosphere in Interrogation Room Two is thick with emotion as the two detectives drill Shawn for information, relentlessly assailing him with a merciless series of questions.

"You two were the only ones left at the scene! You're telling me you saw *nothing*, heard *nothing*?!" growls Detective Sommers in a condescending and arrogant tone. A large and imposing man, Detective Sommers is sure that Shawn and Jessie had something to do with the butchery, and his week-long scruff and sleep-deprived, wide brown eyes somehow lend a sense of credence to his unwavering confidence.

"Look, kid, this is looking really bad for you two," the second detective adds, speaking in a direct but slightly more subtle intonation. "We can place you at the scene, your blood tests prove you were under the influence, and judging by your demeanor, you have guilty written all over your fucking face!" Detective Riley, usually the one to play good cop in the interrogation game, has lost all semblance of emotional balance due to the nature of the horrific incident and joins suddenly in the brutal inquisition.

Both detectives are thoroughly convinced of Shawn's guilt and feel they can take advantage of his timid nature, and with Detective Sommers taking the lead on the investigation, no holds are barred in the ruthless inquiry. "Listen here, you little *shit*!" Detective Sommers begins once more. "I'm going to get some answers out of you if I have to drag you back to the scene and shove your fucking face into the big pile of mutilated flesh that has become of your friends' bodies!" With that exclamation, Shawn breaks down into a state of panic, his hyperventilation becoming so severe that the detectives momentarily stop for fear of his physical well-being.

"Okay, Shawn, relax. Can I get you some water?" asks Detective Riley, feeling a small sense of empathy for Shawn's condition.

"*Fuck this*," Detective Sommers mutters as he gets up to leave the room, tiring of getting nowhere after hours of questioning. As Sommers leaves the interrogation room, he runs into Detective Moore, who has just begun interviewing Jessie. Denise Moore, a sixteen-year veteran of the homicide squad and mother of three, is of a much more self-controlled nature than her partner Sommers. Her approach on this early morning investigation will be one of delicate temperament. "How's it going with Jessie?" Detective Sommers asks Denise, ending his question with a sigh of exasperation.

With a look of uncertainty on her face, she replies, "I'm not sure yet. I haven't spent much time with him. None of this is adding up. I'm going back in now to speak with him."

"Yeah, well...*good luck*. We're getting nowhere with the other one. Kid's a fuckin' mess too. We're not sure he had anything to do with the deaths. I mean... What the *fuck* are we dealing with here anyway? Twenty-four years with the department and I've never seen anything like this. *This is fucking barbaric*!"

Detective Moore looks down at the ground, shaking her head. "The way those kids died... The way their bodies were torn apart... It seems unnatural, almost like powers beyond human capability were at play." Detective Moore looks back up from the floor and into Sommers' tired and sand-bagged eyes. "I need to get in there, talk to you later," she exclaims, ending with an exasperated sigh.

Moore walks into Interrogation Room Three and gently shuts the door behind her. She paces to the side of the table next to Jessie, who is hunched over and tightly clasping the thin blanket around his torso, and sets a can of Coke in front of him. Jessie murmurs a nearly inaudible acknowledgment and remains motionless, slouched over in abysmal stillness. Detective Moore slowly ambles to the other side of the small table and takes a seat. "Jessie, I need you to be completely honest with me. What happened last night in the woods?" Jessie, still frozen in paralyzing inertia, does not answer her question, but she can tell by the tear running down his cheek that whatever did happen has caused him great emotional distress.

Numerous seconds pass and Jessie gradually lifts his head, looking hopelessly into Detective Moore's light brown irises. "I only saw what was left of them... I...I never saw who did it or anything." Once again, he lowers his head back down and sinks into the chair, cradling the blanket around him as if it were a protective barrier. Rumbling lowly from lips partially covered in blanket and pointed to the floor, he adds one more feature to his sparse detailing of the events. "I could feel the hatred. It kind of just hung in the air—thick...like humidity." With that statement, the tears begin pouring down Jessie's face, followed by a whimpering very uncharacteristic of a young man of his otherwise arrogant deportment and brawny, tattooed likeness.

A disturbing sensation overwhelms Detective Moore. She perceives something extraordinarily unsettling about the situation and decides to give Jessie a few moments to calm down before resuming her questioning. As she gets up to leave the room, she attempts to reconcile with the unsettling feeling she is experiencing. Something is gravely amiss, and a deep fear rises within her, causing a strange nervousness unprecedented in its horrid novelty.

As Moore closes the door behind her, she sees Detective Sommers lumbering down the hallway, a strange look of annoyance accompanying his scowling grin. He is not alone; a man donning a black suit, tie, and black shoes so exceptionally shiny that she can spot them across the expanse of the hallway is walking beside him, marching toward her with a stride of entitlement. As he gets closer, Detective

Moore can see he is a man nearing his fifties, around five feet, eight inches tall, average build, short, parted brown hair, and a thick five o'clock shadow that oddly reminds her of cheap whiskey and cigarettes. As he nears her, his hand pulls open his suit jacket, revealing under his blazer the butt of a Glock 19 and a badge wallet next to it, the letters *FBI* reading boldly across the top. "I'm Agent Jerry Norton. Where is Jessie Bower being held?" he demands in no uncertain terms.

"Um, he's right this way... What is this about?" Moore inquires, confused by the man's presence.

"I have some questions for Mr. Bower. Is here in here?" Agent Norton replies, pointing to the door behind Moore. Before she can answer, Norton opens the door and walks in, setting down the black FBI portfolio folder he had been carrying atop the table in front of Jessie as he scoots the chair back to have a seat. As Agent Norton maneuvers the chair inward and adjusts his back upright in the seat, he turns back to Detective Moore and with a slightly beseeching look asks her to get him a cup of black coffee. For a moment Moore hesitates and sneers at him with an incredulous smirk, then heads back out the door to fetch him his drink. Turning his head to the right, he points his attention toward Detective Sommers who followed them into the room. "If you don't mind, I'd like a moment alone with Mr. Bower." Sommers, too, shoots Norton a defiant grimace and stomps angrily out the door, following the hasty exit with a slam.

Jessie's head now lifted from its forlorn and sunken state stares trepidatiously forward at the man before him. "Good morning. You are Jessie Bower, correct?" Agent Norton asks. Jessie acknowledges with a vague nod, his eyes and face red, swollen from an evening and early morning spent sobbing.

Pulling a small recording device from his pocket, Agent Norton peers into Jessie's eyes with a faint sense of skepticism and presses down on the *Record* button before setting the device on the table. "Can you please state your name for the record?"

A sense of foreboding comes over Jessie and he cannot help but question the agent's purpose for the visit. "What's this about? Who... who are you?" he asks apprehensively, his voice cracking during the effort.

"For the record... Your name, *please*," Agent Norton reiterates, further straightening his posture.

"Um...ahem." Jessie clears his throat and continues, "Jessie...um, Jessie Bower...sir."

"You were present during the incident last night, July 17th, in Angeles National Forest in Arcadia, at the end of Brown Mountain Truck Trail, correct?"

"Uh...yes. Sir, what's this—"

Cutting off Jessie from his questioning response, "What were the surroundings in the area like?" Agent Norton coldly inquires.

"Huh?" Jessie responds, confused by the agent's strange question as he adjusts himself upright, loosening his grip on the blanket that still envelops him.

"What were the surroundings in the area like?" Agent Norton repeats himself, scooting the recording device a few inches closer to Jessie. "Did you notice anything odd about the air, wind, or temperature?"

With a quizzical look, Jessie begins, not sure where to start but convinced he should tell the man something. "Well... I... When I woke up... You see, I kind of nodded off for a while. But, yeah, I told the detective... You know, the lady, that umm... It was like a heat wave... I could feel, like, this weird—"

Cut off once more by Norton, "Did you see anything out of the ordinary with regard to the way objects appeared? Anything seem fragmented or perhaps fading in and out of view quickly?"

"*What*? No, it was just like this heat that hung in the atmosphere. Kind of like… This sounds kind of fucked—" Jessie stops mid-sentence, worried by the thought that, if he continues, he might sound insane.

"Go on…" Norton pressures him, giving him a look of persistent encouragement with a slight nod of the head.

"It…it was like a warm hate you could feel. I don't know how else to describe it." Jessie sighs with an exhausted expression.

"What else?"

Jessie hesitates once again, perplexed by the man's apparent lack of surprise to his previous statement, then continues. "The silence," he begins, taking a moment to work through the painful recollection, "a *death-like* silence. You couldn't even hear the crickets… It…it was like even the animals were afraid to make a sound." Jessie covers his face with his hands and buries his head into the table, shaken by the effort.

"Thank you for your time." Agent Norton ends with a succinct abruptness and presses the stop button on his recording device, picking it up from the table along with his folder. The agent promptly exits the room, passing by Detective Moore who is on her way back to deliver his coffee.

"Hey! Where are you going? You're not done already?" Detective Moore shouts toward Agent Norton as he briskly heads in the direction of the police station entrance. Agent Norton does not even offer a passing glance as he exits the building, walking hastily through the glass door while reaching into his suit pocket to retrieve a flask tucked secretly away in his jacket.

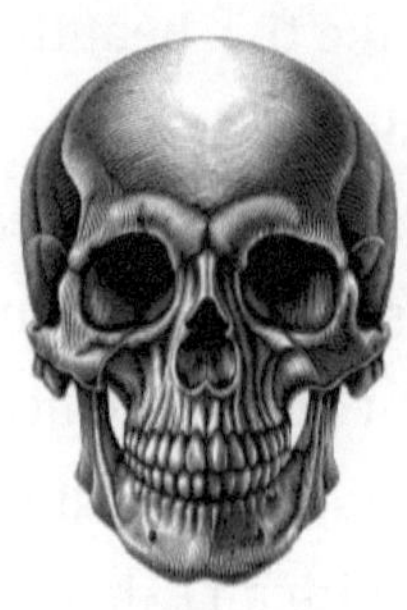

XIV.

The air is thick with a nervous tinge of apprehension in the conference room at Berkeley University this afternoon. The last meeting here regarding matters of scientific discovery, just one week ago, was lauded with the resounding clamor of joyous applause and wonderous excitement at the possibilities ahead. Now, an unease fills the void left over in the absence of celebration—a dread so perceptible that the men and women gathered here utter not a word. They cannot even lift their heads to gaze into the eyes of their fellow colleagues, but instead fumble nervously on their phones or simply gaze silently about the room.

Martin nervously scrapes the bowl of his pipe in the parking lot, silently dreading the meeting he has been summoned to. Wishing he could fill the bowl back up and puff a little longer before entering the building, he instead places it in his front shirt pocket and slowly climbs the steps to the physics hall. He strokes his gray and white beard as he opens the door, a nervous habit he engages in subconsciously when feeling pangs of anxiety. As he passes students in the hallway, he wonders what the meeting is truly about. The phone conversation he had earlier that week with Dr. Jennings seemed a little suspicious, but rumblings among the physics professors at the university suggest that something more profound lies beneath the surface.

As Martin enters the conference room, he can immediately sense the concern permeating the ambiance. Choosing his favorite chair near the far end of the long table, he saunters over and takes a seat. He gives an awkward greeting to his fellow colleague seated next to him while watching as another of the summoned physicists arrives to the uncomfortable silence of the room. Martin pulls his black, wire-framed glasses from his face and starts chewing on the earpiece in anxious anticipation for the meeting to start.

At five minutes past 10 a.m., Jennings opens the conference room door and briskly walks in, followed closely behind by a man donning a black suit, tie, and exceptionally shiny black shoes. All the phones in the room go down and attention focuses on the two men, one of whom stands silent in the corner, while the other, Dr. Jennings, sets his papers down before him and centers himself in the front of the long table. "I have spoken to most of you individually about the matters regarding this meeting," Dr. Jennings begins. "It seems there has been some rather odd happenings occurring in various locations around the country and it was requested that we put together a team of academics to help in the investigation." His words thus far are met with a deathly silence as the members of the conference wait in breathless anticipation for him to continue. "The summary produced by officials from some government agencies, namely the CIA and FBI, state that—and I quote—'Numerous reports detailing unexplained phenomena and occurrences have been documented in recent days stemming from several individual and seemingly unrelated events including, but not limited to, ongoing investigations involving murder, disappearances, arson, delusional psychosis and violence in individuals with no previous criminal record or mental health history, unexplained noises and lights seen in and around sites of disappearances, translucency of objects, events involving gravitational anomalies and physical abnormalities, unnatural bioluminescence involving mutilation, distortions of time coinciding with loss of life and or dismemberment...' Well... that part of the report is unfortunately disturbingly extensive, and I'll save you the detailing of the list in its entirety, but I think you all are getting the picture. I have been provided with some of the case files and met earlier today with a senior official to go over the information they were able to provide. Naturally they were only able to provide us with portions of the information due to the fact that these are ongoing investigations, but I thought maybe we could come up with some theories and reasoning to..." Dr. Jennings pauses in silence and Martin can sense that what he is about to say is something that he would rather not. Dr. Jennings takes a deep breath and continues, "Explain, or perhaps more appropriately, disprove in some fashion the rather disturbing data that I have yet to present. The CIA's Directorate of Science and Technology has a member of its division that seems to think what we are dealing with could potentially have something to do with black holes—"

The silence breaks and one of the physicists bursts forth in incredulous dismay. "BLACK HOLES?! Preposterous!"

"Please, please. Just let me explain," Dr. Jennings pronounces, attempting to quell the outburst. "This individual does have an academic background in—"

"The massive energy requirements," Martin begins, cutting Dr. Jennings short before he can finish his thought, "would be far more than anything we can produce with current technology or by any natural phenomena on Earth. If the energy levels were sufficient, you could, in theory, produce conditions that resemble those of a singularity, but the capability to create those energy levels would be monumental."

"Well..." Dr. Jennings retorts, "yes, but if you'll allow me to provide the reasoning behind... Let me see here..." Jennings, unfamiliar with the name of the member of the DS&T making the claim, stops to flip through the folder laying in front of him, then continues, "Dr. Melvin Humboldt's conjecture, you will see there is a fair amount of data to support his theory, as...ahem...as dubious as it may seem." The room stays silent long enough for Dr. Jennings to open the report and read the summary while most of the scientific minds in the room eye him with crossed arms and looks of profound skepticism. "Dr. Humboldt seems to think, based on his findings, that some of the phenomena reported in recent days could be due to gravitational lensing, Hawking radiation, and gravitational waves. Now, I am not a fan of this idea, but there is more to his report—various artifacts were apparently collected and studied in one of the DS&T laboratories under conditions which they are not at liberty to divulge due to security concerns. The report states—once again quoting—'Using equipment under the Department of Defense and the Central Intelligence Agency Joint Special Military Scientific Advancement Operative (JSMSAO), specific tests have been conducted utilizing spectroscopy, gravitational wave detectors, and various other classified instruments and technologies to observe what may be considered miniature black holes. Objects and areas tested under certain conditions appeared to display altered environmental effects consisting of or resembling detectable changes in the state of close proximity particles in the form of acceleration and radiation signatures not conducive with normal conditions.'"

"What does this mean exactly? What qualitative conclusions are we drawing from this, a singularity? Ripple detection perhaps?" a woman asks from the rear corner of the room.

Before Dr. Jennings has a chance to answer the woman's question,

Martin speaks up once again, this time in defiant consternation. "How is it we are so sure that this has anything to do with black holes? I mean, this is ridiculous... It sounds like science fiction."

A member of the assembly who had thus far been silent speaks up. Stepping to the front of the room, Agent Norton holds up a finger, signaling silence. "Hello, everyone, I'm Agent Jerry Norton. I'm a special agent with the FBI. There are several different agencies currently working together to get to the bottom of this and I have been assigned to three of the incidents in particular—a case in Potosi, Missouri, one in Sugar Land, Texas, and Arcadia, here in California, which I'm sure you all are familiar with from the local news. We believe there is foul play involved. The deaths resemble more of a slaughter than some accident of scientific design. So far there have been two survivors of the US incidents: a man from Potosi, Missouri, and a teenager from Eagle Rock, California." All eyes are now on Agent Norton as he continues. "Now, these are simply leads that I have to follow up on. We don't know exactly what is going on, if any of this is connected, whether biological or advanced technology weapons systems are involved, acts of terrorism...nothing... Right now, all the major agencies are acting quickly to determine what it is we're dealing with. The government is trying to keep it quiet as long as possible, but social media is making it difficult. As a matter of caution, an investigation must be conducted when it involves the loss of life of this magnitude. We don't want to initiate a sense of panic. We have a lot of anonymous tips to follow up on, both here and internationally; some legit, some seem bogus... The important thing here is to remember to keep this quiet and stay calm. This is for national security purposes, and we have assembled you guys because you're the brains that can understand this stuff *if* any of it turns out to be true. These are all simply allegations at this point, and quite frankly, sounds like a bunch of nonsense. But, be that as it may, I have orders to investigate."

Another voice booms from the back of the room. "I don't understand. Some random deaths occur and suddenly they are being tied to black holes and gravitational waves?" the voice asks in a questioning inflection. "This doesn't make sense."

Yet another voice immediately rings out from the center of the room. "If they think the public is at risk, why not just shut everything down, like with COVID?"

"That's a good point, Professor...?" Norton replies, pausing to wait for the professor's name in response.

"Professor Williams," the woman seated near the center of the table condescendingly replies.

"Well, Professor Williams, it wouldn't look too good if we decide to shut down the country, put thousands of people's jobs on hold, not to mention shock the public into hysteria, with no proof minus some bizarre reports of things ninety-nine percent of the public has no understanding of, now, would it?" Norton replies in a sarcastic tone. "As I said, the incidents are incredibly bizarre and, at the moment, we need to investigate every lead we can. Believe me, there are several other agents investigating through more conventional methods, including other agencies... Hell, even the Secret Service has a team working on this. I just happen to be the one assigned to this facet of the investigation. Now, I will need you guys to keep crackin' away on the calculations and data we provided to Dr. Jennings and see if there appears to be any relevance to the information there or if the guys over at the CIA don't know what the hell they're talking about."

The room bursts into a half-dozen side conversations and whispered chattering amongst the physicists as Agent Norton returns to the corner of the room. Dr. Jennings whispers something to Norton then points in Martin's direction. Martin, engaged in conversation with his colleague seated next to him, does not even notice Dr. Jennings approaching. "Professor Patterson, can I have a word with you in the hallway?" Jennings asks, signaling with a waving gesture for him to follow. Martin excuses himself from his conversation with his colleague and follows Dr. Jennings out into the hallway. As soon as the door closes, it opens again, and Agent Norton walks toward them and stands between Jennings and Martin. Dr. Jennings eyes Martin with a stern yet casual look. "We've suggested to Agent Norton that you assist in the investigation. The FBI needs someone in the physics department that can accompany them to investigate the incidents."

Martin looks hesitantly at Norton, then back at Jennings. "Why me?"

"You've come highly recommended by Dr. Jennings," Agent Norton replies with an earnest tone.

"Yes, I feel with your background in theoretical physics you would be the best fit in the department," Jennings adds.

His face flooded with uncertainty, Martin responds, "What about my classes? How long will the investigation take?"

Norton cuts in, "We're hoping just a few days. Long enough to rule out any strange physics stuff... Or, in the infinitesimally small chance that this has anything to do with science gone awry, maybe longer. Regardless, we need a professional in the field to help us sort this thing out."

With a look of skepticism still adorning his countenance, Martin replies, "Do I have to have an answer now?" while stroking his beard in nervous consideration.

"Time is of the essence, Professor," Norton replies, pointing to his watch.

Giving a few moments for thought, Martin agrees. "Just one question, where do we go from here?"

Agent Norton pulls his sunglasses from his suit pocket and places them on his face. "We have plane tickets for departing this afternoon."

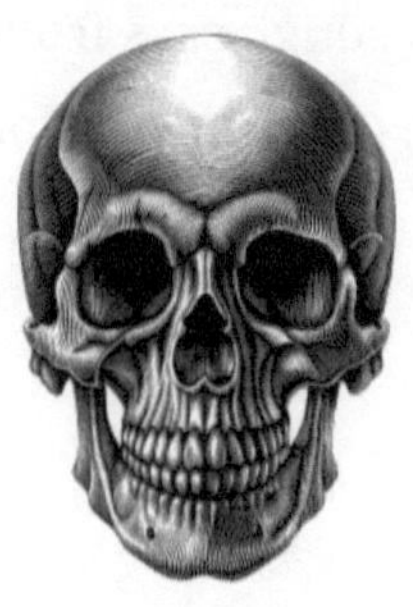

XV.

The bright July sun beams down upon Charles's face as he walks down the extensive stairway adjacent to the entrance of Prometheus Capital Management as he leaves the office for the day. It is a clear and beautiful afternoon, yet the warm sun and cloudless sky are insignificantly vapid in his deliberations for the current moment. Walking toward the small parking area abutting the firm, he heads for the parking space closest to the building with a signpost which reads *Reserved for Charles Kepler*. Opening the door to his beloved Jaguar Project 7, he takes a moment to admire the way the gleam of the black paint reflects in the sunlight, the wax mirroring his image within the illustrious clear coat finish. This thought is fleeting, however, as other considerations captivate his mind. He turns the key and presses the gas pedal, taking a few seconds to admire the engine's monstrous growl while thinking to himself what to do with the annual performance bonus he essentially just signed off on to himself.

The bonus he just acquired, too, is an ephemeral concept, one of hundreds he has received in his never-ending endeavors to achieve financial gain—simply a means to an end. No longer does his outlook on humanity embody simply a misanthropic distancing of himself from those around him. A transformation has taken place deep within his psyche; a longing for something otherworldly and intrinsically antihuman in essence. Charles has become a shell—human by all appearance, yet mechanistic in nature.

San Francisco International Airport is twenty-five minutes away from his firm, but Charles will arrive in fifteen. He is running short on time to make his flight, a consequence of staying late to ensure that the money was transferred from his bonus to the proper account. Merging onto I-280 southbound, he presses the pedal to the floor as the pistons in his eight-cylinder F-Type rise and fall in rapid screaming succession, propelling him through traffic at obscene speeds. No thought of human safety occurs to him, nor would it have any mitigating effect if it did, as he weaves in and out of the lanes ensuring that his arrival will be timely. From San Francisco he will be taking a connecting flight to Yuma International Airport in Arizona, the closest he could get to his destination given the time frame for his appointment. At Yuma, a rental car will be waiting where he will make the hour and a half drive to Athena Laboratories in the Sonoran Desert to observe the preliminary testing of the Singularity Project experiment.

Life has become but a strategy for Charles, a game of chess with only one possible outcome that will satisfy his blasphemous and apocalyptic intentions. The yearning over the years has become undeniable; the obsession so overwhelmingly intense that his conscience has completely left him, leaving a void to be filled with only the darkness that possesses his soul. Beings from beyond the borders of our spiritual realms command his thoughts, actions, and dreams. The creatures that both torment and fascinate his reveries have taken the one human soul worthy of their profane embrace and manipulated its will, a gesture of monumental iniquity and profoundly absent from hallowed favor. All energies are now directed toward a fixed, never-changing point: the liberation of that which was and shall be once more.

Charles's hatred for humanity and mankind's pretentious claim to this universe is of the highest order; millennia spent in a floundering attempt to seize what was never truly ours is, in his view, a farce of scathing satirical irony. For the last millennia in particular, Charles has a profound disdain. Mankind's greatest achievements in philosophy and mathematics are but an egregiously fallacious faux pas from his perspective, an inexcusable blunder in the pursuit to understand something they cannot possibly comprehend—the fact that humans do not see the world in its undiluted form. The actuality of the universe is something humans are not equipped to grasp. This inability to visualize and experience the universe through the abysmally dark lens of nature's hidden reality happens to be a protective trait encoded in man's genetics, for if they saw the truth, they would be driven to extinction under the weight of these horrific truths.

As Charles pulls into the airport parking lot, he veers toward the valet. He spots a man in uniform approaching his car and sneers with a contemptuous glower. His hatred for other humans extends even to the parking lot employees as he skids to a halt quietly cursing the man under his breath. Stopping mere inches from the man's feet, Charles hastily exits the car and tosses him the keys, making sure to warn him about finding scratches upon retrieving his vehicle. He glares at the man with bright blue eyes of intense hatred, a loathing the man can feel as he cautiously approaches the vehicle, apprehensive of Charles's damning gaze and strange demeanor. Turning his loathsome surveyance toward the entrance, Charles marches inside and heads for the flight check-in counter.

Walking through the vast hallway on his way to the counter, Charles eyes the crowds of people around him. Families, children, men, women, plebeians, and subordinates; all sickening him to the depths of his sinister being. His disgust mounts with every step he takes through the contemptable mortal space of the congested airport walkway. Charles passes a mother and father walking their young son through the aisle as he approaches the check-in counter and scowls contemptuously at the young boy, angered by the misappropriation of wasted flesh and soiled spirit the child possesses. The hatred of the great beasts from beyond this plane of existence surges within Charles, fueling his ambitions as he scans the area surrounding the kiosk. He struggles to suppress the abhorrence as he clutches both fists in an attempt to contain the demonic rage boiling within him.

Charles begrudgingly takes his boarding pass and stares blankly through the throngs of people as he heads for the security scanners, his mind silently pulsating with hostility. Through security and onward toward his gate he storms. While the multitudes of other humans shuffling about stifle his passage, he checks his watch: two minutes until boarding. As he arrives at the gate, a prompt sounds across the speakers announcing first-class seating, relieving him for the moment of his existential animosity. Charles boards the plane and takes a seat, the immense reviling disgust within ebbing slowly as he settles into the first-class recliner. The flight attendant approaches him with a smile and a nod, but before she can speak, he orders a scotch on the rocks in a condescending and peremptory intonation, wiping her visage clear of the affable grin she previously possessed.

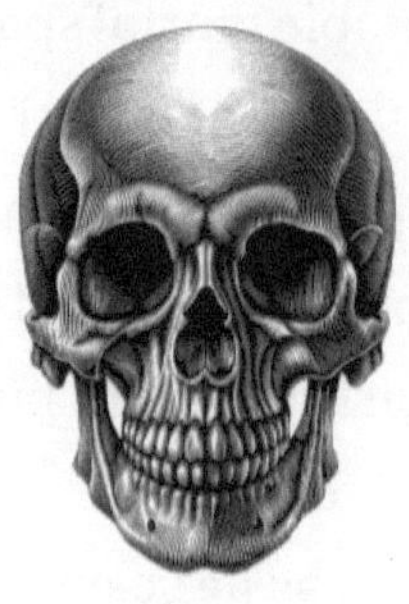

XVI.

For the last two days, Matt has been silent about the cuts on his arms, ineffectively hidden by gauze pads and elastic wrappings that he procured from the local drugstore. On a couple separate occasions, the rest of the band has asked about them, to which Matt simply ignores the inquiry or attempts to explain away the questioning with hurried replies and vague elucidations. Once again, the rehearsal room is thick with an air of despondency, so immensely palpable that the mood amongst the band members is visibly apparent, evidenced by looks of anger and frustration upon each of their faces.

The transcriptions of the texts unearthed in the Al Farâfra district of Egypt have been released steadily since the archeological project began and Matt has been making gradual progress for the lyrics to the new album based on the texts discovered. Until the incident involving him and Erik, Matt's obsessive work on the new album's lyrics had been prolific. Their primary goal is to play a new song from their upcoming album at the show scheduled for this coming weekend, so it is of great importance for them to rehearse the new set list.

The temperament of the members of Nokturnal Skies is not helped at all by Matt's reclusiveness the last couple evenings. Erik understands all too well what happened two nights ago. He is doing his best to rationalize away the scene of disturbing horror he stumbled upon when he found Matt unresponsive in his bedroom and blood pouring from strange cuts on his wrists and arms. But the other members of the band know nothing of the otherworldly events that transpired; they are concerned only with the big show the band has booked and the infuriating fact that their singer does not seem interested in rehearsing for it. Jacob in particular is not dealing well with Matt's seeming lack of interest in practicing. Tending toward nervousness and generally uptight by nature, Jacob likes to be well prepared before a show to mitigate his fears of failure, and more than once this evening, he has yelled at Matt in no uncertain terms to focus on practice. "Get your fucking head out of your ass, Matt! Put down that *fuckin'* beer and pick up the goddamn *microphone*," Jacob snarls at the band's singer for what he feels is the tenth time this evening.

Matt glares back at Jacob with one eye barely visible through the strands of long black hair that hangs in front of his downward-angled face. He tilts his head back long enough to take a long, slow drink from his bottle of Heineken while still eying Jacob with a sense of annoyance clearly painted across his face. Matt keeps the bottle tilted until it is empty and drops it to the carpeted floor, the bottle making a dull clinking sound as it hits the ground and rolls to the side of the room. Matt gradually walks over to the microphone stand, making sure to take his time in an effort to further antagonize Jacob. Sauntering over to the microphone, he picks it up from the stand and holds it close to his mouth, staring at Jacob, who is sitting in irritated impatience behind his drum kit for the duration of the purposefully slow maneuvering. "Okay... Ready," Matt whispers into the microphone, followed by a short belch which echoes with a reverberation through the PA system.

Jacob rattles off a four count with his drumsticks and the intro song to their set list starts with Erik's guitar unleashing a savage riff that ignites the anger-infused atmosphere, scorching the aura of the rehearsal space with an additional layer of energy adding to the dispirited oversaturation. Jacob rolls his sticks across the toms, building upon Erik's intro, all the while staring at Matt with a scowl of contempt, one that Matt willfully returns as he clutches the microphone with an increasing indignation. Steven's bass notes ring out in a low, tempestuous rumbling as the song gains momentum, creating a sinister dynamic that gives rise to a feverish spirit of despondency.

The doom-laden sounds of the song's introduction fade and a raw energy is birthed as the music takes on a new aural spirit of vengeful detestation. Erik begins the riff that segues the song to the next section and the mood within Matt changes; his first vocal line to follow shortly thereafter. Jacob looks over to Matt and waits for his ear-piercing scream, the very action that ignites the blistering speed of his drumming that comes next. Erik's guitar pauses in anticipation of Matt's vocals, and for a moment, all is still. Like a firestorm of erupting volcanic mass, Matt unleashes his hellish shriek, and Jacob lets loose on his kit, playing an infernally accelerated blast over 300 beats per minute double kicks.

As the blasphemous anthem gradually progresses, Matt begins to feel strange, accompanied by a sense of elation coming over his being, as if an unseen force is assuring him that in this moment, everything is complete and absolute in purpose. Matt glances around the rehearsal space, then at his bandmates, stricken by the fluidity of musical craftsmanship as the song continues. His fellow musicians appear to be playing flawlessly and effortlessly, increasing his perception of this temporal purity. He executes his vocal duties with ease and proficiency, bellowing forth his oral facilities as if something else is controlling his actions. Those chants to the forgotten, the ancient scriptures that have obsessed his mind and occupied his lyrics, command the room to life, bringing a mysterious and alluring presence to the impeccability that permeates the air. Everything around Matt—and within him—seems to be functioning in unison, like the universe is one giant, fluent, breathing organism woven together with threads of harmony. Taking another look around the room confirms this notion as his associates appear as if they are moving and merging with each note they play.

All is singular as the seconds turn to what seem like minutes, the minutes turning timeless, all with a fluency that causes Matt to lose himself within the dark recesses of his own lyrics. A conceptual abyss opens in Matt's mind and his physical presence seems to disappear, his spirit tunneling through a portal of black, majestic emptiness completely void of reason, leading him into a barren and hypnotic vacuum of atomic decay. The abysmal gateway widens, allowing for Matt's vision to expand and wisdom to emerge. The commencement of an immortal fiendish genesis unfolds and presents itself to his spirit; this power is not of this world, and it presents itself not to his mind but to his life force, a knowing that sends a familiar fear through his psyche.

Matt takes a deep breath and inhales the dismal abandonment of it all. As he does, he focuses on Steven. While Steven's fingers vibrate across his bass guitar, the melody he is playing gives rise to hues that seem to envelop his body. These colors seem orange at first glance, but curiously change to a reddened shade as an unsettling impression makes its way into Matt's perception. Everything else seems to fade as Matt's focus becomes solely fixated upon these vibrant hues, eliminating the necessity to focus on anything other than the enrapturing colors beckoning his view. The reds become more intense, as does Matt's brooding sensation of dread as reality appears to incrementally tick back into his mind. The scarlet tint abruptly—and violently—is attacked by lacerations of black, mercilessly stripping away the layers of Matt's rapturous sensations with each successive color transformation that occurs.

A faint cry originates in the distance and gradationally makes its presence known. It grows with each passing second, rising from below and tunneling its way from the depths of some unseen cavern with the force of a thousand charging beasts. The sheer terror this scream provokes is unlike anything Matt has ever felt, and it quickly peels away his remaining delusions of serenity. The scarlet hues turn to an unmistakable shade of red as blood spills forth in voluminous fountains of crimson-tinted horror. The tormented shrieks of his anguished bandmate burst their way through the final layer of Matt's tranquility, unveiling the reality of his spurious illusion.

Claws—dozens of them—blackened from countless millennia of undiluted hatred, tear their way through Steven's chest from the inside out, like his body was a despised barrier that could no longer confine the evil that it had suppressed for years untold. The magnitude of these claws is beyond that of Steven's bodily dimensions, bringing a certain physical bewilderment to the atrocity that Matt and his bandmates bear witness to. The ferocity with which they tear through Steven's flesh is without bound, timeless in everlasting and space-altering blasphemy. The contorted faces of creatures unknown to this world appear and disappear, revealing themselves in spontaneous flashes between the furious shredding of bone and organs. Their countenances carry the features of beasts tinged with a profane and rotted semblance, as if they were forced to exist in a realm of torture and vulgarity beyond human comprehension. The hatred with which these beings ravage Steven's body can be felt like a wave of heat emanating vehemently from the pyres of eternal damnation.

Blood, bones, and tissue fly dispersedly through the air and cover the interior of the rehearsal space, spattering the room and the band's equipment with obscene amounts of flesh and gore. The ravaging displacement of Steven's organs is so shockingly appalling that Matt doesn't even feel the chunks of torn skin and droplets of blood hitting his face as his bass player is torn to unrecognizable shreds. A massive arm reaches forth from the inside of Steven's gaping body covered in plated, armor-like, reptilian scales and lunges toward Erik with lengths of intestine clinging to its infernal, blackened claw. The size of the claw itself defies logic, as it is larger than the cavity in Steven's chest that it protruded from. This notion alone captures Erik's fascination, causing a nearly fatal delay in his movement as it maneuvers toward him, swiping and furiously grasping at his leg in an attempt to claim another victim. Erik moves rearward just in time to escape its bloody, entrail-covered grasp, falling into Jacob's drum kit as he leaps backward. The unspeakable horror unfolding before the witnesses of this infernal display of carnage is of nothing that can be conceptualized with human expression—a barbaric demonstration of torturous revelations is beheld by all, an illustration of pure demonic sadism.

For a fleeting moment, Matt's eyes meet with Steven's in between the relentless flailing of Steven's limbs and the horrific slashing of enormous claws. For that brief instant, Matt experiences despair in its purest form; an everlasting glimpse of solitary desolation known only to him in his blackest times of sorrow. A tear forms in the corner of Steven's eye as a look of complete hopelessness comprises the final display of human emotion his spirit will impress upon this mortal plane, and in this moment, the light in his pupils fades.

With an ethereal fluidity, the beasts dissipate and the monstrous claws vanish, as if an abysmal portal—absent from human sight—swallowed the beings into a dark spiritual realm that mortals are not permitted to enter. A vulgar growling can be heard in incongruent echoes emanating from all directions and gradually fading into an unknown distance, almost as if the beasts are cursing this dimension in damning, foul utterances as they bid a condemning farewell. All that remains is a pile of tormented flesh lying motionless in a mucilaginous heap next to the remnants of Steven's bass guitar; that, and the arterial spray and remnants of tissue and organs that now decorate the entirety of the room and the band members' disbelieving faces and bodies.

The look of terror on Matt, Erik, and Jacob's faces is without description as they stand in silence, left aghast at the mutilation they just bore witness to. Aside from the incessant low ringing of Erik's guitar amplifier, the air is hushed—not even the sound of their breathing can be heard. Too shocked to hyperventilate, they stand in stillness, afraid to initiate movement. The eyes of all three band members are fixated upon the mush of crudely torn human remains lying before them. Not one of them can even begin to search their minds for words to utter; in their respective spaces they hold motionless, unified in horrific dormancy.

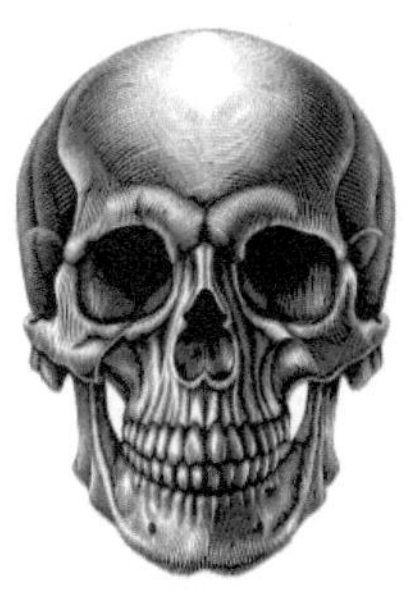

XVII.

The mood is somber in Jessie's basement as he and Shawn pass the pipe back and forth between them, desperately trying to forget the incident two nights ago at the party in the woods. The old brown couch along the back wall has never felt more uncomfortable as Jessie lights the glass pipe again, inhaling a large hit of potent marijuana in the hopes that this puff will be the one to set him free of whatever it was he bore witness to on that terrible early morning. He and Shawn are barely speaking, just sitting in a cloudy haze of smoke, the memories of yesterday's police interrogation still fresh in their minds. Finally, Shawn breaks the silence.

"So... What did you say the man in the suit asked you again?" He looks shyly up from the glass pipe.

Jessie looks over at Shawn, his green eyes now surrounded by red from the weed they have been steadily smoking. "Bro... I don't know what he wanted... His questions were really..." he pauses to motion Shawn to pass the pipe, "they were weird. Like he was trying to gauge my reaction... Almost like he already knew something."

Shawn hesitantly hands Jessie the pipe, then the lighter. "Like he *knew* something? Like what?" he asks in a timid tone, trying his best not to further upset Jessie.

Jessie pauses to hit the pipe, silent for what seems like several minutes as he repeatedly puffs on the glass piece and choking several times as he exhales. "He asked me how objects appeared, and something about...about the surroundings in the area, or some shit." Jessie stops briefly, reflecting on the words he just spoke. "Why would he be asking me stuff like that?" he asks, unsure if he is even recalling the interview accurately.

"How objects appeared? What the hell is that supposed to mean?" Shawn replies with a skeptical look on his face.

"*The fuck if I know, bro,*" Jessie responds in anxious irritation at Shawn's questioning. For the next several minutes they continue sitting in silence, the quietude of the room gnawing at both their subconsciouses in agonizing perpetuity. "And my dad is fucking *pissed*!" Jessie booms, breaking the unbearable silence. "He doesn't know what to think. He's barely talking to me, and when he does, he's just short and pissed-off like." Jessie Senior has seen the strange reports on the local evening news covering the story. The depictions, of course, are vague, as the authorities are attempting to keep the details quiet. But nothing is stopping the social media threads from postulating wild theories and conspiracy-based speculations, and even though Jessie's father does not have any social media accounts, his coworkers have been asking him about the situation non-stop in accordance with what their newsfeeds suggest.

"Last night he made some comment about some guy he works with saying he heard some shit on the internet about kids dying at a drug and alcohol party, then he didn't say a word the rest of the night. What the *fuck* am I supposed to do?" Jessie laments, hitting the pipe again.

"My parents aren't any better about the situation. They told me I couldn't hang out with you anymore," Shawn answers. "I lied to them and told them I was going to work today."

"Yeah, well... Your parents are assholes anyway," Jessie remarks with a grin, the first time he has smiled since the incident took place.

"Fuck you, bro. You going to pass that pipe my way?" Shawn quips while reaching his hand out in anticipation. Once again, muteness ensues. The two sit together, passing the pipe. Not a word is spoken for several minutes as they finish the bowl they are smoking, each harboring thoughts of worry rattling through their shaken minds that they are apprehensive to share.

"Shawn..." Jessie speaks up, breaking the silence, followed by a pause. "There's something else fucking with me."

Shawn leans forward on the dirty old brown couch and adjusts his glasses, the effects of the marijuana so strong that he barely manages to move himself forward to listen to his friend's thoughts.

"I can't tell if it's just me, but..." Jessie stops, unsure of how to finish his sentence.

Shawn looks at Jessie inquisitively for a few moments and then speaks up. "*What*, man?" He rubs his eyes and tries to massage out the dryness caused by the pot. "Go on, *what*?"

"For the last day and a half since that shit happened...I feel like I'm being watched or something."

Shawn looks at Jessie and his eyes widen. "Like...*how*?"

Jessie puts his hand to his head and rubs his forehead in confusion. "I swear there's been a blue van outside my house a lot since this happened. You know, like a cargo-type van with tinted windows and shit." Shawn forces himself upward now, the images conjured in his mind from Jessie's words piquing his interest as he listens intently. "I mean... I've never seen it before, and I know all the neighbors around here. Since that fucked up shit happened, it's just there all of a sudden. I can't tell if I'm paranoid or what." Shawn leans in now, his head turning fully in Jessie's direction, and he stares with a strange look that causes Jessie to react. "*What*, bro? Why are you looking at me like that?"

"*Dude…* I thought I was imagining things," Shawn responds with a relieved yet worried frown.

Jessie, now leaning in toward Shawn, apprehensively yet promptly asks, "What do you mean?" A concerned look forms across his face.

"I saw the same van in front of my house yesterday morning when I got home from the police station." Both of them lean back onto the couch, lost in nervous thought, and Jessie lets out a long, inaudible utterance.

"A *blue* van? Like, tinted windows and all?" Jessie asks Shawn with an almost whispering voice.

"Yup."

"Shit."

Shawn sits up again and looks to his right into Jessie's eyes and asks, "Do you think it's, like, the DEA or something?"

Jessie shoots Shawn a condescending grin. "For what? *What would they have to do with anything*? No, bro. It's got to be that guy from the FBI who came into the interrogation room… Asking all those fucked up questions."

Shawn, now visibly nervous, begins biting on his fingernail. He sits back on the couch and pulls his glasses from his face. "What should we do? You think they still blame us for what happened?"

"*Man, I don't fucking know.* I don't know shit!" Jessie shouts as the stress within him pours over into anger. He stands up as the fear inside him builds to rage, prompting him to kick the glass coffee table in front of the couch, sending paraphernalia and glass shards flying in all directions. Shawn, still seated on the couch, holds his hands up to protect his face from the soaring debris while still clasping his glasses in his left hand as bits of glass pelt his skin. Jessie stomps through the broken shards and off through the basement toward the steps, punching and kicking anything that happens to be standing in his path. Shawn, unsure of what to do, sits there on the couch, listening to the marching of Jessie's feet from the floor above him as they seemingly reverberate through the upstairs hallway straight to the front door. The final noise he hears is the front door slamming shut as he sits in anxious silence, wondering if Jessie plans to return.

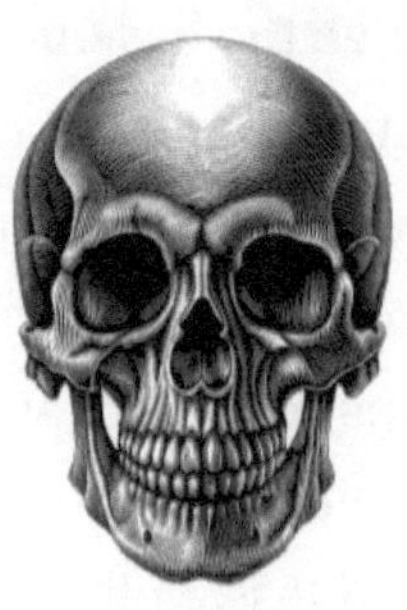

XVIII.

After two connecting flights, an excruciatingly long layover, and a one-and-a-half-hour car ride in a rental from the airport, Martin and Jerry arrive at the Canton Mental Health Facility near Potosi, Missouri. The first stop in their investigation, this incident concerns the bizarre occurrences surrounding events that took place at a family-owned bar and grill in southeast Missouri resulting in twelve mutilations and one surviving victim. The location is in the middle of nowhere on the outskirts of Potosi, seventy miles southwest of St. Louis. Agent Jerry Norton has been complaining on and off for the last twenty miles along the highways and backroads to Martin about how he thinks that it is nothing but a bunch of backwoods Missouri rednecks in this town. The air is moist, and the day is hot; both men are wiping sweat from their brows as they walk from the air-conditioned comfort of their rental car to the main entrance of the facility, the dampness in the atmosphere quickly taking a toll on their bodies in the humid summer heat. As they approach the entrance, Martin eyes the dull grays and off-color browns of the building's exterior, thinking to himself how dreadfully eerie the place looks for a hospital specializing in mental health. Even the landscaping is bleak, with overgrown brush and weeds accentuating the already decrepit ambiance emanating from the dismal colorings of the establishment.

Jerry approaches the entrance first, yearning to escape the misery of the hot summer afternoon, still donning the same black suit and tie he was wearing three days prior. Martin can see the sweat forming under Jerry's armpits even through the darkness of the fabric as he holds the door open for him, a sight that somehow adds an additional layer to his sense of unease. As Martin scurries up the concrete steps in a hasty dash to get through the door, he trips on a broken piece of the step which looks as if it busted free of its original placement years ago and has been neglected ever since. Martin catches himself on the door, narrowly avoiding a fall, and then looks up at Jerry with a gaze of crushing embarrassment. "*Geez*, someone ought to fix that."

Looking down at Martin with a sly smile and through a mien of week-old scruff and sweat-covered face, Jerry remarks, "It looks like this entire building should be remodeled." To Jerry's observation, Martin nods and fixes his glasses, pushing them back above the bridge of his nose toward their proper location. Both men walk through the front entrance and immediately notice a pungent odor assaulting their nostrils with a foul and pervasive offensiveness. The smell is clearly of soiled linens or human waste of some sort, causing Martin to gag and Jerry to scoff at the unknown staff under his breath whom he feels are clearly not maintaining sanitary conditions. Martin, pulling his hand up over his white beard and nose, looks at Jerry with a disgusted grimace and whispers, "*My God*, this place smells awful."

They continue ahead toward the front desk, walking at a brisk pace, hoping the odor will dissipate as they accumulate distance between them and the section of the building they walked in from. As they approach the counter, the stench of human excrement seems to wane and the smell of stale cigarettes takes over. An elderly woman is seated behind the counter adorning a frown and slowly typing on the keyboard in front of her. The lines on her face and the cough croaking from her throat suggest that she has been smoking for far too many years. Her appearance implies to Jerry's mind that perhaps she should have retired by now; to him, she seems far too aged to be of much use in a facility such as this. Martin's first impression of the grizzled old woman is contrary to Jerry's, however; to him, she seems befitting of the antiquated building and, perhaps, has been here as long as it has.

She doesn't even notice the two men standing in front of the counter waiting in anticipation of her attention. After several moments of impatient waiting, Jerry finally raises his hand to his mouth and lets out a subtle cough to garner her observation. With a slow, almost mechanical motion, she gradually cranes her neck up from her computer monitor and takes notice of the visitors. "Hello, how can I help you?" she grates in a raspy voice.

Jerry is taken aback by the pallor of her face and the blank expression in her dark, nearly black eyes. "Umm…" For a moment, Jerry forgets what he was going to say, the look of death in her eyes consuming the thoughts in his mind. "Ah, yes… I am Agent Norton and this…this is Dr. Patterson. We are here to see Dr. Morden about a patient here."

For several seconds, only the sounds of a ghastly wheezing can be heard as the old woman sits behind the counter staring at the men with cold, lifeless eyes, breathing with a harsh exertion and scowling at them as if their presence is wholly unwelcome. Then, with a guttural croak, she finally responds. "Down the hall and to the left. There's an office. He will meet you there." Jerry nods with an uneasy gesticulation and he and Martin begin down the hall, both men relieved to be removed from the awkwardness of the situation.

Martin enters the room first, followed by Jerry, and once again they are greeted with an ominous aura of decrepitude. The color scheme of the room is vaguely off-putting, even though the paint does not seem exceptionally old. It somehow exudes a sense of nauseous decay inspired by the strange choice of hues—dull grays offset by a muddy olive—secreting a strange sense of vulgarity. The room is large but only four chairs are present—the cheap collapsable type with uncomfortable backrests and hard steel frames.

No sooner than both are seated, a man walks into the room, a tall, dark-haired fellow with a stern face and black goatee. In an unfriendly and very direct and emotionless tone of voice, he introduces himself. "Good afternoon, gentlemen. I am Dr. Morden, the director of psychiatry for the hospital." Dr. Morden limps over to one of the two remaining empty chairs and takes a seat, wincing in discomfort as he lowers himself into the chair. He appears to be in fair shape, yet clearly he is afflicted by some sort of painful ailment. He is carrying a manilla folder in one hand, which he gently places in front of him as he eyes the two men sitting across the table. He slowly folds his hands together and rests them on the table with a sullen grimace adorning his face. There he sits in silence, staring at the two with a look of piercing detachment, until Jerry finally breaks the peculiar stillness.

"I'm Agent Norton and this is Dr. Patterson. We're here—"

"I know why you two are here," Dr. Morden interrupts, nearly barking at them with contemptuous haste, as if Jerry's voice had somehow offended him. His sullen grimace turns suddenly to an ominous and curious smile, and he promptly adds, "You are here to interview *the patient.*"

"*The patient?*" Jerry questions, taken aback by the strange reference to the man they are here to see.

"That is what we have been referring to him as," Dr. Morden explains, his smile turning back into a scowling sneer. "I must warn you," he starts, unfolding his hands and placing them flat on the table, "you must take extreme caution in dealing with the patient. He is extremely paranoid and becomes intensely violent when something agitates him." Jerry sits in resolute calmness, not the least bit intimidated by Dr. Morden's warning, but underneath the table Martin's feet begin to shift, nervously tapping at the thought of the doctor's words of caution.

Without hesitation, Jerry looks at the doctor with a sneer of confidence followed by a determinate nod. "We will be certain to take precaution during the interview."

The doctor shifts his head slightly to the left in a strange diagonal manner as if he is adjusting for discomfort and replies, "There's something else... He has been experiencing episodes of narcolepsy." Dr. Morden looks at the file lying before him on the table and picks it up, shuffling it from hand to hand. He looks back at Jerry and Martin, adding, "They still have not identified him, and thus, we have no medical records to refer to. He remembers nothing from before the incident." Jerry and Martin stare at the doctor, neither quite sure what to make of his statements.

Finally, gathering the courage to speak up, Martin straightens his back and looks timidly into Dr. Morden's stern countenance. "Well... Is he available to speak with us now?"

Dr. Morden looks at Martin with a glance of intrigued observance, almost as if he is surprised to hear Martin address him directly, and responds in a low, cold voice. "Let me check." With that, Dr. Morden gets up from the chair, using the table to assist him in standing, struggling as he slowly straightens himself upright. He limps to the door and down the hallway while Jerry and Martin watch him through the windows of the room.

Ten minutes pass as Martin and Jerry sit in the frigid and nausea-inducing room, chattering back and forth in small fragments of spontaneous dialogue to pass the time. Twenty minutes in and still no sign of the doctor or the patient. At this point, Jerry is becoming visibly frustrated, and Martin attempts to lighten the mood with a failed attempt at cracking a joke about the smell of the building when they first entered. Thirty-two minutes into their wait, Jerry and Martin finally see the silhouette of a person appearing on the leftmost side of the windows in the front of the room, moving at a painfully languid pace, further accentuating their restless impatience.

A blonde nurse, probably in her late thirties, walks past the glass and through the door, stopping to hold it open for someone not yet visible through the window. She does not even acknowledge Martin and Jerry, but instead stands at the door looking up the hallway, obviously waiting for an unknown person's arrival. More figures suddenly appear through the glass: two burly orderlies, clad in scrubs and donning callous frowns, walking with a smaller male patient between them. They walk slowly with a cautious gate, careful not to allow the frail man between them to fall. They gradually shuffle the man into the room, and upon entering, Jerry and Martin can clearly see why he needs assistance. He is heavily sedated, drool dripping precariously from his chin, while a straitjacket holds his arms across his chest. More disconcerting than the apparent sedation and the vestment constraining his limbs is the welcoming smile adorning his saliva-glistened and semi-listless face, almost as if he is the only lucid soul in the room.

The patient has messy, darkish brown hair sprouting chaotically in all directions. His green eyes are wide with excitement yet paradoxically lethargic, and sweat covers his face as if he is fixated in a state of drug-induced mania. A man in his mid-fifties, judging by appearance, he is shockingly thin, and his sunken eyes and pronounced cheek bones give his facial features the unusually dreadful resemblance to a fleshless skull. His mouth all the while is suspended in a remarkably warming smile, one that belies his otherwise tumultuous features.

The orderlies seat him in one of chairs at the table, and the blonde-haired nurse takes the remaining chair while the two large aides step back and observe with arms crossed and scowling, authoritative expressions upon their faces. Jerry, anxious to begin, looks at the drooling and bound man with the same sense of professionalism he would extend to anyone else during an interview and sets his digital recorder on the table and presses *Record*. "Good afternoon. I am Agent Norton, and this is Dr. Patterson. We would like to—"

"I KNOW why you're here!" the patient interrupts, his warm smile suddenly turning to a look of staunch seriousness. "You seek penance for your crimes."

Martin turns his head slightly toward Jerry, wondering what his response to the odd statement will consist of. Jerry is used to interviewing some of the toughest criminals, capable of profound acts of malevolence, but he has no experience dealing with a situation such as this. He can see Martin's head turned slightly in his direction and can feel his gaze through the periphery of his vision, and he knows he needs to continue forward with some type of response. "Well, actually, I was hoping we could start with your name, Mr.—"

"WHO I am is of no consequence," the patient starts, an expression of grave sincerity in his wide, sunken eyes. "Your contrition for SINS of the flesh...for CRIMES against humanity...for the DOWNFALL of mankind! These are the ONLY things of any *consequential relevance!*" A new line of saliva begins to drip from the corner of the patient's mouth as he starts to rock back and forth with a disturbingly metronomic cadence while vacillating between shouting and normal levels of speech in his disturbing responses. Martin, unsure of whether he should participate or sit in confounded silence, is hushed by his own nervous incapacity.

Once again, Jerry attempts to bring reasoning to the conversation.

"Sir, we are only here in an attempt to gather information on the incident earlier this—"

"It is *I* who shall *inquire!*" the patient once more breaks in, this time in a bizarre and shrill articulation. The patient's countenance of sincerity turns grim, and a frown of malice adorns his face as he grinds his teeth with vehement intensity. "*Have* you ever conversed with a *demon*? Stared *intently* into a shadow's gaze as you watched a person die?" The patient then shifts his view to the left and stares at Martin with a sobering gleam in his eyes as his frown smoothens and his teeth steady themselves. The man's body calms underneath the straitjacket, and for a brief moment the warm lucidity returns to his being. "The eclipse is upon us, you know. Soon, my friend, when the sun is blanketed in darkness, the shadows will come to life." With that foreboding and baffling declaration, the patient goes limp and his eyes close as he slumps over in his chair. The orderlies, held in stillness all the while, promptly rush forward to save him from falling to the ground. The two burly aides straighten the patient upright in the chair as best they can while the nurse checks his vital signs. It appears that he has suffered another narcoleptic episode, something the doctor warned Jerry and Martin about when they first arrived.

The blonde-haired nurse who has been silent until now looks up from the patient and in the direction of Martin and Jerry. "I'll have to get the doctor." With that terse assertion, she briskly trots from the room and heads up the hallway.

Jerry and Martin survey the patient as he sits limp in the chair, their eyes fixated on the strange man as his still body rests in morbid repose. Neither of them know what to say, and Martin, fidgeting in his chair unable to control his jitters, pulls his glasses from his face and begins to nibble on the earpiece as he often does in times of stress. Jerry, unperturbed by the episode and previous unsane ramblings, sits calmly with his hands folded on the table, the recorder resting in front of them capturing the entirety of the patient's mad discourse.

Suddenly, the patient's eyelids spring open, and with straining, wide optics the patient looks over Martin's shoulder, staring at the corner of the room like some adversary only visible to him has spontaneously appeared. Frantically the patient struggles to break free from his restraints and begins screaming at the top of his lungs with a murderous pitch, one that pierces the eardrums of all four of the occupants near him in the room. The two large attendants, unprepared for the psychotic outburst, do not have time to react as the patient explodes up and out of his chair, knocking the one on his left to the ground as he scrambles for the doorway.

The two burly orderlies give chase, but the fear inside the patient accelerates him down the hallway with an immense velocity, the straitjacket across his chest making no difference in the rapidity of his movements. The patient, now almost to the end of the hallway, trips and falls as Jerry and Martin watch from the doorway of the room, shocked at the explosiveness of the man's agility. The orderlies manage to catch up to the patient and, with a quick and agitated consternation, realize he is bleeding severely from his mouth. As they scramble to subdue the man's erratic and hostile outburst, they see he is bleeding more profusely than was originally thought. With one orderly to the left and one to the right, they attempt to maneuver his body over so that he is facing upward, desperately trying to see where the blood is coming from. All three men wrestle on the floor as one of the orderlies grabs the patient's left leg, which is furiously kicking at the other man with alarming intensity. As he grabs ahold of the leg, he hears his partner's voice and looks up to see a horrified gaze upon his face. "*Mike! His tongue!*" The orderly looks over from his partner's face into the patient's, appalled at the sight before him. The patient, still vigorously kicking and gyrating in an attempt to escape, has his half-torn tongue hanging repugnantly from his lips. With one grinding bite, the patient tears through the remaining portion with his front teeth and spits it at the orderly clutching onto his left leg. The severed organ hits the man in the face along with droplets of blood and smaller chunks of tissue, spattering his mouth and cheek and causing him to shudder in disbelief. Momentarily stunned from the shock of the patient's self-inflicted injury, the orderlies pause, giving the patient a chance to slip away from his partially prone position and once again take off down the hallway.

The end of the corridor is just a few yards away, yet it is closed off from escape by a door on either side, both locked with electronic key card systems. The aides, now back to their senses and once more giving chase, are driven to panic at the thought of the man bleeding to death on their watch, resulting in an even greater incentive to apprehend him at once. The patient looks back one final time at his pursuers with a terrified observance and they are not quite sure if he is peering at them or over their shoulders at something only witnessed through his own fragmented mind. With nowhere to go and trapped by the confines of the hallway's exit-less termination, the patient hurls himself through the second-story window at the end of the corridor, crashing with tremendous force through the glass and steel-frame barrier on the outside. The momentum from the inconceivable leap sends his terror-stricken form arcing to a substantial degree, impaling his body on a wrought-iron fence below, leaving in the hallway above nothing but a trail of blood droplets leading up to his spiritual and corporeal escape.

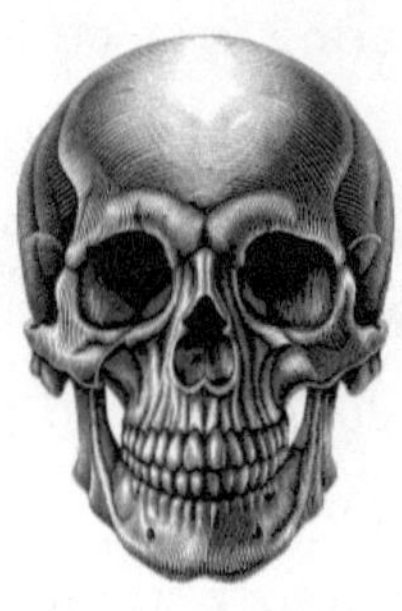

XIX.

The Sonoran Desert this time of year is considerably hot and dry. A July evening in this portion of southwestern Arizona does not offer much respite from the blistering heat; even after the sun goes down, the temperatures can remain above eighty degrees. A barren landscape of desolation and sheer isolation, save for the magnificent and victorious achievement of science and engineering known quite simply as Athena Laboratories nestled unnaturally amidst the uninviting and unforgiving terrain. Athena is home to the world's largest and most powerful particle collider: the Max Planck Particle Accelerator. This crowning achievement of human thought and design was built upon the bedrock of revolutionary physics and empirical triumph, funded by shadow corporations and government agencies hiding behind three-letter acronyms and the darkest motivations. Layers upon layers of shell companies, cryptocurrency transactions, third-party intermediaries, and government grants cloaked in offshore accounts funded the monumental project, but in the end, who would investigate the source of funding for such a massively groundbreaking venture such as this?

The most recently touted success of Athena, of course, is the discovery of a new fundamental particle of nature, the almighty graviton.

With this discovery, scientists hope to better understand the very nature of gravity, down to the smallest constitute—found inherent in the name of the newly observed particle. Discovered less than one week ago, the particle has been named as one of the biggest discoveries of the last several decades in innumerable scientific journals online and throughout countless social media outlets, with Athena being the center of praise amidst the clamor of celebration.

But beneath the surface of celebratory response, and underlying the pure scientific design of the massive facility and its inconceivably intricate design, one finds a startling and blackened truth, a reality that the common person cares not to acknowledge. Corruption seeds the plants that bear fruit in this arboretum, and avarice is the only god that the corrupt bend their knees to—Athena Laboratories is no exception.

Dr. James Hidalgo greets Charles in the lobby of Athena with a smile, pleased to see him once again. He shakes Charles's hand with a firm grasp as he walks through the double doors of the lobby, knowing that Charles expects a strong clasp from any man who is deserving of his respect. As always, Charles is dressed in exquisitely sophisticated attire, this time a dark blue Cesare Attolini suit, which accentuates his bright blue eyes, causing them to appear incandescent in the lightly shaded backdrop of the opulent entryway. Charles flashes Dr. Hidalgo a charming smile, one that is forced but still easily conjured, as he has spent many years mastering the art of deception. Charles's perfectly timed greeting and flawlessly styled blond side part belies the sinister intentions underneath his charisma and beguiling professional deportment.

The two men walk down Athena's main hallway through the administrative area, making small talk on their way to the elevator. Dr. Hidalgo, the leading scientist for the Singularity Project, explains in his Spanish accent the keynotes in the recent developments of the preliminary experiments. A thin man, descendant of Barcelona, Dr. Hidalgo's olive-colored skin and shadowy, dark facial hair convey a sense of congeniality alongside his affable personality and quick-witted, jesting mannerisms. They enter the elevator and Dr. Hidalgo presses button UG3, the level where the research department is located. On the ride down to the third sub-floor of the facility, Hidalgo explains to Charles how grateful his team is for the contributions Charles's firm has made toward the team's scientific efforts. He goes on to explain that the results of the preliminary trials have been nothing short of monumental in terms of the data collected and the implications for the qualitative outcomes projected. As they step off the elevator, Charles smiles at Dr. Hidalgo with a smirk of silent cynicism, knowing that, in time, his malefic intentions will be fulfilled.

Dr. Hidalgo leads Charles through the research department down the hall, past several containment areas and through the technology centers. The area is bustling with scientists, engineers, and postdoctoral researchers, all leering suspiciously at Charles as he walks through the aisleways with a stern aura of importance, a look that suits him well and is befitting of his potent, commanding presence. Hidalgo stops at one of the collaboration spaces to speak with a small group of PhD students that he knows is currently working on the results of the preliminary trials. Charles approaches the students with an overshadowing presence as Dr. Hidalgo introduces him as one of the contributors to the project. They shake hands and exchange greetings followed by a quick summary of the group's research efforts. Charles thanks them for their time and shoots them that ominously pleasant smile, coupled with a wide-eyed gleam from his shockingly bright blue eyes.

Moving onward toward the end of the long stretch of areas within the research department, Hidalgo shows Charles to a secluded office space where he asks him to make himself comfortable and offers a refreshment. Charles declines the offer of a beverage and folds his hands in his lap while crossing his legs, then proceeds to calmly wait for Dr. Hidalgo to expound upon the results of the preliminary trials. The office is exceptionally spacious, exuding a sense of openness, with wide-view windows allowing for the bright desert sun to filter through the tinted glass panes. Dr. Hidalgo takes a chair at the corner of the beige oak table adjacent to Charles where a laptop sits open, the image of a password prompt pasted across the screen. Hidalgo hastily smashes the keys in rapid succession, bypassing the password screen, and opens the files from the project server as he begins to explain the current developments within the project's scope.

"The preliminary experiments are running *flawlessly*. The scientific breakthrough we are on the verge of achieving will change the world forever," he tells Charles with a sense of excitement in his voice and a glimmer of hopefulness in his eye. With a smile of elation that spans the entirety of his face, Dr. Hidalgo continues, "The proof of the existence of gravitons has led to an instantaneous bevy of experimentation that was not available before. The question of whether a black hole is sustainable under experimental conditions is no longer debatable!"

Pleased at Hidalgo's detailing of the experimental developments, a sordid grin appears across Charles's countenance, and he asks, "How soon can I view a collision detection for myself?" in a low and innocuously forbidding tone of voice, his blue eyes large and aroused with a sense of reserved yet surmounting enthusiasm.

Still reeling with excitement from his previous statements, Dr. Hidalgo looks at Charles with a light of exuberance in his visage and responds, "We are ready for another test *today*. Scheduled for this afternoon, as a matter of fact. I knew you wanted to be present for at least one of the particle collisions."

Dr. Hidalgo's invitation pleases Charles, and he acknowledges with a slight nod of the head and a subtle smile. "*Perfect*," he replies while still seated in resolute stillness, hands clasped firmly and steadily in his lap and legs crossed in motionless poise.

"Well then... Would you like a tour of some of the rest of our facility as we wait for the experiment to begin?" Hidalgo asks as he closes the laptop in front of him and rises from his seat.

"I'd love to," Charles responds, finally unclasping his hands and uncrossing his legs with an almost mechanical progression. Dr. Hidalgo walks to the door and Charles follows, straightening his dark blue suit as he marches toward the doorway. Heading back down the long stretch of hallway toward the elevator, Hidalgo begins questioning Charles's familiarity with the technology associated with the particle accelerator, curious as to the extent of his knowledge regarding the equipment. Charles gives a terse response to the questioning, explaining that his knowledge and contributions to the project are based solely on results and the beneficence of scientific achievement.

As they wander through the twists and turns of the research department and around the labs and collaboration areas, Dr. Hidalgo explains further the physics and technology comprising the structure of the main bulk of the particle accelerator complex. He details the electromagnetic fields utilized for energizing the particles during initialization and the boosters that further increase the velocities of the protons as they near the speed of light. Charles listens sporadically with a lackadaisical expression, his interest piqued at times but otherwise making sure to never seem impressed, even when Hidalgo speaks of something compelling; Charles learned long ago to never show astonishment when being introduced to fascinating information, a manipulative tactic that has served him well in the world of finance. Besides, his true intentions are far from the wonders of science, instead residing within the netherworlds of forbidden thought and the ancient horrors of inhuman desire.

Charles is led down the elevator to floor UG5—the technical and systems infrastructure level. There, Dr. Hidalgo explains as he walks Charles through the comprehensive and exhaustive section, is where the cooling systems are housed and monitored that chill the superconductive magnets responsible for creating a pathway for the charged particles to travel where they will collide with one another in a spectacular display of fundamental force detection. Charles looks at the monumental assortment of cooling tanks and helium-containing refrigeration systems in silent awe, their massive and expansive tanks stretching across the large section of the facility as far as his eye can see. "Dr. Hidalgo, at what temperature are the magnets kept?" Charles asks, being sure to phrase the question in a leisurely and professional inflection.

"*Great question*, Mr. Kepler. The cryogenic fluids are kept at nearly absolute zero, roughly -456.15 degrees Fahrenheit. That way the magnets can remain in a state capable of producing superconducting properties with minimal resistance," Hidalgo proudly explains with a look of excitement, thrilled that Charles seems to be taking interest in the tour. As they roam throughout the rest of the technical and systems infrastructure level, Charles mostly remains silent, with a nod or a less-than-enthusiastic acknowledgement thrown in here and there for good measure. All the while he seethes with unholy anticipation for the experimental test to ensue, passing the time in blistering impatience as he begrudgingly goes along with Dr. Hidalgo's tour of the facility.

As the minutes tick by, Charles looks down at his watch in the hopes that Hidalgo will do the same. The hint appears to play on Dr. Hidalgo's subconscious as he checks the time and announces that they should soon head to the Dirac Detection Center to prepare for the safety briefing before they can observe the collision test. Charles once again, in his commanding and unwaveringly staunch demeanor, nods at Hidalgo in agreement and follows him out of the vast maze of cryo-genic cooling systems and toward the aisleway leading to the elevator.

Once inside the elevator, Dr. Hidalgo presses button UG8 which leads to the accelerator rings located ¾ of a mile underneath the bar-ren landscape of the Sonoran Desert. The Max Planck Particle Accel-erator—the largest particle collision detection system in the world—is located in the nauseating depths of this subterranean facility, six hundred feet below the desert surface. Fifty-one miles of closed-loop beam pipes comprised of ultra-rare minerals and alloys make up the circumference of the collider rings, the likes of which seem almost un-earthly in their material composition. The efficiency of the super-con-ducting magnets in their nearly absolute-zero chilled state allow for the tremendous amounts of energy needed to accelerate the particles to velocities that approach the speed of light, a feat that is surpassed only by the facility's state-of-the-art artificial intelligence-driven de-tection systems.

There are several collision points along the expansive length of the Max Planck Particle Accelerator. Sites deep in the facility are ar-ranged around the colossal ring of pipes making up the particle col-lider with sophisticated detection areas, themselves marvels of modern engineering and scientific wonder. There are multiple detec-tor sites and numerous detection systems, all designed to observe dif-ferent types and manners of collisions and constructed around different scientific models and theories in order to observe a wide range of physical phenomena. But there is only one detection site in the Athena Laboratories facility that Dr. Hidalgo and Charles Kepler are concerned with.

The system infrastructures that detect the particle collision results in this particular site are composed of a novel architecture of quantum computing technology instrumental in the exploration of gravity field-related physics. This sector, known as the Dirac Detection Center, is reserved for experimentation associated with secret entities and special financial persuaders, the variety of which typically involves obscure funding and black budgets, mostly military related but not always. The experimental collisions and data collected in this portion of the Max Planck Accelerator are never released to the public. While recent developments surrounding the discovery of the theorized graviton have been causing a stir amongst those of the scientific community, the findings were not conducted in this sector of the detection systems but rather in one less subject to the intensive secrecy that the Dirac Detection Center is cloaked in. None of those involved in the Dirac Center's operations are quite sure how Charles and his firm gained the clearance necessary to set in motion the type of scientific venture the Singularity Project consists of. Those strange and nameless entities at the top of the Athena food chain—the ones whose final say is without question—gave their blessing after the financing for the project from Charles's firm, Prometheus Capital Management, cleared, and no further inquiries were made after payment was received.

Charles and Dr. Hidalgo exit the elevator and enter the enormous Accelerator Access Complex. This immense level is the largest within the Athena Laboratories facility, housing the massive collider rings spanning a total of fifty-one miles. The Accelerator Access area is split into several subsections containing their own detection systems, and walking to the detector sites is not an option. A series of motorized electric four-wheel scooters are parked near the elevator doors and Hidalgo heads for the first one in line, with Charles hopping eagerly into the passenger seat, anxious to witness the experimentation. "The detector site we are visiting is not far from here—about eight minutes or so. Usually, the sites are reached above ground, but...the Dirac Detection Center is different. We should be there just in time for the safety briefing," Dr. Hidalgo explains as he presses on the acceleration pedal and backs out of the parking space.

After an eight-and-one-half minute scooter ride, they reach the Dirac Detection Center. Surveillance cameras line the walkways to the door, and a guard stands present outside the entryway. The detection site is painfully plain and unassuming; nothing but unpainted concrete walls, resembling more of a massive underground parking garage than a highly advanced scientific facility. Dr. Hidalgo approaches and nods to the guard in an oddly silent manner, suggesting that both he and the guard are aware of the secretive nature of the business at hand. Hidalgo swipes his security card across the card reader and the door unlocks with a click followed by a sweeping sound as the door bolt automatically slides out of the catch. He holds open the door and Charles enters, paying no attention to the guard who offered him a nod as a show of respect.

Upon entering the windowless steel door, the appearance of the facility changes drastically. Charles and Hidalgo pass through a sophisticated lobby area clearly arranged for high-profile guests and members of the military elite. Passing by the leather chairs and over the marble floor, directly across from a coffee bar, they enter the Data Collection area of the Dirac site. Walking through this area is the only way to get to their first destination within the Dirac Detection Center—the conference hall, where the safety briefing will be held before the particle collisions begin. Filled with the most powerful computer processors, including quantum-based drives and AI-integrated analysis systems, the Data Collection area is a fascinating sight to behold for most, but in this moment, to Charles, it is only another section of the facility to march through before finally witnessing what he came here to see.

Onward, around two corners and down a fifty-yard stretch of

gloss-white, exceedingly reflective hallway, Dr. Hidalgo and Charles enter the conference hall, where several members of the team responsible for running today's experiment are gathered awaiting their arrival. Charles's outstanding physique and commanding presence when entering the room steals the attention of the occupants for a few seconds, a response he has become accustomed to over the years. "*Hello, everyone.* This is our visitor today, Mr. Charles Kepler. He will be joining us during the second preliminary trial experiments for the Singularity Project this afternoon," Hidalgo explains to the small body of scientists and control engineers. After some key points on safety protocols involving various jargon related to emergency procedures, radiation hazards, and exit locations—all of which Charles paid little attention to—the small team of men and women in the safety briefing gather their belongings and begin filing out of the room and toward the control center.

The control center, somewhat of a misnomer, is less of a controls area and more of a technology hub for viewing the collision results for the Dirac Detection site. Here the sophistication of this clandestine portion of Athena Laboratories is so far advanced that only specialists in the fields of quantum technology are trained to handle and maintain the equipment. The most elite controls engineers from all over the globe are employed by this surreptitious division of Athena, and their tenure here has and always will be strictly covert.

As the team files into the viewing portion of the control center, Charles first notices eight large screens completely covering the south-facing wall of the room with theatre-style seating arranged to the front of the screens in three rows of six seats. Behind the seating arrangements, along the back of the room, he sees towering computer servers and cooling tanks designed to chill the quantum servers which deliver the visual images of the particle collisions on the viewing screens, all of which, Hidalgo informs him, are the only of their kind in the entire world.

The men and women of the small team gather into their seats while Dr. Hidalgo leads Charles toward two empty seats in the front row and center, Hidalgo taking the left and Charles the right. One of the scientists, a woman of seemingly stern deportment, with long brown hair tied in a bun and dark, thick-framed glasses, stands off to the side of the viewing screens. Charles watches her as she picks up a phone hanging near the screens, and by the manner with which she speaks to the person on the other end, appears to make a call to the main accelerator control center. Charles cannot quite make out what she is saying but is certain he hears something to the effect of *two minutes left to initialization*. The woman places the phone back on the receiver and turns to Dr. Hidalgo, confirming Charles's interpretation of the phone conversation by relaying that the process is set to begin shortly. As the woman takes her seat, the top right screen on the display wall suddenly reveals a digital countdown display beginning at two minutes and counting down by the millisecond. Numerous other data sets are displayed on the screen, including temperature readings, energy levels, and various other collider initialization stats. Those gathered wait patiently for the experiment to begin as various new measurements and readings appear incrementally on the monitors lining the wall.

One minute to go now, and a low humming can be heard as the energy levels rise from far away in the complex signaling that energy is being directed to the ring conductors. The towers behind the seats flash colors in flickering pulses as cooling fans kick on, anticipating the quantum computing tower's power consumption spike. Thirty seconds left, and the meters for the energy levels on the power monitor reach the red while the other seven viewing monitors flash to life showing graphs, three-dimensional representations of empty fields, and probability maps for the gravitational particle representations. As the countdown reaches ten seconds, all the digital gauges are pinned, showing the energy fields have reached maximum capacity and the particles are nearing the speed of light. Three, two, one... Everyone is silent, not even breathing is heard as all eyes are on the viewing screens, the seven monitors instantaneously filling up with data as the graphs are charted.

"*There...* You see, Mr. Kepler!" Dr. Hidalgo exclaims, his voice resounding with excitement. ".723 seconds! Almost three quarters of a second sustained! *A full half a second longer than the last black hole!*"

A pleased look and a diabolical smile greet Charles's face as everyone claps and cheers but him. He simply sits in motionless contentment, poised with a deep sense of malignant gratification coursing through his being. For the second time in human history, the team has successfully sustained the existence of an artificially produced black hole, the first being the same day the laboratory discovered the graviton less than one week prior. As the team celebrates the experimental results, only one thing resonates within Charles's mind as he turns his head slightly to the left and leers at Dr. Hidalgo with an austere and fixated glance. "Are we set to proceed with the Singularity Project on the 25th?"

Hidalgo looks at Charles and, recognizing the seriousness of his tone, replies, "Yes, sir. I believe everything will be prepared by then."

"*Make sure that it is.*"

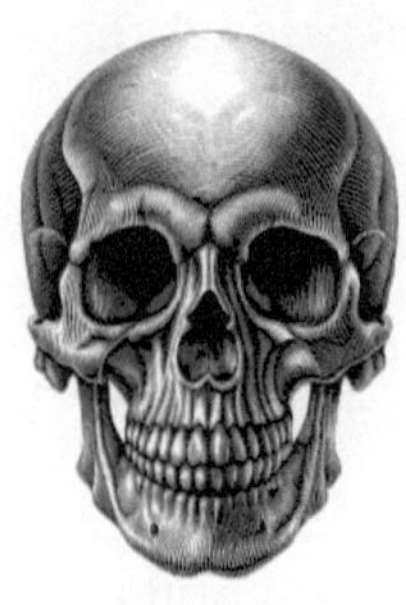

XX.

Room 12 at the Ivy Motel in Oakland smells of stale cigarettes and old milk. Although a faint aroma, Matt can still sense a whiff of it every time he exits the bathroom after emptying his bladder of the beer he has been drinking nonstop since witnessing the horrific death of his bandmate, Steven. Matt has been at the seedy motel since the night before, checking into the room after leaving the police station. The investigating officers have instructed him to stay nearby as they will have some more questioning to conduct soon, however, Matt feels his apartment is not currently an option, instead finding his solace in this rank and solitary room. When Matt last spoke to Jacob, he learned the police had cordoned off the rehearsal space for crime scene investigators, and rehearsal for the upcoming show is impossible without a bass player. All that is left now is to mourn the death of his friend and bandmate; that and drown his sorrows in a pitiful deluge of alcohol-induced despair over his current circumstances and the hideous incident they all bore witness to.

Police are baffled at what has occurred and the media is getting suspicious with the rash of bizarre deaths happening around the country. Potosi, Missouri, Sugar Land, Texas, and now two California incidents involving extraordinarily odd deaths and strange phenomena have taken place. There are whispers on the streets of unexplainable phenomena and mutilations, the news feeds on social media are starting to speak of conspiracy theories, and the evening news in California is reporting on two separate incidents in the same week involving deaths without solid leads. While at the present time these are still small rumors and not garnering widespread attention, the teams of detectives working these cases are feeling the pressure; soon the public will be made fully aware of the strange occurrences and bizarre mutilations, and by then, they fear, a mass panic will ensue. But none of these concerns currently weigh on Matt's fractured mind.

Matt finishes another bottle of Heineken and tosses it across the room, the bottle landing along the wall making a loud clanking sound as it reflects off the edge of the trim. He sits up on the hard mattress of the motel room bed and moves his hair out of his eye while clumsily reaching over to the nightstand to grab another. As he does so he sighs, annoyed that the longneck is just out of reach. "Fuck." Matt sits up farther while pushing down upon the mattress as he edges closer to the beer, realizing that his hand is pressing downward on one of the pages of the ancient text that he brought with him to the room the night before. Many printed pages of that mystical document discovered in a strange tomb isolated from civilization in the Al Farâfra district of Egypt lay scattered atop the cheap and stained blanket of the motel bed. The last couple days have been nothing short of horrific; the one thing still bringing a sense of ease to Matt's distraught mind is his one true passion in life—those forbidden occult writings of times long ago.

Matt began teaching himself to interpret Egyptian and Sumerian glyphs and script in the 8th grade, and even though he's no professional, he always has been quite apt at deciphering their spectrally dark meanings. Along with his curiously strange ability to see beyond that which average humans perceive, the artificial intelligence systems used in transcribing the latest ancient writings have made it relatively easy for him to understand the antiquated and sinister suggestions found within the archaic languages.

Leaning back against the headboard of the budget motel's cheap and uncomfortable bed, Matt pops off the bottle cap to a fresh beer and picks up a page of the printer-copied text as he takes a swig. He becomes engrossed in the novelty of the recently discovered manuscripts; they are unlike anything discovered before, so bizarrely unique in the ways they were written. That oh-so-familiar sense of comfort and warmth envelops him as he reads on—the excitement of pondering the thoughts of cultures past bringing a nostalgic feeling that never ceases to please him. It is almost like a drug for his fractured perception, lulling his mind into a state of peaceful euphoria. These newly unearthed pages of obscure rituals and profane rites are particularly comforting, the Egyptian glyphs seemingly leaping forth from the paper while tempting Matt to join in their ancient and verboten celebrations.

The fact that the page his hand embraces is printed from a website seems utterly inconsequential, for at this precise moment, Matt can feel the texture of the papyrus on which the images were originally inscribed. Many of the symbols are familiar to him, describing sacred deities and spells to destroy enemies; however, some of the characters are completely unfamiliar and exude a maleficent aura around their composition. Matt tries to focus on the hieroglyphs, straining his eyes to focus, but as he stares intently at the figures on the page, he feels a gust of air upon the back of his neck. This sudden zephyr casually warms to a sultry breeze, kissing his skin with a caress of delectation and a subtle hint of insidious forewarning. Is it the soothing effects of the alcohol he has been indulgently consuming, or an event triggered by elements outside of his being causing this glowing warmth? Eschewing the notion, Matt cares not for such inquiry, deciding instead this incident of peculiar relaxation is warmly welcomed and could not have arrived at a more fitting time.

Matt sinks lower into the embrace of the cheap motel mattress as everything but the pages before his eyes begin to fade. The arcane images on the page take on a life of their own, spinning tales of times now forgotten. *Or are they reenacting long lost events?* Matt wonders as his slips into a state of absolute repose. Suddenly, and with the surreal fluency of a dream, the paper that Matt holds within his grasp metamorphoses into a window to the past. Visuals and renderings play out before his eyes as a scene of primitive times reveals itself from the pages like a continuous stream of hallucinatory thought manifesting within the archaic writings.

Matt gazes onward in disbelief as an exhibition of horror abruptly unfolds, a place of excruciating human suffering revealing itself in views tinted with torment and revulsion. Only the soothing sentiments of his initial illusory respite allow him to retain his composure as a visualization of madness ensues, conjuring images foul and disastrous in nature. Matt bears witness to men, women, and children in bondage, forced to toil under the tyranny of ancient oppressors and subjugated by racial conquest—the conquest of the human race. As far as the eye can see, people are laboring, compelled under the governance of horrid beasts wielding ghastly instruments of torture, to construct great monuments in reverence to their diabolical rulers. Piles of bodies—several stories high—reeking with the putrescence of decayed flesh remind those of human descent that they are never thought of with compassion, only hatred. Massive temples christened with the blood of the innocent litter the landscape and assure all who gaze upon them that hope is a stillborn dream put to rest by the reality of sacrifice. Screams and moans of the tormented resonate across the landscape, creating a nightmarishly demonic symphony of unparalleled misery. Clouds of overshadowing darkness blanket the skies, and no daylight can be seen—nor could it ever be seen, for this world has never known the blessings of a shining sun. Only the incandescence radiating from a burning mountain of bodies to cast its morbid illumination upon this land—a sickening pyre comprised of corpses belonging to the frail and useless ones.

Far off in the distance, towering in hateful omnipresence, stands a colossal temple built atop a boundless, blackened mountain. It is hundreds of stories high and vastly surpasses the architecture of anything constructed or envisioned with the limited scope of the human mind. Enormous black pillars are mounted to the front-facing ledges of the cosmic structure, forming an open viewpoint for the imperceivably vile ruler whose unspeakably cruel iniquity compels the suffering throughout this dimension. At the heart of this vast temple, beyond the hatefully black cast pillars, is a mighty throne, constructed of rotted flesh and twisted corpses, about which is seated a monstrous being. Like a statue it sits, still and emotionless, animated only by the slithering creatures that writhe and undulate within its inexpressibly grotesque skin. Eternal fires rage within this entity's eyes, burning so brightly and with such ferocity that they cast light upon the objects before them, illuminating the unholy throne room surrounding the being's unspeakably blasphemous presence.

Beneath this demon's throne of mutilated human bodies is a great chamber, no smaller than a dozen castles, built to contain thousands of tortured captives. Many are chained and dangling from hooks, hanging in incredulous tribulation. Pierced through their genitals, faces, eyes, and tongues hang the throngs of innocent; some are dead, some are dying—all are condemned to subservience. There are no words to describe the agony that resides within this bastille of damnation; only the visual representations of a profound evil, tempering the atmosphere with an inhuman desolation comparable to nothing that can be conjured within the imagination of man.

In an isolated corner, deep within the darkest recesses of this unholy structure, lies the disfigured shell of a man. His eyes have been crudely removed and his lips torn from his face. He breathes in intermittent and shallow bursts due to an impaled spear-like weapon driven several times into his chest. A barbaric, hideous beast stands over him, leering with a seething hatred and covered in centuries of congealed blood and rotten entrails. The monstrous creature raises its enormous hoof and prepares to deliver a final blow about the dying man's cracked and nearly skinless skull, the loathing in its sneering, fanged maw incalculable by any means of reason. The man, in his ghastly state of unutterable pain, slowly gazes upward, his eyeless countenance filled with an anguish that no man should ever know. He slowly raises his arm and points toward an iron window imbedded in the wall with the only digit remaining on his blood-covered arm. His battered and cruelly disfigured face turns toward the blackened skyline in the same direction as his index finger as if he can somehow still see through to the outside world even though his eyes have been removed. Through the bars the sky can be seen, and in the darkened clouds a symbol appears. It is vague yet somehow clear, shaped like a star but not quite fully formed. The sigil floats ominously amidst the black clouds, cloaked in eerily disproportionate and amorphous symmetry.

Suddenly the view vanishes, and Matt finds himself in his seedy motel room afflicted by a hellish sear and the presence of an acrid stench. As he is jolted back to his earthly reality, he quickly realizes the motel room he occupies is ablaze, burning with a nightmarish intensity. The bed he is lying on is engulfed with orange and red flames attacking his legs with a demonic ferocity. The odor of burning carpet and semen-stained sheets is sickening, and as Matt lunges out of the fiery bed he chokes on the foul-smelling smoke. His eyes are blinded by the thick, odorous fumes and tears pour down his face as he heads for the door, all the while choking on the noxious clouds as he frantically scrambles. The room is small, but his sense of panic coupled with the blinding optical irritation of the vapors makes it a challenge to find the exit as he stumbles in the direction of the doorway, tripping over an empty beer bottle along the way. He pushes forward through the darkness of his obscured vision, feeling the caress of the uncaring flames steadily rising around him as he makes the final steps toward his gateway to salvation. Matt slams headfirst into the door and is temporarily stunned by the blow, taking a few seconds to recover from the disorienting impact. He desperately searches for the doorknob, his pulse quickening with each passing moment, while the hellish flames are growing by the second, aggressively assailing his back and flagellating his skin through his burning cotton shirt. The fire upon his back grows hotter and the smoke thickens, intensifying the panic that he feels while every pore in his body overflows with sweat.

Finally, his hand greets the knob and Matt throws open the door, plunging simultaneously through the opening with such ferocity that the door nearly flies off its hinges. He lands several feet from the entrance and turns to gaze upon the fires that nearly devoured his being. As he stares into the burning motel room, a figure moves about the firelight, dancing with the infernal flames in a spectacle of apparitional malevolence. The demonic manifestation glides within the inferno, swirling within the fire as if it is stoking the blaze, an unholy conjuration of stirring, nefarious influence taunting his disbelief as he watches the all-consuming pyre. Its blackened presence exudes a sense of maleficence that makes the fire itself seem altruistic. With time-dilating fluency the apparition disappears and the room collapses, causing a maelstrom of sparks and embers to crash to the ground and scatter in a finale of fiery destruction. With this grand culmination, Matt turns and runs, not once looking back at the blaze still raging behind in his wake.

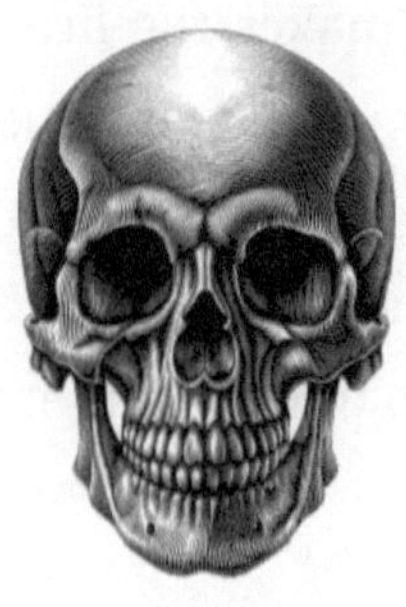

XXI.

As Charles sits stately in his library room, sipping from a wineglass in his tufted leather armchair, he contemplates the darkness he has made Mephistophelian acquaintanceship with. With shades drawn and surrounded in bleak, death-like silence, he ruminates on the elimination of this epoch and the enslavement of man's unfathomable ignorance. Charles takes another long, slow sip of Bordeaux and thinks back on his merciless deeds, all the while savoring the images conjured in his mind of those who have perished by his hands. A smile greets his lips as he closes his eyes and envisions the murders, bringing a profound sense of joy to his apathetic soul. Each death, callously inflicted upon innocent flesh, was not perpetrated in the name of pleasure; Charles's dark affiliations have provided him with diabolical guidance, revealing to him the sinister ways to enlightenment, made clearer with each successive kill. The entities with whom he makes his demonic covenant have chosen a person to help him in his unholy endeavors; one who is descendant of pure proletariat blood. This shell of flesh shall be utilized as a vessel, a portal through which the blackest energies can flow.

Glancing up from his wine glass toward the Howard Miller grandfather clock in the corner of the room, Charles sees that the time has come to abandon his contemplation. He slowly rises from his armchair with morbidly mechanical prowess and sets the wine glass down on the table beside him. As he turns toward the doorway, he pauses to pull his pocket square from his suit jacket, using it to gently wipe the droplets of blood from his black leather Oxford shoe. Charles tosses the soiled pocket square onto the floor and continues toward the door, carefully stepping around the pool of blood slowly expanding from the slain body hanging from a hook in the coffered ceiling overhead.

Across town, ten miles south of Charles's Berkeley Hills mansion, near the Port of Oakland, two men clad in dark clothing are exiting a blue cargo van in an alleyway behind a large, decommissioned factory. Opposite the factory is an old service station that has recently been converted into a small storage warehouse. The moon is almost full, and clouds hang overhead, casting strange shadows upon the ground while the men survey the surroundings before unloading the van. Convinced that no witnesses are present to observe their devious operations, the driver steps out of the van and walks around to the rear, joined on the other side by the man previously occupying the passenger seat. The driver takes one more slow and comprehensive look around, ensuring that the alleyway is indeed void of human presence, then signals to the passenger with eyes of mischievous intent before conveying a final thought as he opens the door. "Let's make this quick." He flings open the back of the vehicle and grabs a person from inside, violently yanking them from the floor of the van. The occupant is shaking, tied, blindfolded, and gagged, and the man forcefully escorts him inside the back door of the building. Following closely behind is the passenger, who drags another occupant across the ground and into the small warehouse, this one whimpering and sobbing as he is pulled.

The inside of the converted service station is dimly lit and has a dank and nauseating aroma, giving rise to further panic within the mind of the sobbing captive. The other captive remains largely silent save for the rapid breathing venting from his sweat-covered nose. *"Where's the tape?"* the larger of the two men—formerly the driver— barks at the smaller as he seats the silent captive on an old wooden chair. The smaller man releases the legs of the sobbing captive, allowing them to drop to the hard concrete ground, joining the upper half of the captive's body already in contact with the floor. He pulls a roll of electrical tape from his pocket and rushes to the side of the larger man, holding it outward in an attempt to hand it over. "No, *stupid*! Tape his fucking hands to the chair while I hold him up," the larger man growls, angered by the smaller man's miscomprehension. Nodding his head in confirmation, the smaller man begins wrapping the tape around the silent captive's already bound hands to the vertical supports on the backrest of the chair, securing them firmly to the wooden spindles. "Now his legs," whispers the larger man to the smaller, leering commandingly at his subordinate accomplice.

Now restrained to the chair by both hands and feet, the once silent captive, too, begins whimpering. The fear of the unknown grips tightly upon his mind as he struggles to breathe through the rag stuffed into his mouth and taped around his head. Thoughts of certain death torment the now chair-bound captive's imagination, causing his heart to pound with adrenaline-fueled intensity. Only a few feet away he can hear the sounds of his friend weeping and sniveling, exacerbating his own sense of panic. Left lying on the cold concrete floor of the warehouse, unable to move and stricken with terror, the other captive begins to hyperventilate, screaming beneath his gag in uncontrollable horror. *"Goddamnit,"* the larger man grumbles as he begins toward a large wooden table sitting several yards away, clearly irritated by the sounds of the wailing. The man storms over to the table with a grimace of contempt plastered across his face, muttering profanities under his breath as he stomps across the floor. Scattered across the tabletop are an assortment of tools and hardware, of which sundry items he picks up a hammer. The man pauses to look at it as if admiring its shape and size, rotating it about as he inspects its curvature. Keeping the tool raised, he makes his way back over toward the captive helplessly bound on the floor, raising the hammer higher with each step he takes. As he approaches the screaming captive, writhing and kicking both legs simultaneously within the restraints atop the ground, he flips the hammer around. Bringing the handle downward with tremendous force, the wood contacts the captive's skull, the ferocity of which knocks him completely unconscious. "*Now, you...* Shut the *fuck* up or you'll be next!" Instantaneously the chair-bound captive ceases whimpering; only the sounds of panting emitting from his flaring nostrils can still be heard.

Time fragments as the chair-bound hostage's mind writhes in fear, twisting and churning with an endless stream of possibilities and horrifying scenarios, the contemplation of which torment his mind as he waits for what seems like hours for his fate to be revealed. The wondering and waiting are agonizing; has the time yet come for his uncertain future to be determined, he wonders, trying his best to control his breathing and keep his panic under control. He can hear his subjugators in the background chatting amongst themselves, laughing in apathetic unconcern, completely detached from the emotional distress of his circumstance. The other captured person remains unconscious on the floor, a condition that the chair-bound prisoner envies in some strange way.

As the seemingly timeless waiting continues to torture his mind, a new fear propels his fragile emotional state to heightened levels as the sound of the door opening behind him echoes across the warehouse walls. The chattering between the two men abruptly stops and only the clacking of footsteps can be heard sauntering slowly toward the chair with an ominous cadence foretelling of dreadful things to come. The closer they get, the quieter the atmosphere seems to become, almost as if a dark presence is commanding the quelling. The sounds of the eerily resonating steps draw nearer and the heartbeat inside the chair-bound man's chest quickens as a droplet of sweat inches down from his forehead, stopping at the bridge of his nose just as the echoes of the footsteps conclude.

"Good evening, sir," murmurs a shallow voice from the direction of the room where the two men stand, bidding a respectful salutation to the person who apparently employs their agency.

"Are they secured?" questions the newcomer with a tone of austere succinctness.

"Yes, sir," answers the dominant man while the other stands in silent stillness, his head aimed at the floor.

"You can leave now. The money has been transferred to the account." No further vocal acknowledgement is returned on behalf of the men; instead, a slight nod is imparted by the larger, accompanied by a hasty exit by both.

An authoritative gleam emanates from bright blue eyes as Charles walks slowly over to the rear of the chair and removes the blindfold covering Jessie's sweat-covered and terrified face. Charles circles around the chair with a gradual pace and stops when he reaches the front. He stares down at Jessie with a towering leer of iniquitous curiosity, his six-foot stature offering a powerful and imposing presence along with the nefarious look in his effulgent blue eyes. As the fear builds inside Jessie's being, it seems to fuel the evil in Charles's visage, causing his demon-like stare to further intensify. Charles steps closer to Jessie and raises his hand, pausing suddenly as he hears a noise from behind. The floor-bound captive releases a subtle but audible moan as he awakens from unconsciousness, disturbing the procession of Charles's actions. Lowering his hand with a look of sheer perturbation across his face, Charles turns around and walks toward the source of the moaning just a few yards away. Jessie's friend, now becoming reacquainted with his current situation, looks around as he awakens and realizes once again where he is. As his memory returns, and the cold concrete of the warehouse floor greets him anew, Shawn glances upward with foggy eyes and slowly stirring awareness just in time to see the face of a claw hammer rushing toward his head before, once again, the world goes dark, never to brighten again.

As Jessie watches the skull of his friend shatter beneath the force of the hammer, he can no longer regulate his scarcely restrained composure. The sight of Shawn's head being crushed by the impact of the steel compels him to scream uncontrollably underneath his gag as Charles repeatedly brings the tool down into the helpless man's shattering cranium. Charles stands, leaving the hammer lodged in Shawn's skull, and turns back toward Jessie, eying him with an intense and feverous eccentricity as he swiftly starts in his direction. Jessie's mind reels in absolute terror, convinced that he is next to die. Charles completes the short distance between Shawn's corpse and Jessie, standing now so frightfully close that his body nearly straddles Jessie's legs as they squirm vigorously underneath the tape that binds them. Charles continues to stare into Jessie's eyes as he struggles to breathe, gasping for air in between muttered cries and saliva-induced choking. Charles glares down at Jessie, his bright blue eyes ablaze with spell-binding hatred, and he grips Jessie's jaw with his blood-spattered hands, forcefully pressing it downward. Jessie's jaw nearly dislocates as Charles holds open his mouth, ripping out the gag as he brings his mouth closer to Jessie's. Their lips nearly touch as Charles begins to violently heave and convulse, his body shaking with a pulsating fury as blackened, swirling shades of demonic eidolon vomit forth from his mouth, infecting Jessie's body with loathsome and vile spirits. The entities fill Jessie's body with a foul hatred far beyond the limits of human resilience, so dark in their iniquitous vulgarity that his skin turns pale in autonomic revulsion. In response, Jessie's body attempts to regurgitate the obscene specters, only for them to whirl and spiral with still greater intensity back down his throat in a vortex of sickening depravity. Charles slams Jessie's mouth closed so violently that two of his front teeth crack under the pressure while his body shakes and spasms in reaction to the perverse spiritual invasion.

The spasmodic convulsing ceases and all is momentarily still, giving Charles the chance to take a step back from Jessie and patiently observe the outcome of his profane undertakings. He watches with callous disassociation as Jessie's eyes close, causing his appearance to give off the impression of death. For several moments the motionlessness ensues and all that can be heard is the panted breathing from Charles's exasperated lungs, fatigued from the exertion put forth during the wearisome invocation. With a savage ferocity, Jessie's eyelids abruptly flash open, as if something beyond corporeal faculty is controlling his physicality. With eyes now widened and facial features possessed of demonic rage, a disturbingly beast-like growl erupts from deep within Jessie's befouled body. The echoes from the monstrous sound fill the tiny warehouse, reverberating across the room with a sinister corruption that can be felt like a distorted wave of putrid radiance. Jessie's mouth shuts, stifling off the blasphemous roar, completely shattering one of his cracked teeth in the process of the forceful closure. The profanatory echoes continue resonating within the room, gradually fading out of existence as if a damning spiritual essence is slowly escaping into unknown regions of space and time.

Jessie's pale skin regains its natural hues, and his countenance seamlessly metamorphoses back into form, erasing all semblance of the ungodliness that transpired. Charles steps to the rear of the chair and rips loose the tape binding Jessie's hands, allowing him to move with autonomy. Not a single word is spoken between the two as Jessie reaches down and removes the tape from his legs, the cold silence broken only by the sounds of the material tearing free. As Jessie stands up from the chair, he looks at Charles with neither fear nor authority, an emotionless blankness instead gracing his demeanor. Free now from the chair, Jessie stands and stares blankly ahead as Charles turns and starts for the door, the clacking of his shoes once again filling the room with an ominous cadence. Jessie follows Charles at a steady pace, his gait and deportment one of unconcern, as if nothing beyond the usual had transpired in the hours since his abduction. As they make their way out of the building, not a word is spoken between them, nor a hint of recognition given by either party; only the faint sounds of footsteps to fill the otherwise silent air of profane ambiance through the dimly lit and morbidly dank room, followed by the slamming of the warehouse door.

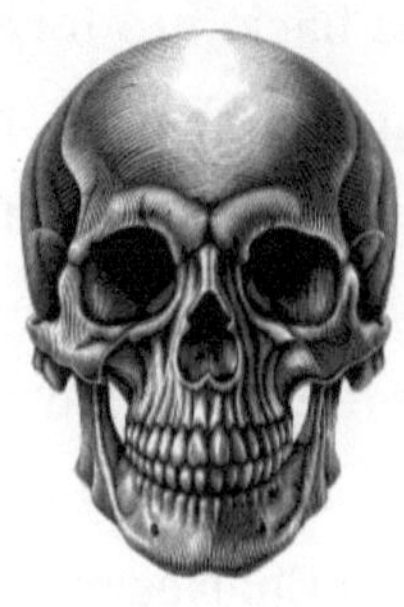

XXII.

The Scotch whisky in Jerry's glass, while still providing the familiar stinging comfort, does little to ease the burdens currently disquieting his troubled mind. It is not the violence of the strange occurrences at the Canton Mental Health Facility that disturbs his mentality, however, but instead the lack of information he and Martin were able to garner from the interview before the man leaped from the second-story window to his gruesome and unexplainable death. Martin, on the other hand, sits in perturbed quietude, deeply affected by the horrendous tragedy he bore witness to earlier today.

It is noisy in the airport lounge where Jerry and Martin await their next flight, and the waitress is taking forever to place their order. Jerry requested a booth in the rear corner of the restaurant so they would not be disturbed by the din of the busy airport eatery, but the seating arrangement has done little to quell the chatter amidst their surroundings. The next flight out of St. Louis for Houston isn't until 8:15 p.m.—another two hours away—so Martin proposed dinner before takeoff, an idea that Jerry quickly agreed to as the thought of a stiff drink entered his mind.

"I am a professor, not a *detective*," Martin snorts, breaking the awkward silence between them. He picks up a glass of water sitting in front of him and grips it with both hands, spinning it around slowly before taking a sip. "I really am unsure of whether I want to continue. I didn't anticipate anything of this magnitude... Seeing that poor, disturbed man leap to his death..." Martin pauses and turns his head in disconcerted contemplation while letting out a deep breath, then continues, "I am a *scientist*, an *academic*. I thought I was going to be examining physical evidence, or maybe drawing conclusions based on some statistical analysis, not...not *watching people bite their own tongues out of their mouths*!" A look of incredulous anger accompanies his face as he glares at Jerry while removing his glasses from his face. He rubs his nose in an attempt to relieve his frustration then looks back at Jerry, waiting for him to respond.

"*Look...* I know that this wasn't what you expected, *hell*, I've never seen anything like that in all my years, but we just started. Give me just a few more..." Jerry stops as the waitress finally arrives to take their order and redirects his attention to her. "Can you give us a few more..."

Martin swiftly interjects, "No, it's fine, we're ready. Ribeye, medium-rare, asparagus, and mashed potatoes... Thank you."

The young server looks at Jerry with inquisitive eyes and begins to ask about his order, but before she can utter a word, he answers, "Just the scotch for me, thanks." The server smiles and turns to walk away as Jerry focuses his attention back to Martin. "*Please*, Dr. Patterson, just a *few* more days."

Martin, still playing around with his glasses, places them back on his face and stares at Jerry with an intense rumination swirling erratically through his thoughts. "Okay, Agent Norton... A *few* more days, and that's *it*." He returns to slowly spinning his glass of water on the tabletop while Jerry turns his attention back to his scotch. The silence between them returns and both stare off into separate corners of the restaurant while the bustle of the airport in the background fills the void between them.

After a few minutes pass, Jerry tires of the uncomfortable quiet and picks up his scotch, finishing it with a final, long swill. He swirls the ice cubes around in the glass and places it on the edge of the table in hopes that it will clue the server to bring another. He runs his hand over the stubble on his face and scratches his chin while looking in Martin's direction. Martin notices Jerry looking his way and focuses his attention, assuming that Jerry is preparing to speak.

"When I first became a detective 18 years ago, long before I joined the FBI, I was working on a case of a missing child—a high-profile case." Martin's interest now piqued, he turns his body toward Jerry and scoots upward in the booth, awaiting with curiosity the details of the forthcoming story. Jerry sees now that he has Martin's focus and clears his throat before continuing. "*Ahem...*" he chokes, looking nervously about the room while simultaneously scanning for prying eyes and putting into check his volume of speech. Apologizing for the sudden pause, he fidgets aimlessly with his hands, nervously fumbling for the courage to proceed. "Sorry. Anyway, she was 10 years old; her name was Emily..." Jerry continues to explain, pausing once more to look for the server as if he is suddenly made uncomfortable by his own story. Martin gives Jerry a glance of anticipation while waiting for him to continue. "Well...anyway... We thought it was a ransom case at first, given that it was an affluent and well-known family. You know, who wouldn't think that at first?" Jerry explains in a questioning inflection while looking to his left for the server to bring him another drink. "A few days after she went missing, the local authorities received a strange handwritten letter from the child. It was done in crayon...*red* crayon, I remember it well. Ahem... Sorry, excuse me," Jerry apologizes after clearing his throat for a second time. "The letter was *almost* pleasant...but in an unsettling way."

"What do you mean by *unsettling*?" Martin questions as he once again pulls his black, wire-framed glasses from his face and places them on the table.

"Emily spoke of being in a place that was like a dream, full of strange weather and what she called '*the shadow creatures*.' She said everything was fine and not to worry, '*it will all be better soon*.'" The server walks by and Jerry stops her to order another scotch as Martin eagerly waits for him to continue.

As soon as the server is out of earshot, Martin interjects, "What did the department make of all this?"

Jerry grabs his finished drink back from the edge of the table and attempts to scrounge a last watery sip from the glass, then continues. "We didn't know what to think. I was just starting out as a detective and even the department veterans had never dealt with a case like this. No clues to her whereabouts...no witnesses...the family didn't appear involved... *Nothing*. We could do absolutely *nothing* but wait."

Both men sit at the table and say nothing for several seconds. In the short interim, the server walks back up and sets Jerry's drink on the table. Jerry turns his head toward her but does not afford her a glance. "Thank you." While looking down at his drink, Jerry swirls the scotch around the glass with his finger, and not bothering to lift his eyes upward, continues. "We heard nothing for weeks. The family was frantic—the mother ended up in the psych ward after pulling all her hair out one night; they had to administer several hundred sutures where she had ripped large chunks of flesh from her head along with the locks of hair." Jerry stops to take a slow drink from his glass, savoring the taste of the blended Scotch whisky and hoping it will ease the discomfort of his morbid narration. He sets the glass down and looks at Martin. "*Finally*, six weeks later…they received another letter. It was strange and made little sense. Emily wrote, 'I am transforming, and I will be coming home very soon, *the gloomy man said so.*'"

Both are silenced by Jerry's last words of recounting, and before either can speak, the server returns with Martin's food. She places it on the table and Martin thanks her with an emotionless and terse acknowledgement. His appetite is momentarily disrupted, and he pushes the food to the side as he looks back at Jerry and waits for him to continue. "*Anyway…*" Jerry starts, breaking to take a long, slow sip from his drink. "At the bottom of the letter was a drawing…a strange one… It was of an eerie symbol… A sort of star, drawn in a dried reddish substance. We had the substance tested… It was Emily's blood." Martin says nothing but studies Jerry's scowl as the words he speaks fall loathsomely from his lips. His eyes remain fixated on Jerry's expression, and he can tell by the disgust forming on his countenance that the horrors of this story do not end here.

"Once again, we heard nothing, this time for months. The mother was released from the psych ward a month after the second letter arrived… Two weeks later, she killed herself. She left a suicide note saying that every night in her sleep she saw Emily—she claimed that Emily was trapped in a bizarre place filled with unspeakable torment. She said she bore witness to Emily being tortured night after night by hideous otherworldly beings and she could no longer handle these… *visions.*"

"Do you believe her? What did you and the department make of all this?" Martin questions with a look suggesting a mixture of nauseated interest and obvious skepticism.

"It…gets much worse," warns Jerry while holding his glass of scotch before his face and slowly spinning it as he watches the ice cubes swirl carelessly within. "Soon after the mother's death, the father began receiving strange packages in the mail—boxes wrapped in materials that were common in the early 1900s, but not sold or manufactured anymore—the packages contained ominous-looking symbols and shapes, fashioned from organic-looking materials."

Martin runs his hand through his white beard as he listens and stops Jerry momentarily to ask, "The packaging materials were tested for authenticity?"

"Yeah, we had...uh...spectrometers, expert analyzers come in... You know, use all kinds of fancy equipment. They don't know where the hell the packaging and materials came from. The packages, though...they weren't the most concerning part..." Jerry stops and knocks back his scotch with a final quaff. "The strange objects inside the packages... We had those tested as well..." A long pause ensues as Jerry sets his empty glass down on the table and looks at Martin with a disconcerted gaze. "They were created using Emily's skin and organs."

"*Why are you telling me this*?" Martin finally asks in a sickened and irritated tone while his food sits untouched on the table, getting colder by the minute.

"*Just...*let me finish. Shortly thereafter, the packages disappeared from the evidence locker. The family was devastated by the entirety of the events; we had no leads, no witnesses—nothing. About a year after the little girl went missing, the father got a phone call... He said it was Emily. The father reported that he could barely understand what she was saying, 'it was as if she was under water,' or 'speaking with something muffling her voice.' He explained that it was '*like she was in another world.*'"

"*And you believed him*?"

"I don't... No, *not at first...* I don't know..." Jerry rubs his forehead in frustration and continues. "He claimed that while she spoke, he heard voices whispering over hers, faint voices talking in the background in some foreign dialect—he said they reminded him of snakes the way they hissed and wheezed. He told us her voice was distorted and seemed to echo. When I interviewed him, I remember him stammering, 'she sounded like she was moving farther and farther away.' All he could make out was, 'I am almost home, Daddy.' And then he said there was a moment of silence—a stillness where even the whispering voices stopped. After a few seconds, he heard growling, like lions or bears, but far more 'hateful.' He used that word...*hateful*... followed by a blood-curdling scream. Then, he said, the phone went dead, and they never heard from her again."

"Well, that's probably the worst thing I've ever heard in my entire life, but I fail to understand what this has to do with me, why you would tell me this, or anyone else outside your department for that matter!" Martin shouts with a scowl of contempt across his face, rousing the attention of others seated nearby in the restaurant.

The look in Jerry's eyes suddenly changes to one of pleading, hinting for the first time since the two met at a sense of compassion. "I used to get a distinctly odd feeling while working on that case, something I couldn't explain. I somehow felt as if I had seen that star symbol before; but not just saw it... It was almost as if... Like I had some strange connection to it. Like it meant something to me. After the girl's last reported phone call, the case went cold, and I never got that feeling again...*until earlier today*." Jerry looks solemnly into Martin's eyes from across the table and Martin can sense the sincerity in their gaze. "I *need* your help on this, Dr. Patterson. There's something very wrong here, with this investigation in general, and I need someone with your background to help me figure it out." Martin says nothing but implies his consent with silence.

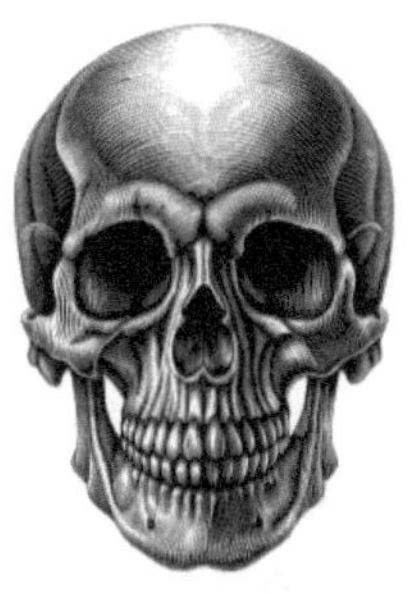

XXIII.

It is just past 6:00 p.m. on Tuesday, July 21st. Eddy's Bar and Grill usually has a fair dinner crowd this time of day, and tonight is no exception. The food here is not notably succulent, perhaps a little greasy even, and the fries are typically soggy, but in this small farming town in rural Kansas, unless you wish to drive twenty miles to the nearest bordering city, this is the closest spot to grab a bite to eat.

The patrons steadily arriving and leaving are the regulars; no strangers in the small establishment this evening, just a familiar crowd having their usual drinks and ordering the same meals they have become accustomed to for years. The servers know everyone by name here, and unless someone decides on a whim to try something different, they also can guess their choices before they place an order.

The country songs playing on the overhead speakers near the bar are the familiar tunes the customers have grown up with, and everyone in the bar tonight knows the Garth Brooks song currently streaming. Two of the men at the bar, relaxing after a hard day in the fields, lift their glasses to each other while singing along, "'Cause I've got friends in low places...'" followed by the man to the left chugging back his beer, slamming it on the counter, and demanding another. The mood is lively in the small-town establishment tonight, even for a

Tuesday, and the atmosphere seems cheerful as the clatter of dishes in the background clang and the sounds of laughter fill the bar area.

Centered in between the liquor bottles and bar shelving hangs a TV which holds the attention of a few of the men sitting at the stools. It cannot be heard over the mixture of chatter, music, and din of the kitchen helpers, but those watching can still make out the weather forecast currently scrolling across the bottom of the screen. The local weather man pipes cheerfully on about things unknown as the temperatures and rainfall predictions continue to appear and disappear while those tuned into the broadcast struggle to make out what is being said.

Suddenly, the weather portion of the news is interrupted and a red banner flashes on the bottom of the screen reading in large letters *BREAKING NEWS*. The broadcast on the screen changes to a new background setting as live coverage of an unfamiliar town is shown across the TV from an aerial helicopter view. "Hey, *Jim*. Turn the TV up, will ya?!" yells one of the patrons paying attention to the broadcast to the bartender who happens to be standing near the TV. The bartender grabs the remote from underneath the counter and turns it up to an audible level as the screen switches once again to a reporter standing on scene. The request to increase the volume catches the attention of some of the other people seated at the bar, and all listen intently to the words emanating shockingly from the correspondent's statements.

"Are we... We're live? Okay. Thank you, Diane. I'm Daniel Thornburgh with WNBT News here in Beaverdam, Ohio, where we begin with breaking news.

"Currently, we are following reports unfolding in Beaverdam—a small community centered on traveler services and agriculture—where the entire population has completely vanished. Reports came in earlier today from sources claiming that police in other departments outside of Beaverdam were getting calls from relatives and friends that they could not reach family members or the local police offices here in Beaverdam beginning earlier yesterday morning and afternoon. After police from other departments attempted to contact the Beaverdam department, they received no answer. When sent out to make contact, authorities reportedly found all homes, businesses, and vehicles deserted. The authorities and family members of the residents in Beaverdam are getting no responses through calls, email, or social media.

"The reports of missing persons came pouring in just after noon yesterday, local time in Beaverdam, Ohio. At this time, no reports of any deaths or injuries. The situation is still developing, and as of around noon yesterday, not a single resident of Beaverdam's three hundred plus population has been located or heard from.

"If you look behind me, you can see a backdrop of the situation. As you can tell, there are numerous police cars and helicopters in the vicinity searching for any signs of the residents. If you look just to my left, you can see cars off to the side of the road in a ditch with no occupants. The same to my right. There appears to be some vehicles at the gas station, but nobody inside. Still, no sign of any of the three hundred residents at this time...

"There is one shocking clue, however. If you can... Yes, pan over to the right a little more... Sorry, folks... On an old warehouse building behind the gas station there is a massive sign scrawled in what appears to be red paint. It is in the shape of a kind of star. As you can see, it is quite large, painted across the entire side of the building... A strange kind of star symbol. It looks like the police have that section of town cordoned off for investigation..."

By this time in the broadcast, all eyes are locked on the television and silence permeates the atmosphere. Not a soul in the restaurant dares to speak; instead, with incredulous awe they hold their breath, save for the cries of a small child softly whimpering from a highchair in the rear corner of the room.

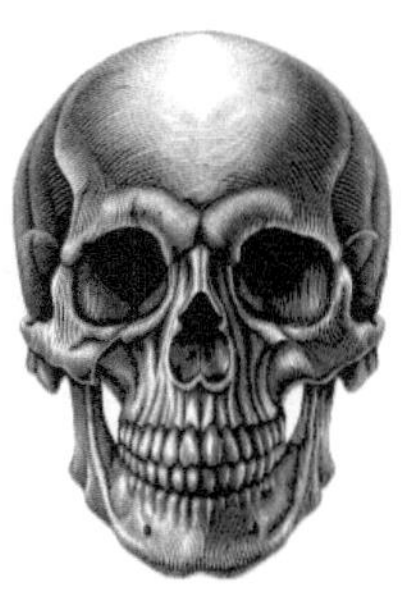

XXIV.

Heading northeast on 73rd Avenue toward East Oakland, just past the Coliseum, Matt steps briskly and with a cumbersome angst weighing upon his mind. He has been walking nonstop in aimless uncertainty since escaping from the fiery collapse of his motel room in the San Leandro Bay area, and with nowhere to go—and mired in restless confusion—he rambles onward precariously into the night.

All was lost in the incendiary ruination of his temporary dwelling, leaving Matt with only the clothes on his back and a few dollars in his pocket. Realizing he has not eaten all day and craving the ephemeral relief of an alcoholic beverage, he decides to make a stop at a liquor store he sees up ahead. As he enters the store, pangs of hunger assail his gut, and so he scans the aisleways for a snack. Matt grabs a bag of chips and heads next down toward the beer cooler. Knowing he has only a few dollars and some change rattling loosely around in his pocket, he grabs the cheapest, strongest tallboy he can find and heads back up the aisleway toward the counter.

Matt approaches the counter and sets the chips and beer in front of the store employee who is eying him curiously from behind the register. Matt shoots him a strained, partial smile and proceeds to fish through his pants for the money while his disheveled long black hair swings carelessly and troublesomely in front of his face. Behind the cashier, a small TV is tuned to the local news and the reporter's voice suddenly catches Matt's attention as he struggles to count the bills and change with his shaking hands. As Matt attempts to tally up the total, the reporter's voice echoes words from the TV speakers that he somehow cannot ignore, and he stops counting to look up at the screen. "Yes, that is correct, Tom, the entire town of Beaverdam has vanished without a trace… If you look behind me, you will see the only thing left behind is a kind of oddly shaped star symbol on a large warehouse which officials have confirmed is painted in human blood…"

Fear seizes Matt's being, the magnitude with which causes him to drop the loose bills and change to the floor. He is no stranger to horrific reverie and eerily perturbing visions, but never before have his otherworldly cogitations been connected to events based in reality— not in this manner anyhow. With a sudden nausea overwhelming him, Matt runs from the store, leaving behind his money and intended purchases on the countertop before an awe-stricken and confused store attendee.

A lightheadedness abruptly overcomes him, and he stops running, feeling as if he is going to pass out. Before Matt gets the opportunity to collapse onto the pavement, thunder cracks across the sky, temporarily stealing his focus away from the dizziness attacking his being. Rain follows the thunder, pouring down with a violent intensity, assailing Matt's body unmercifully as he tries to regain his concentration. He turns to re-enter the liquor store only to discover that the door is locked, which he immediately finds confusing since he was inside only moments before. Matt looks up through the pounding rainfall and to his consternation sees the building is dark and the windows boarded as if the store has been closed for years. Before he can form a proper explanation inside his panic-stricken mind, a bombardment of hail begins battering his body and shelter becomes his only concern. He quickly surveys his surroundings only to find an empty and abandoned town greets his terrified glances.

Horrified and utterly confused, he darts toward the nearest building—a three-story abandoned house adjacent to the shop he failed to gain entry to. Finding the front door to the home locked and seemingly boarded from the other side, Matt scrambles toward the back of the home while covering his head with his hands, trying as best he can to shield himself from the relentless barrage of hail. Just around the corner he sprints, finding to the rear of the house a cellar door entrance greeting his frantic gaze and protruding benevolently from the ground abutted to the foundation. He pulls on the old, rusted handles several times only to discover the door is secured with an ancient-looking iron padlock. The hailstones continue to beat against his skin as his mind races, the thoughts of what to do next coming in waves of fleeting and scattered fragmentations. Trying once again to free the splintered wooden doors from their fastened state, Matt notices the edge of the right-side door pulling slightly upward each time he yanks back. The onslaught of hail suddenly seems more ferocious now, or perhaps it is the intensity of his dilemma causing the illusion of increasing distress; either way, Matt focuses his attention on the corner of the right cellar door, drawing back on it unmercifully until the wooden panels begin to break free from the hinges. After a few seconds of overextended tugging, the door cracks free with a loud, crunching snap and Matt races down the steps into the unknown darkness of the cellar, nearly tripping as he hurriedly escapes the storm.

Once at the bottom of the stairs he can see nothing but blackness before him, and the first thing he notices beyond the dark is the spider webs clinging alarmingly to his face and upper body. Terrified by the thought of spiders crawling undetected over his shirt, he quickly removes it and shakes his hair free of any potential unwanted pests. Matt reaches for his cell phone to use as a lamp and turns on the flash, noticing upon doing so that his surroundings are barely more comforting than the barrage of hailstones still wreaking havoc outside. The dusty old cellar, it seems, has been boarded up and vacant for some time, as the atmosphere of dank and unoccupied desolation that greets his initial glances is overwhelming and without question.

The cellar is large and appears to stretch endlessly onward as Matt slowly traverses the underground labyrinth, a sense of fascination tantalizing his imagination coupled with the gradual unfurling of his sanity. As he twists and turns through the cellar maze, lighted only by his cell phone torch, each corner seemingly connects to yet another unending length of unexplored cryptic space. Not much was left behind by the previous occupants; mostly boxes and half-empty shelves filled with curiously strange-looking items and antiquated, rotting furniture pieces, all covered in what looks like centuries of dust and cobwebs. In various unknown places, Matt can at times hear dripping as he shambles through the dark corridors of the cellar, hinting of water leakage from the storm which no doubt is the cause of the musty fetor. Matt utilizes his shirt to knock free the webs that block his passage, still removed from his upper torso since entering the dripping Stygian abyss.

Matt rounds yet another corner in the seemingly eternal expanse of sub-basement to finally discover something strikingly different in his narrowly lit field of vision. The cellar maze has ended, terminated by a finalizing small room. This culminating area is void of shelving or objects, save for a large antediluvian full-length mirror that somehow exudes a ghastly aura of moribund putridity about its rustic frame and abominably black surface. The linearity of time, Matt suddenly realizes, has somehow escaped his sense of reasoning, and as he gazes upon the lone item before him, he cannot remember how long he has been standing there. As he remains motionless before his image, contemplating the odd notions resulting from his self-reflective inquiry, an even stranger thought occurs—*Where am I?*

Matt gazes incredulously into the mirror at his reflection, straining to catch a glimpse free from the rebounding radiance of the cell phone light held precariously in his hand. He recognizes the long black hair hanging carelessly in front of his face and the shirtless, thin chest reflecting in the mirror's image, but the tired lines in his face and the sunken eyes staring back at him elude his memory's recollection. Confusion grips him deeply and securely in a flash of heart-palpitating terror, and Matt loosens his grip first on his shirt then on his cell phone, utilizing his hands instead to brace his head and face as he falls to his knees in emotional collapse. The phone falls several feet away, casting a strangely elongated shadow across the room silhouetted in Matt's hunkered over and fear-ravaged shape; only the sounds of heavy breathing and a faint dripping in the background offer an unexceptional repose to the stark ambiance permeating the room's maleficent aura.

A cavernous void fills the space where Matt's cognitive functions previously sojourned, and the absence of pragmatic thought would be a curious dilemma for him were he able to contemplate such a concept. A force beyond measure compels him to suddenly lift his head, allowing his eyes to level with the image reflecting before him, lit dimly by the cell phone lamp resting on the abysmally black and vacuously empty floor. If at this eerily incongruent scalar axis of time Matt were somehow able to form an opinion based on observation, he would most certainly recoil at the barely discernable image staring back hideously and demonically from the mirror's surface. Eyes of white fill his orbital sockets, preparing him for the inhuman journey ahead. Now completely devoid of reason and vision, all that remains is a shell with human form—a container of flesh awaiting proprietorship.

The mirror's shine reflects darkly in the scantly lit radiance of the cell phone light and the area surrounding Matt's reflection shifts seamlessly to black ripples of dilation and strange vectors of space-time quanta. In non-sequential fragmentations of movement, long arms stretch toward Matt's motionless body, gripping him with monstrous claws whose disjointed motions can most closely be likened to stirrings caught in strobing light. They are covered in thorn-like protrusions of bone and rotted flesh, like demonic vines cultivated in the darkest recesses of cavernous horrors unknown. They drag Matt's body slowly into the mirror with a velocity so hauntingly paced that, were he able to comprehend this unsettling slogging, he would surely go insane from the vulgarity witnessed therein.

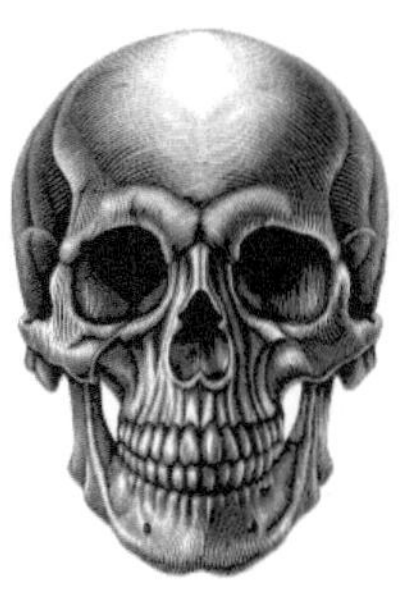

XXV.

None of the four occupants of the blue cargo van make a sound as they head south on Maritime Street through the Jack London Square area of Oakland, California. At this time in the early morning, the area is mostly barren with the exception of the usual street-life variety and local vagrants who call this locale home. Charles and Jessie sit motionless and speechless in the four-person bench row behind the driver and passenger seating. They have no reason to talk and nothing to discuss; they both are intrinsically aware of what must be done, as are the two men seated in the front of the van.

The driver—the larger man earlier responsible for one-half of the abduction team of Jessie and his friend Shawn—steers the van into a large parking lot and around the back of a massive warehouse, the top of which overlooks the brackish waters of Oakland Outer Harbor. A large security fence surrounds the vast property topped with razor wire and surveilled by numerous cameras throughout the lot. The van pulls up to a loading door around the back and stops long enough for the driver to enter a security passcode into the digital entry system keypad; one of two entry options, this one being mounted to a drive-up post, while the other is attached to the side of the door. A large, empty concrete parking area awaits them inside the loading door and the driver pulls the van into a far corner near a doorway to another section of the warehouse.

The driver exits followed by his smaller partner, the echoes of their slamming doors resonating throughout the expanse of the enormous, empty loading area. The smaller of the two men opens the side door of the van, allowing Charles and Jessie to exit into the faintly lit loading zone, no doubt kept dim due to the energy costs associated with a massive structure that is clearly unused for commercial or any other legally viable purposes.

Charles takes the lead and heads through the double doors adjacent to where the van was parked, followed closely behind by Jessie and the two men. Turning a quick left through the building's vacuous darkness, Charles heads through a single door, revealing a staircase illuminated only by emergency lighting casting just enough radiance to make clear the pathway to the next step down into the building's cavernous and hellish depths. The group descends a few floors then enters through another door and down a hallway, which, in turn, accesses yet another stairwell. Onward through multiple series of rooms and doors they advance, dropping several dozens of levels to a deep sub-basement where, at last, they come to a final entryway—a large, hand-carved wooden door.

The carven barrier is clearly not of this century, inscribed in its entirety with symbols and insignias intertwined amidst hideous beings not representative of the human imagination. Charles's accomplices stay outside the entrance while Charles and Jessie proceed though the baleful threshold. As Charles pulls on the barbaric-appearing iron handle, the giant wooden door seems to moan, as if a departed soul were writhing in perpetual agony.

Once past the iniquitous entryway, hundreds of burning candles cast a funereal light upon a dismal setting. The room is reminiscent of an underground auditorium—a theatre of the macabre dug deep into the earth. A large area of the ground—three-hundred feet in diameter and fashioned in the form of a concave circle—has been laboriously excavated and smoothed; completely cleared of all obstructions in order to preserve the sanctity of the space. Black candles burn in groupings at various spots around the massive circular region, spreading just enough radiance to allow one to envision the bleakness of the immeasurably foul surroundings. Most of this tenebrous sanctum is embellished with adornments of nothingness—black, deep, and hollow, a testament to the spiritual void that permeates the atmosphere within.

There exists, however, one thing besides the candlelight and the morbid emptiness pervading the sullen asylum. Far across the vast room, nearly cloaked in darkness, stands a contrivance designed by the hands of depraved minds. Many devices have been built over the centuries to inflict pain upon the human body, but nothing like the dehumanizing characteristics intrinsic to this barbaric assemblage. The machine—constructed from the ashes of the most profoundly hateful funeral pyres—was vomited upon the earth through the toils of forced labor and maniacal human subjugation. There is no record of its existence and no timeline upon which it was built, but nonetheless it is here, existing in all its damnable and blasphemous majesty.

It is twenty-five feet in length, twelve feet tall, and fifteen feet wide, comprised of antiquated gears and shafts, ancient stone masonry, and all manner of royal embellishment. This instrument of suffering was assembled from the mechanical remnants of machinery used only in the most diabolical human exploits, along with various artifacts from statues and other tributes to cruelty; amongst other things, it is an encomium in praise of those who have aided in furthering the destruction and debaucherous ways of mankind. Its cold, mechanized features reek of World War II Nazi weaponry; its framework of human skeletal remains whispers secrets of the Mori-ori Genocide; its ancient stone base, upon which the sickening contraption is mounted, shrieks in remembrance of the extermination of the Amalekites and the Midianites. Every last component utilized in the creation of this clandestine and wholly unconsecrated aggregation of parts was in one way or another applied to the extermination of human beings at some point in mankind's history.

Torture and punishment have always been tools employed by despots and the psychotic alike to achieve one end or another, yet pain is also an avenue to the spirit. All the components of this hellish device encapsulate the purest elements of human torment; only an instrument crafted from the ghastliest human misdeeds can shock the spirit from the human shell, as the soul must confront absolute and total despair to be released from its fleshly prison.

Charles walks slowly around the expanse of the massive circular pit and toward the machine, breathing deep the nightmarish atmosphere, while Jessie follows his languid pace. After making the trek halfway around the circle, Charles stops and turns to Jessie. "I cannot go on. You must approach the offering alone." Jessie proceeds onward along the rest of the darkened, candlelit path with a lack of emotion and devoid of self-will, both callously torn from his infested hull. As he approaches the machine, he begins to feel a warmth building inside his chest, and a novel feeling of madness swirls within his brain as if he is approaching the fulfilment of something he was always meant to embrace.

Only a few yards from the machine now, Jessie notices there is a woman—blindfolded and gagged—bound upon a stone carved table atop the device. As he nears the blasphemous mechanism, he sees there is a small set of stone steps ascending to the level of the table. Jessie proceeds forward, climbing the steps with a mechanical displacement about his gait, and approaches the woman with a faint sense of curiosity brooding within his nearly empty husk of reason. She is affixed to the table with thick leather straps—time-worn and blood-stained—aged by the decades that have passed since they were originally used in the torturous experiments held by SS doctors in World War II. She is naked, shivering, and paralyzed by fear, nineteen or perhaps twenty years of age, and beautiful; *A vision of perfection,* he thinks, a lucid and original thought finally piercing through his infernally possessed mind. A young woman from a prosperous background, she was chosen for her known purity and devotion to her faith. She is a child of God in her family's eyes, and it is no secret amongst her friends that she is still a virgin.

The helplessly bound woman is exhausted and mentally fatigued from the countless hours of anxiety since her kidnapping and does not sense Jessie looming silently over her. Enraptured by her innocence, Jessie reaches over to touch her face, and upon doing so, a panic swells, causing her to twist and writhe violently underneath the leather straps. As fear and distress engulf her emotions, something dismal awakens inside Jessie. The foul blackness that Charles vomited into him awakens and infects his thoughts, resulting in a repulsive and profane counsel of spirits to confer action.

Jessie, in his singular and violently focused frame of mind, leers downward toward the girl before him, no longer perceiving a vision of perfection but instead a symbol of paltry and contemptible filth. An inexorable and furious rage builds inside Jessie as he gazes upon the pathetic creature before him. His ribcage expands and contracts in increasing volume as his breathing becomes more intense with each passing breath. Jessie's fingers begin to clench into fists as an inhuman hatred overwhelms his being. He takes another breath and rips the blindfold from the girl's face, affording her the opportunity to gaze upon a visage of ghastly and demonic vehemence. Instantaneously her vigorous squirming halts and her large blue eyes angle slowly from the waist of her captor toward his face, calmed for the moment under the influence of pure curiosity. She has been blindfolded for several days and her vision is blurry and distorted, which seems to somehow intensify the lucid interval feeding the tranquility of the moment as a sense of wonder fills the void where panic once thrived. She squints and tries to focus, desperately striving to capture a closer look at the face of the man standing before her.

Abruptly her inquiry is answered as Jessie lunges forward and grabs her by the hair, violently pulling her upward as far as the leather straps will allow. Simultaneously he leans over, drawing close his face to hers, while his damning gaze pierces deep into her bright blue eyes and penetrates down into the depths of her purified soul. Even if the girl were not gagged, it would make no difference, for her vocal cords could not possibly orchestrate an appropriate response to the horrific vision of Jessie's vulgarly demonized countenance as she finally catches a glimpse of the possessed human overshadowing her form.

Jessie's breathing is rapid now, heaving with a grim hatred that envelops the terrified girl's being with each exhalation of fetid and damning air. Without warning, his grip on her hair tightens and the girl cringes in terrified agony. Her attacker's mouth slowly opens as she begins to feel hairs being ripped one by one from the back of her head, a result of the furiously intense pulling at her scalp. An inhuman growl erupts from Jessie's mouth with such intensity that it sends shock waves through the skin of the girl's face like ripples through water. In this culminating moment of bestial growling and terror-inducing unveiling, Jessie reaches to the side of the table and instinctively pulls a rusty lever, throwing the machine into operation.

He slams the girl's head back onto the table and jumps down to the floor, landing on bended knee from the height of the plunge. Jessie slowly rises and turns to gaze upon the ungodly events unfolding before him, still seething with a deep and otherworldly rancor. The gears begin to turn as the machine comes to life, grinding with a feverous, preternatural detestation. Antiquated sounds pulsate from its rusted components, churning forth a symphony of mechanized moans resounding throughout the vast candlelit dimness of the warehouse abyss. The dismally lighted ambiance of the background seems to dissipate and is replaced by a cosmic blackness, deep and superbly distant in its vacant, abstract nothingness.

A monstrous arm slowly extends from beneath the hideous contraption, reaching no less than ten feet in length. It is like the skeletal remains of some vanquished demon whose limb was removed in the act of war and fashioned into a bionic instrument of torture. It is fitted with gigantic metal claws—sixteen inches long—designed to painfully scrape flesh in a primitive and agonizing technique. It curls itself over the table and goes to work tearing through skin to cleanse the offering of its exterior restrictions, causing copious amounts of blood to pour from the lacerations it leaves behind. While the arm crudely pulls away flesh, holes open within the table and small tubes fitted with intravenous needles push through. They worm their way into the girl's arteries as if they are possessed with a consciousness all their own. As the giant arm tears away epidermal layers from the girl's body, the tubes supply blood to keep her alive, ensuring she will not perish before the rite is completed.

In the background, Charles delights in the horrors progressing before him, the demons that drive his passion swirling within his spirit, and he feels ever closer to his life-long obsession with those loathsome beings existing in dimensions so cataclysmically deep. The ineffable agony experienced by the poor girl's overwhelmed senses approaches a woeful apex and she begins to pass out. Charles and Jessie both look onward as a chamber above the girl opens and ammonium carbonate is released to awaken her to the evil abound, for the offering must be made with consciousness fully intact. The obscene entities that occupy Jessie's body writhe in ecstasy as their ancient profanity surges forth, forcing their vile presence upon the atmosphere of the warehouse basement and this world—their rightful dominion—further increasing the already colossally horrific blackness, now fantastic in its nefarious profundity.

The once gorgeous girl now lies skinless, awash with an agony that no human being in the history of mankind has hitherto known. Jessie peers onward—or perhaps, the beings that possess him peer for him—as the next stage of affliction commences; Charles, all the while, taking great delight in the girl's ghastly tribulation. A slide opens just to the left of the girl's head and dozens of copper wires slither forth like tiny snakes desperately searching for a place to burrow. They slowly force themselves into the back of the girl's skull as if being driven by unseen hands, gradually drilling their way into the young woman's brain and piercing through her medial temporal lobe and nestling their conductive lengths into her hippocampus. They send electric currents which stimulate her darkest secrets and most painful memories while simultaneously a tiny drill lowers itself from above. The primitive device pierces her prefrontal cortex, precisely boring into the part of the brain that controls positive thoughts, destroying her ability to form a sense of hope.

The girl is frightfully nearer now to the zenith of mental and physical torment, a necessity for removing the soul from its confinement of flesh. Concurrent with the young woman's crescendo of suffering, Jessie's body straightens itself into an expressionless, ridged form and all consciousness seems to vacate his shell. The poor girl's anguish, closer to the threshold of human suffering with each passing moment,

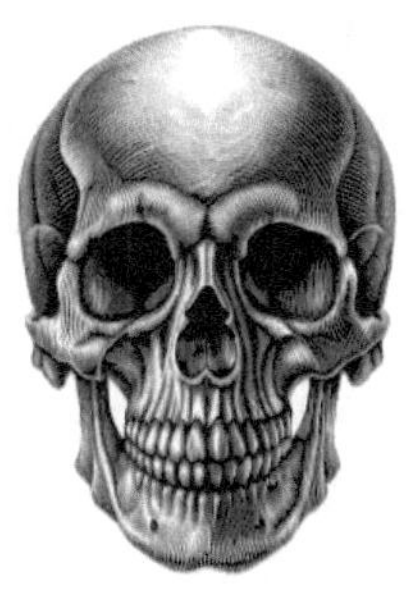

XXVI.

"**S**tupid *fucks*! How the hell do you fuck up a simple car rental?" Jerry storms from the front entrance of the rental car company in Sugar Land, Texas, two hours behind schedule and feverishly angered by what he perceives as a personal slight and an instance of grave incompetence on behalf of the employees working within. Martin, in his jovial and generally agreeable nature, follows Jerry out of the rental car agency perturbed by the setback but not nearly enough to send him flying into an outrage the likes of which Jerry is currently exhibiting. The rental car was supposed to be available at 7:00 a.m., and, at fifteen minutes past nine, they are just now heading to their next location, Saint Mary's Immaculate Conception Cathedral, where Agent Norton and Dr. Patterson hope to understand more thoroughly what happened there earlier this week that caused the deaths of so many people.

"Just try to relax a little, Agent Norton. We only lost a couple hours," Martin reassures Jerry, trying his best to create a sense of calm as they head through the parking lot toward their rental car.

Jerry looks at Martin with a sneer, his week-old stubble causing him to appear slightly unhinged in the Texas morning sunlight. "I know, but things like that shouldn't happen—I reserved that car days ago... This ain't no reg'lar circumstance."

For the first time since they met, Martin notices a hint of Bronx in Jerry's voice. "Agent Norton... Are you from *New York?*"

Jerry steps to the passenger side of the blue Ford Escape rental and places his hand on the door, slowly looking up at Martin as hits unlock on the key fob. "Fuck you," he whispers with a slight grin, realizing that Martin has taken notice that when he is mad his hometown accent sometimes becomes apparent. Martin simply smiles back and runs his hand through his thick white beard as he gets into the passenger seat.

Saint Mary's Immaculate Conception Cathedral exists on the outskirts of the community of River Oaks, an upscale suburb of Houston, Texas, just west of downtown. As Jerry and Martin speed off toward their destination, a lingering air of spectral darkness transfuses the emotional aura of both occupants along the way. Perhaps it is the late start they got on the day as a result of the car rental mishap, or maybe the reports coming out of Beaverdam on the apparent disappearance of an entire town. Quite possibly, their angst is partially driven by witnessing a man's suicide right before their eyes, which is spiraling them into a strange sense of haunting that infects the atmosphere around them. Conceivably, and in all probability, however, it is the amalgamation of all these events combined creating the strange and otherworldly presence they can so palpably and apprehensively feel.

Upon nearing Saint Mary's, Martin and Jerry can spot the massive neo-Gothic structure from several blocks away. As they turn on West Main Street, just two blocks south of the cathedral, Martin notices the portal to the vast entryway appears black in the shadows cast by the surrounding buildings, creating a dismally eerie repulsion around the pointed archway above the entrance. The Texas summer sun seems to fade into the backdrop behind a veil of clouds as they near the parking lot just one block away now from their current position. Jerry can see the church has been cordoned off with police tape and the parking lot is vacant as he slowly pulls the rental car into the front lot.

"Well… Shall we?" Jerry says to Martin as he opens the car door with one hand, his other grasping a folder containing the case reports. Martin gives no reply, simply a nod and corresponding motion of exit. Jerry and Martin head through the large parking lot and toward the front entrance, both grateful that the late morning sun is well hidden behind a wall of darkening cloud cover. The multiple arches towering above the cathedral portal somehow, too, seem black to Martin as he approaches the front entryway, and even though he can clearly see from up close they are an off-gray, something in the back of his mind suggests otherwise.

A triumphant oak double doorway graces the entrance to the cathedral adorned with ornate carvings of angelic beings bordered by quatrefoils and majestic tracery patterns. As Jerry lifts the police tape blocking the door and starts to duck underneath to grab the door handle, he pauses upon glancing upward, suddenly taken aback by what he sees. A single bloodied handprint can be vaguely made out on the exterior of the door shining faintly, yet repugnantly, in the dim sunlight forcing its way through the gloomy skyline. Martin takes notice as well, apprised by Jerry's intermission, but neither says a word; instead, their acknowledgment of the situation is confirmed by silence.

Jerry enters the giant cathedral and Martin follows, allowing the wooden door to slam shut behind him. A rush of air accompanies the slamming door, bringing with it the stench of blood and death. Even though the crime scene cleanup crew has already come and gone, the acrid odor of the deceased persists, along with a ghastly foulness that penetrates the atmosphere. Jerry and Martin both wander about the nave of the cathedral, only the sounds of their footsteps resounding high into the vaulted ceilings and seeming to echo off the networks of converging ribs hanging elegantly over their heads. Saints and martyrs fill the scenery of the stained-glass windows meant to imbue those who gaze upon them with a sense of unyielding faith, yet the dull sunlight filtering through them on this surreal day makes the biblical depictions appear almost unholy in the spiritual destitution of the cathedral turned mourning site.

As Martin follows Jerry through the main aisleway, the pews seem like they are closing in on him. They head toward the altar and Martin stares up at the giant statue of Jesus hanging from the cross. The statue in this setting seems far more lamentable and hopeless than he has ever taken notice of before. Martin cannot help but sense a slight feeling a nausea stirring in his stomach as the stale aroma of blood seems to creep into his nostrils, appearing thicker with each step he takes toward the image of Christ. He cannot tell if it is his imagination or if the scent is authentic, but either way, the feeling of dread accompanying his perceived sense of queasiness is real enough to make him consider turning back and exiting the cathedral.

Jerry stops dead center in front of the giant cross towering triumphantly behind the altar, pulls open the file folder he brought with him into the cathedral, and starts reading aloud from the reports. "So... It looks like we have a mass suicide here—one member of the parish, Jack Clancy, age 46, forced a large crucifix down his own throat until he asphyxiated on blood—a woman who was a member of the congregation, Martha Wellington, 62, drove iron spikes through her own eyes with a wooden hammer with such force that the final blow drove one through the back of her skull—oh, *Jesus...*" Jerry stalls for a moment, stunned by the atrocious detailing of the next account. "Nicole Madison, 12 years old, climbed up to the top of the large crucifix behind the altar and dove off, her face hitting the floor and snapping her neck inches from where her dead father lay—Jacob Madison, age 39, father of, carved his common carotid artery from his neck using a pocket—"

"Enough! Just stop!" Martin yells, no longer able to stomach the graphic accounting of the police reports. Martin glances around quickly for a path to the restroom but before he can move, he doubles over and vomits onto the limestone floor of the cathedral. Jerry pauses his reading of the reports to look over at Martin.

As Jerry watches Martin, he suddenly notices a gust of frigid air rushing into the nave aisle and toward the altar. A sinister and dismal moaning follows the rush of cold which seems to grow more despondent as it approaches. A sickening fetor accompanies the moaning, like a mixture of burning sulfur and putrefying flesh, gradually intensifying as the moaning gains resonance. The lights inside the cathedral extinguish and the nave becomes dark—so dark that it is as if the sun has been removed from the daytime sky, slowly fading away until the light no longer shines adequately through the stained-glass windows. Only a single ray of sunlight seems to shine through the end-most panel—an image of Judas Iscariot illuminated diabolically in the back corner of the first archway. The grim illumination casts a sinister radiance in its pathway, lighting up the image of Christ behind the altar. A disturbing howl seems to emanate from the image of Jesus—an unearthly and abysmal yowling like that of some malevolent entity being tortured by a far more obscene being. Along with the howling comes something that both Jerry and Martin are not quite sure is real, yet all the same they look onward, Jerry from full standing position and Martin from bended knee, still wiping vomit from the corner of his mouth. As the howling echoes from some unknown region of space beyond the depiction of Jesus, blood begins trickling from the eyes of the statue, almost as if Christ were weeping for the mournful events soon to come.

Martin slowly climbs to his feet and looks over to Jerry, who is standing only a few yards away. An expression of horror is painted across Martin's face, a look that Jerry can appreciate given the present circumstances plaguing their surroundings. Jerry inches away from the altar as the howling grows louder, and he drops the files from his hand onto the floor as his body prepares for flight. Jerry slowly turns back toward the cathedral entrance and away from the altar while Martin follows suit, both men prepared to run as soon as the timing seems right. Jerry pivots his right foot behind him and plants it firmly into the floor, anticipating that soon he will run. His calf muscles tense up and his right quadriceps flex as he takes off full sprint down the nave aisleway with Martin panic-stricken in tow.

As he passes the first several rows of pews, Jerry can hear the howling getting louder, its eerie resonance getting deeper as it seems to gain on his heels. Flashes of flinting specters fire past the two men as they run, swirling and haunting their pathway, as if they are on the same trajectory of time and space as the two. Midway down the nave, the glimmering spectral presence ceases and the single ray of light shining through the stained-glass image disappears. Simultaneously a deafening stampede of sounds coming from the direction Jerry and Martin are running stops them both dead in their tracks. A rumbling builds, akin to the trembling of an earthquake yet sounding more like a herd of large beasts rushing through the relatively confined space inside the cathedral. A fear mounts inside both men that topples over into undiluted panic as a barely discernable and translucent force presents itself before them in an inexplicable yet inescapably tangible demonstration of raw energy.

Both men are frozen in awe at what stands before them. Towering in horrendous vulgarity, notwithstanding the dubious nature of what their eyes perceive, the vague outline of some creature can be seen— tremendous in stature—standing almost as tall as the forty-foot-high cathedral ceiling. Its features are obscene—so vile, in fact, that Martin nearly passes out from the sight. Hundreds of horns can be scarcely observed as Jerry and Martin's eyes struggle to focus on the horrifically diaphanous beast. Teeth by the thousands can be validated by Martin and Jerry's vision, but where the mouth begins and ends cannot be confirmed. Its hooves are caked with rotten blood and entrails and the stench of decay is overpowering, but how many cloven feet it possesses is wholly unclear. A fetid warmth is felt by both men standing in its presence, a warmth that reminds one of freshly gutted entrails steaming ethereally on a cold winter day.

The epinephrine pumping voluminously through Martin's bloodstream is perhaps the only thing preventing him from collapse as he stares up incredulously at the terrible thing that presents itself so monstrously before his fragile and mortal being. But if the horrid blasphemy taking residence within the hallowed nave of the cathedral were not enough to instill within Martin a sense of fright beyond comprehension, the thunderous growling and storm-like undulating that accompanies its presence surely offers a solution to this frivolous uncertainty. As Martin gasps and cowers at the sickening and violent shaking, the colossal entity vomits forth foul sounds and vulgarities that no words can quite express.

Amid the thunderous echoing bellowing forth from the infinitely mouthed creature, Martin falls backward onto the cold floor of the nave aisleway as he watches Jerry levitate into the air, seemingly hoisted by the repugnant energy spewing forth from the demon's profane essence. As Jerry ascends into the thick air stifling the cathedral atmosphere, the ground beneath him glows with a ghostly luminescence hinting incandescent hues of red strangely mixed with shades of black. The colors beneath his elevated body exhibit no semblance of structure, but instead exude amorphous shapes and strange energies that shroud Jerry in a state of suspended animation. Martin lies in a state of shock on the cathedral floor, staring in disbelief as the symphony of cataclysmically blasphemous happenings shatters his imagination.

With a lightning strike of instantaneous terror, all noises and occurrences converge, and a single blast is heard resonating with demonic intensity throughout the cathedral. Instinctively Martin closes his eyes and covers his head with his arms and hands as if preparing for the fallout from an explosion. The hideous yowling and sadistically monstrous growls seem to fade away like they are receding back into the strange dimensions from which they came.

Martin cautiously lowers his arms and adjusts his glasses while slowly opening one eye, followed by the other. With profound apprehension he peers around the room to find Jerry lying on the floor several yards down the aisleway from where he himself embraces the cold limestone. Martin rises to his feet and once more glances around the cathedral, only to find that all seems to be just as it was when they first entered the building. The dull sunlight once more shines softly through the stained-glass windows and the blood no longer stains the face of Christ from behind the altar. Martin lumbers over to Jerry, shaken from the catastrophic events, and intending to wake him from unconsciousness, instead stops when he notices something odd about the ground atop which Jerry lies. A strange star symbol marked in what appears to be blood is scrawled on the cathedral floor beneath Jerry's body where the ghostly luminescence before illuminated the ground in strange red and black hues. As Martin stares at the oddly shaped thing in a perplexed and semi-psychotic trance, Jerry awakens to a state of utter disassociation and confusion.

"Where are we?" Jerry stammers as he stumbles to his feet and looks around in a clutter of mental disorganization.

Martin, still entrenched in paralyzing bewilderment, is not quite sure how to answer but manages to piece together a reply. "We're in the cathedral... Texas... Houston."

Jerry wipes a spot of drool from his stubble-covered chin and climbs to his knees as the memories of the past few minutes begin to assemble indeterminately within his mind. He glances around the cathedral nave and shakily stands, nearly falling as Martin steps in and grabs his arm to steady him. "What's this..." Jerry starts, looking down to see a red substance covering parts of his arms and pants where he previously lay atop the strange symbol marked blasphemously upon the limestone floor of the holy premises. He stares at the ground in consternation to see a symbol he knows all too well, a sigil he hoped never to lay eyes upon again. The unholy memory—*the missing girl*— *the strange connection—that damned star-shaped symbol*! Jerry recoils in horror as he gazes upon the floor of the cathedral in disbelief, not sure if what he sees is reality or some spurious illusion conjured forth from whatever haunts the space within the church's blackened ethereal boundaries.

Jerry looks away from the ground and at Martin's face. He can see the fractured sanity lining Martin's countenance and knows that something outside the realm of human influence is impacting this world—manipulating—exerting control over mankind's existence. Martin looks back at Jerry with a woeful gaze. "Let's go, Agent Norton."

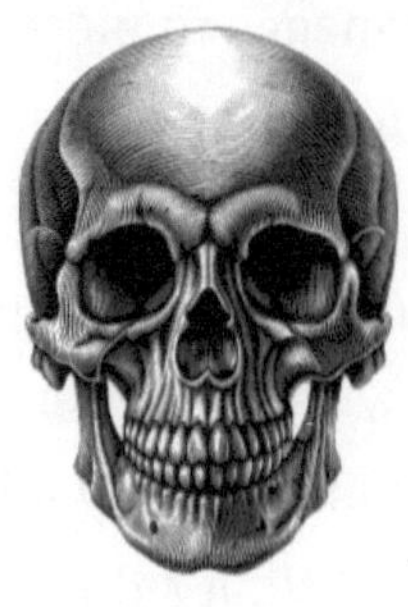

XXVII.

The Oakland container yard ground is scorching hot in the California sun and the sear of the concrete in between the container stacks where Matt lies awakens him to a stark new environment far removed from the last he remembers. How he got there is one question among many currently plaguing his tortured mind, but many more must be answered to even begin quelling the dark uncertainties swirling tormentedly through his fragmented consciousness. Something far more appalling than his awakening in the shipping container facility wrestles with Matt's reasoning.

A mixture of realities somehow manifests in all he sees as he observes his surroundings, his vision now a combination of this world and some unknown space of barbaric transcendence. Towering mountains and a background bereft of light—yet somehow visible—superimposed in a preternatural materialization over the world he is used to creates a terrifying new existence for his perception to grasp.

Matt jumps to his feet and rubs his arms and chest frantically, trying to massage away the burning sensations inflicting his skin from where the hot concrete roasted his extremities while he lay unconscious for an unknown timespan. As he glances around the port yard, he tries in earnest to remember anything that can explain his current circumstances. *Where is my shirt?* he wonders. In disintegrated flashes, memories flicker in and out of his mind, taunting his sanity with torturous reverie. Matt holds his head in his hands for a moment, trying to force coherence into his thoughts only to be shut out of his own mind by a vexing and sinister subconscious influence. He moves his hair out of his face and tries to think. In a flash of retrospection, he recalls the liquor store, the hail, the house, and finally, the mirror. He gasps at the reality—or perhaps, fabrication—of what has transpired.

Once again looking around, Matt can see stacks of shipping containers in rows around the port yard, but there all semblance of reality fades. The ground he stands upon is black molten rock, the backdrop comprised of black and red-tinted peaks topping massifs that seem to stretch infinitely into the nightscape. Matt falls to his knees and covers his eyes, weakened from the shock of the visualizations. He opens them again, this time sure he will awaken, but the same horrifying sights once again greet his disconsolate gaze.

"FUCK! God damned *flickering!*" His mind surges with pulsations of energy as he screams aloud in mental anguish, the flashes of images vacillating between other worlds and his more familiar reality overcoming his sense of existence. A phantasmagorical stream of images and words from the texts discovered in the Al Farâfra district of Egypt are coursing through his thoughts intermixing with glints of the unearthly realms and the world ordinary humans see. Matt, in a fit of rage-induced perplexity, begins punching himself in the head, unable to think of any alternative means of coping with the horrifying gravity of his existential dilemma.

As Matt thrusts his fist into the side of his head, still kneeling atop the port yard ground, a yard worker happens upon him while walking through the area. A large man, domineering in stature, bearded, and covered in prison tattoos, his appearance gives off the impression that he is not easily frightened. Still, the sight of a shirtless, long black-haired man kneeling on the ground while fiercely pounding the side of his head with his bare hands is enough to make him hesitate before approaching. Gathering his pride and composure, the yard worker, thinking Matt must be a drunken or perhaps mentally ill vagrant, shouts from afar, "Hey! You fuckin' *bum*! What are you doin'... Get out of here before I call the cops!" then proceeds to walk in Matt's direction.

The punching stops and Matt remains kneeled and motionless, fixed in place with his head aimed toward the ground. "*Hey*! Did you hear me?" the man shouts, now angered further by Matt's seeming disregard of his authority as he marches forward. Almost within arm's reach now, the worker decides to give Matt a final forewarning as he steadily closes the distance between them, his frustration gaining momentum with each step he takes. "Listen, you *fuck*. Get your ass up and take it the fuck outta here before I beat the shit outta you... *Last* warning." Matt gives no implication that the man's threat is perceived and instead responds with the same static pose, seemingly unmovable by words alone.

The man—a hefty six foot three inches and teaming with muscle, prison tattoos, and a beer gut—grabs Matt by the arm and violently pulls him from his knees. In a boiling rage, the yard worker drags Matt over several feet to the nearest stack and shoves him headfirst into a shipping container. Matt's head collides with the metal wall of the container with a repulsive, fleshy thud, a sound so sickening that even the enraged man finds it disturbing. The worker follows his merciless aggression with a harsh reproach, warning him, "Now get the *fuck* out of here, you crazy bum, before I *really* beat the shit out of you!"

Temporarily stunned by the brutal collision, Matt slowly regains his footing, stabilizing himself on bent knee next to the container his skull just greeted. With a stop-motion-like bizarreness, Matt cranes his neck around and upward, meeting the man's eyes with his own. The port yard worker's rage-filled countenance transforms into one of shocked disbelief, his goateed, cigarette-stained mouth left agape at what he sees. As the man stares into Matt's seething gaze, a longing to look away floods every fiber of his being. As deepening feelings of perturbation fill the man's emotions, somehow he cannot find the will to avert his attention from Matt's eyes—pitch-black yet filled with a world of depthless horror. An orgy of torture and twisted flesh seethes within his pupils, bursting forth in relentless hostility. Visions of thousands of tormented human beings, subjected to unfathomably hellish misery, bleed from within his blackened optics, painting a tapestry of never-ending suffering.

The yard worker, frozen in speechless terror, stands motionless, unable to form a comforting thought. Suddenly, he feels his insides begin to warm as Matt glowers with accelerating intensity into the man's horror-stricken visage, his facial expressions growing more hateful with each passing second. Paralyzed with fear, and imprecated with a swelling abdominal inflammation, the man's legs give out from under him, and he crashes to the ground, doubling over in pain as his gut begins to boil in agony. Matt slowly climbs to his feet, his movements smooth, like the slithering fluency of a serpent uncoiling its predatory lengths. He towers over the worker, focusing on the terrified man's suffering, the boundless mourning playing out in his blackened optics projecting an exhibition of measureless torture. Pressure builds within the man's robust ribcage, and he gasps for air while helplessly peering again into Matt's soulless gaze, hoping for mercy while he begs with pleading eyes. The man is forced to look away as the visions of mutilation within Matt's pupils continues to display sights beyond human comprehension, a suffering far more sinister than his own.

He clutches his chest with his right hand while frantically feeling around for a grip on the container next to him with his left and desperately tries to climb to his feet. His lungs expand and contract uncontrollably and he chokes up blood, covering his overalls with the crimson hues of life's essence. The yard worker's panic intensifies as Matt's visage transcends the boundaries of human emotion, darkening the atmosphere around the isolated corner of the port yard. Matt's cheeks hug the sides of his face tighter with each passing second as his well-defined cheekbones clench vehemently in furious intimidation, and now the man knows more than ever that his death is near.

The air shifts and the ground hums in an unsettling vibrato as the once fearless, prison-inked port yard worker slowly levitates from the ground several feet into the air. A low, spirit-crushing moan begins to resonate from deep within the earth, thundering echoes of damnation and unholiness. A trembling within the ground beneath them accompanies the moan as if an unseen entity were charging forth from depths unknown, sounding a battle cry of unbridled torment and apocalyptic annihilation.

Sweat beads upon the yard worker's forehead as he gazes down toward the ground he no longer embraces, the concrete now at least twelve feet beneath him. Terror explodes within his mind, fueling a frenzy of flailing limbs that cannot seem to guide him back to the container yard surface. He offers himself a second's repose from the panicked thrashing of limbs to glance toward his sinister disciplinarian.

If the poor man's sanity had not been shattered thus far, what he now witnessed surely would disembody his metaphysical self from any grasp on reality. Beneath him, on the sunbaked, far-off port yard ground where Matt once stood, is an abhorrently appalling beast pulsating with demonic rage. Several times larger than an average man and chiseled from the likeness of a Greek sculpture's musclebound frame, the monster stands, commanding dominance over the space it occupies. The hellish entity seethes with iniquity, its diabolic features echoing the semblance of a dragon's maw and donning horns atop its hideously shaped skull. Adequate description fails within the yard worker's interpretation of the being. Devoid of eyes, nose, and all other facial attributes is this unearthly tyrant—only a gaping hell of fangs adorns its cranial profile.

However, something infinitely more pernicious than simply teeth alone fill the monstrosity's jaws. Spewing forth in unholy rage is a maelstrom of blackened apparitions, the nebulous crypts from which they charge forth breeding unequivocal measures of barbarous horror. The spirits vomit in violent agitation from the gaping mouth of the beast, rushing toward the hovering man's body with a godless velocity. A tear falls from the affrighted worker's eye, followed by several more, as the foulness of the spiritual vortex rages toward his free-floating and helpless mass.

The first infernal apparition plunges into the yard worker's awe-stricken mouth and rushes down his throat, cauterizing the man's esophagus with its torrid foulness. The man hovers in suspension as dozens of blackened specters follow the first, each successive demonic spirit more ferociously ravaging than the former. In paralyzed tribulation, the worker's body hovers as he chokes on the scrofulous entities, each one further despoiling his mortal shell. The vulgar black spirits, shapeless in their cursed form, hiss blasphemies in ancient tongues while entering the man's abdomen, causing their horrified host to vomit in revulsion. The once brazen man regurgitates the contents of his belly as the rancid stench of rotting flesh that emanates from the spectral beings causes his stomach to churn in sickened repugnance. Countless apparitions continue to spew from the mouth of the unholy beast below and into the man's body as his limbs cease flailing, the yard worker now too engorged to continue moving.

Abruptly the onslaught of rushing spirits ends, and the monstrous creature below stands poised in silence—mounted to the earth in statuesque antiquity—its jaws still gaping as if frozen in time. Reality seems to pause, and the entire area goes silent, as if the universe waits in singular anticipation. The man's body floats motionless in midair; even the numberless incorporeal beings that occupy his shell seem to have ceased all activity in peaceful reverence to this moment's reprieve. Amid the ubiquitous calm, one stirring disrupts the tranquility. While the conciliating moment freezes his body in peaceable levitation, the man's eyes slowly roll back into his head, gradually exposing the white which surrounds his hazel irises. They languidly continue upward until no color can be seen, leaving behind a milky sea of lifelessness.

In triumphant, unconscionable extravagance, an explosion rocks the landscape, sending chunks of flesh, huge sections of skin, and bones flying across the container yard at fantastic speeds. The yard worker's entrails launch through the air in all directions as hundreds of foul, demonic spirits surge outward from within the confines of the man's fleshy bounds, gushing forth like a sickening geyser of nightmarish iniquity. Blood and fragments spatter the landscape, spraying everything in the vicinity with gobbets of human remains; even the ancient statuesque beast is baptized in sanguine particles, christening its ungodly fanged jaws with crimson gore. The port yard worker's body is blown so far into the air that it takes several more seconds for all the pieces of flesh to finally stop scattering across the landscape, the moments between impacts growing further apart as each bit of matter falls from the sky. The last clump of flesh is heard greeting the ground many yards away as the blackened spirits swirl in all directions, evanescing as they scatter into the landscape. With the final demonic entity disappearing into the backdrop, only the gore-drenched beast remains, still planted atop the earth in hateful defiance.

Without warning, the monstrous being shatters its stillness and opens wide its immense jaws, bellowing an otherworldly growl with such force that it rattles the shipping yard ground. The enormous beast then swings its mighty arms upward, grabbing its lower jaw with one claw while gripping its upper row of fangs with the other. The creature proceeds to rip its maw apart, screaming in demonic rage as black blood sprays the already saturated landscape. It tears its entire body in two from its hellish mouth downward, leaving two massive mounds of partially connected flesh. The sickening piles of profanatory gore fall to the ground with an impact that shakes the containers surrounding it, revealing within another creature standing poised with unholy purpose. Matt calmly walks away from within the folds of fleshy carnage as the remains rapidly decay and disappear into the ground, leaving behind no trace of the ancient beast's corporeal existence.

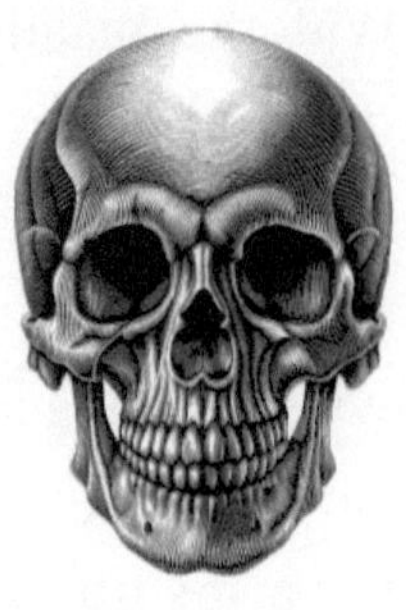

XXVIII.

Once again, the conference room at Berkeley University is filled with emotion and nervous anticipation, but this time it is not tinged with hope and endless possibility as was the case in their first gathering one week prior, nor even the anxious disbelief and palpable unease which permeated the consciousness of the second. The room is thick with an atmosphere of fear-driven angst; shouting, bickering, and all manner of discontent are on shameless display as the group of physicists vent their concerns amongst each other in an irreverent show of unadulterated dread. As in the previous meetings, the revered Dr. Phillip Jennings heads the assembly, and this time an expression of grave concern damns his visage with a look that no matter how hard he tries he simply cannot conceal.

Between the random acts of violence and inexplicable phenomena, the entire town of Beaverdam, Ohio, disappearing, the story Martin and Jerry are telling, and now, countless reports of people going insane, the physicists present in the conference room are overwhelmed beyond belief. The upheaval within the room borders on chaos as Dr. Jennings attempts to speak upon a point relating to the presentation he has prepared. Two men arguing in the corner of the room, oblivious to Jennings' talking points, begin to raise their voices so loudly that two other attendees stand and walk toward them to quell the dispute before blows are thrown. Simultaneously, Agent Norton, standing center of the lengthy table, begins shouting at three physicists, overcome with rage, indignant over their doubt toward Martin and Jerry's tale of demonic intervention at the cathedral. Sundry other disruptions cast a presentiment aura over the conference room while one lone scientist listens with partial attentiveness to the point Dr. Jennings attempts to make clear during his underappreciated seminar, albeit while scrolling apprehensively through his Facebook newsfeed.

Finally, the lone scientist listening to Dr. Jennings with vague receptiveness explodes. "*Everyone*, SHUT UP!" The clamor slowly begins to fade into hushed clusters of whispering as Martin stands up out of his chair holding his phone in his right hand. Taking his free hand, he straightens his glasses, then proceeds to run it briefly through his beard in preparation for what he plans to say next. "Have any of you checked social media in the last hour?" Several puzzled looks come from the room as the twenty or so members of the conference gaze amongst themselves in confusion, each trying to comprehend where Dr. Patterson is going with his inquiry. "I didn't think so… Here, let me pull up a news report from about half an hour ago," Martin begins in a condescending intonation, unlocking his phone before continuing. "'Looting and Riots Begin as Reports of Mass Hysteria Overcome the Streets of Maine…'" Martin pauses long enough to look up from his phone, making certain that everyone is listening carefully and free from their piddling squabbles. He scans the room and carefully eyes the occupants with a moue of contempt, ensuring that his words are taken with the utmost gravity before proceeding in a commanding tone "'In a press conference just fifteen minutes ago, Mayor Jim Broderick of Allagash has declared a state of emergency. The entire town is on lockdown after violence between residents of the rural area broke out following the discovery of a massive pile of bodies along the St. John River in the remote community of Allagash, Maine. Authorities have confirmed that the bodies are the remains of the entire 380 residents of Beaverdam, Ohio, that went missing less than two days ago. The residents are in a state of panic and the mayor is urging everyone to stay calm. Due to the outbreak of violence amongst the citizens of Allagash, Mayor Broderick has requested assistance from the National Guard. The mayor also stated that he has requested additional federal aid and resources from the White House.'"

The entire room is now silent; not even the sound of breathing can be heard amidst the sepulchral taciturnity. Martin next begins to scroll through his phone, pulling up a video he saved that was posted live just ten minutes prior. He maximizes the volume and turns the screen around for the room to see. What follows breaks the silence in the room, replacing it with gasps and utterances of shocked disbelief. The video depicts footage taken from a bystander as throngs of people in downtown Chicago attack one another in a murderous frenzy, their faces possessed of what can only be considered inhuman and diabolic dominion. The shredding of flesh amongst the seemingly psychotic legions is so vulgarly prolific that in one corner of the screen blood can be seen washing down the street as if a heavy rainfall was pouring voluminously from clouded skies. The hordes of people savagely battling can be seen attacking one another, not with weapons, but their bare hands—ripping, clawing, gouging—by the hundreds, perhaps thousands, as if an archaic battlefield filled with beasts of ancient rage suddenly exploded within the city.

"*My God*," Dr. Jennings gasps, joined not a second later by similar dispirited exclamations from other members of the conference:

"*This*...this can't be happening..."

"IS THIS REAL?"

"What are we going to do?"

"Dr. Patterson, is...is there a plan in place to... Some kind of *military*...*"

Agent Norton disrupts the flurried outbursts in an attempt to bring some sense of calm to the panic slowly building within the minds of those gathered. "Everyone! *Please*! In two hours I have an emergency meeting with DOD officials and members of the CIA to discuss the situation. I assure you the White House and Pentagon have this under control..."

"*Under control?*! Are you fucking kidding me?" a woman yells from the back of the room. "That video showed an entire city of civilians tearing each other to pieces! Like *animals*, or worse! How is everything..."

Jerry raises his finger to hush the woman as his phone rings. Looking down at the screen, he sees it is his boss from the agency. "This is Agent Norton," Jerry says into the phone, turning his back on the room and walking toward the doorway. Martin watches Jerry in silence, disturbed by the video he showed the room, yet somehow still calm on the outside, that ever-present stillness of deportment bringing a small sense of comfort to those seated next to him. Notwithstanding his short outburst when garnering the attention of those about the conference, he somehow feels a strange sense of sound reason amidst the chaos.

Jerry finishes his short phone conversation and motions Martin to join him outside the conference hall while the attendees of Dr. Jennings' assembly turn once again to quarreling amongst themselves, this time with a feverish intensity. "We have to go, a chopper is waiting," Jerry tells Martin as he exits the room and before he fully enters the hallway.

"I'm not going *anywhere*," replies Martin in an obstinate tone, straightening his glasses and continuing. "I gave you what you wanted. Three full days… That's what you said, *yes*? A *few* days?"

"I just got off the phone with my boss… Top military officials with the Department of Defense along with members of the CIA are waiting to hear from us. This is *not* optional."

Martin stares into Jerry's eyes, returning the cold, implacable gaze that he himself receives while stroking his beard of white and gray. A time now looms for deep contemplation before offering a calculated response, and Martin thinks briefly yet considerately before answering. "Step outside with me, Agent Norton." Jerry nods in agreement and both men walk down the hallway, their footsteps the only sounds pattering awkwardly and heavily between them.

Once outside the physics hall, Martin pulls his cherished blue Savinelli billiard pipe from his pocket and begins packing it with a fresh bowl of cavendish, something he realizes he has not done since Agent Norton's arrival. Jerry, realizing Martin needs a moment to relax, sits down on the steps of the physics hall entrance and enjoys the breeze blowing refreshingly through the hot summer veil while Martin flips the top to his pipe lighter and stokes the ember within his bowl. Martin sits down next to Jerry with his pipe hanging loosely from his mouth, small clouds of sweetly scented smoke billowing intermittently from within. They say nothing, both men enjoying the cool summer breeze as if it is the last they shall ever know.

After a minute or so, Martin takes the pipe from his mouth and speaks. "Agent Norton…"

"Jerry."

"What?"

"Just call me Jerry. No need to keep it formal."

Martin takes a few more puffs from his pipe and turns his head toward Jerry. "Well then, *Jerry*… Call me Martin."

Jerry smirks and nods, turning his head briefly in Martin's direction then back to the view ahead.

"I don't know what to make of any of this, Jerry. The things we've seen—the Beaverdam incident—the videos from the internet—has the world gone mad? Is this the apocalypse? What happens next?"

Jerry sighs and turns his head back to Martin, saying nothing for several seconds but speaking volumes with his eyes. He looks away from Martin and mutters a strained reply. "I don't know. This isn't what I thought it would be, that's for damn sure."

"What did you think we were getting ourselves into?" Martin questions, puffing passively away at his pipe.

"When I got the initial briefing, before I came to see you... It sounded like... Well, *honestly*, like bullshit."

"How?"

"It was real hush-hush. I knew from the start some other agencies were involved. I thought maybe it was some military thing, related to China or Russia. Some secret weapons deal. You know, maybe that's why the CIA was involved. I was briefed on some new experiments they were concerned with. Something about black holes. I mean, *come on...* Sounds like *Star Trek sci-fi bullshit*. I thought, what the hell do they need me for, I'm just a run-of-the-mill bureau agent. But now I'm starting to think otherwise..." Jerry suddenly trails off and simultaneously looks at the ground, letting out a subtle exhalation reeking of annoyance, concern, and frustration.

"What do you know that you're not telling me, Jerry?" Martin asks, putting his pipe down for the moment to focus on Jerry.

Jerry pauses and closes his eyes, taking in deep the cooling zephyr gracing his skin. "I keep thinking back to that girl that went missing years ago. *They knew.* The agency knew about that case... It was years before I ever joined the FBI, but they questioned me about that case when I agreed to this one. It was...almost like they picked me for this assignment."

Martin returns to his pipe, joining Jerry in scanning the horizon straight ahead, neither bothering to speak for nearly a full minute while Martin draws on his pipe and Jerry watches the skyline in stillness. Martin pulls his briar billiard piece from his mouth and turns to Jerry, letting out a small plume of smoke as he speaks. "I'll ask again. What are we getting ourselves into?"

"Friend, I don't know. But something darker than the human mind is behind whatever is happening."

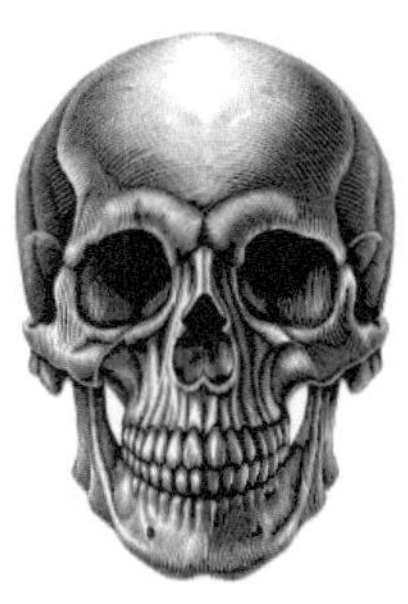

XXIX.

Charles reposes amidst the candlelight glow, cross-legged and naked, the eerie, almost tranquil absence of sound filling the void with a deceivingly peaceful stillness. A specific room was designed when his mansion was constructed, its dimensions and shape chosen to harness energies undetectable by conventional scientific methods. The space inside this portion of the home is sharply repellant in architectural wholesomeness. Aside from Charles, only the engineers and carpenters who undertook the project have been inside the maledicted chamber, and even those unfortunate souls were only contracted for small portions of the job and, in all likelihood, bequeathed cantles of their souls in the process.

The strange shapes of the walls stretching to the elliptical ceiling angle purposefully in obtuse and unsatisfying degrees, playing tricks on the mind as they curve back inward in seemingly sporadic and intermittent patterns. Meant to capture the potency of ancient and forbidden powers, the obscene curvatures of the partitions act as spiritual barriers trapping demonic energy inside and preventing it from escaping.

Ritualistically inspired formulations of blasphemous alchemies were utilized in the creations of the alloys that coat the walls in off-hues of blackened tint. The metals, chosen for their symbolistic purity, were painted upon the oddly constructed walls with brushes of bone and skin while still molten, an eons-old method of application long forgotten by modern man, and rightfully so, as the cruelty used in fabricating the tools is barbaric beyond comprehension. The transmutations of the base materials used in the unconsecrated pigments create elements unknown to scientific minds of this day and age; their compositions were discovered ages before man walked the earth by long-dead races of monstrous beings whose arcane wisdom knew no bounds in its foul dissoluteness. Charles's profoundly unholy meditations and otherworldly affiliations have shown him the rites which unlock these formulations—a depraved ceremonial journey along a path sodden with the blood of the innocent.

The anomalously shaped walls and the accursed coatings upon them would be useless were it not for the morbidly symmetric ceiling that forms a confluence of the two, elongating into a perfect ellipse that curves upward into the attic above. There, into the major axis of the forty-foot span, is where the true power of the room is displayed. One could not tell from entering the room, but the outer limits of the strangely shaped walls are curved, meeting the semi-major axes of the ellipse in a cleverly hidden, architecturally sound, broad cylindrical formation. The esoteric nature of the elliptical ceiling shares similarities with ancient occult fascinations, many of which concern themselves with the planets and their orbits, a significance that is shared here in the diabolically inspired craftsmanship of Charles's meditation room. The reasons behind the architecture, even to Charles, are not wholly clear, but the unholy creatures that drive his motivations assure him through the most fiendish intellection that, in time, all will be known.

In this nefariously excogitated section of his deeply malign manor he sits, contemplating the infinite and deliberating upon the final portions of the Al Farâfra translations. All is singular in his darkened mindset as he sits silently—breathing—musing—transfixed in abysmal depths of horror. One final piece is still missing, however. Those texts of old, discovered by mistake in a forgotten tomb, have thus far shown Charles the way. Over the course of the unearthing, the translations have been rapid, and the assistance of AI-driven software has made the release of the texts to the public a nearly instantaneous reality. However, not all of the strange and dreaded compositions have been exhumed from the desserts of Egypt. Some things were never meant for mortal eyes, and the finality of such a profoundly dark and vast enlightenment is beyond the percipience of all but one.

They speak to him at dismal frequencies through the accumulation of energy waves in the room. Who *they* are is of no concern to Charles, as these beings are beyond the grasp of his current corporeal manifestation. In dreams they have visited him many times, and he knows their kingdom well. Deceit and non-linear visualizations mark their presence in his demonic reverie and many times over they have toyed with his mind, revealing themselves in hints and fragments only partial even in their ominous splinters. The frequencies with which they spread their baleful communications resonate within the architecture of the room, and as Charles sits deep in meditation, he can sense their debaucherous influence inside his mind. Over many years the bloodshed has been thick, laced with tidings to other realms and deeds accomplished in the name of the forbidden and unknown. Those with whom he now converses directly have no misgivings of his dedication—enough innocent flesh has been sacrificed and sufficient offerings have been made. The entities from beyond the portal reach through by only spiritual means at present, channeling their thoughts into Charles's mind and guiding him toward the final translations. The ones whose ancientness exceeds that of the Earth direct his cogitation and show him the keys to the gateway beyond, finalizing his diabolical journey as man and preparing him for his passageway to the abyss.

Still breathing—slowly—deeply. Charles can sense the energy about the room as a hum of reverberation steadily swells with a fluidity that seemingly metamorphoses the sound into a color not previously known to his mind. The hue intensifies and the swelling of the energy simultaneously fades while all things in the periphery seem to crinkle away, almost as if time itself was fragmenting, taking with it gravity's effect on matter. Breathing—slower. The length of time between respirations stretches as Charles feels a oneness with the absence of gravity, allowing the sharpening coloration to absorb his shifting perception. His vision straddles the line between this world and beyond, and for a brief moment, the two dimensions merge, creating a coalescence of interdimensional abstraction. No longer breathing. The world Charles was born into is now wholly beyond his reach as his sight fixates on the landscape he has known only in his unholy dreamscapes.

As he awakens anew unto this blasphemous creation before him, a being of astronomical proportions greets his unbelieving gaze. Its size is such that it cannot be determined where the creature's body begins and where it ends, but one thing is certain—it is a devourer of worlds. Its presence is so vastly apocalyptic that even Charles is awestricken by its catastrophic nature, forcing him, if only for an instant, to question his ambitions. The entity is a magnate, or perhaps even a god amongst its race, for its triumphantly baneful omnipotence is terrifyingly clear to Charles by way of its ancient and imperious stature.

Its declamations of hideous blasphemies are spoken in thunderous growls, commands so powerful they seem to vibrate Charles's body from the inside of his mind. The draconian beast demands to be free from its universal constraints, not by speaking to Charles in its befouled and monstrous tongue, but by the thrashing of its countless immeasurable limbs. Charles feels dismally weak in the entity's unbounded presence, and he cannot tell where he stands in the great being's hierarchy of significance. The horror and enlightenment within Charles's newly born conceptualization surges as the confrontation between his own infinitesimally diminutive mortality and the endlessness of the abysmal beast edges onward into circumstances unknown. Thus, Charles looks away from the great being, his understanding of its black and hideously profane desires solidified, and onward instead into the world that surrounds it.

The mountainous being is immersed in a land of writhing and rotting flesh, accompanied by a rancidity so foul, the reek of a rotting carcass seems pallid by comparison. As far as the eye can see is a landscape of cavernous trenches, mountains, and rugged terrain. It appears barren to Charles at first glance, yet upon closer inspection he can see it is filled with crawling and desperately loathsome movement. Bizarre creatures are slithering, bellying, and darting through, over, and amidst the environment, similar to no beings Charles has before imagined, with alien speeds and motions that are difficult for him to fully comprehend. Everything seems to be built from the remnants of dead lifeforms: a never-endingly expansive topography of bodies in various stages of decomposition make up the composure of the land, peaks, and gullies below.

The panorama of decay brings not repulsion but a sense of unification into Charles's transubstantiated consciousness. An unrelentingly profound desire to delve further into the obscurity of this unholy dimension begins to flood his malign quintessence with a dark and brooding intensity. He can feel a shifting deep within his mortal shell as he floats passively and mysteriously through the membranes of the outer worlds. Sights granted to no mortal eyes are bestowed upon Charles and the endless enigmas of immeasurable epochs unfold before his unflinching spirit as he traverses the infinitude of that which man has never known.

As Charles glides ethereally through the carnivorous zephyr of the accursed aerial space, he notices the slithering in one region of the decaying terrain moving strangely in relation to the rest of the surroundings. Charles's soul flashes with a burning and disruptive contempt inspired by an unrecognizable source, and instantaneously he finds himself gazing downward on one area of especially putrescent landscape. He feels his essence shine with a powerful and mysterious fervor while the undulations of the writhing land seem to synchronize with the magisterial energies surging inside him. A hyper-fixation culminates, and Charles becomes one with this moment in time, as if the continuity of space-time collapses for his formless essence but continues for all things outside of his being.

As he watches with hateful, continuum-lapsing enthusiasm, layers upon pulpy layers of mutilated flesh and bone start to separate as that parcel of fetid ground splits wide open like it was stricken with an enormous unseen cleaver. From the cleaved opening of the rotting terrain, black fluids gush forth in profuse volumes accompanied by a treacherous stench that fumes with vapors of unknown and revolting diaphanous toxicity. As the grayish vapors gradually dissipate, a stirring beneath the rancid folds of terrestrial flesh can be seen. The movements begin to intensify, and sounds can be faintly heard, ones that seem to echo sentiments of a delirious and terrified nature. As the clamor grows, clawing, too, can be discerned, followed by a panted breathing that clearly portends fear. A being flashes abruptly from the furrows of otherworldly flesh with a burst of panicked intention. With an excruciating and fear-driven yearning for self-preservation, the lifeform explodes into a sprint and begins across the tormented landscape fleeing from whatever hellishness resides below.

From his incorporeal vantage point, Charles can see the defector is a subjugated creature, human-like, but not of the human world. Attempting escape from its unknown castigation, the hopes of only a moment's reprieve floods its tormented and crudely contorted countenance. The terror that comprises the essence of its fears can be felt like an arctic wind inside Charles's mind. This death-like chill kisses his black soul and excites his darkened spiritual aspirations, further heightening Charles's awareness of the hate-fueled spheres of abandon encapsulating the dimensions he is now permitted to occupy.

Unworldly speeds are achieved as the creature bursts across the gore-soaked terrain, moving the being at velocities that rival Earth's fastest mammals. The rate at which the terror-stricken biped moves is not without good reason, however. Upon reaching full speed, an explosion rocks the landscape, and a second entity bursts through the hole that the first being fled from. Thorny osteoid protrusions, infernally blackish flames, severed appendages, and an endless abstraction of unspeakable horrors decorate its foul, skeletal form. The enormity of its size and strength overshadows its evader by tenfold as it stomps mercilessly across the land, crushing the decaying ground with each monstrous fall of its titanic cloven hooves. It, too, moves with a ferociously rapid pace, its goliath, ground-shattering strides quickly closing the distance between them.

The gargantuan monstrosity swiftly shortens the divide, and once within striking distance, splits the back of the fleeing creature's head in two with a sharp and depraved instrument of torture. The wounded being crashes to the ground and flips several times over as the sudden loss of balance causes its extreme momentum to engage violently with the rugged terrain. The disabled lifeform's tumbling comes gradually to a stuttering halt with the pursuing beast now above the former. Looking down with an expression of pure, vehement loathing, the behemoth seethes now with a hate not known to man. Standing motionless, save for a deep breathing that expands and contracts within the monster's chest, the beast respirates with disturbing heaves, concurrently emanating a low and unutterably powerful growling. The leg—if it can so be called—of the nightmarish demon pulsates with a grim and hideously vascular system of biological conduit and muscular tissue, over what can only be described as a skeletal system completely devoid of flesh. It is no less than three times the fallen being's size and appears even larger now raised from the ground, poised in a static position over the lesser creature's severely maimed cranium. The inexorably appalling beast thrusts its hoof downward onto the dying being's visage, crushing its skull into the pulpy fleshiness of the disconsolate ground with a force that shakes the immediate surroundings.

Charles watches in apathetic silence from his ethereal view, taking in deep the madness of this wretched and decaying world of barbaric existence. He can feel the spite of the beast below him as if they are one and senses instinctively what is to come. The hellish creature once again pulls his instrument of torture from some unseen scabbard and crudely splits the biped's abdomen wide open, exposing strange and unfamiliar organs swimming in viscous fluids and curiously anomalous tissue. The demon attacks the corpse's open wound with a ferocious and terrifying intensity, tearing entrails and viscera from the gaping cavity while roaring blasphemies in an ancient and horrifying tongue.

Abruptly the carnage ceases, and the beast utters its final profanation. It begins to breath once more in gurgling tones of underworldly rumblings while its optics gleam with a reddish and hell-conjuring intensity. The demon extends its skeletal-like arm toward the emptied abdomen of the slain escapee and reaches into the torn carcass with its enormous viscera-soaked claw, pulling something from the depths of the corpse which resembles a crumpled page. Charles closes his eyes and raises his arms as he embraces a telepathic connection with the mighty creature below, allowing raw and sinister energies to move freely throughout his spirit. The demonic entity below raises the leaf of papyrus above its body and releases a thunderous growl of hate-filled victory, its conquest one not simply over the enemy slain before it but over the transcendental ramparts that prevent their kind from crossing over. Charles rises even farther into the bleak atmosphere, riding high upon the triumphantly unrighteous power gifted unto him. An orgasmic and tyrannical sensation of spiritual omniscience inundates his essence, and he can feel the truth and legend behind the fallen being's predilections and fate.

The now expired and viciously defiled being was of an immeasurably old and mysterious universe of which few worlds have known, and even fewer conscious beings have understanding of. Its kind knew of things that cannot be acknowledged by modern man—things archaic and esoteric, but sympathetic to lifeforms both familiar and beyond human conception. Their race were keepers of a vast and secretive knowledge, cosmically significant and universally profound. Their collective wisdom foresaw that which may come as a result of the ideas laid out in the text—the ubiquitous horrors that these concepts suggest. So, it was decided amongst them to make hidden these arcane and world-ending scriptures, so that time and dust might conceal them in a world filled with ignorance of their power, wiping clean the memories of their existence. One special protector was to guard the designs contained in the final ancient text—a creature whose existence was the last of its kind.

The rotting ground around the dead biped's carcass begins to quake and radiate as if the blood of the poor dead creature is exciting it. Charles's unification deepens, creating even greater cohesion with the outer world he embraces, the togetherness with the wretched landscape boiling over into demonic lunacy as the ground below his floating form gurgles with a disgorging animosity. The butchered flesh and fragments of bone and gore seep into the land, fueling an undulating rhythm of ghastly arousal, and all things beyond this portion of damnable terrain begin to fade from Charles's sight. The blood and hacked up foulness disappear into the fetid soil and so, too, does Charles, plunging downward into the black and timeless depths.

Immersed in sub-terrestrial visions, Charles feels as if he *is* the otherworldly realm his mind embraces. Within the subconscious abstraction of this metaphysical hellscape, his head is violently thrust backward along with the length of his spine. His chest bursts open and his rib cage explodes outward, allowing his skeletal structure to fuse with the slithering spawn surrounding him. Charles's limbs—numerous and appalling in absurd dexterity—crawl through the deep with ravishing agility, feeling and interpreting the nightmarish worlds far beyond and below. Mouth removed—no need for words in these catacombs devoid of symbiotic unification. Eyes put to rest—nothing to see now; only contemplation remains. A boundless meditation of depths unwanted and the eternal repulsiveness that exists on the other side of mankind's tiny and insignificant reality. With arachnean finesse he traverses the planes of iniquity, his body now resembling the contemptable, seething foulness his spirit has always paralleled.

A frozen cauldron of misanthropy and hatred for living beings, in this world and all others, is here to be explored. A draconian journey ensues for an epoch lasting beyond time's constraint and many abominations are witnessed. Charles is stripped bare of his humanness as he infinitely descends, downward, further into the bottomless stretches of antipathy and extermination. Time is lost here; this universe has a physics to its constructs that does not heed a fourth dimension. Further still, he transcends the boundaries of imagination; all thoughts are now fed into his mind through a collective conscience. They think for him. The brutality of this plane of existence drives his will—motivating, terrorizing, assassinating all outside influence. A moribund reality of excruciating condemnation toward all dictating forces beyond this mutilating landscape has appropriated and manifested itself for now and all eternity to come within his new form.

Charles's sense of human reality is no more—only the horrific realities of mankind's outcome remain; and what now must be done.

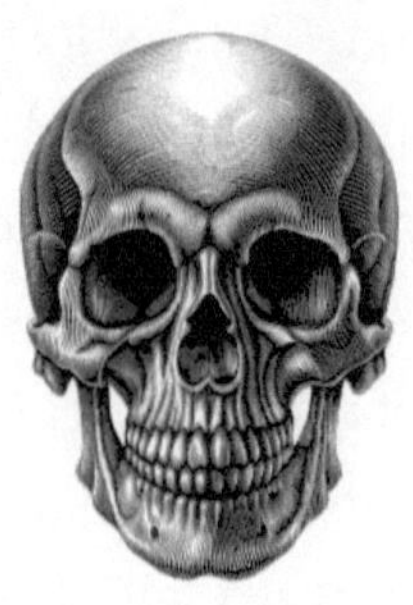

XXX.

In the Southern Windhoek Hospital, central to Namibia and located in the midst of a valley enclosed by the Khomas Highland plateau area, a TV plays for no audience, only a ransacked waiting room and the empty, tossed chairs surrounding it. The flat screen itself probably would have been taken too, had it not been secured by large bolts to a steel frame mounted upon the hospital wall. Although the rest of the surroundings have been ravaged, it is still plugged in and working, airing emergency bulletins for the city to a vacant building, save for the dead and dying littering the hallways and ICUs, screaming and bewailing unanswered pleas for help. It was left on a news channel by some unknown person, possibly hospital staff, or perhaps a patient awaiting admittance when the chaos initially broke out. Through the cracked screen and raspy speakers, a reporter can be seen and heard speaking in English, although subtitles scroll across the bottom in Afrikaans and German.

He is middle-aged and has a mustache and glasses. The dark brown closely cropped hair dancing in the breeze atop his head is not well managed, as if he has not had any time for grooming. His tie is loose, and his upper shirt button unfastened, probably in an attempt to cool his sweat-covered body. His British accent suggests the broadcast may be taking place in England or somewhere near that region of Europe. He attempts to hide his unease as he fumbles with his paperwork, words spilling from his mouth in a garble of repetition and frequent stuttering:

"Reports are still coming in at a frantic pace as cities all over Europe, the Middle East, and Asia are describing scenes of horror. Killing, looting, robbery...killing—murders—widespread...arson, the list goes on... Complete *mayhem* has taken over most of the major cities in Europe and the reports seem to indicate the violence is quickly spreading across Africa as well. Citizens are *strongly* urged to seek shelter and protection... We...we just don't know exactly what's happening yet..."

The dithery news anchor pauses as a blonde-haired petite woman stoops by his desk in a shiftless attempt to hide from camera view. She hands him some papers, whispers something, and disappears out of sight.

"Breaking reports just in... It appears—" He stops mid-sentence and turns away from the camera at an unknown person with a look of shocked disbelief adorning his sweat-covered and pale countenance. "Is this right? This *can't* be right!" Receiving an affirmation from some unseen source, he turns his head back toward the camera and swallows slowly before continuing with a droning and hollow cadence. "Sources at the Brazilian Ministry of Defense claim reports are pouring in from Brazil..." He turns once again to his off-camera colleagues. "Are you *sure*? Has this been confirm— It has? Members of the viewing audience, my sources tell me that reports of the mass killings of children by their parents and families is occurring in Brazil and other parts of South America..." The reporter pauses and glances away from the camera once more with a look of unmitigated disgust smeared across his face. He says nothing for several seconds and glowers apprehensively back down at the report, then back up at the camera, a repulsed sorrow filling his eyes as if his insides are churning. "Hundreds of eyewitness accounts are coming in detailing *shocking* brutalities taking place in a large favela in Rio de Janeiro, Brazil. I'm told children are being killed by the hundreds—shootings, beheadings—" He stops and touches his earpiece, pressing it into his ear to ensure he is hearing the incoming information accurately. "I'm now being told residents of the favela have built a huge fire, a dozen stories tall or more, and they're throwing...throwing...the children onto it..."

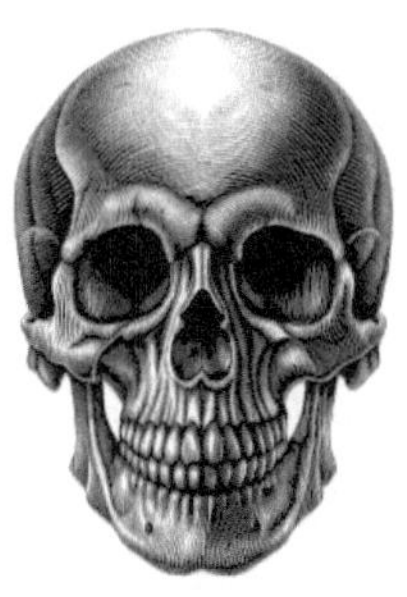

XXXI.

Outside of Base Alameda on Coast Guard Island, nestled within the Oakland Estuary, Jerry stands alongside a training center wall, preparing to sneak a drink after the helicopter ride over from Berkeley. The bottle he acquired came from a liquor store purchase several days prior, hidden conveniently in his suitcase for a planned evening's nightcap that he never got the chance to enjoy. It is 6:45 p.m. and their meeting with the Department of Defense and officials with the CIA begins in fifteen minutes. The military have chosen this spot as a temporary haven for special operations, a request that the base had no authority to deny. The sun warms Jerry's face as he leans against the hard red brick of the building's exterior, allowing him, if only for a moment, to take in a flicker of reprieve before he meets with his determinate superiors. Jerry takes a long breath, inhaling the subtle warmth as if it is his last and only chance while simultaneously reaching into his suit jacket for the pint of scotch stashed readily inside his inner pocket. Just as his lips greet the edge of the bottle, Martin slides around the corner, startling Jerry to the point of spilling warm J & B down the front of his wrinkled and sweat-soiled button down. "Damnit!"

"Sorry, did I frighten you?" Martin queries with an uneasy, half-attentive smirk while pulling jerkily at his pipe, trying to free it from his front pocket.

Jerry's anger quickly fades as he sees the disquietude in Martin's eyes. "Yeah, uh, *no*... I mean...it's not a big deal." Jerry continues watching while sipping from his bottle as Martin finally frees the pipe only to find the tobacco has spilled into the lining of his pocket. The look of disappointment in Martin's gaze as he stares solemnly into his empty pipe and then at the mess in his front shirt pocket for some odd reason overwhelms Jerry with pity. "Would you like a drink?" Jerry offers, holding the bottle out toward Martin in a companionable show of sympathy.

Martin suspends his fumbling and looks at the bottle, thinking to himself for a few seconds before reaching his hand out in acceptance. "Sure. Now seems like as good a time as ever for a drink." Jerry shoots him a smirk that Martin does not even see and returns to embracing the sunshine while leaning the back of his head against the warm red brick. "*So*, what's the plan? Has anyone given you any type of briefing or anything? Did your boss say anything during the phone call?"

Jerry pulls his head away from the wall and takes the bottle from Martin, tossing back one last swig before screwing on the cap. "I don't know. All I was told was to get my ass over here—you and me both."

"Realistically, what do we have here? Another pandemic? Did Wuhan create a strain of COVID that causes people to go insane? Biological warfare from Russia or North Korea, perhaps? But then how do you explain the strange phenomena—black holes, entire towns vanishing then reappearing dead...whatever the *bloody hell* it was we saw in the cathedral?" Martin begins to work himself into a distressing unease. Recognizing the anxiety building, he abruptly stops talking and begins stroking his beard and straightening his glasses as he often does. He takes a deep breath while pulling his tobacco pouch from his pocket and begins filling his pipe, silently hoping Jerry will say something to calm his nerves.

"Look, friend, I *wish* I had some answers for you. I'm in the same boat you are. You know what I know. Russia, China, science, the devil... I have no clue. All I know is now the DOD is involved and that means this is being taken as seriously as it can be. In less than ten minutes we're going to find out just how fucked we are."

With Jerry's response, a cold wind suddenly dismantles the exchange, enveloping the air as clouds roll past the shining sun, blocking its warming rays. A woman's scream is faintly heard in the distance carried on the wind from Oakland's direction and both men stare at each other in a wordless conciliation of concern. "It's happening here too," Martin claims in a listless murmur.

"It's just the wind, Martin."

"Who are you kidding, Jerry?! You heard what I said in the meeting. Violence and chaos are spreading. A pile of bodies STORIES tall...full of...of...*Beaverdam residents*! I even saw something online not ten minutes ago about parents murdering their kids in Brazil, by the hundreds...*thousands* perhaps. It's here—the end of the world! The god damned *apocalypse*!" Martin tries to light his pipe, but the wind fights the flame. Angered by several failed attempts to ignite the tobacco, he chucks the lighter as far as he can while both men watch the plastic and metal casing bounce, shatter, and disappear into the distance. Jerry puts his head down and heads for the door. "Let's get to that fucking meeting."

Through the double doors and starting down the hallway, Jerry can see his contact waiting for him at the end of the long passageway. As he works his way through the corridor, Jerry feels a rising presentiment of dread, possibly stemming from the authoritative look cast upon him by the man clad in military dress waiting in seeming impatience at the end of the aisleway. Or, perhaps, it is the dull grays and nauseatingly light hues of blue separated by a long, abhorrently dark orange stripe spanning the length of the walls on either side adding to his already beleaguered mentality. Jerry ignores the fear welling inside his core and straightens his back and shoulders. He quickly checks behind him to lay eyes on Martin's position, which he sees is only a few steps trailing.

Jerry reaches the end of the hallway and nears his contact, a person he has never met but instinctively discerns to engage. A shorter but commanding specimen of a man in his early fifties, accompanied by buzz cut hair and covered in military ribbons, he greets Jerry and Martin with a stern and unforgiving acknowledgment. "This way, gentlemen."

The two men follow him into the adjacent room where they are met by four others seated at a table and one woman standing authoritatively near the entrance. "Dr. Patterson, Agent Norton, I am Lieutenant General Robert Larson, Director of the Chemical and Biological Defense Program for the DOD, and this is Dr. Shelly Masters, Director for the Advanced Defensive Research Projects Agency." Stiff handshakes are shared by Martin and Jerry with the two directors, and awkward glances are given by both men toward the other four unintroduced attendees staring eminently from their chairs behind the table. They all join the seated members of the collaboration while the air in the room seems to adjust to the seriousness of the occasion.

General Larson wastes no time in getting straight down to business and, once formalities are expressed, inquires immediately about Jerry and Martin's findings. "Agent Norton, can you give us a briefing on the evidence you and Dr. Patteson have collected? As I understand it, you two were assigned..." the general pauses to look through his folder and paperwork for the locations before continuing, "the Arcadia incident, Potosi, and...Sugar Land."

The occupants of the assembly all look in Jerry's direction awaiting his answer. Not one to typically feel pressured in any situation, at this particular point in time, Jerry can feel the sweat dripping precipitously down his right armpit as he fumbles for words within his mind on how to begin. "Well, um...*yes*, of course... I first visited with the lone survivor of the Arcadia incident. There were two, actually, but one individual, Shawn Townsend, age 20, was never actually present on scene or near enough to the incident during or after the incident occurred to be of use. The other...a..." Jerry stops to clear his throat and loosen his tie, feeling the eyes of his interrogators upon him with scathing deliberation. "*Ahem...* Excuse me. The other, a Jessie Bower, age 18, reported awakening in the woods at a gathering to find everyone deceased. He also reported a heat that seemed to hang in the atmosphere accompanied by a 'deathlike silence.' He was quoted as such, sir... A '*deathlike silence.*'" Jerry watches nervously as the occupants of the meeting take notes in their notebooks and on their laptops, waiting for someone—anyone—to say something.

The general straightens his posture, uncrosses his arms from in front of him, and stares at Jerry with an emotionless leer. "Heat in the atmosphere? I see. And silence? I'm willing to bet he mentioned the animals in the woods surrounding the area. No sounds, correct?"

"Yes, sir," Jerry responds with a slight hint of intimidation in his voice. "Just like my briefing prior to the investigation suggested." With that statement, Martin fixes his gaze in Jerry's direction, a look of anger fused with puzzled mistrust smeared across his face. Jerry catches Martin's glare of disapproval and shoots him a cynical eyeing of his own, alerting him without words that now is not the time.

"And the second case you were assigned—Potosi, Missouri?"

"Well, sir... I didn't get anything from the survivor of that incident quite like the briefing suggested or the Arcadia teen. He was...

mentally disturbed. Rambling on about demons and so forth. Before he…"

"Yes, killed himself. Very unfortunate."

"What about the Sugar Land site?" Dr. Masters finally asks, breaking her silence, her dark brown eyes burning analytically from behind thick black glasses as she waits for an answer.

Jerry looks at the table, then back at Dr. Masters, followed by a glance back downward that does not reverse. "Perhaps Dr. Patterson should answer this one."

Both the general and Masters turn their gaze toward Martin, who is sitting solemnly and passively next to Jerry trying his best to appear collectively calm. Martin straightens his glasses and clears his throat while situating himself upright in his seat. "I have no expert opinion, nor do I have any direct evidence to even begin explaining the phenomenon I witnessed in Saint Mary's Immaculate Conception Cathedral."

"*What the hell is that supposed to mean?*" Lieutenant General Robert Larson asks with a condescending smirk.

Martin, slightly offended by the response and accompanying smirk, looks the general in his eyes and fires back. "*Unexplained sounds*, like howling and growling—*earthquake-like vibrations—visual and auditory hallucinations*—monstrous…*things*—a stench that I cannot even *begin to describe*—then, to top it off, I watched this man sitting next to me floating in mid-air! *Things like that, SIR!*"

The general sits back in his seat and crosses his arms, clearly annoyed by the seemingly ludicrous nature of the event's portrayal. "Agent Norton… What is all this nonsense?"

Jerry, still staring at the table, slowly lifts his head and briefly makes eye contact with Dr. Masters, then, for an even shorter moment, with the general, before angling it back down toward the table. "That's…that's about the gist of it, General."

A voice from a man seated two chairs behind Jerry breaks the tension. "Dr. Patterson, can I ask you to leave the room for a moment?"

Martin cranes his head strongly to the left to see who exactly is now asking him to leave the meeting he was ordered to attend. The man appears a little young to be in the room, probably late twenties or so, as best as Martin can tell, adorning a face so smooth that he gives off the impression that growing a beard is probably not even an option. With an equable compliance, Martin calmly stands up and exits the room.

The man two chairs behind now pushes his laptop aside and clasps his hands in front of him while looking directly at Jerry. "Agent Norton, I'm Devin Haronshaw, analyst for the Science, Technology, and Weapons Division over at the CIA."

"Yes, I know who you are," Jerry coldly starts. "I saw you during the first briefing."

"Of course. Well then, down to business. I asked Dr. Patterson to leave the meeting because we need to discuss some things that are confidential and of national security."

Jerry immediately bursts into laughter, summoning glowering visages from both Devin and the general. "HA! *National security*? You must be joking. The world is in utter chaos right now and you're worried about national security... Jesus. Okay, look, what is it *exactly* that you want from me at this point?"

Devin unclasps his hands and places them on the table as if he is bracing himself for some action unknown even to him. "We are fully aware of the gravity of the situation, Agent Norton, and since *you*, not Dr. Patterson, but *you* have been briefed and signed the non-disclosure agreement, and *you* have the clearance and are privy to certain details regarding these matters, you may stay. *However*... I am required to ask anyone who is *not* cleared to leave when speaking upon these matters. Now... We have reason to believe that a new type of military technology is being used to create the conditions and circumstances being experienced across the globe—"

Devin is stopped cold as Jerry once again erupts into laughter, this time uncontrollably, causing Devin to throw up his hands mid-sentence and begin chewing on a pen laying on a pad in front of him.

"Agent Norton!" General Larson shouts in a disgruntled and commanding voice. "I would advise you to take this matter seriously."

"*Seriously*? Are you kidding me? I fully agree, *sir*! These matters should be taken with the utmost seriousness, but I can assure you that the military is not what we need to deal with this situation," Jerry responds with a subtle smile that gradually transitions into a frigid and stoic expression.

The general looks at Jerry with a demeanor of demanding intensity, his eyes alight with a mixture of interest and fury. "Then what exactly is it we need, might I ask?"

"To fall to our knees and beg God for deliverance," he responds.

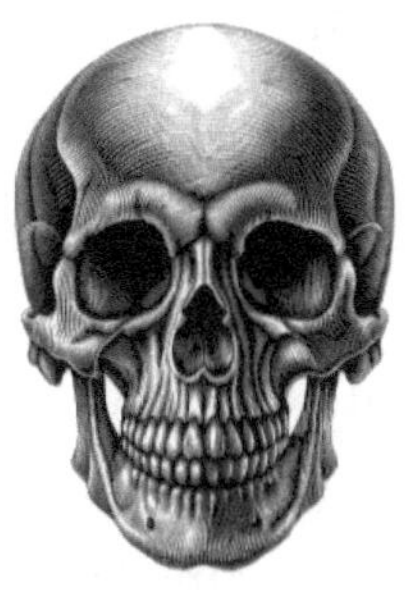

XXXII.

The phone rings for what seems to be an eternity, the incessant jingling sounding in Charles's ear with a tempestuous clamor further aggravating his lack of patience as he waits in anger for someone to answer. After several dozen chimes, a receptionist finally answers with an angelic voice and an inflection which sounds enthusiastically apologetic. Her greeting is met with one of apathy and completely void of kindness. "Dr. James Hidalgo, please." While the world is ensorcelled in madness, a small portion of scientists, engineers, and other researchers who live on site at Athena Laboratories carry on as usual, as if nothing outside their encapsulated world exists; only their singular purpose within the facility walls to concern themselves with, and the scientific advancements with which they hope to achieve.

"Dr. Hidalgo here," a voice gently articulates into the phone after a five-minute hold made even more unbearable by the irritatingly atrocious piano music played in a loop while Charles awaited the call to be transferred.

"Dr. Hidalgo, it's Charles. Are we still set to run the experiment on Friday?"

"Well, Mr. Kepler..." Hidalgo begins, straining for words as he pauses in consideration. "You've no doubt been paying attention to the news, yes? We're concerned about continuing forward with any accelerator experiments at this time. A lot of our staff have left over the last twenty-four hours and—"

"*NO*! Absolutely not! Don't even say it! I have contributed copious amounts of money and resources to this project, not to mention your personal research, and the only thing I want to hear coming from your mouth is, *Yes, sir*, the project will be carried out on Friday at 9:45 a.m.!"

"Well... I understand your concerns, sir, but..."

"*No buts*! 9:45, *Friday*. Must I remind you of the ramifications should you choose not to proceed?" Charles warns in an obstinately indignant tone. "When everything blows over and things are back to order in the world, do you want the public to know about the details of our endeavors?"

"Come now, Mr. Kepler, there is no need for threats. And *remember*, you're just as guilty as me," Dr. Hidalgo responds, raising his voice into the phone with a hint of confidence and contempt.

"Are you sure you want to test the waters there, James? I have the resources to *fucking* bury you... What exactly do you have? A few scientists and a paper trail leading to offshore bank accounts for entities that don't even exist. *Friday*. 9:45 a.m. That time *precisely*. Less than thirty-six hours from now." With that, Charles waits for a reply, relishing in the finality of his statement and knowing that the next words from Dr. Hidalgo's mouth will be ones of compliance.

"9:45, Friday... The experiment will proceed as planned," Hidalgo shamefully responds, his voice trailing off into deferential regret as Charles presses the end call button on his phone.

The darkness enveloping Charles's body seethes in a vortex of rhythmic, ancient iniquity. His corporeal shell is halved, consisting partially of flesh with the remainder a twisting and loathing cauldron of black specters. The parts of him that are comprised of bone and matter drop the phone to the floor of his lavishly decorated bedroom, the phone case bouncing and cracking onto the Persian silk carpet beneath his amorphous form. Charles glides across the room effortlessly in a fluid motion, not quite walking, yet not fully drifting. His movements are chaotically synchronous and purposeful as the ancient beasts guide his way. He is not quite sure where he is being led and simultaneously wholly aware of the obligation before him.

He knows the syzygy must be made to run concurrently with the experiment; a total solar eclipse to blacken the Earth as the gateway is opened. The Singularity Project—devised in spirit by those ancient beings inconceivably foul—was set into motion eons ago in preparation for the new beginning; a beginning which in turn signals an end. Demented thoughts of neurotic spiritual detachment pixilate within Charles's mind as he is led down the hallway; images of human annihilation along with all forms of life on Earth ending in cataclysmic rapture boil within his subconscious. His bodily half quivers and twitches as the shadows swirl in ecstasy, ushering him down the stairway and into the main hallway. Still unknowing of his destination, but in tune with the evil abound, he can sense that another being not present awaits his calling.

Charles has envisioned the final page and knows the ancient text holds the key, but the writ alone will not suffice. An opening must be made, and mankind's greatest minds have bridged the gap, providing the means with which to throw open the gateways to beyond. Still embracing the darkness, and holding firmly onto his introspection, Charles dreams vividly of the eclipse's darkening of the Earth as the entities of black guide him toward the kitchen, all the while stoking the reverie of demonic guardianship, allowing his focus to shift to a protector on this side of existence.

He glides with a ghostly ease into the kitchen of his palatial mansion home, led only by the fiery light of a profane influence through the darkness of the unlit room. Thoughts of blasphemous proclamations, a blackened Earth, and the final accelerator experiment mix fluently within his cognition as those from beyond this realm force his left hand—the only of the two still solid in structure—onto the handle of a large kitchen knife. The diabolic perversions encompassing his partially material form are palpably felt and wholly in control as the legion of dark spirits from unknown spaces direct the knife into his stomach, spilling forth what remains of Charles's corrupted and bifurcated intestines. A bizarre and curious display of viscera flows forth from the gaping wound across his spectrally amalgamated abdomen as the blade rips slowly and forcefully from one side of his hip to the other, allowing his insides to gradually pool into a sickening accretion atop the kitchen table. Charles gazes downward as the last of his innards ooze forth from the gash, realizing with an illuminous and euphoric finality the meaning behind his nefarious spurring.

The darkness within his mansion is absolute, yet the flames alight within his mind allow him sight, as the glow emanating from the outlines on the tabletop reveal to him a map drawn in entrails and gore. Once again, like so many times before, the ancient ones of time's forgotten past have shown him the pathway to enlightenment. His journey, long and arduous as it has been, draws one step closer to the end as he gapes down at the chart etched in blood and intestines, embracing silently the definitiveness of what lies before him. The location where he shall be gifted the final page of text, that scathingly detested rite of life's damnation, has now been unveiled before his blackened and demonically awakened eyes.

As the knowledge he acquired solidifies unto his being, the specters leave him, disappearing into the already darkened corners of the room and tainting further the mansion with a ghastly and insidious hate. Charles's body coalesces with a burning unlike he has ever known, causing a pain so severe that he collapses onto the floor in an accumulation of his own blood. The hour is late, and daybreak draws near, summoning a dark and restless reverie inculcated by even darker influences.

With the break of dawn, he finds himself nude and rightfully whole, still lying in a puddle of partially congealed fluid. Charles gathers himself from the floor and heads upstairs to dress, preparing himself for his excursion to the envisaged location.

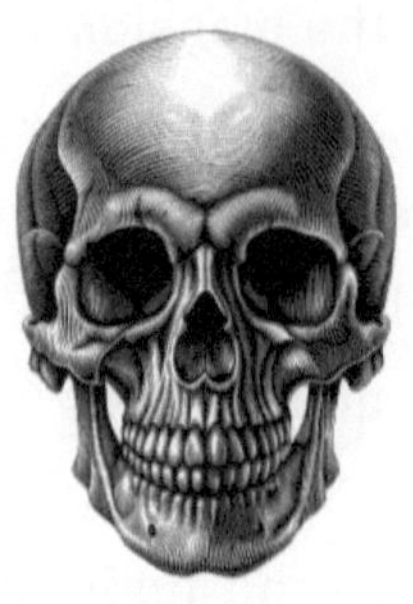

XXXIII.

Strange and forbidden things are occurring atop an immensely elevated, grass-covered hill situated on the edge of Tilden Regional Park, just east of the San Francisco Bay. Acres upon acres of rolling knolls are scattered sporadically throughout the surrounding area, yet none are quite as blissfully appealing as the highland to the west of the main roadway, rising majestically above the foothills below. The sun seems to shine with a whimsical radiance on this bewildering morning, illuminating the curious scenery beneath it with a traitorous and beguiling consolation. The summer breeze here is tainted by the stench of decay, a subtle attar, one that plays more on the subconscious than on the nostrils; still, its foul putrescence instills within the erudite spirit a sense of the damnation at hand.

The vast hilltop is not without its own clandestine and tumultuous past. For over two hundred years, tales have been told of its paroxysmal and blood-soaked history. Beginning in the late 18th century, Spanish explorers embarked on their quest to map out, colonize, and convert the native peoples in an attempt to further their own expansion, yet in some cases their attempts were met with a dreadful and hostile resistance. The rumors of slaughter and pillaging, rape and defilement, mutilation and degradation, all effected by the hands of the explorers unto dozens of Ohlone families, circulate still to this day amidst soft-spoken lips and whispered tales. Even the ground along the hilltop seems sullied by the blood spilled during those blackened times. Until today, not a tree existed along the expansive stretch of flat high above the screaming slopes. Before today, only the blankets of green grassland could be experienced; that, and the secrets bequeathed by the olden summer wind.

However, on this ineluctable summer morning, late in the month of July, something of enormous stature can be seen sprouting in moribund repugnance directly in the center of the once treeless and sullen ground of the hilltop in Tilden Regional Park. Its colossal and towering frame stretches high into the air, begging the question of just how and when it started to grow. A shadow is cast ominously over the surrounding landscape by the nightmarish tree-like growth, darkening the region with a foreboding and terrifying outline. It is organic, yet lifeless, and unlike any plant indigenous to Earth, weaving spells and incantations most hideous with the curling and twisting of its hardened, innumerable limbs. From afar its base appears almost skeletal, as if its still-growing form was aging in reverse, born unto a rotten shell and gradually culminating from within. The boney protrusions extending horrifically from the mid-section can almost be witnessed slowly burgeoning, if one concentrates intently on the hellish appendages shooting upward into the affrighted sky. In certain spots the growing monstrosity has developed a type of bark, leathery and abusive in its blood-red and grotesque appearance. What exactly is causing it to grow can only be hypothesized, but those gathering on the hilltop share stories of human sacrifice—the spilled blood of children shed so vigorously within the last couple of days.

A celebration of sorts is underway, and the revelers are gathering en masse, making their way up the hillside to pay reverence to the strange and hideous growing thing. A superbly unsettling atmosphere seems to permeate the undercurrents abound, but most don't even notice as they gather 'round the tree, smiles painted across their lips and semi-delirious joy about their faces. They sing and dance, paying homage to the towering monolithic entity; some celebrants joining hand and hand in frolicking circles, others sitting with guitars and bongos playing in trance-like veneration to the proliferation above. As more and more arrive, the joy is spread further, touching each new arriving participant with the gift of completion. Some bring food—fruits and lavish spreads—others, gifts and offerings of majestic splendor, leaving them at the base of the ghastly and enigmatic growing entity. The offerings seemingly cause the sprouting behemoth to grow further still, as if the tree can somehow sense the glorification from its ever-increasing idolaters.

As the throngs steadily multiply, increasing by the hundreds every hour, the jubilation intensifies, causing an ever-expanding aura of excitation that borders on the lines of mania. The smiles and faces of some can be described as ones of elation and pure serenity, while others can be witnessed crying tears of euphoric bliss, perhaps felt for the very first time in their lives. Families gather along the hilltop, bringing along the elderly and small children, all carrying with them the promise of hope and freedom. They arrive in fleets of cars, or on foot, motorcycles and buses, the temptations of some unknown salvation drawing from afar those who seek enlightenment by the masses.

On one end of the vast hillside, along a peculiarly steep and angled slope, an old man with a walker is spotted trying as best he can to make the arduous trek to the top, no doubt entranced by the lure of the tree. He struggles and toils all with a smile on his lips, yet the intensity of the incline precludes his advancement. Other new arrivals spot the old man's drudgery and stop what they're doing to help him to the top. No one labors alone on the high hillside this day, as if the draw of the strange boney growth's unspoken promise has brought an unaccountable peace to the people.

As the hours wear on and the crowds thicken still, the wind begins to whisper as if divulging secrets and myths. Children prance and play amidst the masses as smaller groups gather together, joining in the celebration under the menacing shadow of the haunting and colossal structure. Between the romping of small children and the sighing of the once silent wind, it is at times hard to discern whether the children's voices are coming from the laughter of the dallying youth or the zephyr gently blowing through the tree's crooked and mysterious limbs.

Drones fly through the air gathering photos of the eerie growing thing, operated by locals who have taken an interest in the anomaly. Concurrently, multitudes of selfies and pictures are shared across social media platforms, spreading quickly the news of the strange and wonderous happenings. Curiosity peaks as people see their friends and family posting images of their whereabouts, prompting even more new groups to gather on the hilltop under the ever-increasing hideous entity. For the moment, it is as if the horrendous atrocities of recent days had not even taken place, as the cheer and frivolity spread contagiously with each new arrival.

Atop the hill, underneath the skeletal living monument, capacity is reached, yet still more arrive. As the wind picks up, so does the whispering, repressed in volume yet still audible to the reconciled mind. The celebration ensues and seems to grow in fervor as the hours pass, fostering an ambiance of almost neurotic contentment. Some of the participants exude a nearly trance-like state of euphoria, seemingly tuned to the frequency of the atmosphere. Near to the base of the trunk—if one were so inclined to refer to it with such intention—a young woman strips completely bare, shedding her clothes in celebration. She dances around the morbidity and gently rubs its hardened exterior, gracefully tiptoeing and thrusting without shame or restraint. Several yards away, a gentleman plays a flute in harmonic reverence, quickly changing his tune to carry along with her movements. Many take notice and some join in her bareness, uncladding themselves to join in her unveiled merriment.

While some revel in nakedness, others speak in strange tongues, shouting unrecognizable exaltations in honor of the tree. What their words lack in comprehension they make up for in ardency, and just as in the woman's dancing, they seem to entice others to enlist. With every performance and each added partaker, the whispering breeze seems to grow louder and clearer. Talk amongst the people begins to manifest rumors regarding the voices and soon the idea becomes certain that the whispering is in fact real. Smiles, creepily adorned upon faces of the rumormongers, spin tales of the origins and generations of the eerie whispering. It is told amongst the revelers that the secrets carried upon the wind are the voices of the sacrificed children whose blood has been so vigorously shed in Brazil and other parts of the world. Although shocking and revolting in a manner unutterably profound, the smiles do not fade as the celebrants share with each other the sickening notions behind the breeze. Instead, the rejoicing continues and seems to increase further still, almost as if the revelation is cause for an acceleration in reverence.

The morning stretches into noon and the sun sits high above the horizon. The hilltop below shines in a brilliant radiance embellished by song and dance, praise and offerings. All things atop the grassy hill are held deep in the embrace of a manic lucidity. Only the strange, ever-expanding tree-like growth seems to mind the warmth of the glowing sun, as if its twisted and rotting form somehow knows all too well of blacker things to come.

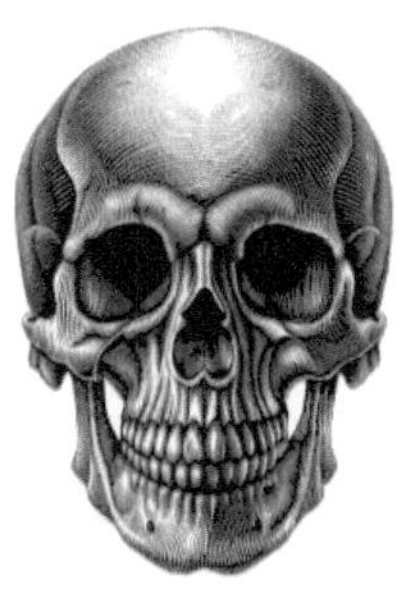

XXXIV.

A desolate place of tormented depravity fills the view reflecting back into Matt's eyes as he scans the landscape scowling with an incomprehensible hatred. He marches forward through the barren and bleak lifelessness of the pathway before him, enlightened by a sense of profane guidance. His strides are large and swift, much greater and more pronounced than possible with his human form, this shell of demonic barbarity befitting more appropriately of his unearthly surroundings. In another dimension of existence, his footfalls would land upon the area of Oakland, California, but in the embrace of his alternate self, all he can envision is the horror that lies beyond the dreaded gateway.

Singular his objective, and destination wholly known, Matt makes his way through the nightscape on the other side of reality. Craters, massive boulders, and fragments of what surely were once living structures pulsate with a slow cadence, giving the land a death-like animation. Through the dimensional membrane his presence makes no impact. The environment on the mortal side of existence is unaffected by each step his monstrous form takes, unlike the plane beyond the separational rift where his thunderous footsteps reverberate through the dark and tortured environment. Matt's nightmarishly enormous body passes through valleys of immense hopelessness and inconceivable blasphemy, lined with skeletons of vile creatures which protrude wretchedly through the rotting ground. A massive skull—frozen in scream as if slain by an ancient enemy—gawks as Matt stomps by, almost as if its long-vanquished visage is alarmed by his presence. On humanity's side, passersby don't notice the stench of decay that assaults Matt's nostrils; they have no inkling of the depravity that lies beyond their vision of this universe. Too few are left on the streets to be concerned with Matt's oddly loathsome and pitch-black eyes as he walks fearlessly through the alleyways and avenues. Those still roaming the city seem to be more content looting and marauding than concerning themselves with a bedraggled and enraged character such as Matt currently represents.

The trek across the necrotic terrain is quite effortless in Matt's transmuted mind. Tilden Regional Park is still miles away, yet the timeless fluency of an everlasting yearning burns deeply within his possessed spirit. The ancient beings that drive his will have waited countless eons for this period to arrive, and their unholy beckoning is one of patience and elaborate design. So onward his travels continue, into the darkness of the abyss and, consequently, forward through the downtown streets of Oakland, toward the hillsides of Tilden Park.

The day is well into the afternoon and approaching early evening as Matt—or, perhaps more fittingly, the human form he is perceived as in this world—approaches the edge of the hillside. Those gathered in attendance now number in the thousands, and the celebration of the unearthly growing thing has reached near hysterical proportion. It is difficult to tell madness from joy as the multitudes dance and throw their hands to the sky, all in reverence to the almighty tree. The growth itself has reached portions of unparalleled heights, rivaling even the mighty redwoods of northern California with its vast, twisting limbs and still-expanding skeletal trunk.

The police and local media have taken an interest in the strange happenings as well in recent hours. The potential for violence cannot be ruled out with the sporadic outbreaks occurring throughout the country. While the number of officers dispatched to the scene is low at the present moment, other precincts have been alerted and are on standby should things take a turn for the worse. The news stations not covering other spontaneous episodes of chaos throughout the city have also gathered around the site of the eerie skeletal thing stretching farther and farther into the sky. Unlike the handful of police officers camped out below the hillside, some of the reporters have chosen to make the trek to the top to see for themselves the magnificence that is the tree, none of whom have been heard from since, creating a sense of panic amongst their colleagues back at the news stations.

Upon reaching the periphery of the thick and boisterous crowds, Matt stops for a moment to inhale the blasphemy of the horrid sight. He gazes upward to the top of the hill and lays his mortal eyes upon the panorama before him. On the other side of his vision, past the splitting membrane of dimensional separation, he envisions a scenery far removed from that of the human experience. The torturous revelations of the reality his otherworldly sight grants him are incomprehensibly barbaric in their cruel iniquity; however, to his blackened and demonic mindset, the beauty that he witnesses is inconceivably sublime. He stares intently up the hillside and scans the backdrop beyond with eyes so black and lifeless that their obscurity seems to curse the terrain they envisage.

His summoning to this forbidden ritualistic celebration is not without cause, and no sooner than he arrives the revelry accelerates rapidly, as those in attendance begin constructing an altar in reverence to the tree. From the bottom of the hillside, adherents can be seen carrying large stones and cinder blocks from some unknown source in a formational line, handing them off one by one all the way up the hill and placing them at the base of the tree. The construction moves rapidly as an ominous foreboding fills the air, too faint for most to sense its presence creeping slowly upon them. That thing—that ever-expanding tree-like curiosity—now towers at over five hundred feet tall, and still it grows, gaining even more adoration from its devoted followers. It seems to feed on the worshippers' energy, growing slightly more with each section of altar amassed. Matt stands rigid in form, his long black hair blowing wickedly in the breeze, as he watches the disciples lay the final stones.

Ready for action and remaining on high alert, the police presence below the hill is tinged with a sense of dread as they watch carefully the happenings beneath the towering necrotic growth. For the moment they simply observe and stay poised to engage should something beyond the portentous activity currently transpiring ensue.

The altar has reached completion, which seems to please the vile growth; meanwhile, cheering and chanting can be heard amongst the throngs of people, echoing inauspiciously throughout the valleys below. Tongues spoken in reverberating unison sound repulsively from those surrounding the altar. The unknown language is hideous in its ungodly articulation causing some small children to wail in uncontrollable fear. The chanting grows louder and fiercer while the air seems to thicken, as if an unearthly wave of hellish radiance suddenly pierced through the ether from a universe beyond.

A man, clad in nothing save for an eerie symbol carved freshly into his chest, breaks through the crowds holding within his arms a small Rambouillet lamb of which the origin is not known. As he places the creature upon the altar, the symbol upon his chest becomes more readily visible. It depicts a type of star, oddly shaped yet mysteriously symmetric. Another person makes their appearance known before the altar, this time a female, donning a curious and unsettling mask with horns that extend several feet above her concealed visage. She, too, adorns nothing beyond the dreadful coverture hiding her face, and upon her left buttock is graven the same ghastly star, bleeding steadily from the fresh incisions that created it.

The sun still shines in hallowed resplendence upon the crowded hilltop scenery and the glint shimmering from the blade held high above the woman's head validates the brilliance of its radiance. All eyes above and below are now focused on the altar as the chanting grows to deafening volumes and the atmosphere seems to densify further. A breathless anticipation embraces the worshippers gathered atop the hill while the final words are spoken from lips unseen through tongues unknown. The woman stands firm before the altar, the dagger clenched tightly within her hands, as she lifts her head toward the skyline and shouts praises in infernal tones. The blade comes swiftly down upon the lamb and its blood is shed, covering the stone altar in a crimson spatter of unconsecrated and desacralized fluid.

With the plunge of the blade, thunder cracks the sky—a morbid and deafening thunder unlike that which aligns with the storms of an ordinary weather pattern. The sound is fantastically overpowering, such that nearly all the people in attendance shield their ears from the terrifying roll. Matt stands catatonic as he watches the throngs of adherents writhing in aural agony, waiting for something not yet conceptualized by the masses here gathered. As the last echoes fade away, and the people regain their composure, the hordes of revelers turn their attention toward the heavens in a fearful yet curious gaze. An ominous dejection permeates the mood, so palpable in abject intensity that some of the celebrants begin to weep. A trenchant hopelessness devours the spirits of all gathered atop the hill, robbing them of any sense of self-command.

The sudden outbreak of grievous detachment is mitigated by a forceful bright light that abruptly pierces a portion of blackened clouds above. So brilliant is its radiance that it leaves everyone in attendance awe-stricken, a look of jubilation adorning their faces in a universal moment of psychotic delirium. Abruptly, the radiance disappears, replaced seamlessly once more with clouds of black. With the return of the blackened sky, something inhuman takes over the will of the people, and forthwith the compulsion to die can be felt by all. The human sacrifices begin and blood spills upon the altar as one by one the worshippers throw themselves unto the stone platform to be slaughtered for the great and hideous growing monstrosity.

The infernal praises spewing wretchedly from the mouths of the worshippers are thunderous and intermix unsettlingly with the shrill howling of the dying, as the horn-masked woman thrusts her dagger repeatedly into victim after victim, covering the ground beneath the tree with rivers of sanguine fluid. The blood flow is copious, yet seems never to accumulate, as if the roots of the tree below the earth are feasting unquenchably upon the stream.

Officers from below the hill rush their way through the crowds, shouting for backup from all available units in police code while panicking over the prospect of putting a stop to the egregious bloodshed. No response is heard over the police radios as the few onsite units make their way to the top, struggling through the crowds and fighting the steep hillsides in an effort to reach the altar. The first officer to conquer the hillside's sloped and overcrowded encumbrance bursts through the chanting throngs, pushing and shoving and shouting, largely to no avail. The adherents of the tree show little interest in allowing easy passage for the officer—and, moreover, little interest in anything whatsoever—as the majority stand in morbid stillness chanting hymns in tongues of ghoulish incoherence. Nevertheless, the officer breaks through the forest of human bodies and nears the dreadful stone altar where he can begin to see through the last rows of human obstruction and toward the bleak reality of the situation. From the bottom of the hill the bloodshed was not plainly visible, and although the officers could tell even from that distance certain atrocities were occurring, nothing could have prepared the man for what he was seeing through the thinning layers of people separating him from the sacrificial platform as he steadily moves closer.

As the policeman pushes his way frantically past the final row of consciously destitute and maddeningly motionless adherents, for a brief moment all goes quiet within his mind, and the chanting and screaming seems to end. While he focuses on the horrific vista before him, he tries to make sense of the vile panoramic atrocity that his eyes perceive, yet it is as if his mind will not allow for an experience such as he gazes regrettably upon. From the bottom of the vastly sloping hillside, one could not possibly have seen nor understood the gravity of the horror that was occurring at the apex of the grassy mountain, and would he have known beforehand, it is quite possible that his trek to the top might never have been made. The blood spilled upon the ghastly, extemporaneously constructed stone platform is indeed profuse and covers the area in extravagant and immoderate volumes, not even to make mention of the droplets which have flung as far as twenty feet away in the egregiously performed stabbing by the masked and star-marked woman. However, it isn't the morbidly excessive amounts of life fluid that shocks the officer to the core of his spirit, but rather the use of the bodies once they have been adequately emptied.

Those gathered immediately around the altar who have for unknown reasons not been sacrificed have taken to disemboweling the bodies of the slain victims, followed by a morbid utilization with the deceased that the officer can barely begin to comprehend. In a great circle, just beyond the skeletal growth and past the altar, they dance in nauseating and obscene rhythms, wearing the gutted corpses of the sacrificed followers as vestments around their naked bodies. The way they gavotte and shuffle with the remains brings an unspeakably horrific feeling from deep within the officer's being, forcing him to look away for fear of vomiting in revulsion.

Seconds later, two more officers make their way through the columns of worshippers, pushing aside the chanting hordes and laying their unbelieving eyes upon the ghastly scene. One of the policemen immediately throws up the contents of his stomach upon visualizing the horror before him, while the other rushes toward the altar with gun drawn and pointed toward the masked woman's head. "Freeze, bitch! Drop the *fucking* knife *now*!" he commands with a stream of adrenaline-induced saliva dripping laggardly from his consternated visage as he stops a few feet from the altar. As if the woman is not even aware of his presence, she commences her ritualistic endeavors, seemingly commanding a fresh sacrifice to be placed upon the platform in a diabolic and indecipherable tongue. Those lined up to be slaughtered, too, seem undeterred by the police presence, almost as if the officer's corporeality is nonexistent. "I said *stop*! I'll put a *fucking* bullet straight into your *fucking* face, lady!" Once again, his order goes unanswered, and the ritual continues as two naked men surrounding the woman help another human offering onto the sacrificial platform.

The officer, left with no choice but to eliminate the threat, makes the decision to shoot and begins to move his forefinger from the outside of the trigger guard to the inside in preparation to fire. As he slowly starts to squeeze, he can feel a heat surging through his veins, the adrenaline within his body pumping increasingly with each millimeter the trigger moves. As the trigger travel approaches the end of its range, the time for the firing pin to meet the bullet primer is deathly near; only the sounds of the officer's own pounding heartbeat can be perceived inside his thoughts, along with the anticipation of release. What comes to pass could not, however, have been foreseen, as the echo of gunfire is not heard. Instead, only a bizarrely peculiar crushing sound resonates through the officer's eardrums, accompanied by a mounting pressure upon his skull, the intensity with which he has never experienced before. The last thing the policeman sees as his vision seems to tumble inward on itself in a collapsing, telescopic deformation is the congregation of enormous claws gradually closing from the back of his head around to the front, culminating in the compaction of his face.

The two remaining officers, having reached the altar, gather composure from their shocked and horrified initial reactions and stand in morbid rigidity at the sight of the vile beast poised in majestic enormity before their fellow colleague's lifeless body. Gone is Matt's humanness—replaced by the corruption within—and now his true purpose overflows with nightmarish and unspeakable cruelty. The gaping hell of fangs which adorns its inhuman cranial profile adds a superfluous layer of terror upon the already horrifying idea that, apart from its barbarically hideous maw, no facial features are present—only that monstrous horned skull, embellished with innumerable dagger-like teeth.

The thought to reach for his sidearm does not even enter his mind as the vile entity rushes toward the first of the two men, grabbing him by the arms with a violently terrific intensity. The size of the creature's limbs is easily that of the officer's entire body, thus its claws wrap his arms from his hands down to his elbows as he hangs helplessly in the air. The sounds of the man's flesh ripping apart can be heard over his own screaming as the creature pulls his torso in two sections, leaving a pile of innards and crudely torn halves in the spot where he stood. As if the monster's presence were a mere backdrop to the scenery, the throngs of worshippers offer not even a glance as the sacrifices and chanting continue on the periphery of the beast's carnage. The enormous creature raises its faceless and horned head toward the sky and stretches wide its hellishly extensive jawline, releasing a thunderous growl that shakes the landscape.

The remaining policeman pulls his weapon and begins firing at the beast, trying his best to aim steadily amidst the pulsations of his adrenaline-fueled body's overwhelming trembling and the disbelief clouding his mind. The demonic entity charges explosively in his direction as he commands position over the ground upon which he stands, poised with gun drawn, steadily pulling the trigger in rapid succession. The bullets rocketing from his weapon seem futile as the beast continues forward with increasing momentum, leaving no time for the officer to alter his course of action. The demon's footfalls tremble the earth as it crushes the soil beneath it, each stride covering enormous spans of ground as it closes the short distance between it and the policeman. Stopping less than a foot from the man's now cowering form, the beast angles its cranium downward, as if staring through the terrified officer's soul with its optic-less, blasphemously horrid face. The being's towering body is poised with nefarious fervor, and when the horrified man looks up into its iniquitous countenance, his eyes seem only to focus on the rows of sharp teeth shining inexplicably through the mysterious growth's baneful shadow and the darkened clouds above. The entity's musclebound frame pulses with destructive incitation as it breathes in the man's fear, its chest expanding and contracting in quickening succession while streams of saliva steadily pour from its horned, reptilian-like skull. The officer drops to his knees as weakness overwhelms him, his acquiescence to death trampling his will to survive. As he closes his eyes, he dreams of the next life, and silently says a prayer while waiting for the beast to strike.

From behind, the man suddenly feels a hand upon his shoulder enlaced with a bower of tenderness. For the briefest of moments, he feels a sense of ease, calming his thoughts as a glimmer of hope creeps crescively into his mind. The officer looks down and to his left, and he can tell it is a woman's hand resting warmly upon his collar. Her soothing touch conjures a semblance of nostalgic reverie, reminding him of the way his mother would soothe his unease as a child. Somehow, the gargantuan beast towering repulsively over his pitifully helpless shell escapes his notice, as he places his hand upon hers in a propitious yet distorted show of reciprocity. In an abrupt reversal of fortune, the embrace of her palm is suddenly superseded by a disobliging sting, followed by the sensation of fluids rushing onerously down his trachea. The taste of blood fills his mouth as his neck splits wide and the stark realization occurs to him that his throat has been slit. As the officer chokes on his own gushing vitality, he topples to the ground, landing on his back while instinctively clutching the wound, trying to seal off the gaping incision. His vision fades away as the scenery dissipates from view; however, his mind allows for one final hazy image. The ghastly sounds of his gurgled choking resound sickeningly throughout the officer's failing consciousness, yet even through the unsettledness of his consummating mortality, his final contemplations assemble upon images of the horn-masked woman standing in grim willfulness over his departing spirit.

The slain policeman's draining life force slows to a decrescent trickle, and ultimately ceases, leaving the area where he fell saturated with the last of the required blood offerings. The beast stands poised in silence, as does the woman, as do the multitudes of worshippers.

The quietude of the hilltop is inconceivably sinister, and quite remarkable, in consideration of the numbers there gathered. Only the strange growing thing atop the hill seems to make any discernible sound, yet not one that can be heard through human audition. The sound it produces resembles more closely a vibration—a kind that cannot be felt, but experienced inside the soul. The tree—that monumental structure now reaching heights nearly one thousand feet into the sky—discharges a demonic energy that resonates with a blasphemy most undeniably profound. Not a single movement can be discerned among the masses; it is as if the tree holds dominion over all gathered beneath its skeletal, twisted formation.

Amidst the silence and strange stillness of the ghoulish panorama, the slightest of movements can abruptly be observed. Just beyond the hideous growth, the top of a man's head can be seen clearing the hillside and moving casually up the steep and crowded grassy mountain. As he makes his way to the flat of the hilltop, his pace increases slightly, and his posture stiffens, seemingly adjusting for the encumbrance caused by the suit he dons upon his well-poised form. The once still throngs silently clear a pathway without so much as a glance in his direction, as if they can somehow sense his presence. Charles walks briskly through the human parting and approaches the tree, stopping a few steps away from the vast circumference of the unearthly skeletal base.

He does not notice the countless sacrifices strewn about the hilltop, or the great beast still standing in hideous and undefinable iniquity near the tree, nor does he care—the next step in his wicked journey alone envelops his mind with a singular wholeness. As he stares at the vile, ominous thing, he ruminates upon the essence of its existence—a seed, sown eons ago by creatures unspeakably profane, watered by the blood of slain children, and finally, cultivated by the sacrifices atop the great hill whose past knows intimately well the foulness of humanity. Charles inhales deeply the putrescence of the evil permeating the hilltop and continues to fixate on the tree, focusing his energies on the darkness sealed within it.

Like a flash of lightning tearing violently through clouds of black, a thunderous snap erupts from inside the twisting growth, so powerful in volume that it echoes through the valleys below. A crack appears through the tree's center and continues along the vertical span of the trunk, stretching all the way to the branches above. The growth begins to creak and moan with a blistering howl as it splits in two tremendous sections, almost as if it is wailing in tortured agony. As the two goliath portions of tree begin to separate and fall to the earth, the stillness amongst those gathered below remains constant. Hundreds of bodies are crushed as the tree crashes to the ground, its enormous length stretching too far for eyes to see. An otherworldly amalgamation of substances ooze and spill viscously from within the torn base, covering the hilltop with a rancorous stew of carnage not comprehensible by the human imagination.

Charles remains calm and unmoving, still only a few steps away from the base, unperturbed by the ground-shaking crash and resultant outpouring. The appalling mixture of indescribable elements within the tree's halved base empty onto the ground and what is left prompts Charles to move forward with graceful consent. He inches closer and peers down into the trunk of the vile growth, his eyes alight with a fervorous wonder. As his eyes brighten, so does his countenance, not from emotion within him, but rather as a result of the illumination emanating from inside the shattered growth's yawning fissure. Charles reaches into the crevice and removes the artifact so brilliantly shining, an object that brings a malevolent grin to his loathsome visage. In triumph, he holds high the article retrieved and lets loose upon the hilltop a hate-filled scream—a victory cry in praise of the acquired final page.

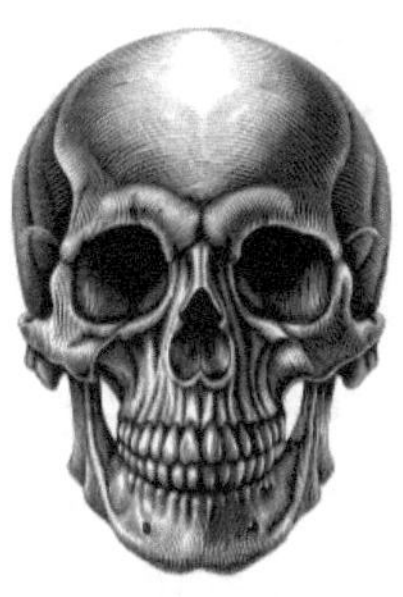

XXXV.

The swirling, blacker-than-shadows vortex of raging and abysmal entities moves violently in color-draining maelstroms inside the gateway as Charles gazes into the infinity of horror beyond. The churning, unimaginably bleak pathway that connects this world to the other side is inconceivable in its inhumane capacity and unutterably devastating in cataclysmic potentiality. The warehouse is much colder than ever before, both in temperature and atmosphere on this direful Friday morning. Nothing matters apart from the evil that resides within that deep, eternally expansive space before him.

At 9:45 a.m., a mere three hours away, the path of totality will darken the Earth, including the warehouse encapsulating the doorway to places beyond the grasp of mankind's most profoundly ruinous conceptualizations. The total solar eclipse is more than a subtraction of light from the gateway; it is a symbolization of what awaits humanity in the moments that follow. The beings that lurk in the endless and abominable depths on the other side of the portal yearn with an unmanageable hostility to reenter this unrightfully occupied realm, their seething hatred for mankind accepting of no limitations in perpetuity.

The world outside the warehouse walls is steeped in chaos, destruction, and unprecedented despair. Animosity and dissension dictate the actions of the human population in every country on Earth, and with each hour that passes, the enmity of man unto man grows more powerful and threatening. Looters and warring factions now rule the streets and towns of every city in every nation; the smell of death is quickly becoming an indelible aroma within the atmospheric temperament of hate, rage, and fear. Mankind is decaying from within the confines of its own flesh—and the beings crawling and slithering in the mire of their own loathing from beyond the dark gateway are pleased.

The hour of blackest summoning draws near and Charles knows well what must be done. When the path of totality casts its demonic obscurity upon the gateway, and the infinitude of gravitational pull curves such that not even light can escape, only then can the spells be uttered forth from the mouth of the ordained. Charles, however blessed by the creatures lurking hideously in realms inconceivably dark he may be, possesses still a spirit too pure to recite the blasphemies at time of totality. He must rid himself completely—and with finality—of the human soul.

It has been said for centuries by the spiritually erudite that the pineal gland is the seat of the soul. Dismissed by some as metaphysical absurdity and championed by others with a less empirical rationale, the dividing line between faith and scientific theory is not always as clear as one might wish to think. To many, the soul resides in the place where belief holds firm, a region neither abstract nor confined by walls of the flesh. Charles thinks—therefore, it must be—that the space within his being to be removed is centered behind the midbrain, between the thalamic bodies. To be rid of his pineal gland is to be cleansed of spirit, thus fully preparing his corporeal shell to act as a vessel for the final rite.

A corner space within the hellish depths of Charles's Jack London

Square area warehouse on the subterranean lower floor has been prepared in recent hours for the surgical procedure to take place. Visualization systems utilizing various mirrors, cameras, and monitors have been procured and arranged in such a manner that Charles may carefully observe the self-imposed operation in detail. Perioperative instruments are carefully laid out on a sterile drape in front of a neurosurgical chair fitted with a custom Mayfield headrest allowing for his head to remain completely still while he performs the removal. Among the equipment set out before the chair lie a craniotome and a rotary bone saw, both used to cut through the skull; several scalpels, forceps, and scissors, intended for slicing through and manipulating tissue; and a titanium mesh plate for covering the hole that will be left in his cranium. A table next to the one upon which are laid out his surgical instruments is covered with sundry antibiotics: Cefazolin, Cefuroxime, and Metronidazole. Shockingly absent from the preparatory collection is any form of anesthesia, analgesic, or other pain-reducing medications; only the cathexis for dark energies beyond measure to quell the agonizing experience to come.

The corner of the massive warehouse lower floor where the procedure is set to begin seems abundantly more illuminous than the shadowy blackness that surrounds it, almost as if the black energy within the gateway has sanctioned particles of light for the occasion. Candles are lit, glowing eerily around the operational space, but until now they seemed not to glow for fear of the evil resounding hatefully throughout the nightmarish domain.

As Charles approaches the operating chair, he disrobes, dropping his suit attire and other articles of clothing along the way with no regard for where they fall. He sits down into the seat and glowers at his reflection in one of the mirrors, the candlelit image staring back heeding only a hate-filled expression of contempt for his mortal essence. Charles adjusts the braces and fastening components of the mirror system to calibrate the proper position. As he does so, he examines the portion of his head to be incised, looking through his perfectly combed hair to inspect the surgical region. A series of monitors and cameras are prepositioned to aid in the surgery, all of which are wholly ready for use. Charles studies the system of mirrors and then observes carefully the two monitors, reassuring himself that the view is sufficient. Satisfied with his findings, he picks up a can of shaving cream and begins spreading it copiously atop his scalp.

As Charles begins to make strokes across his skull with a straight razor, he chants in low and tormented murmurs utterances of eons-dead blasphemies. With every pass of the blade, a new level of heightened awareness is reached, allowing for access to greater and greater acuity within himself. Accompanying the final length of hair removal is a rush of omniscience, one that provides anatomical perspicacity and grace. With this renunciation of will, the procedure now begins.

Between the cerebrum and the spinal cord, Charles makes a mark on the back of his skull, carefully watching the monitors and mirrors as he lays down the ink line. The tip of the pen is cold on his shaved skin, but it's a sensation that somehow thrills him as he proceeds marking the area. Checking the mirrors once more, he ensures for accuracy, then reaches for a bottle of antiseptic to gently cleanse the area. The bone saw's steel handle is pitiless in his grasp as he positions it carefully to the rear of his neck, making sure to line up the blade's teeth with his marking. The sound of the saw powering on is unbearably exhilarating, a sensation that drives the blackness within him to hellish extremes as the flesh on the back of his cranium awaits to be ruptured. Charles puts the saw blade to work, listening blissfully to the sound of the motor intermixed with rending skin and skull, creating a medley of sickening composition.

He utters not a sound nor does his countenance waver as an elongated opening is made in the rear of his head. Blood drips down from the wound onto his back and Charles answers the release with a blot from a towel, drying the area so he can continue the operation with clear observance. Next, a pair of retractors are attached to the upper and lower end of the incision as he watches carefully the images shown on the monitors from the cameras set up on the rear of the chair. The skin now sufficiently parted to allow for access to the bone, two more cuts into the skull must be made to fully remove the portion necessary to reach the cerebellum, the section of brain which must be maneuvered around in order to access the pineal gland. Once again, Charles powers on the bone saw and begins cutting into his own skull, a feat that would drive most men to madness or defeat. The flap now completely cut, he sets down the blood-spattered tool and this time reaches for forceps in its place. Charles again soaks up the blood from the back of his head and stares ominously into the system of mirrors fixated on the surgical region to be entered. Utilizing the forceps with a maniacal finesse, he carefully pulls away the portion of detached skull, exposing his brain to the bleak atmosphere pulsing restlessly within the warehouse walls.

Charles pauses and looks menacingly into the mirrors and monitors, admiring the work he has accomplished thus far. He turns his head slightly left, then to the right, tilting it as he does to ponder upon the intricacies of the human brain. He focuses specifically on the layers of meninges enveloping the exposed cerebellum and grins in horrific pleasure as he reaches for a scalpel. The layers wrapping his mind's capsule separate with ease as the blade makes contact, partitioning into splitting sections the soft membranes that protect the organ within.

Now completely unobstructed from his depraved tampering,

Charles reaches in—not with an instrument, but with his own forefinger—as he begins pressing upward on his exposed occipital lobe. Forcing his finger in between the occipital lobe and cerebellum, he works his way into the middle of his head, making sure he can feel the third ventricle just before reaching the final destination. The images displaying apathetically back into the monitors from the camera system would without question cause a normal man to acquiesce to the defeat of collapse; however, the dark ones of times most ancient guide Charles's impulses and strengthen his resolve, fortifying his resoluteness with powers immeasurably profound.

Charles can sense with the tip of his finger the edges of the pea-sized gland—the pineal, fabled seat of the soul—as it embraces the end of his appendage and releases a stream of sensation unfamiliar to his befouled essence. Almost as if a last ounce of remaining purity is pleading for mercy, a feeling of endearment, not hate, floods Charles's consciousness with a deluge of overpowering emotion. Taken back by the wave of sentiment, he struggles to regain his composure. Stuck within the snare of unresolve, Charles slowly removes his finger and glances forlornly at his image in the mirror before him. Thoughts swirl with excessive rapidity inside his mind as he sits atop the surgical chair, a large section of skull missing from the back of his head and brain exposed. A teardrop forms in the corner of his eye as he glances over at the bloody scalpel lying on the surgical drape, wondering remorsefully if his death should follow.

The room's darkness hums with a spectacular intensity, creating a pulsation of rhythm unlike that which can be heard through the air. Although he cannot see the spiraling gateway in the center of the room, Charles can feel the beings within the portal charging their energies with steadily increasing magnitude. The aura in the black, portentously seething atmosphere of the warehouse's lowest level teams with animosity toward Charles's hesitation, and he can sense the disapproval of the ancient ones. His volition was renounced when the utterance of blasphemy was made at the beginning of the procedure, thus relinquishing his will to the powers beyond the gateway. His heart pounds relentlessly inside his chest and doubt swarms his mindset as Charles ruminates on the sensation released upon making contact with his soul. A sudden throe of impulse grips his reason and he reaches instinctively for the scalpel while looking regrettably at the reflection of his neck in the mirror. Suicidal compulsion overtakes his thoughts, but as he plunges the blade toward his jugular, his eyes become awash with black.

A growl of incalculable proportion erupts from Charles's mouth as his jaw stretches to the point of dislocation. The surge of untold power vomiting from his unhinged maw creates waves of unrestrained energy throughout the skin on his face and causes his eyeballs to nearly pop free from their sockets as they bulge repulsively outward concurrent with the rumbling sound. The roar echoes beyond the limits of the warehouse walls and into the streets of Oakland as Charles loses all control of voluntary motion. The archaic forces from within the space of the gateway act for him, causing Charles's arm to reach around to the back of his head and violently dislocate his right shoulder. With inhuman dexterity, the foul creatures lurking hideously from beyond the portal guide the scalpel still embedded in his hand into the opening in his skull, lodging the blade directly into the center of his pineal gland, avoiding none of the surrounding elements.

The blackness within Charles's eyes fades back to white as a look of pitiful subservience adorns his still gaping visage. His life kept intact, but now without soul, he slowly raises himself from the surgical chair, drained mercilessly of emotion and vigor. Blood spills from the opening left agape in the back of his head as he fumbles for a roll of gauze on the end of the table. As he gradually and carelessly wraps the fabric around the site of the surgery, he is cast away into thoughts of untainted nothingness, coiled in a spiritual vortex of black.

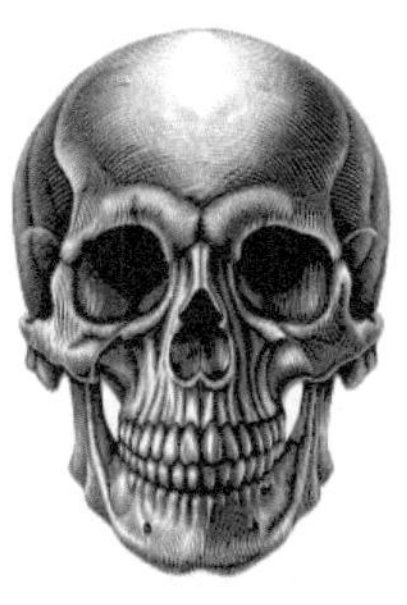

XXXVI.

B ase Alameda on Coast Guard Island is, under ordinary circumstances, a location embodying strict rules of order and tight military-like dictation. A place where routine and procedure are upheld in determinate succession, and anything less is subject to stern scrutiny and the potential of disciplinary action. Things are far from ordinary this morning on the base, however, and the hours preceding the current time have been wrought with a chaos that no man could have foreseen.

The room occupied by Dr. Patterson, Agent Norton, Lieutenant General Robert Larson, Dr. Shelly Masters, Devin Haronshaw, and the other three agents from the CIA is saturated with the stench of perspiration and urgency, a potent mixture of fear-induced uncertainty compounded by silent unresolve emanating shamelessly from each member of the group. The table they have been gathered around for hours now is covered with notes, folders, laptops, and every conceivable arrangement of disorder, all in the hope of coming across something in their joint efforts to extract a direction in which to turn for answers. It is 6:30 a.m. and all have gone without sleep, adding on top of their anxieties a level of frustration that can be felt in the atmosphere.

The general pores tirelessly through a stack of folders military intelligence operatives have gathered in the past week, searching for something, anything, that can point them in the right direction while intermittently referencing phrases and terms from the reports to Martin in the hopes of singling out anything of potential importance. Jerry stands over two of the agents as they scroll through files on a laptop, sneaking the last sips from his scotch in between scouring thin and ineffectual leads acquired from the agency's gatherings. Dr. Masters argues heatedly with Devin and the other agent from the CIA, debating the uncertainties pertaining to advanced weapons of unknown and unprovable origin. All eight of them are exhausted and tapped of vigor, red-eyed from scanning innumerable documents, and hoarse from talking endlessly of theories leading nowhere.

"Okay, okay...just hear me out," Devin begins, pausing to take a drink from his water bottle, and silently hoping this time they will pay closer attention than the previous three times he proposed an idea. "If..." Devin gasps, struggling to swallow his water, half-choking in haste as he forces the words from his mouth before he is ignored once again. "*If* the Russians were utilizing weaponry based on some type of gravitational device...say, a beam of gravitons, *in theory*, couldn't that create a small singularity? Dr. Patterson... Thoughts?"

Martin looks up from the stack of papers in his hand upon hearing his name, confused by the sudden vie for his attention. "I'm sorry, what?"

"*Jesus*! Is anyone listening?!" Devin, accepting defeat for the moment, throws down a pen clumsily gripped between his fingers onto the table and storms out of the room in frustration.

"My apologies, what just happened?" Martin questions the general, confused as to what caused Devin to leave.

"Not sure. *Look...* This, right here..." He entirely ignores Martin's inquiry into Devin's exit. "Two months ago, we learned from one of our intelligence operatives that the Military Intelligence Department in Beijing has been working on unmanned fighter jets controlled by AI systems, not just for piloting, but for something called 'gravity assist.' The report claims something to the effect of 'utilizing anti-gravitational launch assist and quantum propulsion—'"

Martin holds up his finger, interrupting the general mid-sentence. "General, should I be examining these documents? I thought this stuff was classified."

"Dr. Patterson, at this point, what choice do we have?"

"I don't think it matters anyhow, sir. To me this sounds like some sort of takeoff or landing assist. I don't think this is the type of technology responsible for what we're seeing."

Angered now by his inability to formulate a lead, the general barks in response. "Well how the hell should I know? I'm director of biological and chemical weapons, not this *Einsteinian gravity nonsense*. Who the *hell's* idea was it to examine gravity as the culprit anyhow?"

Alerted by the outburst, one of the CIA agents defensively speaks up, addressing the insinuation regarding his earlier suggestions about the potential use of gravitational weaponry. "What else would cause miniature black holes? *A fucking M16?*"

"Gentleman, please," Dr. Masters cuts in. "We're all tired. Let's take a break and reconvene in ten." The room lulls to a low blend of sighs and groans as Jerry and the general exit to get some fresh air and the others sit back in their chairs or pace nervously about the room.

Devin, unable to relieve his mind of the obsession to continue looking through the data, re-enters the room. Sitting back down in his chair, he leans forward and begins to scan the document next in the stack. For some inexplicable reason he finds himself whispering aloud as he reads the description of some experimental testing underway currently at Athena Laboratories. Information gathered by a case worker investigating some data that was red-flagged by the agency several weeks earlier raises questions in his mind and alerts his senses to something peculiar in the record. The employee overseeing the investigation seems not to have much technical knowledge, as can be discerned through the reading of the report, but something does stick out that raises the hair on his neck as he continues sifting through the file. A phrase that keeps repeating—more specifically, the name of an experimental test: "The Singularity Project."

Devin does not seem to notice that he is reading aloud—in a whispered tone, but one that is audible through the silence in the room. "*Wait...* What did you just say, Mr. Haronshaw?" Martin asks, his face flush with attentiveness.

"Huh? What? Oh... This report. Something caught my eye here—some kind of experiments they're running over at the Accelerator Complex in the desert. Something called 'The Singularity Project,'" he repeats once more while reading the name from the page.

Martin bursts up from his chair and rounds the table, hitting his foot on a chair and nearly falling in the process. "Ah, damnit!" Martin snarls, momentarily stunned by the impact. "Where does it say that?" he presses, limping his way over to Devin as quickly as he can.

"Right here, *and here*. Something one of our agents was investigating. Looks like something was red-flagged during some type of offshore funds transfer. They managed to interview one of the engineers working on the project, but something happened... They weren't able to follow up with him. He couldn't be located, it looks like. A project headed by a Dr. Hidalgo."

Martin starts reading the report hurriedly while bending over the table, kicking his foot as he peruses the document to try to shake off the pain of stubbing it on the chair. Abruptly he stops and lays the page on the table and begins stroking his beard while looking at the ceiling, thinking to himself as everyone in the room waits for some kind of response. Martin suddenly lowers his head and gazes at eye-level toward everyone still in the room while removing his glasses. He closes his eyelids and rubs his eyes, seemingly attempting to remember something specific.

"A couple weeks ago, just before the discovery of the graviton at Athena, a colleague, Dr. Whitney Bridgeport..." Martin stalls and places his glasses back on his face, letting out an exhalation of trepidation as he does so. "She is a member of a special research team over at Athena—not typical research, advanced theoretics, stuff that—" Martin, interrupted by Jerry and General Larson's re-entry into the room, briefly stops speaking to allow for them to hear what he has to say. Seeing that all eyes are now on Martin, Agent Norton and the general both stand poised in piqued interest. "Anyway... Dr. Bridgeport and the team were working on something she was concerned about, something she wanted to tell me, but I could tell she was hesitant to completely divulge. She refused to give me details... She just sort of hinted at things. I didn't even take her seriously. In all my years as a physicist, I've never... Nobody has ever said things..." Martin wears a look of disbelief as he gathers the courage to continue. "She wouldn't come out and say it, but I think she was concerned with creating unprecedented levels of energy, the kind that could not be constrained. Well, *shit*, I couldn't make much of what she was saying...but then she mentioned something—something patently strange. She mentioned a name in indirect reference. But that was not the strange part of what she said." Martin breaks from his thought, carefully planning next what to add. "A name, yes, and by inference, *a date*."

No longer able to bear the anticipation, and drowning in sleepless angst, the general demands in no uncertain terms, "*Well*, Dr. Patterson? Spit it out!"

"She said the final accelerator test would be performed when the path of totality casts its demonic obscurity upon the gateway."

"What the fuck does that mean?" Jerry quickly retorts with a look of recoiling perplexity about his face.

Martin blankly stares at Jerry while recalling the odd conversation as best he can from memory, then replies, "At the time I wasn't sure, but now it's clear—the eclipse."

Devin, this time, responds before anyone else has the chance, fumbling forth a stammering and murmurous question for Martin to expand upon. "And the...the name? You said she indirectly referenced a name?"

"Many times throughout the conversation she kept saying 'project.'" Martin pulls his glasses away from his face and once again begins to rub his tired eyes. "Every time she would refer to it—'project, project.' She refused to tell me the name of the experiment, but she was so upset and seemingly confused that at one point I heard it." Martin takes a breath and slides his glasses back on his face. "She accidentally called it 'singularity.'"

"What does this have to do with what we've been seeing recently?" asks Dr. Masters in a genuinely inquisitive tone. "You're talking about something that has not even occurred yet. So what if an accelerator experiment is set to run today during the eclipse? The phenomena we are seeing started two weeks ago."

Martin looks at Dr. Masters with a grave and concerned countenance, a look that sends shivers through her body as she stares back in nervous expectation. "Dr. Masters...the preliminary accelerator trials also began two weeks ago."

"*Martin*, why didn't you mention this before?" Jerry demands with a disbelieving sneer.

"I...I mean... It *didn't* occur to me. Dr. Bridgeport was so vague when expressing her concerns... I wouldn't even have remembered the words she said about the project if Mr. Haronshaw wouldn't have mentioned it!"

A deathly stillness grips tightly upon the aura of the room, holding captive the eight members of the assembly with an embrace so chilling that not a word is spoken in response. One can only guess at the thoughts swirling aimlessly and sporadically through the minds of the occupants as each one thinks of something to say. Finally, with great hesitation, Devin breaks the cessation of sound. "What time does the solar eclipse start?"

Martin slowly cranes his head to the right and answers while sympathizing with the solemn expression in Devin's eyes. "Totality will be reached in the East Bay region at 9:45 a.m."

The general looks at his watch and then at Martin, glowing with an intensity about his tired and time-weathered face. "It's ten 'til 7. Martin, you're coming with me in the chopper!"

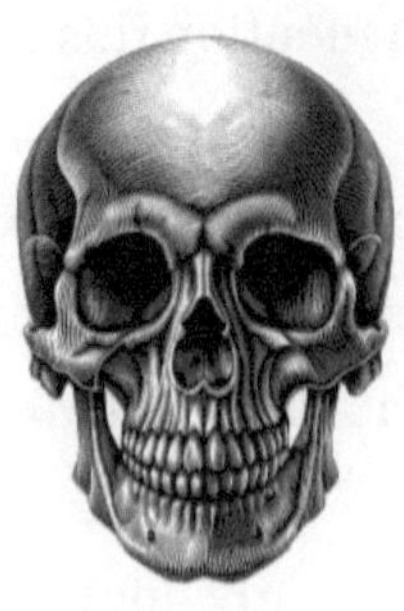

XXXVII.

The thumping of the air around the MH-60 Jayhawk can be heard easily through the window of the room as Jerry watches the helicopter containing Martin, General Larson, and six battle-hardened, combat-ready Marines leaving for Athena. The helicopter was chosen over the Blackhawk the general arrived in, a choice based on the fuel capacity of the Jayhawk over the Blackhawk. The room itself seems eerily serene with the absence of all other members of the impromptu conference, most of which have wandered off to find a spot to rest after a long night and morning of endless dredging through mountains of information.

It is 7:15 a.m. and with a bit of luck—or, perhaps more appropriately, a stroke of divine intervention—the chopper carrying Martin and crew to Athena Laboratories located on the edge of the Sonoran Desert will make it before the eclipse is set to occur. Jerry nervously bites at his fingernail as he contemplates alone in silence, the first time he feels he has had a chance to think in solitude for many days now.

Nicotine has been one of Jerry's greatest challenges throughout his lifetime. Quitting for what was supposed to be the final time two years ago, suddenly the thought of a cigarette flashes into his mind. Perhaps it's the overbearing tension of the world's uncertain fate, or maybe it's an excuse built on the notion that, *If mankind is doomed anyway, why not?* Either way, Jerry decides to take a walk around the complex in the hopes of finding a smoke to bum.

He wanders back down the long passageway and through the dull grays and nauseatingly light hues of blue separated by a dark orange stripe covering the walls of the walkway. He is still sickened by the odd choice of paint, but the prospect of puffing away on a cigarette soothes the off-putting feelings arising from the coloring. Once through the doors leading to the outside world, he takes a deep breath and savors the cool breeze blowing through the wind and upon his face. Jerry looks to the left out over the estuary and across the San Francisco Bay and wonders what will become of this world.

Shaking off the thought, and deciding it is better not to philosophize at this moment, he turns his attention back to finding a cigarette. Looking around the area, not a soul can be seen. The parking lots seem barren for a coast guard base. *Most everyone must be home with their families*, he thinks, *or worse.* Too many thoughts are coursing restlessly through his brain, he decides. Giving up the lust for nicotine for the time being, he instead heads back inside, thinking perhaps a cup of coffee will suffice in place of a smoke.

Jerry shambles back to the room he started in and pours a cup of coffee from the pot in the corner, taking the last of the brew now several hours old. The Maxwell House tastes bitter on his tongue, but with no Folgers available, he'll take what he can get. As he sips from the Styrofoam cup, he paces about and scans the view from the meeting room windows, looking once more over the bay and the nullity occurring therein. No boats are moving, no birds flying overhead, nothing—it is as if the area is absent of life.

Jerry sits back down in one of the chairs and takes another sip, sweeping his eyes across the mess of paperwork and files scattered carelessly over the entirety of the table. With everyone gone now, he decides to flip through some of the documents, glancing in particular at the ones labeled *Classified*. Previously authorized to be allowed access to some of the CIA and military's findings, it was made clear at certain points throughout the laboriously tiring process that he was not to lay eyes on certain things gathered by the Department of Defense. However, with the general and Dr. Masters absent, and the others taking rest in separate areas of the facility, compounded by the notion that the world's current circumstances are beyond human control, the temptation to peruse uninterrupted through the guarded information is exceedingly tempting.

Jerry begins flipping open folders, searching for anything particularly fascinating while every now and then stopping to listen for footsteps in the hallway. To his disappointment, most of what he discovers is of little interest, primarily reports seemingly gathered on subjects that can be heard on any substandard military-themed podcast.

After ten minutes of cautiously scouring tepid and unspectacular records, Jerry tosses the last folder he wishes to examine on top of the table, scattering several other folders beneath it into an unorganized clutter of loose papers. "Shit." He sets his coffee on the table and slowly begins to straighten the pages, arranging them back into their respective folders as best he can. As he does so, something catches his eye, sticking provocatively out from underneath several of the scattered papers. That old, distinctly odd feeling rises inside his gut—that strange connection; familiar, yet wholly unwelcome. Jerry abruptly sits back in his chair as the memories return. The girl—the case—*that damned star!*

He leans slowly forward and pulls the page from underneath the cluttered pile, causing the remaining papers resting precariously on top to fall to the floor. It appears this file was the one Devin was previously examining, the same folder he found the Singularity Project information in. Had the former occupants of the room given themselves more time to thoroughly look through the remaining reports, they would have found an additional piece of information. As he looks apprehensively at the dreaded star-shaped insignia, he sees that it is part of a company letterhead—specifically, the company's logo. Contact information on the Singularity Project is not addressed to the lab where it is to be conducted, as the address states a location in Oakland, California. Something fiercely overpowering wells up inside Jerry's being, abruptly and beyond his control. The urge completely overwhelms him to get to the contact location for reasons that supersede explanation. Jerry quickly pulls up Maps on his phone to check the address, surprised that, despite the world's tumultuous state, cell service is still available. To his utter consternation, the address is a warehouse in the Jack London Square area, only a few short miles away from his current location.

Knowing full well that the streets right now could be dangerous or perhaps not even navigable due to rioting and looting, Jerry can only think of one way to arrive at his destination. He wonders at the prospect of getting a helicopter lift to the location. *Is there even anyone left here to pilot the damn thing?* Charging from the room, Jerry turns down the hallway and toward the center of the building, searching frantically for Dr. Masters, Devin, or anyone he thinks may be able to get him to the warehouse. As he runs, he pulls out his phone and checks the time: 8:45, one hour until the eclipse. Jerry slides around a corner shouting for Dr. Masters, eagerly trying to garner a response from one of the remaining people in the building. Only his voice echoes back through the empty hallways as he turns down another, the thought of getting to the potential contact addressed on the document swirling through his mind in a virtual whirlwind of desperation. He calls again, this time to Devin, then to anyone who might be listening—all met with an absent response, which only heightens further his sense of urgency.

Jerry stops, "Fuck it," and turns around, heading back up the hallway and toward the main entrance, hoping that by the time he makes it to the helicopter pad he will run into someone that can help him get to his destination. As he bursts through the doors to the outside, he stops and scans the scenery, still not catching a soul within his frantic sight. Accentuating his panic is the vision of the moon edging over the horizon, the path to totality coming alarmingly into view. He picks up his pace once more and runs down the empty roadway toward the north end of the island, the area where he could see the landing pad from the meeting room window. As he sprints down the vacant roadway, he looks to his left and can see the cutters and patrol boats parked on the west side of the island, the dismal image of the moon hovering ominously overhead. They, too, are devoid of human presence, ushering in thoughts of hopelessness within Jerry's mind.

Past the last building blocking his view, and between a cluster of trees, Jerry can finally see the landing pad and a chopper parked off to the right. He slows to a jog and his breathing becomes labored as the distance between him and the helicopter decreases. The area still appears vacant, but he sees two cars parked nearby, one at the end of a lot and the other near what appears to be sheds. A glimmer of hope graces his senses as he sees the shed door is open, perhaps due to the employment of someone inside. He continues to jog at an even slower pace as he nears the outbuilding, his lungs heaving in labored discontent. As he approaches the open shed door, he once again checks his phone, seeing that the time is now 8:55.

"Hello..." Jerry manages to barely force through his strained breathing, catching two quick breaths before continuing. "Anyone...in there?" As inside the original building, no response, a disquieting follow-up to such a hopeful initial sight. Suspecting this area to be unoccupied as well, he steps inside the shed to confirm his assumptions.

To his surprise, he finds a person standing with their back turned at a workbench, tinkering with some manner of mechanical part. Better still, the man appears to be donning a flight suit, a sight that rejuvenates Jerry's urgency once again.

"Excuse me, *sir*." No response, the lack of which drives Jerry's nerve to extremes. "Sir!"

"Huh?" Startled, the man turns around and removes an ear bud from the left side of his head, the loud music blasting through the speakers being the apparent cause for his lack of response. The man's look of surprise turns to one of slight fear as he mentally absorbs the frantic appearance plastered across Jerry's countenance.

Before the man has the chance to say anything more, Jerry bursts, "I need a helicopter ride, *now*!"

"*What*? What do you mean you need a helicopter ride? Are you insane? Who the *fuck* are you and what the *fuck* are you even doing here?"

"Special Agent Jerry Norton," he starts with an authoritative demeanor, "FBI!" Jerry reaches into his pocket and pulls his badge, practically shoving in it into the man's face. "I need you to take me across town, *fucking now*!"

"Well, Special Agent *Jerry*, I'm not authorized to take you anywhere, nor would I even if I could. What the hell are you even doing on this base?"

"Look, I don't have much time! I'm here with Lieutenant General Robert Larson and Dr. Shelly Masters. They took off in a chopper earlier and now I need to get to a warehouse in the Jack London Square area—it's only a few miles away!"

"Oh, you're with those military and CIA assholes...the ones who just decided out of the fucking blue they would commandeer our base—"

Jerry cuts him off, deciding the time to argue has passed. A feeling within him he cannot rationalize ignites, the desire to make it to the warehouse before the eclipse occurs flooding every pore of his being in a deluge of irresistible compulsion. Jerry draws his Glock 19 and aims it at the man's face. "Fire up that chopper now, *motherfucker.* You're taking me to that warehouse!"

The man slowly raises his arms and backs away, hitting the workbench behind him as he does so. "Whoa... Calm down, mister... I...I can't just take the chopper, we have protocols..."

A shot rings out and the man covers his face while cowering, realizing moments later Jerry has fired a round into the workbench next to him. "The next one will be into your leg, then your other leg," Jerry warns, eyeing him with a look of pure malevolence.

"Okay, okay... Let me just—"

Another shot rings out through the outbuilding, echoing loudly in the confined space. This one is dangerously close to the man's leg, missing it by mere inches. "Now, *move!*" The man exits the shed and walks cautiously toward the helicopter, with Jerry following closely behind and gun pointed steadily at his head. Jerry ensures the man enters first, then walks around the outside of the chopper, all the while keeping the barrel aimed directly at the man's face. Once both men are inside, the pilot sets the throttle position to idle and calmly looks over to Jerry. "Look, I'll take you... But can you please point that away from my face?"

"Shut up and start the fucking chopper," Jerry replies casually, keeping his firearm steadily aimed in the man's direction.

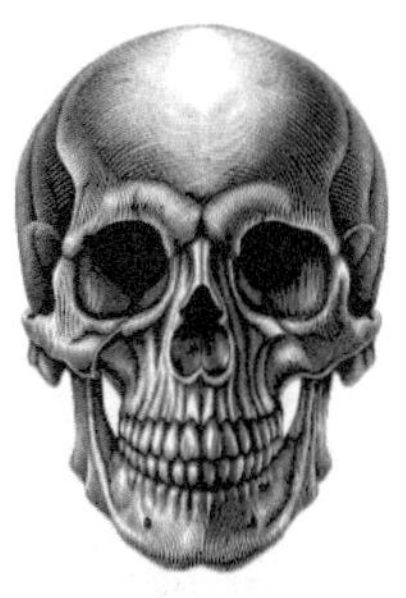

XXXVIII.

The sun is still partially visible as the moon rises steadily between the Earth and its star, casting a dimness ethereally chilling upon the western edges of the desert's barren and nearly empty landscape. Totality will not occur in this location; however, the path of partial eclipse still beckons within the observers feelings of dread that cannot be obscured. The helicopter containing Martin and crew hovers over the parking lot of Athena Laboratories as the pilot surveys the massive complex for a place to land. The parking lots are ominously empty for such a large facility due to the majority of employees being absent as a result of the worldwide chaos ensuing throughout the planet. Where they are and what manner of activity they are engaged in is unknown and fully incomprehensible; at this point it is difficult to say who is embroiled in the madness and who is tending to their loved ones and communities during these unprecedented and tumultuous times. Even though the lots are mostly vacant, save for a few vehicles parked intermittently and sparsely upon the vast concrete slabs of empty blacktop, the powerlines and light posts make it hard to find a safe place to set down the chopper between the randomly parked vehicles and lengthy expanses of high voltage wires.

"Dr. Patterson, where the hell am I going anyway? What part of the facility houses the area you're trying to get to?" the pilot yells back to Martin.

Pointing in the direction of a large building near a large piece of artwork representing a pair of entangled photons, he replies, "Over there, I think... That building is where the main entrance is. See how close you can get us to it."

The pilot looks at Martin, then at the general, and with a confident glare, starts, "I'm going to set us down in that grass off to the right of the building," before adding with a cautious inflection, "I hope we can clear the power lines."

The general gives a nod and the pilot proceeds, navigating slowly over to the area of grass-covered space, carefully maneuvering between a light post and building to the front. Martin checks the time and feels a shock of nervousness shoot through his body as the clock on his phone reads 9:30, a sensation of alarm multiplied by the darkening sky. The chopper lands with a jerk, lightly making contact with the earth, and the pilot sets the throttle to idle while Martin, the general, and his fire team of battle-ready Marines exit the aircraft. They jog across the lawn and head toward the main entrance, leaving the pilot behind, both Martin and Larson praying they are able to gain access to the building.

Upon reaching the main entrance of the facility, they burst into the lobby doorway, not giving a second thought as to whether the doors will be locked as they throw themselves into each side of the double entryway and through the lightly shaded backdrop of the opulent Athena threshold. The area is vacant and comprised of many different hallways, prompting the general to question with haste, "Which way?"

"Follow me," Martin replies as they pick up their pace, searching for a person to guide them to whoever is running the Singularity Project. "There are several access points to the accelerator ring," he explains as they hurry down the hall, rounding a corner to make it to the elevator. "The problem is, I have no idea which one to use... I've only been here twice before, so I'm not that familiar. I do remember the elevator can get us to the main accelerator floor, but from there it can be miles in any direction."

"*What*?! Miles? We don't have that kind of time!"

"We're just going to have to hope God is on our side, General."

As they turn down the last corridor before approaching the section containing the elevator, Martin spots it at the end of the hallway. "There! Now we just—"

"Hey! Stop!" a voice shouts from behind, initially alarming the men and causing the Marines to take aim. The sudden surge of adrenaline quickly turns to relief for the general and Martin, as the soldiers keep steady their weapons, ensuring the man they have within their crosshairs is not one of the afflicted. "*Whoa*. Easy, fellas," the now startled man replies, not expecting to see armed military personnel in his building. "Who are you with?" the security guard cautiously and quietly asks. Apparently making his rounds about the building, he just so happened to catch Martin and crew before they entered the elevator and were perhaps lost in the enormity of the complex's massive subterranean expanse.

"Thank God!" the general exclaims with a look of frantic relief upon his face. "We are looking for a Dr. Hidalgo. It's about an accelerator test they are running in less than fifteen minutes. We need to get there *now*!"

"I can't just take you to meet Dr. Hidalgo, he's in a restricted area today. You would have to—"

"Look, asshole! You see this?" General Larson pulls his credentials from his pocket and shows them to the man, looking him dead in the eyes with a commanding glower as he does. "Department of Defense,

United States Military! You are going to take me to him, and I mean now, *God damnit!*"

The security guard, fearful of causing trouble for Athena and the possible repercussions of disobliging actions toward a US government official—not to mention the six M4 carbines pointed in his direction—agrees.

"Yes, sir. This way."

The guard begins in the other direction, opposite the elevator, prompting Martin to question his direction. "Where are you going? The accelerator is down the elevator!"

"Not that elevator," replies the security guard. "Dr. Hidalgo and everyone still on site are in another location... I told you, he's in a *restricted* area. We need to take the service elevator to UG8, then a scooter to the Dirac Detection Center. If you're lucky we'll get there right about when the test is starting."

"*No!*" yells the general. "We need to get there *before* the test!"

"I'll do my best, but once we get to the ring it's about an eight-minute scooter ride to Dirac."

They run through the hallways, down three long stretches and several smaller corridors, sliding around corners while huffing and panting in exhaustion, before finally reaching the elevator. As the doors close, Martin checks his phone for the time.

"Well?" asks the general as he sees Martin checking.

"9:36!"

"*Shit!*"

The elevator reaches the ring and all nine men run for the nearest scooter. The general hops in the passenger seat and Martin takes the rear. "The scooters only seat four," exclaims the guard, panting heavily in between breaths.

Looking at one of the Marines, the general barks, "*You*, come with me. The rest of you, wait here," before turning his attention to the guard and ordering, "Step on it! Get us to Hidalgo, *now*!"

The security guard smashes the pedal and the electric motor whines off down the north passage of the ring corridor toward the Dirac Detection Center while the incertitude of the future builds increasingly and unbearably inside the minds of all.

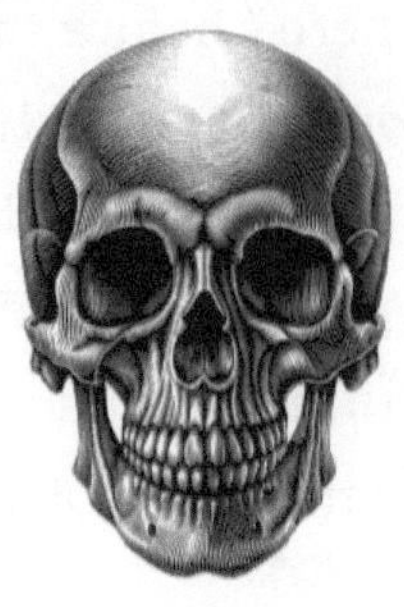

XXXIX.

Sitting with legs crossed, naked upon the surface of the warehouse floor contemplating nothing before the swirling, blackened gateway, Charles is frozen in stillness, dimly lit by the black candles scattered sparsely throughout the massively cavernous space. The back of his head, still leaking from the missing portion of skull through the clumsily wound bandage, drips fluid and blood onto his bare back as the darkness before him seethes restlessly in anticipation. The horror of the gateway's loathing is incalculable, the depths of its abysmal bleakness unfathomable, and were it even possible to ponder the infinitude of dark possibilities before him, charging relentlessly inside the hellish vortex, Charles no longer possesses the ability. The irreversible damage caused by the surgical procedure has rendered him a tool—a puppet of flesh for use as a vessel for the final translation of that ancient and forbidden text unearthed in those strange tombs of Egypt.

In a dark corner of the massive warehouse subfloor, confined inside a space only faintly more illuminous than the darkness within the gateway, the beast hides within the shadows. The eyeless, faceless, innumerably fanged creature that Matt has become protects the obscurity within the periphery of the gateway, ensuring that no harm comes to the vessel that shall utter aloud the final transcription. The time of totality is near; at 9:45 a.m., less than five minutes away, as the sun's light is obstructed from the portal, and the translation is spoken, and the accelerator generates the blackest of holes, the gateway will open, allowing those inexpressible things from times of ancient horror to break through from their dimensional prison into this world—their rightful dominion. All will know soon the torment that awaits.

Outside the warehouse walls, the thumping of a helicopter can be heard landing inside the large security fence topped with razor wire that surrounds the vast property. "Stay here and wait for me!" Jerry yells to the pilot as he jumps out of the chopper, nearly tripping as he runs toward the loading door entrance. As soon as he gets several yards from the helicopter, he hears the sound of the engines accelerating and he turns to see the pilot leaving him there. "Fucking asshole," Jerry mutters resentfully as he swings his head back around toward the building.

Making his way to the rear entrance, he wonders if this wasn't a waste of time. Surveying the back lot, not a car can be seen, nor does it look like the warehouse has been used for many years. Jerry looks to the darkened sky and, seeing that the moon now nearly covers the sun, knows with morose certainty that time is catastrophically short. As he rounds the corner he spots a Jaguar, some type of luxury sports model that he does not recognize but which instills within him a sense of hopefulness. Running up to the door, he immediately begins pounding and shouting, but after only a few slamming knocks decides instead to fire two rounds into the digital entry system keypad, shattering the bolt within. He thinks it strange that such a seemingly old warehouse would have a sophisticated keypad system, but the thought is fleeting as he bursts through the door, bypassing the lock.

Once inside, he realizes he has no idea where to go and begins immediately shouting to gather someone's attention. Nothing but his own echoes resound throughout the loading bay area—that, and a strange sensation of familiarity for the aura within. He checks his phone and sees that he has four minutes until totality, a sobering yet somehow familiar thought.

Still unsure of what he came to the warehouse to accomplish, he rushes through a single-doored entryway, revealing a staircase illuminated only by emergency lighting. Something inside him takes over, almost as if he is guided by powers unknown, and he races down the stairway into the building's cavernous, lonesome depths. A peculiar governance leads the way, descending his movements down a few floors then through another door entering a long stretch of hallway. The hallway, in turn, leads to yet another stairwell, lit even more faintly than the previous one, almost as if the descent is taking him into deeper levels of blackness, reminiscent of a symbolic spiritual decay. Onward through multiple series of rooms and doors he advances, bounding through the underbelly floors as fast as his legs will allow, dropping several dozens of levels to a deep sub-basement, guided all the while by a force he cannot understand. Three minutes until second contact—the beginning of totality—and straight ahead he sees a large, hand-carved wooden door inscribed with symbols, insignias, and awful, unearthly, hideous beings.

Jerry stops, frozen by the appalling nature of the carvings, momentarily caught in the rift between urgency and fear. Overcome by the will of something outside of reasoning, he pulls on the iron handle and apprehensively enters through the carven threshold, only to be met with a blackness the likes of which he has never experienced before. His lack of familiarity with the darkness therein is quickly superseded by the presence of a three-hundred-foot diameter concave circle, swirling in barbaric, vortex-like animosity. The hatred within the vast area of tempestuous seething can be felt like a wave of unparalleled heat upon his skin, something like the radiance of a blast furnace but somehow colder—darker. So dark is the churning spiritual maelstrom that the areas surrounding its iniquitous circumference seem to be lightened by comparison, a visualization that chills his spirit to the point of panic but, stranger still, seems to excite a part of him that he has never been acquainted with before.

Abruptly his vision is averted, turned now toward a man whom he vaguely sees through the dull candlelight, sitting naked off to the side of the whirling and blackened vortex of inhuman, smoldering hate. As Jerry adjusts his eyes, he focuses on the bloody bandage wrapped carelessly around the man's head and sees it is dripping continuously with blood and oozing fluids. The man seems as if in a trance, fixated on the maelstrom before him in some strange state of demonic meditation. Unbeknownst to Jerry, Charles is beyond the ability to reason; void of the capacity to think for himself, he is now but a pawn comprised of flesh and driven by the blackest of unearthly will.

Before Jerry has a chance to think or act, the man rises to his feet holding a piece of what looks to Jerry like an ancient page of text. The gateway churns in magnificent horror stoked by the approach of totality as a monstrous humming fills the abysmal warehouse space. Jerry knows the sun's light will soon be obstructed, and something within him can sense the madness that will shortly ensue. As if frozen in a state of disembodiment, watching his own self from some otherworldly dimension, Jerry cannot seem to move his vocal cords to utter a sound, even though the magnitude of fright within him surges in erratic and overpowering pulsations. He knows he is supposed to put a stop to the insanity he envisions before him, but some unfamiliar kinship to the darkness abound abates his every intention.

The humming metamorphoses into a thunderous growl followed by howling and screaming from an unseen legion of otherworldly sources. The waves of heat intensify as the swirling spirits unite, bringing about a singular black whirlwind upon the inner circumference of the terrible mass of beings within the gateway. As Charles's lips begin to move, a voice emanates from his mouth uttering the final translations in an unearthly language and tone not capable of being produced by the human larynx. The sounds coming so hideously from the naked man's mindless visage send shockwaves of terror through Jerry's body but simultaneously draw him in closer through means of some unidentifiable vicarious symbiosis. A violent shaking begins, and the ground trembles in response, seemingly agitating further the growling, the screaming, and the volume of the words erupting from the mouth of the man. The energies within the circle accelerate and the vortex shifts, forming the shape of a funnel inside the darker-than-black portal before the two men.

Jerry can feel now that totality is nearly complete as a welling deep within him arises, bringing to the darkness about the room another level of corruption to behold. A oneness with the evil circumvents all else within his spirit and Jerry can feel it lifting his essence up out of the constraints of mortality. An ethereal void inside him is filled with a blasphemous seething as Jerry views from above a being he had not previously taken notice of. A great beast, faceless and hideously fanged, rushes from a dark corner and directly toward the naked man. The naked man moves not and instead continues reading from the page in a tongue so vile that a cloud of blackness emits fumingly from his listless countenance. As the beast charges forward, the final words are spoken, a finality that Jerry is assured of as the monstrous creature tears the man in two.

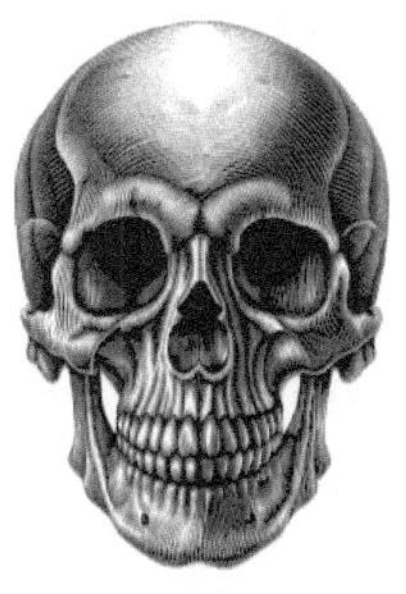

XL.

The hinges to the control center door of the Dirac Detection Area nearly break from the jamb as the Marine kicks it inward, sending small pieces of wood and paint chips flying across the room. The faces of those gathered around the monitors in the viewing area on the other side of the room are speechless, drawn temporarily away from the countdown screen that currently reads *2*. For the briefest of moments, everything seems to move in slow motion as Martin watches in silence the surreal nature of the events unfolding before him.

He can vaguely hear General Larson shouting in overbearing tones to stop the experiment immediately. He can see in fragments the eight large screens completely covering the south-facing wall of the room displaying images, graphs, and sundry other technological data currently in progress. He nebulously beholds the towering computer servers and cooling tanks designed to chill the quantum servers—the only ones of their kind in the entire world—shining with an illustrious yet distant sophistication, surrounded by engineers whose minds are well-acquainted with the advanced technology housed within. He contemplates obscurely the triumphs of science merged seamlessly with groundbreaking advancements in technology so frivolously wasted on mankind's thoughtlessness and ignorance of the greater lessons to behold.

He stops. His mind goes blank as he gazes in seeming disregard while the clock on the screen changes from *1* to *0*. Martin's gray and white beard and black wire-framed glasses go neither stroked nor removed. No need for anxious fidgeting or habitual stress relief. Tranquility is now achieved.

A deafening humming can be heard as the energy levels peak from directing unprecedented amounts of power to the ring conductors. The cooling units flash in rapid succession as the fans move at full capacity, trying to keep up with the heat generated within the quantum computing towers. The meters for the energy levels on the monitors spike the red indication zone and the other viewing monitors spark to life showing pinned graphs, three-dimensional representations of filled fields, and probability maps for the gravitational particle representations—all reaching never-before-seen pinnacles of data retrieval. Every digital gauge is at maximum capacity, provoking incredulous looks on the faces of several of the physicists viewing the screens. The monitors instantaneously display charts and graphs of unprecedented data, a sight that raises concern within the room.

For the moment, it is completely forgotten by all the intrusion of only moments ago, and Dr. Hidalgo speaks first, his voice resounding sentiments of utter disbelief. "Sustained... The black hole is...sustained."

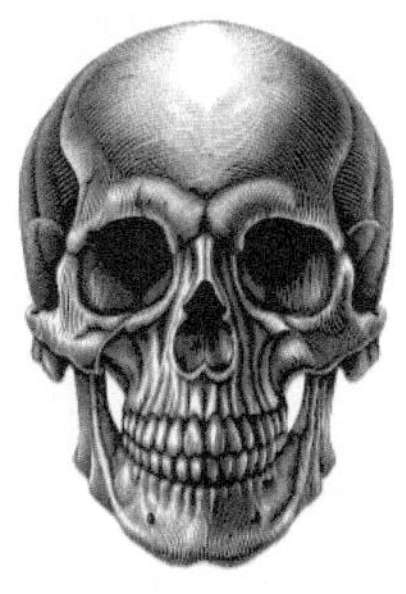

XLI.

The swirling is no more, leaving behind a gaping and limitless chasm filled with an abysmally hueless black, the depths of which can never be measured. The connection between their world and mankind's world is no longer a division of membranous separation, but a manifold of singularity stretching infinitesimally from dimension to dimension, portal to portal. The entanglement of gateways, now terrifyingly certain, is bound forever more, not by distance, not by time; Athena's entryway now belongs to the ancient ones. The antecedently swirling maelstrom of hatred, one and the same.

Jerry stares into the black beyond. Now fuller of wisdom than any human before him, he sees the truth. The smallest fragments of nature, the quantum reality that represents all matter—a design by nefarious corruption. The beings from beyond the gateway—creators of all things foul—cursed long ago our environment with the means to observe. Our science is their deceit, a blueprint for summoning. Time, intelligence, advancement—tools gifted by beings of a gentler disposition, manipulated by spiteful creatures whose tormented intentions are unrivaled in boundless perpetuity. The true nature of reality being wholly outside of their grasp, they instead employed means of spiritual warfare through eons of dimensional tampering and the falsification of ideas.

The gateway moans with spiritual declension and yawns wide with blasphemous foulness, silent to the ear, but felt coldly by the soul. Humanity's end is now in the past, culminating with the gateway's awakening. A new dawn for mankind has begun, filled with a suffering so profound that the mind cannot conceive of its iniquity.

For Jerry, too, a new beginning awaits, one wrought with a series of transformations everlasting. A light shining brighter than a star suddenly beams in implausible splendor from within the gateway's center, illuminating the surroundings with a radiance of fathomless bound. He cannot discern whether he is floating or standing, for the absence of a relative reference point has stolen away his sense of dimensional reason. From within the light walks the silhouette of a person, seemingly small in stature, which defies his lack of position. From photos of times before, he recognizes the face and can even recall a name—one he could not possibly forget. Eighteen long years it has been, but the event he could never release from memory—that case—that star—that child. Emily walks forth from the light, illuminated like a being divine, and stretches forward her small hand, awaiting the embrace of his own. As she leads him through the gateway the light abruptly fades away, initiating the first of endless transformations while the blackness swallows deep the essence of his being.